EIGHTEEN HELLS

Volume Five of *The Continental Divide*

Alanson Rand

Acknowledgments

Special thanks to Joey Clark and Debbie Witt for pointing out when I was making no sense.

Copyright 2016, 2021 Alanson Rand
Cover art and design copyright 2016 Timothy Stead
Editor: Timothy Stead

Rose Island Press LLC
www.roseislandpress.com
info@roseislandpress.com

ISBN (print edition): 978-1-946843-09-8

Also by Alanson Rand:

KEY FIGURES IN THE REVOLUTION OF 2043

Victoria Lang MD, a former director of Chalys Pharmaceuticals
Ada Lang, her daughter
Krista Warner, Activist leader
Arista Molle, a television journalist
Sergeant Mark Mason, a highway patrol officer
Tiara King, a newsfeed reporter for NewsPulse Los Angeles
Timmie Topuha, a videographer for NewsPulse Los Angeles
Lt. Jon Gilsig, Platoon Leader, First Platoon, Bravo Company, 184th Infantry

Rear Admiral Adam Harris, Commander, Submarine Force, US Pacific Fleet
Captain Zachary Caldwell, Admiral Harris' Chief of Staff
Captain Juliette Bricker, Commander, USS *Patrick Henry*
Commander Ennis Quinn, Executive Officer, USS *Patrick Henry*
Lt. Commander Tala Ripley, Strategic Warfare Officer, USS *Patrick Henry*

Gabriel Cheyn, President of the United States
Sara Hogue, Former NSF Tactical Chief
Noah Hayborn, Speaker of the House
Enrico DaCosta, Governor of the State of California
Maryann Heilmann, (a.k.a. Mother Mary Ann Christ), mother of The Profit Joseph
The Profit Joseph, Archangelist leader, purportedly the son of Jesus Christ

National Security Forces
Bob Downs, Former Watcher
Raphael Vinola, Watcher
Philip Cochon, Deputy Watcher
Ari Stein, Night Chief – Intelligence
Hideki Buta, Day Chief – Acquisition
Ryan Beckmann, Night Chief – Acquisition
Piet Vark, Day Chief – Tactical Operations
Tom Riddick, Night Chief – Tactical Operations
Peter Mochyn, Day Chief – Cybermeasures

IMPOSSIBLE LIGHT

Day 51
Thursday evening, October 8, 2043
Fair Oaks, California

Bob Downs stood at Fair Oaks Boulevard and San Juan Avenue noting relevant details: A convenience store to one side bustled with customers, a dentist's office across the street was closed, and no pedestrians walked on San Juan Avenue.

He pulled his tablet from a pants pocket and called up the area's aerial image. The tablet still worked, despite the blast it had taken from Warner's incendiary device, because it was built to military specifications and could even withstand a nuclear detonation. However, his hands were built to human specifications, and tapping the screen brought excruciating pain.

The aerial view showed that Mark Mason's house was located at the end of San Juan and bordered by high shrubs, which would conceal the operation from the neighbors. Nevertheless, he needed the visual obscurity of early dusk and planned to wait until the Blue Hour began around 7:30 PM. He glanced at the tablet's clock – it was 6:36 PM, so he had over an hour to evaluate the tactical environment before beginning the operation.

He strapped on his backpack and started walking south toward the house, admiring the sunset. After years in the color-sapping fug, he was delighted by the palette of blue sky streaked by orange and yellow clouds, complemented by the dark violet of night rising above the Sierras. The sight cheered him so much that he began whistling the tune from *Duck and Cover.*

A sudden flash bleached the colors from the sky, and pain stabbed from his eyes to the back of his skull. Then the ground shook as if he were surfing a wavy sea of concrete, and he reached for a light pole to steady himself just as pressure hammered his side and propelled him into the air. Despite the impossibly bright light, he opened his eyes as he was blown across the street: A small car bounced end over end along Fair Oaks, the roof of a house peeled back like it was mere cellophane, and the street trees bent until their tops touched the ground. His last thought before he struck something hard and his world faded to black was *What Hell is this?*

MARK AND ADA STOOD TRANSFIXED on the patio and watched the column of fire and smoke twist into the sky.

"What happened?" Krista asked, her speech slurred. She tightened her hold on Mark. "Somebody talk to me, please. Please, I'm scared."

Mark was hypnotized by the vision before him: The black dust spread throughout the white mushroom cloud like veins of dark blood, and lightning flashed again within it. A second later, thunder cracked and echoed across the valley.

Krista grasped his arms and shook him. "Somebody tell me what's going on!" she shrieked. "What happened?"

He started to describe the sight but then realized she wouldn't hear a word. He turned to Ada, who gaped at the boiling white cloud. "C'mon, we need to haul ass, kid." She wiped her nose on her shirtsleeve and gaped at the expanding cloud as if she hadn't heard. "Ada!" he yelled.

She rubbed her ears. "Gotta get far away," she croaked.

"I know! That's what I…forget it! C'mon!" He dragged her and Krista into the house. They stumbled into the living room and to the sofa, and he lowered Krista gently onto the cushions. She curled into a ball and sobbed.

"There's a temperature inversion up there. The fallout's coming this way," Ada rasped.

"Look, can you watch her? I wanna pack up some stuff before we go."

She sat beside Krista, and Mark ran to his bedroom. He found a canvas duffel bag and picked up the clothes he and Krista had strewn about earlier, and then he ran to the small bedroom and did the same with Ada's gear. His bag was still half-empty, though, so he dragged it into the kitchen and threw boxes of food and bottles of water in. "How are you two doing over there?"

Ada was guzzling from a water bottle. "Did you ask how we're doing?"

"Yeah."

"My hearing's coming back," she said. "We're holding on, but we need to get going. If we're here when the black rain falls, we're dead. We have fifteen minutes max."

"Got it. I'll be back in two." He opened the door to the garage and flicked a switch, but the lights were dead. One hand in front of him, he shuffled to the gun safe, but the numbers on the safe's dial were invisible in the dim light from the door.

He sidled along his car to the front of the garage and pushed the door opener button, but as with the lights, nothing happened. Waving his hand around in the dark, he snagged the emergency release cord, gave it a yank, and hoisted the door up.

His patrol car sat outside, caked with dust and covered with small branches, and wisps of smoke rose from piles of smoldering leaves on the driveway beyond. Every leaf was blown off the old oaks, and the top branches of one burned. Although he wanted to turn from the surreal vision, he was unable to move even his eyes.

He remembered that the fallout was coming and ran back to the gun safe. After a few tries, he hit the right combination and reached inside for Krista's tablet, the Cryogenie, and Ada's papers. He stuffed these into the duffel bag and then pulled out his spare badge, service pistol, and a box of ammunition.

After dropping the bag at the front of the garage, he walked outside and searched the front yard, but he couldn't find Thomson or Lopez. He ran back into the house, where Krista and Ada were still huddled on the living room sofa.

"Don't rub them," Ada was saying. "You're flashblind. That'll go away on its own in a few hours." She turned quickly when Mark walked into the living room. "What took you so long? You were gone for ten minutes."

"I was trying to find Thomson and Lopez."

"Dabney was sitting on the stone wall when the shockfront hit," Ada said. "He's probably dead."

Mark swore and looked through the patio door.

"Can we go now?" Ada asked.

"Yeah, I got everything, but I wanna to check you both for injuries before we –"

"Later," she said. "We're okay for now, but we won't be if we don't get outta here. Once the black rain starts, we're as good as dead here."

"Black rain?" he asked. "No, forget it, tell me on the way. C'mon, we'll take my patrol car. You two can spread out in the back." He helped Krista to her feet. "You think you can travel?"

She looked at him with unfocused eyes and felt his face with her fingers. "You're okay?"

"I'm fine. Can you travel? We gotta get moving."

She nodded and took his arm. He helped her through the front door and Ada followed, wiping her nose with a bloody towel. They weaved around the debris on the lawn – burning leaves, shattered roof tiles, and a smoldering porch umbrella from a neighbor's yard – until they reached the patrol car. He climbed in and thumbed the ignition pad, but the car wouldn't start.

"It won't work," Ada said. "Strong fission emits a powerful E1 electromagnetic pulse that scrambles unshielded electronic circuits. It might start if you reboot the car's computer from new software, but we don't have time. We'll have to hoof it."

"I don't understand what's wrong," he said, flicking switches and pushing buttons.

"It's dead, Mark. We'll have to walk." She peered at the mushroom cloud, which was creeping closer. "We need to move north, like *right now.*"

"All right, yeah." He climbed out of the car. "I'll carry the bag. You walk with her." He walked to the garage and shouldered the duffel bag. "Let's go."

Ada pointed at the oddly painted sports car in the garage. "What's that?"

"That's my dad's 'Stang." He reached up for the handle of the garage door. "I should close this. The thing's a classic, and I wouldn't want it ruined."

"So classic that it doesn't have circuit boards?"

"Circuit boards didn't exist when this baby was built." He yanked down on the door and then stopped halfway and whooped. "Oh, right! I get it!" He ran to a pegboard, pulled off a key, and jumped into the driver's seat. The engine cranked a few times and caught with a throaty rumble. "There! We have wheels!"

"You're so smart," she said. "What would we do without you?"

He pushed the patrol car away from the garage, rolled the 'Stang out, and tossed the bag on the front seat. "You two get in back. I don't want her to be alone. It's a tight fit, but it's gotta do."

"I wouldn't think of leaving her alone," Ada said. She took Krista's hand and guided her into the backseat. "See? There's plenty of room. Let's roll."

"One more thing." He ran to the patrol car and pulled a large white case from the trunk, and then he dropped it on the front seat too. "My medikit. We're gonna need this." He slipped the car into gear and maneuvered around his patrol car.

"Where are we going?" Krista asked.

"Someplace safe." Ada stroked her hair and kissed her forehead.

"I wish I could see what was going on." She rubbed her eyes, but Ada pulled her hands away. "All I see is white."

"Just leave them alone and they'll be okay, I promise."

He stopped at San Juan Avenue, where trash cans, branches, and roof tiles covered the road as far as he could see. Plumes of thin smoke rose from piles of rubble that had blown against the street-side shrubs. A black assault rifle was lying under one of those shrubs, and he looked for Lopez, but the street was empty in both directions. He rolled down the window and listened for a human voice, but he heard only inhuman sounds: The wind rushed and moaned toward Sacramento, and the yellow sky crackled and fizzled like an ancient, untuned radio. He drove up the street and looked into the houses, which were as devoid of life as they were of glass.

The destruction grew worse as they approached Fair Oaks Boulevard. The street trees along the boulevard had been blown over, and most were burning. Dense smoke blocked the fading sunlight, while the light from the blazing tree trunks set the hazy air aglow. Leaves and dust covered every surface. Cars were scattered across the road, and some had flipped onto their roofs.

However, a few people had survived the devastation. A young man climbed from an overturned pickup and staggered to the side of the road, and people pulled children from a van that had crashed into a building. Inside a dentist's office at the corner, a man writhed on the floor. "The buildings formed a shock funnel here," Ada said, looking up and down the road. "The shockfront was concentrated. It wiped out everything."

"It really wasted the place," Mark said. "I don't even recognize it."

"I wish I could see," Krista said. "Tell me what it looks like."

"The telephone poles were blown over like matchsticks, and they all point in the same direction," Mark said. "Everything's burning or smoking. There's little whirlwinds of dust everywhere."

Krista leaned forward. "We've got to document this. Mark, do you have my tablet?"

"Sure." He reached into the duffel bag and pulled it out.

She sat back in the seat and initialized it, and after the welcome window chimed, she handed it to Ada. "Photograph everything. The world has to see this. Snap everything that catches your eye. Is there enough light?"

"Everything's on fire," Ada said. "It's like a sunset out there, so there'll be enough."

Mark opened the door and turned to get out. "While you're taking pictures, I'm gonna help get people outta those cars. I gotta do something."

"No, you don't," Ada said.

"I'm a public safety officer and this is a –"

"This isn't just a freakin traffic accident!" She looked through the window at the mushroom cloud. "Our only priority is to get us and the vaccine outta here before the black rain starts, which should be soon from the looks of that cloud."

"Black rain? What's that?" Krista asked.

"It's radioactive debris that attracts water up in the pyrocumulus cloud and condenses. Each drop is death." Ada looked up at the cloud again. "And this was a low airburst, so there'd be a lot of radioactive debris even if it was a clean nuke. But it wasn't – that bomb was the dirtiest ever made, and its cloudshine is six times as bad as a conventional nuke's. Once the upper thermals blend with the cold air layer I see up there, it'll get bad down here."

"Like the bomb wasn't enough?" Mark asked. "Are you saying it's gonna rain radioactivity too?"

"Yeah, and the only thing you can do is get away. If these people are out in the open when it falls, they're dead. You can't prevent that."

"I hate not helping them out. It's heartless to abandon them." He sat back in his seat and sighed. "But I guess we gotta be practical."

"When it comes to radioactivity, you're either practical or dead, Skid."

He looked through the windshield, but the city was devastated in every direction. "All right, but where do we go? Everything I can see is wrecked."

"The plume is heading south-southeast. Go north or east," Ada said.

"Okay, I know some people in Roseville, and we can crash with them. That's north of here." He pulled into the intersection, weaved around a jumble of fallen telephone poles and power lines, and then drove north on San Juan. Less debris clogged that side, although stalled cars blocked the way, and he had to maneuver around them. "I just don't get it, though. Why would anybody do this? Who would do something this terrible?"

"A monster," Ada said. "The worst kind of monster."

FADE TO WHITE

Day 51
Thursday night, October 8, 2043
National Tranquility Center, Fort Belvoir, Virginia

Ryan Beckmann swiveled in his chair to face the podium. "Multiple malfunctions being reported on Blackeye 21, Phil."

"What's up with it?"

Beckmann pointed up at a white screen on the Wall. "All main cameras are transmitting pure, noiseless white. The sidescan cameras are transmitting imagery, but the mains are sending us zip."

"What's Airship Ops say?"

"They're running diagnostics right now, but they've never seen anything like this. They also say the positioning thrusters are non-responsive and it's drifting southeast, so they're thinking of landing it at Fort Irwin and checking it out. We might be going without Central California visuals for a while."

"This is a bad time for a major equipment failure," Cochon said. "We still have teams in the field for the Senate project. We need eyes on Sacramento right now."

"They're working as fast as they can."

"I want visuals by sunrise. I'll send them to clean up Tonopah if they're too incompetent to get…what is it?" Cochon turned to the Cybermeasures chief, who was waving his hand in the air. "This isn't a kindergarten classroom. Pipe up if you have something."

"The NSA feed is reporting unusual cell phone activity in central California. The cell networks are overloaded. The activity centers on Sacramento, but there's no cell activity *in* Sacramento." He pressed his headset to his ear. "My contact says most of the conversations refer to an earthquake or some sort of explosion. The NSA just flagged it as a Level One Emergent Incident, Phil."

Cochon walked the perimeter of the dais with his hands behind his back. "Ryan, check the sidescans from Blackeyes 19, 20, and 22. Can you pick up any long-distance imagery on central California?"

"I'm working on it now." He accessed the data, but the sidescans from the Seattle and Phoenix airships were obscured by cloud cover. However, the airship over Los Angeles showed a clear image. "Oh, Jesus."

"What?"

Beckmann sent the image to the Wall, and everyone in the Watch Room gasped: A bright fireball rose into the sky atop a column of swirling fire as a pressure wave radiated from Ground Zero and flattened the city. Then the fireball faded, and the column of flame and smoke spread into a mushroom cloud.

"What? Where is this?" Cochon asked.

"That's Sacramento – or it was," Beckmann said.

After a second viewing of the bombing, Cochon remembered his duty. "Go to Level Red. Clip this and send it to the White House recommending a Continuity of Government evacuation. Send it to the NSA, NSC, and FEMA too. Transfer our data to Mount Weather, and place Pocatello and Fort Carbon on ready alert. Move two companies of Collaterals and all available drones to each base. Let's go, move it, people! We have a job to do!" He pulled his tablet out and dialed Raphael's number. "And somebody task the Syllogic Engine on this! I want a list of probables in one hour!"

DISPATCHES

Midnight Sun
News Post of October 8, 2043

CATACLYSM IN SACRAMENTO

We are receiving reports that a massive explosion occurred in Central California at 6:36 PM Pacific Time.

Dispatches from San Francisco say that an earthquake of catastrophic magnitude struck the area, but Witnesses in Vacaville and Auburn report that a flash of bright light preceded the tremors.

The Edmonton Teleseismic Monitoring Office says preliminary data suggest a local magnitude of 6 to 7 on the Richter scale at a depth of fifty feet. Privately, our Edmonton contact says the wave amplitude and profile are more consistent with a nuclear detonation than an earthquake.

Viewers of a live NewsPulse broadcast from Sacramento say the reporter didn't mention ground shaking and that her broadcast ended abruptly in mid-sentence. Contacts at NewsPulse San Francisco say the reporter's satellite connection terminated at 6:36 PM.

Ham radio operators in Vancouver also note that all broadcasts from Sacramento stopped at 6:36 PM and haven't resumed since.

As further information comes in on this developing story, we will report it immediately.

EIGHTEEN HELLS

Day 51
Thursday night, October 8, 2043
Fair Oaks, California

San Juan Avenue was clear as they drove north except for people who stood on the road, staring at the looming mushroom cloud.

Because the streetlights weren't working, Ada's photos were coming out murkier as they drove away from Sacramento's glow. She decided that she'd taken enough photos and laid the tablet on the seat just as a warm drip tickled the end of her nose. "This nosebleed just won't stop."

"You hurt it?" Krista asked.

"I'll say. I faceplanted into the patio after the shockwave dissipated."

"Pinch it just under the bone. That always works for me," Mark said.

"My mom used to smack the bottoms of my feet twice," Krista said.

"Hunh? What'd that do for a nosebleed?" Ada asked.

"Nothing, but they always go away on their own anyway. I wouldn't be worrying about it."

"Yeah, I get these during growth spurts," Ada said.

"*You* get growth spurts?" Mark asked.

"Oh, is that sarcasm I hear? Can I napalm you now?"

"I wish you guys would just shut up," Krista snapped. "Jaysus, is this ever the wrong time to do the dozens on each other."

"I'm not up for it anyway," Ada said. "My stomach feels weird. Did you bring anything to eat?"

"I brought that box of Oatie Ohs," he said.

"Fine. Maybe it'll settle my stomach."

As he reached for the duffel bag on the floor, the side windows exploded and showered him with glass. "Get down!" he yelled. "Gunshots!"

He yanked the wheel hard and stepped on the gas at the same time, swerving the car down the road. He spotted a side street ahead and turned into it without slowing, sliding around the corner on two smoking wheels, and then he gunned the gas. "Is everybody okay?" he yelled over the rush of wind from the broken windows.

"Fine," Ada said. "We're both fine back here. Don't worry."

"Hold on!" He skidded into a parking lot behind a row of stores, stopped the car, and then climbed out with his pistol raised. After scanning the area for shooters, he leaned back inside the car. "I think we're safe now," he said. "That was a little scary, huh?"

"Nope. So how about those Oatie Ohs?" Ada asked.

He reached into the bag and handed her the box. "Probably saved my life, bending over to get those. That bullet musta been aimed at my head."

"You're welcome," Ada mumbled through a mouthful of cereal.

"Why were they shooting at us?" Krista asked.

He rubbed the knots out of his neck with one hand. "Dunno. You can't tell with scumbags. Most of them have Cranial-Rectal Inversion and can't even tie their shoes. What these kids need is some good old-fashioned biofeedback, that's what –"

"You have the only car in the city that runs, and they want it," Ada said.

His hand froze in mid-rub. "All right, yeah, that's it. I'll have to stay off the arterial roads from now on. It's like driving in a shooting gallery." He looked at the back door of the store in front of him. "Hey, I know this place. Dani's dad owns it. I bought my widescreen here last year."

The store's back door creaked open, and two young men walked through carrying a TV. "Damn it, they're looting! The place gets nuked, and the first thing they do is boost?" He grabbed a baton flashlight and shined the beam in their faces. "Police! Drop it and raise your hands over your head! *Levanten la mano!* Now, punks!"

The two men squinted at him and lowered the TV to the ground. One of them said, "Hey, *pitufo*, you got no backup. Why doncha just suck me off, man?"

"You wanna play it hard, *pachuco?*" He flipped the flashlight in his hand and held it like a club. "Okay, I'm in. We'll kick things off with an aluminum massage." As he stepped forward, the thieves kicked the TV toward him and sprinted around a corner. He jumped over it and chased them.

"What's going on? Where'd he go?" Krista asked.

"He's being a cop again and chasing crooks," Ada grumbled. "Mr. Do-Good can't resist being a hero." Gunfire and shouting echoed from the front of the building, and she swore and climbed into the driver's seat. "There has to be a picture of this guy in Darwin's notebook. Right next to the freakin dodo bird."

She yanked the shifter into drive and gunned the gas. When she reached the front of the store, he ran around the corner, and she locked the brakes to avoid hitting him. He jumped into the passenger seat as the car was still sliding. "Go! Back up! Get the hell outta here! There's hundreds of 'em!"

She'd just found the reverse gear when a mob of young men wielding sticks turned the corner. They pointed at the car and ran toward them screaming.

"Move it, Twink!" he yelled. She punched the gas pedal and the car rocketed back into the street, leaving some of the muffler behind. She stopped and tried to slip the transmission back into drive but couldn't make the shifter work. "It's stuck!"

"Lift the button! The button!" He reached for the shifter, but a young man jumped onto the hood, and Ada looked through the back window and jammed the accelerator to the floor. The thug slid off and tripped a few of the oncoming men as the little 'Stang roared down the street in reverse, slewing from side to side. The mob chased after it.

She whipped the car around a corner but spotted stalled cars on the road as soon as she made the turn. "There's a car in the way!"

He glanced through the rear window. "We're stuck!"

"I can see that! You just had to play Sergeant Freakin Justice, didn't you?"

The mob surged around the corner waving sticks and pipes over their heads. "You'll have to drive right through them."

"You need Krista behind the wheel for that, bub." She hooked her arm over the seat back, looked through the rear window again, and gunned the car backward, slipping between two stalled cars with just inches to spare on each side. A second later, she swerved around more cars, sending Mark and Krista sprawling across the seats.

"What are you doing?" Krista groaned.

"Not now, honey, Mommy's driving," Ada said. She swerved again, and Krista slid across the car. "Just lay down and stay there!"

He sat up in his seat and pointed through the windshield at the approaching mob. "We need to get outta here!"

"I'm working on it!" She swerved one more time, and then she saw an intersection and slid the car around the corner. She turned at the end of the block and then again at the next street.

"Whatcha doing?" he asked.

"I'm trying to lose them," Ada said. "Gimme a minute." She punched the gas and the little car rocketed to highway speed.

"Slow down!" he yelled.

"I'm getting us the hell out of here!" she yelled.

"Stop already! We're far enough away!"

"Shut it! You're distracting the driver! And you said distracted drivers are dangerous!" She took another turn on two wheels, and the force threw him into her lap.

"Jumpin Jesus! Enough already!" He pulled the keys out of the ignition, and the engine turned off.

"What'd you do that for?" Ada asked as the car rolled to a stop. "They're right behind us!"

"No, they're not, we're safe now." He laid his head back against the headrest and let out a shaky breath, and then he opened the door and looked around. They'd stopped beside a park surrounded by small homes, but the streets were silent, and he saw nobody on the walks. "Looks okay· here. Let's get out and stretch for a minute."

"Absolutely. If I don't have a smoke soon, there's gonna be a body count," Krista said.

Mark climbed out and checked the surroundings again. "And Twink said she couldn't drive. Seriously."

"It's Opposites Month, so maybe I can only drive backwards," Ada said. "But I did good, huh?"

"Yeah," he said. "A little too good." He reached in and took Krista's hand, and she stumbled out onto the pavement. "How's the eyes doing?"

"I can see shapes now but no details." She leaned against the car and fumbled inside the robe for her cigarettes. Mark flicked the lighter for her, and she took a long, hungry drag. "From what you guys described, I'm glad I can't see anything. I don't need more nightmares."

"We can't stay here for long," Ada said, turning in a circle and scanning the street. "There might be other mobs around, and I'm still worried about the black rain." She peered up through the trees at the cloud, which caught the light of the fires beneath it and flickered orange. "I can't tell what's going on up there since the sun set. I don't wanna take any chances."

"We'll get moving as soon as we're done," he said. "We definitely have to avoid the main roads from now on." He looked around the park. "The only problem is that I have no idea where we are."

"You're lost? In your own hometown?" Ada wiped her nose with a blood-soaked towel.

"Yeah, this part of town's like the Devil's Triangle. You come in here without a satnav system, you can't ever get out. Only the locals know the secret."

Ada peered through the trees again and pointed to the southwest. "The glow is that way, so that must be Sacramento. We just have to head in the other direction."

"Right. We'll eventually hit a main road and find out where we are," he said. "It should be pretty easy."

OVER AN HOUR LATER, they were still lost in the maze of suburban streets and were rolling down one of the few straight roads they'd come across.

"How many fingers am I holding up?" Mark asked.

"Umm…five?" Krista asked.

"Four. The thumb's not a finger."

"Well that's a little picky," she said.

"Nope. Twink says it's actually a digit, not a finger," he said.

Krista leaned toward Ada. "Why are you poisoning his mind?" she whispered. "Can't you think of anything better to do?"

"I was bored."

"That's cruel. You know how impressionable he is."

He pulled to the curb, removed a pair of binoculars from the duffel bag, and looked down the street. "I see an arterial road up there. I don't see any mobs on it, so that's good...aw, hell."

"What?" Krista asked.

"That's El Camino Avenue up there," he said.

"El Camino Avenue? 'The Road' Avenue? Seriously?" Ada asked.

"Hey, it's California. Look, we musta got turned around. We haven't been going north, we've been going west. El Camino runs along the north side of the city." He dropped the binoculars into the bag. "I'm not going back into that maze. I think we oughta take El Camino to Route 5 and then head north to Roseville. It's only a few miles."

"I just want to get far away from here," Krista said. "Whatever gets us outta this hellscape is fine with me."

Ada leaned through the window and peered up at the cloud. "As long as we don't get any closer to Sacramento, we oughta be okay. But do it fast. We're being irradiated every second we dawdle."

He slipped the car into gear and turned onto El Camino. As with Fair Oaks Boulevard, the road was littered with glass and crossed by downed telephone poles and power lines. The street trees were smoldering and stalled cars dotted the road; some had flipped over, and most were burned. Stores lined the street, and while the ones on the south side were just missing glass, the ones on the north were devastated – storefronts and roofs had been ripped away, leaving behind only twisted steel skeletons. Burning clothes and papers fluttered across the road, and a light haze of smoke drifted in the air from unseen fires to the south.

Ada looked up at the glowing underside of the cloud again, which cast a soft glow over the city. "We're close to Sacramento. The cloud looks hot, and the cloudshine's cooking us. We shouldn't hang around long."

"Yeah, I know. I'll get us outta here as soon as I can."

He crept along the road and steered around the rubble, and he had to muscle the little car over telephone poles lying across the pavement a few times. Ada picked up Krista's tablet and snapped photographs of the destruction while Krista gaped. "Jaysus, this is terrible. Look at that building over there – it looks like somebody hit it with a feckin humungous baseball bat."

He slapped his hand on the steering wheel. "Aww hell, I wonder who else the Reds hit. I didn't think of that. Krista, can you do me a favor and call my mom?"

She took the tablet from Ada. "Sure. What's the number?"

He gave it to her, and she spoke the numbers into the tablet. She raised it to her ear, frowned, and then tried again with the same result. "I can't get through. I just get this staticky warbling sound."

"She lives outside San Francisco, and if they got hit too…" He ran his fingers through his hair and puffed out his cheeks. "Look, I gotta make a change of plan here. I need to go check on her."

"Okay," Krista said. "It doesn't matter to me at all."

"Anywhere else is better than this," Ada said.

"Thanks. We can pick up Route 5 and go west through the farms." He steered around a stalled car and stepped on the gas. "I hope she's okay. Christ, I never thought anything like this would happen. Could you try the number again?"

She did, but the call didn't go through. "Nothing. That doesn't mean San Francisco got hit, though. The phones might just be dead."

"Don't bother trying," Ada said. "The electromagnetic pulse blanked out the switching stations and uplink sites."

The road widened into a divided highway clogged with more stalled cars. They drove west past large malls with cars piled against the storefronts, but nobody was in sight. He maneuvered around a stalled bus and looked inside, which was also empty. They pulled up to a deserted bus shelter soon after. "Where'd everybody go? This is always a busy place."

Ada saw a row of ashy gray cones piled against the shelter's back wall, and she gritted her teeth and turned away. "They're still here."

"Where?"

"You just don't see them. Let's get away, all right?"

"Right, yeah," he said. "Move along, nothing to see here."

After the malls, the road climbed a long bridge over a rail yard. As they rose higher, they spotted a dark pillar of dust swirling over Sacramento backlit by the orange glow of fire. The stem of the mushroom cloud had dissipated, although tendrils of golden flame shot up from the ground beside the dust pillar. Tall whirlwinds of black dust spun in the distance, and silver light flashed inside them. Heat still streamed from Ground Zero and bathed their faces.

"I am become Death, the destroyer of worlds," Ada whispered with tears welling in her eyes.

"I know what you mean. This is like looking into the pits of Hell," Krista said.

"This is worse than a Base-M hallucination." She covered her face with her hands and sobbed, and Krista hugged her. "Oh, my god, I never thought it would be this bad."

"It's gone," he said. "The whole place is just gone. You can usually see the skyscrapers from here, but they're gone. It's all just dust now."

"It's radioactive dust," Ada said, wiping her cheeks. "Don't go anywhere near it."

"No, no, we'll pass right by. Route 5 is only a few miles ahead, and then we'll be going away from it." He glanced to the south again. "Christ, I feel like I had a limb amputated or something. The city's been there my whole life. It can't be gone."

"Please, just get us far away," Ada said. "I don't want to see any more."

"I'll second that." They drove through a cloud of greasy black smoke, and Krista gagged and covered her face with her robe. "Jaysus, what's that stink? It's like burned plastic or something."

"I can't smell anything," Ada said.

He pulled his shirt up. "It really reeks. I'd close the windows if I had any. Wow, my eyes are watering now."

"We've got to get out of here," Krista croaked. "It's even coming through the robe."

He wiped his eyes and tried to see through the windshield. "I'm going fast as I can."

Ada coughed, causing her nose to start bleeding again, and she covered it with the towel. "My nosebleed's getting worse," she said.

"Let's see." Krista pulled the towel from her nose and gasped. "Jaysus! This thing's totally soaked! You're pouring blood!"

"There's something wrong. My nosebleeds don't usually last so long."

"Okay, lie on your back and pinch your nose hard," Krista said. "Try not to cough. That'll just open it up again."

She coughed again harshly. "It's hard not to with this stink." She barked another cough and reached for the towel.

"Do you have any more towels in that bag?" Krista asked Mark.

He handed her a roll of paper towels, and she ripped strips from it. "Stuff these up your nose. I'll give you more when they're soaked." She leaned into the front seat. "We've got to get someplace safe and take care of this. No more sightseeing, okay?"

"It's not like I'm taking you on some damn tour! I'll get us out as soon as I can!"

On the other side of the bridge, they found a neighborhood of homes that had been blasted into rubble. After a few minutes of steering around and over pieces of the shattered houses, the road widened into a tree-lined parkway. Its trees were leafless too, but their branches blocked the wind and the stink, and the only obstruction was a long caravan of stalled cars. He drove onto the shoulder and picked up speed.

Krista lowered the robe and sniffed the air. "Good. That's a lot better. Now let's see how you're doing." She pulled the strips from Ada's nose and handed her fresh ones. "It's slowing down. Still, I want you to lay there and not move. Just relax and let it stop."

The parkway ended after ten more minutes of driving. Piles of sticks dotted the side of the road where homes once stood, and some of them were aflame; at one, an elderly man calmly sprayed the blaze with a garden hose. Aside from him, nobody combated the fires.

Once they passed the neighborhood, Mark spotted an intersection in the distance. "That's the entrance to Route 5 up there. It looks like there was a pile-up at the traffic light." He slowed as they approached it and saw a pile of twisted, smoldering metal a hundred feet long. "Looks like a thirty, forty vehicle carbecue."

"Don't be a cop, Mark," Krista said.

"Yeah. It's not worth it anyway. No one survives that kinda collision unless Heavy Rescue is on it fast." He turned onto the ramp for Route 5 North. At the highway, he stopped and looked in both directions – the bridge to the south had collapsed into the river, and cars were piled in the wreckage.

He steered around a stopped truck and drove to the empty HOV lane. Soon after, they were cruising north with fresh air flooding the car. The road curved to the west a few minutes later, and they crossed a long bridge over swampy farmland.

Ada sat up and looked through the back window – the glow and the cloud were still there, but they were now far away and getting further every minute. She sat back, turned her face into the wind, and let it wash away the burned stink.

When the bridge ended, he slowed and found an opening in the jumble of stalled cars and trucks. He drove onto the shoulder and took an exit.

"Why are we getting off?" Ada asked. "I kinda liked going fast for once."

"This is our exit. To get to my mom's house from here, you gotta go through Woodland," he said. "We'll head west over the hills using the back roads. That way we can avoid Route 80, which is a disaster on a good day."

They drove onto a main street running through a small, dusty town. Men were clustered on the street corners, each armed with a rifle to repel an enemy that had already come and gone, and they eyed the car as it drove past. They passed through the town and were soon racing through an orange grove.

After traveling a few more minutes, Krista tapped his shoulder. "Can we pull over?" she shouted over the wind noise. "I think we're safe!"

"How about here?" He spotted a parking lot with a decrepit wooden fruit stand at one end, turned into it, and stopped in front of the listing building.

"I've got to have a potty break and a long stretch," Krista said. "And a cigarette, and some water, and a whole lot of other things." Ada opened the door, stepped out, and reached back for Krista. "A little first aid wouldn't hurt, either. How's your nosebleed doing?"

Ada wiped her nose and looked at the towel. "It stopped. Wow, that was a bleeder for the record books."

"You smacked it hard," she said.

"Yeah. It was so bad that I feel a little weak now. I lost a lot of blood."

"Your color is coming back, though." Krista reached into the duffel bag, pulled out three bottles of water, and passed them around. "I'm parched. The air is so dry that my throat hurts."

Mark took a bottle and looked at Sacramento. "I can't wrap my mind around this."

"I know, right? I had the same problem when I figured out Cheyn released the virus on purpose. It was too big and too bad to comprehend."

He frowned and pulled out the medikit. "Yeah. We gotta take care of ourselves right now, though. It helps to focus on this instead of thinking of that." He hooked a thumb over his shoulder. "Why don't you two go take care of business? I'll set up here. I wanna check you both for injuries before we go on."

Krista took Ada's hand and walked behind the wooden shack. When they were done, he cleaned and dressed small scratches all over their bodies. Krista found her jug of painkillers and poured a handful for herself and Ada. "So how are we doing, doc?" she asked.

"You're both beat up. Twink has a lot of bruises on her right side, and that's gonna ache tomorrow." He shined the light on their faces. "It looks like you both have first-degree burns, but just on one side of your body."

"They're flashburns," Ada said. "They'll fade in two or three days."

He leaned against the car and crossed his arms. "You know a lot about nukes, kid. Why's that?"

Ada's face tightened, but Krista didn't notice. "She knows all sorts of nuclear stuff, Mark. It's good to have a whiz kid around at a time like this, isn't it?"

Ada glared at her, spun on her heel, and stalked to the fruit stand.

"What's up with her?" He scratched his head and watched her go. "Sensitive, isn't she?"

"I'd cut her some slack. She's had an awful day."

"We all have." He looked at the glow on the horizon. "Her problem is that she knows too much. Me, I'm kinda grateful to be ignorant of the details right now. It makes things simple, y'know? All I gotta do is survive for the next minute and not think about stuff like black rain."

"Sometimes it's a curse to know too much. And when it comes to that, the kid is truly cursed."

"Yeah, but kids get over stuff fast." He let out a long sigh and sat by the front fender, and she curled up with him and laid her head against his chest.

"While we're waiting for her pout party to end, can you call my mom again?" he asked.

Krista pulled out her tablet and dialed, but she heard only the same warbling tone. He frowned and looked away at the skyglow, and she wrapped her arms around him. "I think it's just a communication glitch. She's probably okay," she said. "Don't worry yourself."

"Yeah, but I will anyway." He ran his fingers through her hair. "How are you doing?"

"I hurt everywhere, but I'm alive and I'm with you. I feel crazy grateful for that."

He pulled her close, breathed a noseful of citrus, and watched the light from Sacramento flicker across the distant hills. "I don't know what I woulda done if you'd gotten hurt or…worse. I'm trying to keep you safe, but Fate keeps throwing more and more at you. Now it's nukes. How do I protect you from nukes?"

"As long as you're around, I'll be safe. You're like my bodyguard." She rested her head on his shoulder and yawned. "I had a bodyguard when I was a kid, and he always kept me safe no matter what. He threatened to tear a kid's head off once for hitting me with an iceball." She murmured a contented purr and draped an arm across his chest. "Gave me a little tingle."

"Well, I'll do my best, but all I can do is hope it never happens again." He ran his fingers up and down her arm. "There's one thing I kept thinking about, driving through that hell," he said softly. When she didn't answer, he bent over to whisper in her ear. "When bad things happen, it makes you think about the good things. It makes you not care what people think and makes you look at what's important. And what's most important is having you with me, Krista." He gave her a light peck on the forehead. "I love you and I always will, till the sun goes out and the stars go home."

She answered with only a soft snuffle. "Okay, I don't deserve to say that, and you're right. I don't deserve you at all. But I can't help how I feel. Are you mad at me? Am I getting outta line?" She didn't answer, so he reached down and turned her face up to his. She was sound asleep.

He turned his face to the stars and laughed, and a few minutes later, he rested his head against the fender and closed his eyes.

MARK'S EYELIDS FLUTTERED OPEN, and he saw a field of stars on the edge of a dense, orange cloud. He'd hoped that the devastation of Sacramento had just been a bad dream, but the ghastly cloud brought his memories back in terrifying detail.

The stench of burned plastic was overpowering. He tried to wave it away from his nose, but he still sneezed, blowing a cloud of dust off Krista's head and waking her. "Whuh?" she asked.

"Hey there, sleepyhead."

She blinked and yawned. "I was asleep?"

"Yeah, we both were. I dunno how long."

She pulled out her tablet. "Jaysus, it's one in the bloody morning!" He got up and helped her to her feet, and she saw the glow of the fires to the east. "That wasn't just a nightmare?"

"No. I wish it was." He looked around the parking lot. "Where's Twink?"

"Last I saw, she was stomping off to that shack. I'll go look."

"Wait." He reached into the car for his pistol. "I'll go first."

They walked around the shack and found Ada sitting on a fruit crate, looking at the ground. "Hey," Krista called. "There you are. It's time to hit the road."

"You go on without me," she said. "Just leave me here."

"What?"

"I want to be left alone, okay? Can't I have my space?"

"Sure, sure. I'll take the left seat and you take the right."

Ada scowled and looked away. "Don't joke around. Look, I can't go on anymore. Just respect that."

"And leave you in the middle of nowhere? You're the one who's joking. C'mon, hop in the car. We'll talk this through."

Ada shook her head.

"You're serious?" Krista asked.

"Yeah." She looked up at the foothills, illuminated by the faint, flickering light from Sacramento. "It's the end of the line, sister." She smiled, but her eyes were moist and sad. "Thanks for the wicked pissin ride."

Krista turned and whispered into Mark's ear. "This sounds bad. I've got to talk her around this. Wait at the car, wouldja?" She watched him turn the corner and then knelt next to her. "You sound real depressed."

"With good reason."

"It's about the bombing, isn't it?"

Ada nodded once.

"Then let's talk it out. You'll feel better if you do."

"The last thing I want is to chat."

"So we'll talk about something else," Krista said. "It might help take your mind off the bombing."

"*Nothing* will take my mind off that."

"Right," Krista said. "I know how you feel."

"No, you don't. Just respect my wishes, okay?"

She took Ada's hand. "I *am* respecting your wishes. You wanted me to talk you out of this. If you didn't, you'd already be walking through that dark field over yonder where I couldn't find you."

Ada sniffed and then laughed softly. "You suck."

"And if I like the guy, I'll swallow."

"Eww!" She shivered and covered her mouth. "You're gonna make me spew! I can't believe you said that!"

Krista gave her a wide, white smile.

"And you're proud of it? God, you're such a slut!"

"God, you're such a virgin!"

Ada poked her in the chest with a finger. "Hey, not by choice, sister!"

Krista grabbed the finger and laughed. "There you go – now that's the Ada I know and love!"

She wiped the tears from her cheeks with her sleeve. "You're the kinda person my mom warned me to stay away from. Why do I hang with you?"

"Because I'm the person your mom warned you about, dummy." Krista squeezed her hand. "Come with me. We'll see San Francisco. We'll see Chinatown together –"

"No way. I lived in China. Total suckitude."

"Then we'll ride the cable cars, and we'll talk whenever you're ready."

"I'm not in the mood to sightsee. I've had enough of that for a lifetime."

"I know, but things will get better," Krista said. "Right now, we're at the bottom, and it looks pretty damn depressing. But it won't always be like that."

"I wish you were right."

"I know I am. From here, the only way out is up. Come on." She held out her hand.

Ada looked from her hand to the skyglow of Sacramento, and then she wiped the tears from her face again.

A MILE OUTSIDE VACAVILLE, Mark found a dirt road and began a slow climb through a canyon. At the top, the trees were stripped bare, and leaves swirled in eddies around their trunks. Light tan dust coated every surface.

A few minutes later, the trees thinned and they climbed to a grassy ridge, where they found a turnout for a scenic viewpoint. He pulled in and stopped near a line of radio towers with bent and twisted dishes swaying loosely in the breeze.

"We're on Mount Vaca," he said. "After this, the road goes through the hills and comes out north of Napa, but the surface is really rough. I gotta stretch my bones before I try that."

"Good," said Krista. "We need a break. Are we safe here?"

"Yeah. We're fifteen, twenty miles west of Sacramento, and we're upwind. I gotta get the medikit and check out Twink's wounds again too, see if they finally stopped bleeding." He climbed out and opened the passenger door, and Ada tumbled out and sprinted for a clump of bushes at the lot's edge. He helped Krista out, and she stood and stretched, pulling the dirty robe around her waist. "How are you feeling?" he asked.

Krista forced a smile. "Sore everywhere. Ribs hurt like hell too, but I'll be okay. I'd love some ibuprofen, though."

"You got it. How's the eyes?"

Krista blinked a few times and looked around the lot. "Everything still looks fuzzy, but with this dust all over the place, I can't tell. There's still a blank spot in the center of my vision too, and it's driving me nuts. Where'd Ada go?"

"Over there." He pointed to a thicket of bare branches.

Krista reached into the duffel bag and pulled out a roll of toilet paper. "Be back in a minute."

"Need help?"

"I don't. I can handle this if I go slow." She hugged him and then shuffled to the bushes.

He reached into the car, pulled out the binoculars and the medikit, and carried them to a picnic table overlooking the valley. The glow from Sacramento was so bright that he didn't need a flashlight to find his supplies in the kit.

Ada walked from the bushes shaking leaves from her hair. She noticed some scratches on her new boots, scowled, and then plopped onto the bench.

"You know, on a clear day, you can see everything from here," he said, looking through the case for skinspray and painkillers. "Sacramento, Redding, even the skyscrapers in San Francisco."

She stood and looked around. "Where's San Francisco?" He pointed west, and she picked up the binoculars and focused on the city. "The lights are still on, so it hasn't been nuked. That means this wasn't World War Four."

"You mean World War Three?"

"No, that was mostly over by 1957. World War Four is next on the hit list."

"Well, whatever you call it, I'm glad it didn't happen, and my mom's okay." He sprayed wound cleaner and antibiotic on her scratches, but the wounds still bled freely. "You've got a few stubborn bleeders, Twink. You hurt anywhere else?"

She shook her head and walked to a stone wall. When she saw the mile-wide circle of glowing coals that had been Sacramento, she gasped and covered her chest as if she'd been punched in the heart. "Omigod," she whispered, lowering herself to the bench slowly.

"You okay?" he asked, and she shook her head. He walked to the wall and watched the devastation below, the light of the burning city flickering across his face. "Jesus Christ. This is gonna be in my nightmares forever."

She nodded and looked into the dirt at her feet.

"I don't understand why anyone would do this. I mean, Sacramento wasn't a world power center like Washington. It was just a small town. It's pointless to blow it away."

She shrugged but didn't answer.

"I'll bet the Reds did it," he said. "Well, I hope we turned the place into an ashtray."

Still looking into the dirt, she said, "The Reds didn't do this."

"Yeah? Then who did?"

"Us."

"What?" He spun around and gawped at her. "What did you say?"

"*We* did it, Mark. Americans."

"What? Like we did this to ourselves?"

"Yes," she said in a small voice. "I know that's hard to believe, but it's true."

"That's impossible." He sat on the stone wall and shook his head. "Look, you're real smart, but you're wrong on this one. I don't believe we'd nuke one of our own cities."

She let out a tremulous sigh. "A fact is a fact, no matter what you believe."

"But it doesn't make any sense. Why on Earth would we do that?"

"I don't know! Why can't anybody figure things out for themselves?" She rested her elbows on her knees, pulling at the roots of her hair. "Why do I have to give all the answers? Why me?"

"Cuz you're the only smart person we got?"

"Oh, fuck that." She doubled up until her face touched her knees and sobbed. "Fuck everything. Nothing matters anymore. Don't ask me for answers."

He stood and gazed at Sacramento. "I just don't think Americans would do this kinda thing."

Krista walked from the car, buttoning her hoodie. "What kind of thing?"

He paced along the wall and kicked up clouds of dust. "Twink's gone off the rez. Some delayed shock reaction or something. She's got this weird-ass idea that it was an American bomb."

"Oh, Jaysus." Krista sat on the bench beside her. "Are you sure?"

"Oh, c'mon, don't tell me you believe her," he said, and Krista shot him a warning glance. He grumbled and sat on the wall.

"So it was American?" she asked.

Ada nodded, still looking at her feet. "It was a W104 Mark Eighteen strong-fission warhead with a yield of 950 kilotons. It was delivered by a Lancet cruise missile launched from one of our Patriot submarines."

"This is getting ridiculous," Mark said. "How can you be so certain about that?"

Ada looked up from the ground and wiped away tears with her sleeve. "Because I designed the W104 warhead."

KRISTA STOOD SLOWLY and walked to the wall, watching the embers and absorbing Ada's revelation. "This was Baby Bang Bang, wasn't it?"

"Basically." Ada nodded slowly and gazed at the toes of her boots again. "It was my particle trigger but not my bomb core. Los Alamos modified the Black Betty core from the M209 man-portable nuke instead. They wanted the higher yield-to-weight ratio even though it's the filthiest bomb ever made. I argued against that, but they were under lotsa pressure from the White House to deliver an ultralight warhead for the Lancet missile. They ignored me."

"But how can you be sure this was your bomb?" Krista asked.

"I saw the open-air test of the W104 Mark Three at Punatayu Atoll four years ago. It was a dual flash – the fusion implosion was blue and the fission burst was yellow, just like I saw tonight. I felt a double overpressure wave too, and that's the W104 detonation signature. Only one device on the planet does that. And I designed it."

"Well, shit," Krista said.

"Yeah, shit." She lit a cigarette and exhaled slowly.

"I thought they were waiting till you had your doctorate."

"They lied," Ada said. "And I lied to you. We all lie, we're all liars, and we all have stupid secrets..."

"It's okay. I understand. Everybody lies, Ada."

"Not for the reasons I do. I lied cuz I didn't want you to know I can wipe out the world, not cuz I stole your lipstick or something." She took a fierce puff and watched the cloud drift away in Ground Zero's orange glow. "Here's the truth – they took me away a month after Bumfuck Wyoming and never let me go. I've been flying to Los Alamos nearly every weekend for five years, and I spend two solid months in the lab over the summer. I'm there so much that I bought a house in White Rock to get some privacy. And now I'm the chief physicist of the Lightweight Devices Lab, and we're designing all sorts of nasty shit that would give you a coronary on the spot if you knew. We're even working on the W104 Mark

Twenty, an *improved* variant of this little firecracker, cuz the Mark Eighteen wasn't badass enough."

She looked at her hands for a few moments, wringing them slowly, and then she pointed to Sacramento. "And you think this is bad? Oh, no, I can do even worse. I can make a light fifty-megaton warhead the Navy can pop on a Lancet. It's a string-fission device, and stringchain reactions don't generate a shockwave like other ultrahigh-yield nukes. It just burns a hole in the Earth's crust and triggers catastrophic earthquakes. With that, we could melt any silo or command center the Reds have. Los Alamos will crank me hard to build it once they find out I know how. And when that bomb's done and all those Patriot subs are finished, we'll be able to wipe out any country's land-based nuclear capability. Instantly. With no warning. You think the Reds will let us build that?"

"Naw," Mark said. "They'll blow us away first."

"Wrong. They'll try, they'll fail, we'll retaliate, and here comes Doomsday. Get used to looking at Ground Zeroes, Skid."

"So we just keep you outta their hands," Mark said.

"That's not so easy. You don't know what they're like. The only thing I can do is get that bomb design outta my head before they realize I can build it. And how can I forget something I already know?"

"We'll keep you safe," Krista said, wrapping an arm around her shoulders.

"I just wanted you to like me, but you wouldn't have liked me if you knew what I really was. What I was really running away from." She nodded to herself and then spoke softly. "If I go back, there'll be even more Sacramentos…"

"Stop. You're not responsible for the whole world," Krista said. "You're not God. You're a kid, and you're a good kid, and I love you, and I won't have you bashing yourself. Just because somebody else was a monster with what you made doesn't make you one."

"Thousands died cuz of me, maybe millions." Ada ran her fingers through her hair. "What's it matter, thousands or millions? What's the difference in the end? I'm still the worst murderer ever."

"Sounds like you're taking responsibility for what the scumbags do," Mark said. "You can't. Their ugly isn't your fault, it's theirs."

"Right. You didn't do this," Krista said, hugging her tight. "I want you to repeat that till you believe it, and if you don't, I will – you didn't do this. You wouldn't have. You're no monster. Somebody else is the monster, somebody from our side." She gazed at the glowing embers surrounded by a ragged ring of fire. "Cheyn, I'll bet."

"Our own president nuked us?" Mark asked.

"He's a cold-blooded bastard. I know the sonofabitch, and he'd do this. He's got no heart."

"But why? Why attack his own country? Is he off his rocker and just…" He stood and looked into the valley. "It makes no sense. He's our president, for chrissakes. He's on our side."

"He's on his own side," Krista said.

"But I don't get it. What's he gain from this?"

"What's he gain?" Krista asked. "Congress would have impeached him if the state seceded, right? Well, he stopped that. They didn't vote, they didn't secede, and now California's not his problem anymore."

He glared at Sacramento, a muscle twitching in his jaw. "I'd shoot the bastard myself if he was here." His hands balled into fists, and he kicked a rock so hard that it shattered against the wall.

"Calm down," Krista said.

"Don't tell me to calm down!" he said. "Try me again next year!"

Krista nodded and looked at Ada, who was staring glassy-eyed at Sacramento again. "How are you doing?"

"I'm fine," she said. "I can take care of this. May I have a moment alone with Mark, please?"

"Sure, I'll go get some water and let you two talk." Krista shuffled to the car, while Ada walked to the wall and stood beside Mark.

"Don't bust my chops right now," he said. "I'm not in a great mood."

"All right." She took his hand. "Mark, are we friends?"

"In that tough-love kinda way, yeah."

"So you wouldn't want to see me hurt, right? If something was going to hurt me, you'd try to stop it?"

"Sure, yeah."

"Then I need a favor from you. Promise me? It's the only favor I'll ever ask for."

"Okay," he said. "I'm a little confused here, though. What are you talking about?"

She dropped her cigarette into the dirt and crushed it with the toe of her boot. "I want you to kill me."

"What?"

"Take me into the bushes and shoot me in the back of the head. Make it quick. Just don't let Krista see my body, please? Leave it here, go to San Fran –"

"I'm not gonna shoot you!"

"Please, I want you to. I *need* you to."

"Fuck no! Look, Twink, you gotta get over this kinda –"

"There's no getting over this!" she shrieked.

"Get control of yourself!"

"I *am* getting control of myself!" She reached for the pistol in his waistband. He batted her hands away and tried to grab her, but she twisted out of his grip and whirled to face him. "You sonofabitch!" she screamed. "I'll do it myself if you won't!" She jumped over the wall and ran downhill toward Sacramento's radioactive cinders.

Krista ran up to him. "What's going on? What's she doing?"

He vaulted the wall and ran after Ada without answering. She watched them run for a moment and then followed. A grove of bare trees forced Ada to slow down, and he grabbed her around the chest and lifted her into the air with her legs flailing.

"Lemme go! Lemme die!" she screamed. She twisted and bucked until even he couldn't hold her, and then she dropped to the dirt and clutched her stomach. With a groan, she sank to her knees and spewed yellow vomit across the grass.

"Ada!" Krista wrapped her arm around her. "What's wrong?"

"Lemme go," she said weakly. "You have to lemme go. If you love me, you'll lemme die –" She convulsed again and vomited, and this time the liquid was dark.

"What?" Krista glanced at him.

He shrugged and knelt in the dust beside her. "We gotta get her outta here," he said. "You get her legs, okay?"

He picked her up again, and Krista grabbed her legs. They carried her back up the hill and sat her on the bench.

"Don't do this to me, please," Ada said. "Please."

"Do what?" Krista asked.

"Don't make me live. If you love me, lemme die."

"What? What are you talking about?"

"That's what she was saying just before she ran." He pulled a foil packet out of the medikit, ripped it open with his teeth, and then slapped a patch on her arm. "This oughta quiet her down. It's a benzodiazepine."

Ada's eyes widened. "No! No patches, please, I hate zombie patches!"

"You need this," he said. "You'll relax in a minute."

"I don't want to relax…I don't…" Her eyes became glassy and her breathing slowed. "Don't do this…to me. I want to…" She closed her eyes, and her head sagged onto Krista's shoulder.

"What was that all about?" Krista asked.

"Probably something about the bombing, I guess. She just flipped out."

"The patch should help her. Her mom used them to stop her panic attacks. I hope that's all this is."

"I dunno, but those patches are powerful. She won't be freaking out for four hours." He flicked a finger against her cheek. "In fact, she's totally out. That was fast."

"Well, we can't leave her like this. Help me get her on the ground." They picked her up and laid her in front of the bench, and Krista sat and rested Ada's head on her lap. "I love the hell out of this kid. I hope this was just a panic attack."

"I dunno what that was. That was an impressive barf, though, like frat-boy-grade spew. That was weird."

"She's just a puker. Once the stress hits, her digestion slams into reverse and up comes dinner. I'm more worried about that breakdown. I've never seen her crack like that, and we've been through a lot together."

"Naw, don't worry. She'll get over it and move on soon. Kids are resilient."

"*She* is, that's for sure," Krista said. "Every day is a new day to her." She stroked her hair, and Ada's head relaxed on her leg. "What I wouldn't give to be able to do that."

He rested his hand on her knee. "How about you? How are you feeling?"

"I feel like someone just threw me against a tree. I'm half-blind and half-deaf. I'm red on one side and white on the other. My best friend just tried to kill herself." She gave him a wan smile. "I'm not handling any of this, Mark."

He daubed cream on her face. "That should help with your burns. I can give you a magic carpet ride if you want. I have some serious painkillers in my box."

"I could use a handful later, if it's no trouble." She ran her fingers through Ada's hair. "And how would you be holding up?"

He sat back against the bench and rubbed his neck. "I'm exhausted. I can't keep my eyes open. Maybe her panic attack just drained me or something."

"Well, make yourself comfy." She tapped her thigh. "I'm a good pillow. And it looks like we're going to be here a while."

"Yeah, I should rest. The road ahead is rough." He laid his head on her leg and yawned. "I've got a hunch that today's gonna be a lot better than yesterday. Kinda has to when you think about it."

She nodded, looking at the blasted hole of Sacramento. "I wish I could take it one day at a time like you."

"It helps if you're shallow and simpleminded. You're in California now, so you might try to fit in." In a few minutes, his head grew heavy on her leg, and he began to snore softly.

She lit a cigarette, which tasted terrible mixed with the stench of melted plastic, but the smoke overwhelmed the stink after a while. She found the binoculars and focused on the wasted circle of annihilation, and beyond it, the devastation they'd driven through. Every telephone pole she saw was flattened and pointing away from Ground Zero. Trains and buses lay on their sides, and thick plumes of smoke rose from the airport. A wind gust picked up from the north, stirring a small dust storm that raced along the base of the hills and moaned a lonely, hollow sound.

The horizon began to lighten over the distant mountains, and she spotted a splash of white on a hillside a few miles away; she turned her binoculars toward it and saw the tail of a passenger jet surrounded by crumpled metal. Wisps of smoke rose from the wreckage and were whipped away by the wind. She scanned the area around the debris field, but she saw no survivors, nor any rescuers rushing to the crash site. With a shiver, she realized they never would – a plane crash was insignificant compared to the night's other horrors.

The Life Force needs you, Figment said. *It needs you to describe this horror to humanity. Don't be gentle. Atrocities like this can never happen again.*

She nodded and pulled her tablet from her pocket. Although it couldn't find a satellite link, it picked up a weak signal from one of the bent cellular antennas behind her. She began to write, not caring if the Federals learned where she was.

○─□─□─□─○

The Rake
News Post of October 9, 2043

EIGHTEEN HELLS
We've finally seen the enemy's face. It was in the mirror the whole time

The sun won't rise today on Mount Vaca. Sacramento will block the light.

I see the city drift to the southeast. It floats high above the valley, scraping the mountain crests, a black cloud of ruin built from blasted dreams of life and love. Sacramento has become a plume of poison that will kill all it touches.

I see the broad valley spread out below. It was once filled with a living city and its suburbs, but through the smoke clouds, I now see only the myriad flickering of flames glittering in a mockery of life.

Ground Zero doesn't seem real. It looks like some science fiction world, an alien planet where the land glows with embers, some place where giant creatures scratched a grid of roads into the burning soil and then departed. Outside this other world is a circle of fire, but I see no emergency lights there or quenching jets of water. Everything just burns, and everything in this ring of fire will be consumed soon. Nobody will fight the flames, I fear, because nobody has survived to fight them.

I see monsters stalking this alien world – great swirling clouds of black dust spinning with terrifying flashes of silvery lightning, monsters that search out and destroy what life may have survived the blast; they meander through the ruins, these devils of dust, followed by smaller, whirling columns of bright flame that dart about and flare bright when they find even more to consume. They stroll this landscape as if they own the land, and they do. This valley belongs to Satan now, and it belongs to these monsters marching through this fire of Eighteen Hells.

And through the smoke, I see bright silver clouds that float above the ground; phosphorescent and shimmering, almost alive and sentient, I think these might be the souls of the dead seeking their loved ones or a release from Hell. I don't know what they are, and I may never know. I don't want to know any more than I do, so I turn my eyes away and look at the sky.

Above me, I see the deathly cloud stretching to the east. The light from the burning land illuminates it with hues of dead yellow and orange, and the thing seems to eat these colors and absorb them as it has absorbed all else.

I was blinded for a time by the impossibly bright flash of the blast; my sight is now returning, but as I look in the valley, I wish it wasn't. Even though it corrodes all hope inside me, I can't turn away from this vision because the horror hypnotizes and captivates me. I fear I'll never become free of it.

I hear nothing but the whispers of the dead as the hot wind blows through barren trees. I hear an unnatural rustling, too, like paper being crushed in a rough hand. I have no idea what makes this sound, but it's terrifying and lonely; I think it's a deathsong, and it frightens me. I wish it would stop, and I yearn to hear a cry, or a siren, or anything at all that says life dares to remain.

But I hear nothing that sounds like life. I was deafened for a time, and I can now hear, but I wish I could be deaf an hour longer so I might hear in my mind the happy sounds I remember. I cover my ears and I still hear that rustling. I fear that this sound has burned into my brain.

I smell a foul wind, a hot, dry, and dead gust that washes over me and clothes me in the stink of the burned city, a smell of scorched dirt and molten plastic that stings my nose and eyes and makes me gasp for air. Although I hope I can forget this death smell, I know I never will.

I want my nightmares back. I yearn for my boogeymen and golems to rescue me, to banish this most terrible of visions – the nightmare of our own creation.

Yes, we made this nightmare. Sacramento was destroyed by an American bomb.

A Navy thermonuclear device detonated over Sacramento last night, a W104 Mark Eighteen strong-fission warhead with an explosive force of 950 kilotons. It was delivered by a Lancet missile launched from an American submarine.

Why would Americans do this? I believe that Sacramento was destroyed by Gabriel Cheyn to stop California's secession vote. For that insignificant reason, he wasted a city and its life.

A million people died in fiery anguish, and you should feel every death, Cheyn. I make this solemn promise before all the deities in every pantheon ever conceived: If I find you before the assassins do, I'll drag you down to Hell's flaming pits myself and savor your screams, even if I spend eternity melting in unholy fire.

Because Hell doesn't scare me anymore. I've seen Sacramento.

-KLW

Dream Krista crouched in a field of vividly green grass, and a man stood at a distant line of tall trees. Between them was a child – she couldn't tell if it was a boy or a girl – with curly, flame-red hair even brighter than Krista's. She called to the child, who stepped toward her and then closed the distance until he or she fell into her arms with a squeal of joy.

She kissed the child's head and then froze – helicopter blades tortured the air not far away, and the sound was coming closer. She snatched the child and ran for the trees as the Federal helicopter's backwash whipped the grass.

Her eyelids snapped open; a few hundred yards to the south, a white helicopter with 'SFPD' painted on the side hovered over the mountain. She drew a relieved breath and picked up her binoculars.

The sky remained as dark as night to the east, but it had brightened to the north and south, and a red dawn spread across the horizon. No clouds drifted across the sky except the black one.

The valley wasn't empty of people, as it had seemed earlier. Helicopters hovered over an encampment north of the city, and the twinkling of red lights showed that fire engines and ambulances were at work. Under the debris plume, the Sierra foothills were still clothed in darkness, and she couldn't tell if anybody had survived there.

More helicopter blades chopped the air, and another SFPD aircraft crested the hill. It rose above Mount Vaca, hovered for a moment, and then dove into the valley.

Ada stirred on her lap. She pulled back a lock of hair and saw that her eyes were open. "Good. You're awake," she said.

"I'm awake."

"How do you feel? You had a bad night."

"I had a bad night."

She sat up and Krista noticed her flat and empty eyes. "You okay?"

"I'm okay." She stood shakily and ripped the patch off her arm. "Freakin zombie patch."

More helicopters flew by, and Mark walked over from the car. "It's time to haul ass. We're gonna have reporters up here soon, and we don't wanna give interviews." He looked at Ada's eyes. "Hey, you okay?"

"I'm okay."

He took her arm, and she stumbled beside him to the car. Krista dusted off her robe, glanced one last time at Ground Zero, and then turned and followed.

AFTER HOURS OF RUMBLING OVER DIRT ROADS, they crossed a small river into Marin County, and the world returned to normal. Cars motored on roads free of wreckage, light poles stood erect, and traffic signals flashed green and red. The gum-sweet scent of eucalyptus drifted on the air, not melted plastic and burned earth. Along the sidewalks, joggers jogged and dog-walkers walked dogs, oblivious to the holocaust only miles to the east.

"Is this a time-warp thing?" Krista asked.

"Nah, it's just that nothing's real in Marin County," he said. "We call this place North Egypt. It's the Land of Denial."

"Ah, now, I love Denial," Krista said. "It's my favorite river."

"It's mine too," Ada said. "I'm trying as hard as I can to stuff last night into the deepest, darkest Sanity Cell I can find, but a heaping helping of denial would go a long way."

"You've got to let me borrow some of those Sanity Cells. I could use a lot of forgetting right now," Krista said. "Okay, how about we make a pact

– last night never happened. There's nothing to worry about and we're safe."

"It's a deal," Mark said, holding out his fist, and Krista and Ada bumped it.

He drove for another half hour, and they watched the scenery slide by until he spotted the Tiburon exit, where he turned off and drove along a waterfront road. The early morning sky was cloudless, and the water was deep blue; sailboats tacked against the onshore breeze and cruised across the bay.

"Yeah, Denial's a beautiful place," Ada said.

"You're catching it from me," Krista said. "I knew I'd be a bad influence."

"Oh, you won't be a bad influence on Belvedere Island," he said. "You've got enough money for these people to…oops!" He turned at a fork in the road. "I always miss the turn. I think the islanders like that the only road onto the island is so hard to find. And it works. I've been driving past it for years." After a minute of driving along a sailboat-studded shoreline, he turned and climbed a road to the island's interior.

"Your mom must be rich," Ada said.

"Nah, she's poor as dirt," he said. "She can't afford this place, and that's probably why the locals hate us. They call us the 'Belvedere Hillbillies.' They used to whisper it, but now they just say it to her face."

"Now that's rude," Krista said.

"Yeah, rich people can get nasty," he said. "Anyway, she inherited the house from Lucky, and she couldn't afford to live here otherwise. I don't think she would if you gave her a choice."

"Who's Lucky?" Ada asked.

"Her first husband. He was a real good high-stakes poker player. In fact, that's how he met my mom. He was taking a break at the blackjack tables, and she was one of the dealers. They hit it off right then and there."

"Ahh, another Vegas romance," Krista said. "I've heard about them."

"It wasn't in Vegas. It was at a casino in Pago Pago."

"Pago Pago, in American Samoa?" Ada asked.

"Yeah. You know where that is?"

"I went through it on the way to Punatayu Atoll," Ada said. "What little I saw from the airport was beautiful."

"Never seen it myself," he said. As they climbed to the top of the island, the road narrowed. Rhododendrons and azaleas crowded the lane and brushed the car as they drove past; behind the bushes, tall homes clad in glass stood proudly.

He passed a stucco garage, its white paint flaking and a bright silver chain dangling over the door, and stopped at a stone wall. "Here we are," he said, opening the door and holding out a hand.

Krista climbed out and then helped Ada, who wobbled on her feet when she tried to stand. "I'm fine now," she said. "I just got dizzy from the zombie patch. So where's this house?"

"Over yonder, behind the garage."

She looked around, caught a flash of the morning sun, and sneezed violently. Blood started to flow from her nose again, and Krista reached into the duffel bag and grabbed the paper towels. "I thought you were done with this." She wiped the blood from Ada's face and handed her a wad of fresh towels.

"I thought I was too."

He reached past them and dragged out the duffel bag. "We can take care of that inside. C'mon, follow me." He led them past the garage, and they crossed a short bridge to a door set in a vine-covered wall. He punched a code into an alarm panel and opened the door, and they walked into a small foyer with a staircase descending to a lower floor. A wide, tall room cluttered with furniture was beyond the foyer, with floor-to-ceiling windows framing a panoramic view of San Francisco.

"It's me!" he called as he walked into the room.

A low wall at the far end separated a kitchen from the rest of the long space. He walked to a large cooking island in the kitchen, set his bag down beside it, and waved for Krista and Ada to come over.

"I have no idea where she is," he said. "Maybe she's out swimming. She does that some mornings." He peered through the window wall onto a balcony. "Oh, there she is."

He swung the door open, and an unseen woman shrieked. "Markie! You're all right!" She shrieked again and he murmured something in reply.

"That was a big welcome home. Like moms everywhere, I guess," Krista said, sitting on a stool at the island.

"Not *my* mom. She'd tell me off first, slap a patch on me second, and then *maybe* hug me when I was safely zombified."

"Oh, I don't think so. I think you two will fall into each other's arms and never let go."

"I hope so. If I ever find her, that is," Ada said. "I just got a helluva lot further away from that."

"It's a setback, that's for certain," Krista said, pulling paper towels off a roll on the counter. "We'll get back to it as soon as we can, but right now we need to take care of this bleedin bleeder. Sit on this stool and relax."

"This is an epic bloodshow," Ada said as Krista stuffed strips of paper towel into her nostrils. "This isn't just a nosebleed. It's a freakin nose period."

"It's got to stop sometime. Now pinch your nose and tilt your head back. That seems to help."

Ada looked up at the wooden ceiling. "This is a nice place," she said. "When we came in, I swear I saw the top of the Golden Gate Bridge."

"You did." Krista said, peering through the window again. "This is a grand view. No wonder they made the whole wall glass."

"All I'm seeing is the ceiling," Ada said. "What I want to see most is the inside of my eyelids. How long will this reunion take?"

As if in answer, the door opened again. Mark walked through with a petite, tanned woman not much taller than Ada; as she came closer, Krista saw that the light bronze was her natural skin color. Her long hair was almost black, as were her almond-shaped eyes, and she appeared to be no older than Krista. "This is my mom, Marissa," he said.

"*This* is your mom?" she asked, looking from her up to Mark.

"I know, it's hard to believe this big man came from me, but he was a lot smaller when he was born." She held out her hand. "Marissa Savu."

Krista shook it and smiled. "Pleasure to meet you. Krista Warner."

Marissa shrieked again. "The rebel? Tell me you're the rebel! Is she that rebel, Markie?"

"Yeah, Ma."

She danced a small jig, whirled to a cabinet and pulled out an immense mug, and thumped it on the counter in front of Krista. "Drink coffee. Tell stories."

"Ma, we haven't slept for four days. Can you interrogate her later?" he asked.

"That's what the coffee's for, Markie, but you can run along if you want. Don't let us keep you up. Oh, who's this?" She looked past Krista, and Ada held out her hand.

"Ada Dang. Dice to eet you."

"Do you have a nosebleed, dear? First, never tilt your head back." She opened the refrigerator door, took out a package of bacon, and pulled off two slices. "Stuff this up each nostril, and it'll stop just like that!" She tried to snap her greasy fingers.

Ada looked at the meat strips with one eyebrow arched.

"No, it really works," Mark said. "But it makes your nose feel weird."

She eyed the bacon, shrugged, and stuffed it in her nostrils.

"Ma, she needs to get some sleep," he said. "Can I put her up in the guest bedroom?"

"Sure, go ahead. Just throw my stuff on the floor."

He opened a door across from the kitchen. Right after, swearing and the sounds of heavy objects falling came from inside.

Marissa pulled a carafe from a coffeemaker and filled Krista's mug to the rim. "What do I need to do to hear your story, Wild Woman?"

Krista sipped from the mug and sighed. "I haven't had a decent cuppa in weeks. Just keep the brew coming, and I'll keep talking." She slipped off the stool and drained her cup. "Okay, refill me and let's go."

"It's a deal!" Marissa said. "Out to the balcony! No time to waste!" She turned for the door but stopped when she heard footsteps thumping up the steps. "Here comes Mikey. You'll like him, dear," she said, patting Ada's shoulder. "He's about your age."

Ada's eyes widened, and she plucked the bacon out and rubbed her nose clean. "I'm a mess! I can't be seen like this!" She turned to bolt for the guest bedroom and saw a boy standing in front of her wearing a Blac Sacrament T-shirt.

"Seen like what?" he asked.

"I…umm…" Ada stammered, and her heart stammered as well. He was a few inches taller than her, but he had the same bronze complexion, dark almond eyes, and full lips as his mother. His long and glossy black hair was pulled back in a ponytail. Without thinking, she licked her lips and tucked a lock of hair behind her ear.

"You're beautiful. Don't change a thing." He held out his hand. "Name's Micah Wright."

"Ada Lang." After a moment, she took his hand.

"Hey, you're all shaky and stuff. No reason to be nervous around me," he said, and then he looked down at their clasped hands. "You can let go now."

"Sorry," she muttered.

A door slammed behind them, and Mark called out, "Watch out, Mikey, she's a biter! Don't make eye contact!"

Micah turned around and hugged him. "Ma was worried sick about you, but I told her you were too stupid to die. Guess I was right. So what was it like?"

"It was like nothing. Nothing happened last night. We're sticking to that story, okay?"

"Okay. You still gonna say that when you go all mutant?"

"If I was gonna mutate, I'd change into you," Mark said. "I don't feel myself shrinking down to your size yet. My underwear still fits."

Micah reached up and ran his fingers along Mark's hairline. "At least the radiation made your lobotomy scar disappear."

"I'm impressed you can reach that high now. And you're not even wearing your elevator shoes!"

"Boys!" Marissa warned, and they examined the floor sheepishly.

"So really, what was it like?" Micah asked.

"I don't wanna talk about it, Mikey. Leave it."

"It sounded hellish. I just read the post that Warner chick wrote on *Midnight Sun* and looked at all the pictures. It was way beyond bad. I couldn't even recognize some places. Did you see those pictures she took?"

"Didn't need to. I was with her the whole time." He pointed to Krista, who gave Micah a small wave. "Krista, meet Micah. Micah, meet That Warner Chick."

"Jesus, *you're* Warner? You're here?" Micah turned to Mark and fist-bumped him. "Yowza, dude! How'd a simian like you pull that off?"

"It's a long, weird story," he said.

"Which I'm going to hear right now," Marissa said, yanking Krista toward the door. "You can come along and listen in if you want, Mikey. Grab a cup."

"Oh, yeah. Wouldn't miss this for the world." As he filled a mug, he asked Ada, "Are you coming?"

She shook her head. "Sorry. I'm beat, Micah. But it was nice to meet you."

"Yeah. Maybe I'll see you later." He smiled back at her. "I wanna hear your story too."

CROSSING GEHENNA

Day 52
Friday morning, October 9, 2043
Fair Oaks, California

As helicopters awakened Krista on Mount Vaca, Bob Downs was regaining consciousness.

The ceiling above him was blurry, and he tried to straighten his eyeglasses to bring it into focus, but they weren't on his face. He began to sit up to find them but almost blacked out from the pain it brought.

His head spinning, he laid back on something that felt like carpet and checked his surroundings. To his myopic eyes, he appeared to be lying in a bland office lobby, and he saw no threats except for the stocky, white-clothed man standing by a desk and holding a halberd at his side.

Slowly, he reached for the pistol in his belt holster and found that his captor had left him his weapon. The white clothing had to be body armor, and his guard was so confident of it that he hadn't bothered to disarm him.

He looked up at the ceiling again – that made no sense. In fact, nothing made any sense, but he knew one thing: The only safe enemy was a dead one. Trying not to alert the guard, he slipped his finger into the trigger housing, and then he pulled the pistol up and nailed him between the eyes. He dropped like felled timber.

Downs dragged himself across the dirty carpet to his kill. When he was a foot away, he saw that it wasn't a guard but a grinning molar holding a white toothbrush in its hand. Carved beneath the smoking hole in its wooden forehead were the words DR. EMMETT WHITE – THE SMILE FACTORY.

He pulled himself up on his arms and rested against a reception desk. *I'm in a dentist's waiting room*, he thought. *Why? But threat assessment comes first, Downs. Keep it together.*

If he was inside a dentist's office, he had defensible shelter and medical supplies. His glasses were missing, but he had his sidearm and his backpack, so he could defend himself. Threat-wise, he was safe for the moment.

Next, he assessed his condition. The bandages on his hands were gone, but the raw wounds were caked with light tan grit that had stanched the bleeding. He hurt everywhere, but his left arm hurt the most – bolts of pain shot from his shoulder and down his arm when he tried to raise it. He pulled back the collar of his shirt and examined the joint; the skin around the front of his shoulder had sunk into a hole where the bone had been.

"Anterior dislocation of the shoulder," he said, recalling his senior year lectures at MMU. Speaking those few words made his vocal cords ache, though, and he grabbed his canteen and gargled. Once his throat no longer hurt, he pulled the emergency medical kit from his backpack and opened it. He swallowed a few painkillers and then filled a syringe with anesthetic and injected it around the hole.

After he began to feel numb, he lay on the floor, rested his left forearm on his stomach, and rotated it up until it was perpendicular to the ground. Wrapping his other hand around the injured arm's elbow, he pulled gently toward the shoulder joint, clenching his teeth and trying not to scream as bolts of pain shot from his shoulder. After five minutes of agony, his arm popped back into its socket and the pain abated.

"Thank you, God," he whispered. He sat up against the reception desk again, and then he reached for his backpack with his uninjured arm and dug inside for his rations. He found a meal packet, tried to read the label, then gave up and pulled the heating strip out. As he waited for it to warm up, he pulled his tablet out and groaned: The screen said it was 9:17 AM on Friday. He'd been unconscious for half a day.

Outside, gloppy rain pattered on the pavement, and the air stank of burned plastic, ozone, and dirt mixed with the piney woodsmoke of a campfire. Spooning lukewarm, tasteless chipped beef into his mouth, he looked through the broken door at the weak light, which was the ominous brown color of a thunderstorm at dusk. He tried to recall how he'd ended up in this alien place and gotten so badly injured, but all he found was a blank spot in his memory. The last thing he remembered was walking past a convenience store the previous evening.

For a moment, he wondered if he'd accidentally stumbled through a wormhole lurking on San Juan Avenue and landed on some stinking, brown-skied planet where a sparkling white smile was as desirable as it was on Earth. But if so, what would he do next? How would he survive? Did he just need a toothbrush? The more he worked to find some rational explanation for what lay outside the door, the more his temples throbbed.

He spotted something moving and looked outside again, but he was effectively blind without his glasses. Tossing the empty meal bag to the side, he unzipped his pack and slipped out the carbon-fiber case holding his custom-made fifty-caliber Dornitz sniper rifle, which was fitted with an all-vision scope that corrected his myopia. He assembled it and scanned the room for his glasses but found nothing except shattered glass and dusty carpet.

He crawled to the door to find what was moving, but he immediately forgot about it once he saw what lay beyond. The world out there had been squashed flat – trees, light poles, and signs had been pushed to the ground, and the convenience store across the street had disappeared. Despite his disorientation, he still recalled its bright yellow roof and flashing neon signs. He blinked and looked again but only saw a concrete floor where the building had stood.

Jumbles of overturned cars covered the street as well as pieces of wood and shingles; the roof of a building across the street had torn off and was waving in the breeze. He decided that was the movement he'd seen and let out a relieved breath.

Slushy black ice splatted on the concrete walk outside the door. The rain was unlike any he'd ever seen, with huge, dark drops falling so sporadically that he could count them.

Resting against the doorframe, he squinted at his tablet screen, which showed a secure connection to the military comsat network. At the very least, he now knew that this place was somewhere on planet Earth. He dialed Raf's number.

"Bob?" Raphael asked when he picked up. "Are you all right?"

"I have no idea what happened to me or where I am, my friend. Brief me if you know."

"Well, what happened is that you were nuked."

"Nuked?"

"Nuked."

He looked through the door at the flattened street and rubbed his sore shoulder. "Like Hiroshima?"

"Might be more like Hiroshima than you think."

"I can't handle riddles right now, Raf. I'm not in great shape."

"I wish I was joking, but I'm not."

"You're serious? It was a nuke?"

"Yes, a nuclear weapon detonated in Sacramento last night around 6:30, but that's all we can confirm right now. Are you hurt?"

"A few minor injuries. I'll be mobile in a few hours." Downs shook his head, still scanning the devastated street. "Holy Son of Jesus."

"Yeah, we're having trouble absorbing this too."

"Can you extract me?"

"No. From the emergency crew chatter we've picked up, they've established a no-go zone eight miles from Ground Zero, and you're deep inside it. It's too radioactive for our personnel to go in there. You and anyone else who survived, well, you're on your own, Bob. Sorry."

"I can manage on my own," Downs said. "Was it a Soviet Bloc strike?"

"They're denying it, of course, but they might be telling the truth. Sacramento was the only target hit, and they would've fired off everything they had in a first strike. The White House also seems to think so. There's been no counterstrike yet."

"What do our intercepts say?"

"We can't find any pattern to the chatter, but I'll learn more this afternoon at the Elder's Synod. I'm looking forward to that. We're meeting in the Rosecliff Room at the Museum of the Corporate-American. I hear the statuary is legendary."

"Have a fabulous time. Do you have any suspects?"

"None. The Engine spit out probabilities, and it said no person or entity had a compelling motive to waste Sacramento. The most popular theory floating around is Warner's. She says Cheyn wiped out Sacramento on purpose."

"That's preposterous," Downs said. "So Warner survived? Can't anything kill that roach?"

"Apparently not. She survived the bombing and took a bunch of pictures, and she has inside information on the weapon itself. I don't know what to make of her accusations, though, and the White House hasn't confirmed or denied anything yet."

"It's possible that the Activists bombed the city, and Warner's just lying again to cover it up." Downs looked at his burned hand. "I wouldn't trust a word she says."

"I don't think the Activists are responsible," Raphael said. "And Cochon agrees. If they had a nuke, they'd flatten Washington with it, not Sacramento."

"True. Does Cochon have any guess who did this?"

"He thinks Warner's right, that Cheyn did it to stop the secession vote."

"If Cochon thinks Cheyn's behind it, then I'm changing my mind – Cheyn's guilt is just a fact waiting for confirmation. And something like this shouldn't be hard to confirm, so Noah should be able to impeach him now."

"Actually, he can't. Noah says Cheyn had a legal right to nuke Sacramento."

"What?"

"That's what he says. As long as the president notifies Congress that there's an insurrection in a state, he's legally empowered to use any military force he wants, anywhere in the nation. And Cheyn sent that letter last week, so he can get away with it. It's ironic that Noah could impeach him for jaywalking but not for wasting a million American lives, isn't it?"

"A million?"

"At least. The bomb detonated over the State Fairgrounds, and there were seven hundred thousand people there alone."

Downs set the tablet down and rested his head against the doorframe. A million Americans murdered – not just the weak and the obsoleted, but the good, the innocent, the faithful. He murmured a silent prayer as a muscle twitched in his jaw, and his hand balled into a tight fist.

"Bob, you still there?"

"I'm going to kill Cheyn, Raf. I'm going to kill him long and slow and ugly."

"Well, take a number and get in line, friend. But you have to get out of there first."

"Correct. And then I have a mission to complete." He closed his eyes and thought for a few moments. "If this bombing was an isolated event, then the Transition is still underway. I still need to redact Warner and destroy that vaccine before she finds someone who can make it."

"You need to work on your focus, man. You've got the attention span of a goldfish."

"This incident isn't my mission. Warner is. Track her by Blackeye and give me her location. Once I'm mobile, I'll find her and finish this. And after that, I'll take out that sonofabitch Cheyn."

"Holy shit! Did you just swear?"

Downs rubbed his sore shoulder again and reached into his medical kit for more painkillers. "Then I'm going to Gitmo for a few weeks. That sounds really appealing right now."

"Anytime you want some sun and broads, it's there for you, man," Raphael said. "Hey, I wish I could locate Warner for you, but I can't. Blackeye 21 is down. The detonation flash wiped out the main cameras."

"We're blind?"

"We're dark from Fresno up to Portland except for sidescanning from Blackeye 22," Raphael said. "However, we backtracked her escape route from Sacramento by looking at the photos she posted. She went west. She was at Mount Vaca an hour ago, west of Sacramento."

"Excellent. Send me the route she took."

"She's long gone, Bob."

"Understood, but she found a safe route out of the city, and I plan to follow it. If this place is as bad as you say – and from what I can see, you're right – then I'll need all the help I can get. By the way, where am I?"

"It looks like you're at the corner of San Juan and Fair Oaks."

"That's where I was when the bomb went off, I think."

"You're not sure?" Raphael asked.

"I must have shock-induced amnesia. That doesn't matter, though. I'm fully engaged in the present situation. We need to find Warner's probable location, so have somebody check into Mark Mason's background. Find his known associates and family west of here. That's where she went."

VICTORIA LANG LISTENED before opening her eyes: She was lying in a large room filled with the susurration of many subdued voices. She smelled antiseptic drifting on the air, which barely masked the reek of body odor and feces. With an effort, she lifted her heavy eyelids and saw a banner hanging from the ceiling above that said LODI FLAMES 2041 DISTRICT CHAMPS.

She turned her head to each side and saw hundreds of beds. In the aisles between them, people in lab coats checked the charts and intravenous tubes of other prone patients.

She wasn't surprised to wake up in a hospital; after the bright flash, the car's brakes had failed, and she rammed into a trailer at forty miles an hour. Her last conscious thought as the airbags enveloped her was that she'd be lucky to survive such a severe accident. What she hadn't expected was to wake up in a field hospital beside hundreds of others. Something more than a pileup had occurred.

She was taking an inventory of her limbs, toes, and fingers when a young woman wearing a stethoscope knelt next to her. "Good morning," she said with a dulcet Spanish accent. "You're up at last. How do you feel?"

"Weak," Victoria said. "My arms and legs feel heavy, and it's hard to move them. I have a headache and my neck feels stiff."

"You're slightly anemic. Everybody here is," the doctor said as she tapped on her tablet. "I'll increase your iron supplement. Right now, though, you need food and rest. Don't try to get out of bed yet."

"All right. Why is everybody anemic?"

"You don't know what happened?"

"No. I was just driving, and then a bright light flashed. Right after that, I hit a truck and got knocked out."

"You must have been in one of the collisions." The doctor scrolled through her tablet and raised an eyebrow. "You were in the big one on I-5. You're one of the few survivors. Luck must be on your side."

"But all these people couldn't be accident victims. Why is everybody here anemic? Why am I in a field hospital?"

"Those are excellent questions." She looked down at her tablet, avoiding Victoria's eyes.

"Yes, they are, and I'd like excellent answers."

"Tell me something first," the doctor said, her brown eyes soft with concern. "Do you have any family or acquaintances in Sacramento?"

"I believe my daughter's there. Why do you ask?"

"Just a question." She pulled a syringe from her pocket and injected a sedative into the IV tube. "When you're well, I'll fill you in on the details, but right now I want you to sit up and eat."

"All right, but –"

The doctor held up a hand. "Eat first, then sleep. That's my prescription."

DOWNS WATCHED AIR BUBBLES ESCAPE from the canteen he'd submerged in the nearly empty toilet tank. When the bubbles stopped, he lifted it out and poured water over his head.

Drying off with paper towels, he examined his naked body in the bathroom mirror but saw no more radioactive dust to wash off. Every wound he'd found was treated and dressed, and he'd swallowed a rainbow of antibiotic pills to prevent his burned hands from becoming infected. His shoulder was sore, but it no longer ached thanks to the Synthopia pills he found in the dentist's supply closet. He was as mission-ready as he could be.

He shook out his clothes in the hallway. Seeing no more dust, he dressed and returned to the toilet to refill his canteen. He couldn't drink enough water – the air was so dry that his tongue had cracked and bled for an hour.

He walked to the shattered front door and looked out. The sky had lightened to a golden haze, and the last drop of black rain had fallen an hour ago. It was time to begin his trek.

Bracing one hand on the door frame, he knelt on sore knees and prayed to be judged worthy throughout the coming trial. God was challenging the strength of his faith by removing him from the NTC and casting him into this Gehenna; he was surely being tested for a greater role than the capture of the troublesome Warner, and he sensed the Almighty's design on the edge of his knowing.

However, to discover God's plan, he had to cross Sacramento's cinders first. Hoisting his pack on his good shoulder, he scanned his threat environment through the scope and concluded it was clear.

He stepped over the rubble that had settled by the doorway and walked to Fair Oaks Boulevard. Since it was twenty hours after the detonation, the trees no longer burned and the debris piles no longer smoldered, although the pervasive burned-plastic smell caught in his throat. He strapped a surgical mask over his nose and mouth, but it did nothing to cut the reek.

He hopped over a fallen utility pole and tiptoed through the wires to a clear spot in the center of the street. As soon as he turned to the west, though, a hot, arid wind blew over him and coated his eyes with fine-grained dust. He turned away and poured water on his face, letting some run into his eyes, but the wind was so dry that his back hairs prickled and poked at his shirt.

Ignoring the sensation, he turned back into the wind, head down, and walked west down the center of Fair Oaks Boulevard, which he was supposed to follow until it crossed El Camino Avenue. Raf had seen no people in Warner's photos of El Camino, so he assumed he'd have a safe journey from there, but he was unsure what threats he might face before then.

While the rubble from the explosion had mostly been blown to the sides, the middle of the road was covered in shattered glass that glowed orange in the dull afternoon sunlight filtering through the dusty air. After a few steps, the dust thinned, and the light set the glass shards glittering like coals. He shielded his eyes with his hand and trudged on, but the wind picked up, carrying with it the reek of melted plastic and putrescence. He gagged and pinched his nose, struggling to draw air through his constricted throat, but it seemed no wider than a straw.

His chest muscles tightened the harder he tried to breathe, and suddenly, he couldn't draw any air at all. He realized he could asphyxiate on this street and nobody would come to his aid. His heart thudding, he staggered to the roadside and found shelter in the lee of a metal gas station canopy crumpled against a stucco building. After a few minutes of concentration, he relaxed his throat and chest enough that he could fill his lungs.

A gust sent a dirty yellow, thirty-foot-high dust devil whirling up Fair Oaks toward the dentist's office. He crept further under the canopy, knowing that the whirlwind was just a freak of the air currents but also unable to keep from shrinking away. The dust devil wandered to the intersection, and he edged from the opening until his back touched rough stucco.

A balloon bounced up the road from Sacramento, its vivid blueness nearly glowing against the dead browns of the street's ruins. It meandered through the plaster and concrete rubble as if seeking a child to play with. The vortex sucked it in, and it spun around the whirlwind a few times and exploded.

Closing his eyes to the street's horrors, he rested his head against the stucco wall and tried to concentrate on his breathing. He sniffed roasted chicken, a smell so potent that it even overwhelmed the plasticky stink, and he looked for the source – and saw the blackened torso of a man with a metal strut skewering his chest, lying atop a pile of charred wood in the canopy's shadows. He skittered back to the opening to take his chances with the malevolent dust devil, which was now spinning down San Juan.

His pulse raced as he realized that these ravaged streets had been overfull with life mere hours ago, and that the dead yellow sky had been a vibrant, dark rainbow of purples. He saw his future in these wastelands: He'd fail God's test, the parching wind would choke the life from him, and his desiccated corpse would lay here beside the man-kebab, forever forgotten, until he turned to dust and the yellow whirlwind scattered his remains. His heart pounded harder, and he wanted to run, stopping only when his heart did.

He rested his head in his hands. The impulse to run was pure cowardice, he knew. He was witnessing this horror for a reason, and he couldn't let it weaken him.

Sipping from the canteen and watching the whirlwind fling trash into the air, he realized that God had set before him the most terrible tribulation: Was he strong enough to walk into a deathwind, one that had to emanate from the Gates of Hell itself, and emerge whole and pure?

He wasn't sure, but he knew he was no coward. It was time to determine his caliber.

He sipped water and wet his eyes again, and then he pulled the surgical mask over his mouth. After asking God for whatever succor he could spare, he crawled from beneath the canopy. The dust devil whirled around the corner toward him, but he turned his back to it and walked onto the road of glassy coals.

Resisting the urge to look behind him, he scanned the road west through his scope, which seemed clear except that a man was standing sentry a block away. He approached with his hand on his holster, but the precaution was unnecessary; the man stood still on the sidewalk and gawped at the sky over Sacramento as if he were still watching the mushroom cloud rise. Dust covered his shoes to the ankles, and the only sign that he was alive was an occasional blink of his eyes.

"Why?" His voice was barely more than a whisper.

"I don't have any answers, friend," Downs said, but the man didn't acknowledge him. He waved his hands in front of the man's eyes, but he didn't react. Downs looked closer and saw that his pupils were wide open despite the bright daylight.

"Why?" he asked again.

Downs left the man to his vigil and continued down Fair Oaks. When he turned onto El Camino, only steel and concrete walls still stood by the roadside. All that remained of the stately palms he'd seen yesterday were the charred outlines of incinerated trunks on the sidewalk, all pointing away from Ground Zero. Everything could burn had – he couldn't see a tree, light pole, or even a stick of wood anywhere, only a carpet of dirt and shattered roof tiles.

El Camino was enveloped in a light brown mist that swirled in the faint breeze, reducing the visibility to fifty yards. He turned away from the wind again to wet his eyes, and then he looked up at the sky. It was unearthly – literally, since in all his days on this planet, he couldn't recall ever seeing such a sight. Dung-brown clouds swirled above, and in the center of the vortex, the sky glowed yellow and cast perfectly shadowless light. He held up his canteen, and it cast no shadows on his hand; looking down, his body cast no shadows either. His heart racing, he looked up again at the glowering eye in the sky, expecting to see tentacled monsters descend through the hole to complete Earth's ruin, and he slowly backed to a concrete wall by the roadside and leaned against it to collect his wits.

His heart stopped pounding after a few minutes, and he rested his head against the wall. It was oddly smooth, and he ran his fingers across the surface; it was a plastic gas station sign that had melted into the concrete. Looking around the lot, he saw concrete with broken metal pipes sticking out of it where a convenience store once stood. Thick bolts protruded from the pump islands, but he didn't see pumps or a metal canopy. Further from the road, cars were crumpled against the concrete wall, and every surface facing west had been completely stripped of paint.

Seeking a break from the apocalypse, he stumbled around the smoking crater where the fuel tanks had been buried and sat on the pump island. Wisps of smoke rose from the ruptured gas tanks, and he watched the tendrils dance in the swirling breeze, trying to draw his focus away from the warscape of the city and the malevolent yellow sky. His hand trembling, he raised his canteen for another sip of water, but then his peripheral vision caught motion in the distance. He pulled out his scope and spotted a group of people walking single file up the road from Sacramento. It looked like a military patrol, and he ran to the crushed cars by the wall and crouched into a dark gap between them.

The patrol trudged past a few minutes later. It was a dozen men and women in shredded clothing, their faces as slack and drained of vitality as the man he'd seen earlier. Downs crawled out from between the cars and walked up to them, but they didn't acknowledge he was there. They seemed interested only in plodding away from wherever they'd been.

All of them were filthy, and most were injured – the skin on one man's face was burned off, exposing a white cheekbone. One older man walked with his eyes closed, resting his hand on the shoulder of the man in front of him, and Downs saw that his shirt had melted into the skin of his back and tattooed a floral print into it. A young woman followed, wearing a dress so tattered that he could see her underwear. Around her neck, she wore a baby sling that was as tattered as her dress; the sling was empty, but she held her hand under it as if an infant were still inside.

The column passed and soon receded into the brown mist. Downs continued walking west and tried to erase the vision from his mind, but a block later, he sank to his knees and vomited his chipped beef into the gutter.

DISPATCHES

Midnight Sun
News Post of October 9, 2043

WHITE HOUSE TO CALIFORNIA: COMPLY OR DIE

The White House Press Secretary confirmed today that a nuclear weapon detonated over Sacramento last night, and that it is unclear whether the attack was the act of the Soviet Bloc or a terrorist organization. Although the Bloc has denied involvement, the White House has ordered US military forces around the globe to Defcon Two and has activated the Civil Defense bomb shelter system. Civilian shelter drills may begin next week. The Press Secretary reiterated that the White House has the crisis under control, and citizens should not panic.

Conditions in the Sacramento area are still undetermined, he said, and the White House is awaiting reports from state officials there. When asked if Federal emergency relief forces had been sent to the stricken area, the Press Secretary said they had not because Federal aid to the state was suspended when California passed its tenpez recall. He said Federal resources will be released, though, upon a formal request by the state government and a repeal of its tenpez recall.

A reporter asked how a vaporized state government could request aid. The Press Secretary said California must nevertheless satisfy those conditions to receive Federal assistance.

CATACLYSM IN SACRAMENTO: DAY TWO

Guy LaRonde, professor of Applied Military Sciences at the University of the Upper Northwest, believes the bombing was a military act: "From Warner's account of the event, it's obvious that the weapon detonated in the air. Her photographs show a small crater at Ground Zero, which is consistent with a three-hundred-meter-high detonation. Further, she describes flash-blindness, which means she witnessed an airburst. Because of this, I believe this wasn't a terrorist act but a military one. Getting a weapon of this size into the air involves more planning and equipment than terrorists have access to."

No reporting is coming from the scene. NewsPulse San Francisco sent a helicopter to the area, but it was driven away by Air National Guard aircraft. Print reporters have been turned back by police blocking Route 80 at Vacaville, and they are reporting that electronic communication there is impossible. Some experts believe that the SatStream satellite serving the area was damaged by the electromagnetic pulse of the detonation.

The police at the checkpoint said that the Sacramento area is now operating under martial law, and civil law enforcement is being directed by the 184th Infantry, a unit of the California National Guard. We have been unable to reach California authorities to confirm the martial law order.

Our Witness in Auburn reports that he saw a mushroom cloud rising over Sacramento, and that he has discovered high-frame-rate footage showing the detonation's flash. When *Midnight Sun* receives this clip, it will be posted promptly.

Dry fallout and black rain are falling southeast of the State Fairgrounds, which is believed to be Ground Zero. The affected areas are primarily in the lightly populated Sierra foothills between Auburn and Lodi. The air monitoring station at the Rancho Seco nuclear power plant, southeast of Sacramento, has been recording increasing levels of cesium-137 and strontium-90 throughout the day.

A GHOST ON THE SEAFLOOR

Day 52
Friday morning, October 9, 2043
Pacific Ocean, 310 miles east of Petropavlovsk, Russia

"It's just a ping party out there, Skipper. We have five skimmers out of Vilyuchinsk lighting up the ocean," Jackson said with a frown.

Commander Ennis Quinn leaned against the rubber-lined bulkhead in the acoustic operator's nest. "Why are they making that racket? They have to be falsing half the time."

"That's what's so odd. With all that sonar propagation, they can't read a damn thing. Unless they have some new discrimination technology I haven't heard about." He pulled off his headgear and leaned back in his chair. "I wonder if it's a deliberate strategy to mask the approach of a stalker vessel using passive acoustic."

Quinn noticed the blinking blue light on his monitor. "Listen for that stalker, okay?" He sat and tapped the message screen, which said that Bricker wanted to see him in the conference room. After scanning the status monitors one last time, he stood and turned to Tala Ripley, who sat at the Strategic Warfare console checking the Mushroom Farm's status for the umpteenth time. "Mister Ripley, you have the conn. I'll be in the conference room if you need me."

He walked down the narrow passageway to the forward conference room. Captain Bricker sat at the far end of the table, watching him with her hands steepled. "I've seen that look before," he said. "It means you're worried, which means I'm going to be even more worried soon."

"If you aren't worried right now, you're nuts."

"Oh, I'm plenty worried," he said as he sat beside her. "We have at least five Red skimmers looking for us, and they're filling the sea with so much sonar that my watch is running backwards."

"Do you have a theory?"

He sat back and rubbed his chin. "The Reds are panicking, which usually happens when somebody in the high command gets involved."

"Exactly." She laid her palms flat on the table, which normally meant that she felt in control, but he saw one of her fingers trembling. "If our bird hit somewhere inside the Soviet Bloc, they'd be busy fighting World War Three right now. Instead, they're searching for us. Why?"

"Because World War Three didn't happen."

Bricker nodded. "Correct. And that means our bird didn't land on Red soil. How are the missile techs coming on cracking that launch server?"

"They're still working on it," he said. "Whenever I ask for a status, they say they'll be at zero percent until they're at a hundred percent. That's their way of telling me to shove off."

"Push them till they scream. In the meantime, another problem is evolving." She called up a surface map on the bulkhead monitor and swiveled her chair to face it. "Ennis, you know that feeling you get after hitting your thumb with a hammer? That feeling that it'll hurt like hell in a second?"

"All too well."

"I've had that feeling all day." She walked to the monitor and traced her finger along two parallel lines heading southeast. "The *Rockefeller* has been paralleling us for twelve hours, and we're not following our assigned course. Why? How do they know where we are?"

"It looks like we're being shadowed by our own side. Maybe it's a coincidence?"

"Or not."

"Or not. And in that case…"

"In that case, we've been set up to take a fall, Ennis. We delivered a nuclear warhead to the target per orders, and now our own ship is keeping within strike range so they can destroy the evidence."

He walked to the back of the room, unlocked a cabinet, and poured two glasses of whiskey. "That's a possibility. An unlikely, somewhat paranoid possibility," he said, handing her one.

"But still a possibility, Ennis." She swirled her whiskey, absorbed in the eddies and whorls for a moment, and then she looked up at him. "What's your take? Have I gone paranoid?"

He sat back in his chair and studied the map. "Concluding that you're paranoid is only possible after we know all the facts. And we don't. Right now, a conservative reaction is reasonable. Everything about this mission feels wrong."

"I hope *I'm* wrong."

"But in case you're not, we should go dark and disappear, Julie. Let's dive below the thermocline and leave the *Rockefeller* and the Reds behind. It's the prudent response."

"Gut reactions aren't enough," she said. "No, we'll wait and see. I'll give the missile techs till tomorrow to crack that server and find our bird's target." She looked at the monitor and sipped her drink. "If they don't, I'll contact Adam and see if he knows what's going on."

IN HIS OFFICE AT BANGOR, Admiral Adam Harris replayed a video clip and pointed at the monitor. "This came from a high-speed camera on Pilot Hill outside Sacramento, where some college was recording a test. *Midnight Sun* just published it. Tell me what you make of this."

"All right." Captain Zachary Caldwell leaned over the monitor on his desk, which showed a metal tower with Sacramento in the background. Seven seconds into the video, the sky over the city flared bluish-white and then yellow. The image dissolved into gray static, and Caldwell jerked upright. "Jesus Christ! Did I really see that?"

"What did you see? Tell me I'm not making this up."

"The double flash. Play that again."

Harris replayed the clip, and Caldwell gasped again at the seven-second mark. "Zack, I can play it a thousand more times, but it'll always show the same thing. You know what that means?"

Caldwell sat on the desk and stared at the wall. "That was the detonation flash of a W104 warhead."

"Maybe Warner was right. Maybe it was one of our nukes. Show me the position of our boats as of 6:36 PM Pacific time yesterday."

Caldwell walked to the wall monitor and called up a map. Six dots glowed on it: three along the north coast of Russia, two in the Indian Ocean, and one off the Indonesian coast.

Harris tapped on the dot blinking in the narrow Strait of Makassar near Indonesia. "The *Paul Revere*. Jimmy Columbo's bending the rules again."

"He's taking the short way home, Adam. The Indonesian Gauntlet cuts nine hours off the trip."

"It's dangerous, and I told him only to do it in an emergency! When's she due in?"

"The *Revere's* scheduled to take the *Hale's* berth right after she leaves next Tuesday."

"I'll talk to that three-balled bastard the instant he sets foot on land. I've had enough of his edge-of-the-envelope shit. This is insubordination, and it'll stop right now if Columbo wants to keep his command."

"You won't do that, Adam. You'll swear, you'll break a few tumblers, and then you'll shake Jimmy's hand because he's the best commander in the Submarine Service."

Harris walked to his bar and filled a glass with rum. "That's it, Caldwell, I've had enough of you. I'm sending you to McMurdo. You'll like Antarctica in the spring."

"And who'll keep you from shooting yourself in the foot?"

"I'll buy steel-toed boots." Harris pointed to the map while sipping his rum. "The *Revere* was the closest boat to Sacramento on Thursday, and it's still out of range. Not to mention that if they'd released a Slick in the Strait of Makassar in mid-afternoon, a thousand people would have reported it. There's more surface traffic in the Strait during the day than Times Square." He gulped his drink and slammed the glass on the bar. "Which is why I keep telling that thick-headed wop to stay out of it!"

"Calm down and focus. They were all out of range – as far as we know."

Harris looked at him sharply. "These positions aren't confirmed?"

"All except for the *Henry*. She lost her comm buoy and hasn't confirmed her position since she entered the Kara Sea."

Harris looked at the blinking dot northeast of Moscow and shook his head. "They couldn't be involved. Julie would have had to reposition to get in range and then deliberately release the missile. That's impossible."

"Nothing's impossible." Caldwell gazed at the wall monitor, his lips puckered as he concentrated on the boat dispositions. He tapped a finger to them in time to the ticking of Harris' grandfather clock.

Harris glared at the monitor too. After a few minutes, he turned away and rubbed his neck. "All right. A W104 detonated over Sacramento, which could have only come from one of our boats, and the *Henry* is the only one we can't eliminate as the launch platform."

"Correct. We have to assume our own boat may have attacked an American target."

Harris sank into the sofa and glared at the far wall, his face tight. "Okay, we're totally screwed," he said, and then he pulled his tablet from a pocket. "I need to inform Naval Operations."

"I wouldn't do that."

"No?"

"No, because they haven't called you. If we figured this out, they did too, so why didn't they at least pick up the phone and have a chat? That's suspicious. You should lay low till we know what's happening."

Harris rubbed his neck again. "Wonderful. I'm starting to smell a shitshow coming on, Zack. This has 'shitshow' painted all over the side in blinking neon letters."

"When you figure out how to paint blinking neon letters, let me know." He walked to the bar and poured a tall drink, and then he took a sip and leaned against the bar. "But you're right. Nothing about this makes sense. While it's reasonable to suspect that the *Henry* was the launch platform, reason ends right there. I can't imagine Julie doing this even with a gun to her head."

"Julie couldn't have launched an unauthorized attack, nor would she. Neither would Ennis or Tala. They would have grabbed that gun and pulled the trigger themselves before they attacked American soil." He thumped his fist on his chest. "I know it in here. I know this in my heart, Zack."

"And I believe you. The *Henry's* Blue Crew is the most stable in the service. Psychometrically, they always score at the top." Caldwell watched the fern leaves quiver in a light rain for a few moments, and then he downed the rest of his drink and set the glass on the bar. "There must have been a catastrophic FUBAR somewhere. In the universe of possible error, though, I'd bet more on a human fault than a system fault. The *Henry* underwent a Schedule A diagnostic before sailing, and its launch systems and every bird passed. The results were perfect."

Harris looked into his eyes and then into his glass. "Perfect, yeah. That could be our FUBAR right there."

"Mind explaining that cryptic comment?"

He rested his head against the couch and stared at the ceiling for a moment, and then he held out his glass to Caldwell. "We're not drinking enough to talk about this. Fill me up, would you?"

As Caldwell walked back to the bar, he said, "I suspect my day's about to get even worse. I didn't think that was possible."

"Nothing's impossible." Harris let out a long breath, still gazing at the ceiling. "This stays between us, okay? What I'm about to tell you is M-Level sensitive compartmented information."

"I'm only cleared for K-Level nuclear info. Maybe I shouldn't –"

"You need to hear this. If this is our FUBAR, you need to know." Harris leaned forward and clasped his hands into a ball. "Three years ago, the *Hale* released two unarmed Slicks out in the Pacific, both fitted with destruct devices. We wanted to see if the new Generation Four Aegis radar would acquire them."

"That's not much of a secret. I read the report. The radars couldn't lock on the target, and every interceptor missile they fired missed."

"Right. What the report didn't say is that we triggered the Slicks' destruct devices when the test concluded. Then something weird happened." He took the glass from Caldwell and motioned at the armchair. "Sit. It's better than passing out standing up."

"Enough of the foreshadowing. What happened?"

"One Slick self-destructed. The other disabled its destruct mechanism and went on to hit its target."

"The missile disobeyed orders?"

"No, the flight controller obeyed its initial order and ignored any subsequent instructions that would have kept it from reaching the target, which luckily was just open sea. Zack, I think the damn thing *wanted* to hit its target."

"Jesus, Adam! And we still deployed them?"

"We had to. We were getting pressure from the White House, and what were we supposed to tell the president? That the thing works *too* well, so we shouldn't deploy it? But after the deployment, we took the flight controller software apart line by line. The sharps in Silicon Valley simulated eighty thousand flights, and they said it was flawless – and that the software had somehow spawned an agile learning intelligence in the flight controller that discovered purpose and determination fast. And that makes sense.

Every line of that programming teaches the flight controller to adapt and make the choices necessary to succeed at its mission, so why be shocked that it realized triggering the destruct mechanism would cause a mission failure?"

"Then rewrite the software so it doesn't adapt and make choices."

"We simulated that. The bird couldn't respond to the thousands of flight variables it encountered and crashed. After that, we just left it alone." Harris gazed at the far wall of the office, swirling the rum idly in his tumbler. "There's a ghost hiding in the machine, Zack. If one missile had it, it could be in others."

Caldwell walked to the bar and returned with the rum bottle. He topped off their glasses and sat back in the armchair. "Okay, putting aside that bowel-watering prospect for a moment, a ghost doesn't explain the Sacramento strike. The flight controller just operates the missile in flight, Adam. It doesn't launch it."

"And that's what has me worried," Harris said. "What if Sacramento was nuked because the ghost infected the *Henry's* Missile Release Control System too? What do we do then?"

Caldwell emptied his glass, set it on the end table, and then leaned forward with his elbows on his knees, examining Harris' rug. After a few long moments, he asked, "So were you serious about that transfer to McMurdo?"

RIPLEY LOOKED AT THE MAP of the *Henry's* and the *Rockefeller's* courses on the bulkhead monitor in Quinn's cramped cabin. She raised the glass to her lips and sipped his contraband whiskey, and then she edged around his knees and sat on his bunk. "Okay, we're totally screwed."

"We might be. The situation is confusing, to say the least, and I don't like confusing situations," Quinn said.

"You're right to be concerned," she said. "What's happening on the surface doesn't fit any war model I've ever seen, nuclear or non-nuclear. This is a brand-new model, one we've never prepared for."

He nodded and propped his feet on the desk. "That's why we need to disappear till we're sure what's going on, but Julie's being conservative. Too conservative." He ran his hand through his hair. "Don't tell her I said this, but this is the perfect time to panic."

"Exactly. We definitely left some paint on the iceberg back in Petropavlovsk. Why can't she see that?"

"I don't know. If this were my boat, the *Henry* would've vanished already. Stealth is our greatest defense. I wouldn't be exposing us like she is."

"She's not your boat, though."

"No, she's not, and there's nothing more I can do." He dropped his feet to the deck and rested his elbows on his knees, looking at his shoes. "I don't know why I ever wanted to be CO of a missile boat, Tala. When I get back, I'm taking my name out of the running. I'm not built for this."

"It's normal to have doubts, especially after what we've been through. Give yourself time to get over this. Your ambition will come back."

"I'm not so sure. Anyway, thanks for listening. It helps to talk, and I don't get the chance very often. An XO is supposed to be a stoic, stone-faced technocrat. Always. No matter what."

"That sounds hard."

"It is, but it's necessary. Submarine crews are a little…internal, and emotional displays from a boat's command disturb their readiness. It's best to keep crises to yourself. But sometimes…" He shook his head and sighed. "I don't know why you want this job. You're out of your mind."

"C'mon. I'd love to have your problems." She pulled her wad of gum off the rim of the glass and popped it into her mouth, and as she stood to leave, Ennis's screensaver flicked on his bulkhead monitor. "Oh, that's just pathetic."

He looked up and saw Krista Warner's graduation picture on the screen. "Oh, that. It's not what you think."

"You mean you don't have a crush on her, but you use her picture as a screensaver now? Gimme a break."

"Hey, she's a pretty woman, and I'd like to meet her astounding gozangas someday, okay? That doesn't mean I have a puppy-love crush on her." He watched her face slide slowly across the screen. "No, she's up there because she's a piece of a puzzle I've been trying to solve, or at least I was before the comm buoy got ripped out of the hull. Here, I'll show you." He tapped the monitor a few times, and a picture of a young girl appeared next to the graduation photo. She had short auburn hair, big blue eyes, and was sticking her tongue out at the camera. "I knew this girl when I was growing up."

Ripley looked from one to the other. "You knew Warner when she was a kid?"

"Yeah, and that's the puzzle." He tapped a knuckle on the girl's picture. "I didn't know Krista Warner. I knew Keira Kellen."

"The one who went missing, and nobody figured out what happened to her?"

"The same one. The Kellens lived in my building's penthouse, and I lived down on the second floor. We called her Princess Pucker because she never hung out with the crowd, and everybody figured she was stuck up. But it wasn't her fault – she had this huge bodyguard that made sure we never got within six feet of her, so you needed a megaphone if you wanted to talk to her. That put a real lid on things. But she came down to the resident's garden every so often, and I met her there a few times. Man, did she ever have a smart-ass mouth." He laced his fingers behind his head and grinned. "I used to have snowball fights with her, and I remember one time I nailed her right in the forehead with an iceball. She went down like a sack of potatoes, and her bodyguard pushed me against the wall and said, 'I see you with a snowball again, I'm gonna rip off your head and piss down your throat.' And I think he would have."

She snorted a small laugh. "Sounds like he was a Marine."

"Uh-huh. Thick neck, thick head. Anyway, I went off to Annapolis after that, and then her mother died and Keira vanished from the face of the Earth. I always wondered if something bad happened to her, but now I think she just ran away and changed her name to Krista Warner."

"Well, it's a spooky resemblance, but that's not much to go on," she said, squinting at the picture.

"Oh, no, there's more. Keira's history stopped when she was eleven, but Krista's started then. There are no public records of a Krista Lune Warner anywhere before the age of eleven – no birth certificates, no school records, nothing. Zero. She didn't exist."

"Huh. You're really obsessed. You even searched her records?"

"If I don't obsess about this, I'll obsess about the pickle we're in, and I can't do anything about that. And I can't exactly take a walk in the park to clear my mind. It's a kind of therapy, working this puzzle."

"No, you're a stalker with a crush, and I'm gonna set you up with all the other lechers in trench coats when we get back to shore. There's gotta be a support group for your type –"

"You're an asshole, Ripley." He picked up a dirty sock from the desk and flung it in her face.

"Nuh-uh. I'm a truthteller!"

"You are? That's great! I'll take you up to Bricker, and *you* can tell her she's wrong, truthteller."

"No way. I'm just a junior officer, pal. That's way above my paygrade."

He propped his feet up on the desk and laughed. "Right. Truthteller, my ass."

FUGUE IN B NEGATIVE

Day 52
Friday afternoon, October 9, 2043
151 Golden Gate Avenue, Tiburon, California

Krista and Marissa walked in from the balcony around noon. "I'll check on Ada and then turn in," Krista said as she sat on a stool at the island.

"Good luck trying to sleep with four cups of coffee in you."

"Oh, I can do it. Don't worry about that at all."

Marissa rinsed out their coffee mugs. "Mark's bedroom is down the stairs, the next to last one on the left. I'm gonna take a swim."

"Do you have a pool?"

"Oh, no. I swim to Angel Island and back every day, a total of two miles." Marissa smiled as she dried her hands. "Regular exercise keeps you young." With a wink, she turned and walked to the foyer.

Krista opened the guest bedroom door and peeked in. Except for the bed and a small aisle beside it, the room was cluttered with spears, shields, clay pots, and tribal masks.

Ada lay on her side on the small mattress. Krista crept to the bed to pull the blanket over Ada's shoulders and then gasped – blood was flowing from her nose, and it had soaked the pillow and the sheets. She swore and ran to the kitchen.

Micah stood at the island buttering a slice of bread. "What's wrong?" he asked when he saw the look on her face.

"Her nosebleed came back." She pulled a handful of paper towels from a roll next to the sink.

He opened the refrigerator door and pulled out a plastic-wrapped package. "You wanna stop a nosebleed, you need bacon. Works every time."

"Bring that in, wouldja? I'll go mop up the blood."

She ran back to the room, knelt by Ada's side, and gave her a shake, but she didn't awaken. She shook her again and then stuffed a wad of paper towels under her nose, which immediately turned red.

Micah walked in carrying two neatly rolled pieces of bacon and looked at the pillow. "Holy cow! You weren't kidding."

"I'm so sorry about the mess."

"Not your fault. Wow, I've never seen a nosebleed like this before."

She squeezed the bacon into Ada's bleeding nostril. "I'm thinking there's something wrong." She pulled off the bloody blanket, exposing the bruises on Ada's arm.

"That's a hell of a bruise."

"The shockwave threw her into a stone wall." She unfolded a fresh blanket and laid it over Ada. "Considering all she's suffered, she's not doing bad, but I'll have to take her to a hospital if this bleeding doesn't slow down."

"This all started after the bombing?"

She nodded. "She told me she bashed her nose when she hit the patio."

He reached into a pocket of his shorts and pulled out a small tablet. "Lemme check something. It'll take me a few minutes cuz this thing's kinda old. I think Sputnik made it." He turned on the tablet and tapped the screen, and then a woman clad in fluorescent orange rubber suddenly appeared at the bedroom door.

"I'm going for my swim," Marissa said. "I'm using my new wetsuit today. It's supposed to increase my visibility in the water."

"Knowing how those boaters think, it makes you an easier target," Micah muttered.

"I know! And that's what makes it so exciting! Without that, it's just swimming!" She spun on her foot and bounded to the front door.

He tapped on his tablet for a few minutes and then sat on the floor. "Okay. Does she have Glanzmann Thrombasthenia?"

"I've got no idea what that is. Is it a disease?"

"Yeah. It's a rare kind of nasal hemorrhage."

"She never mentioned anything like that," she said. "I think she doesn't. She seems as puzzled by this bleeding as I am."

"Then all that's left is radiation poisoning. She's got most of the symptoms. Was she exposed to radiation when the bomb went off?"

"I guess so."

He squinted at the tablet. "It says here that if she was out in the open, she might have gotten a full-body dose. If she was behind something, she wouldn't."

"She was lying out on the patio, and I was next to a stone wall. Maybe that's why I don't feel sick." Krista pulled a lock of Ada's hair behind her ear and away from the bloody pillowcase. "She probably got more than I did. Is there a cure for it?"

"Oh, yeah. There's lotsa things doctors can do."

"All right," she said as she stood. "Go wake up Mark. We've got to take her to the hospital right now."

Micah ran downstairs while Krista wet more paper towels at the sink. She returned to the guest bedroom and shook Ada until her eyes fluttered open.

"Whuh?" Ada said as she sat up.

"I just want to clean you up a little," Krista said. "Your nosebleed came back while you were sleeping."

Ada put her finger to her nostril and sniffed. "You baconized me?"

"It stopped the bleeding, at least." She pointed to the pillow, and Ada looked at it and swore.

"Something's wrong. This isn't a normal nosebleed, Krista. This is something else."

Krista wiped the blood from the side of her face and reached for a new towel. "Don't worry. We'll take care of you, sister. Once Mark gets here, we'll get you to a hospital and let them patch you up."

"Yeah, I'm sick of dripping blood everywhere." Ada sniffed and scowled. "And I'm totally sick of having bacon tampons shoved up my schnoz."

"I had to. You were bleeding buckets."

"Yeah, it's almost like I have –" She stopped short and gulped. "Oh, hell, I have all the symptoms of radiation poisoning. That damn zombie patch wiped my mind. That's why I didn't think of it before."

"That might be the problem, but Micah says it's treatable. Don't worry about it."

"You're worried about it, so why shouldn't I be?"

"We'll get you to the hospital quick as we can and get you treated, okay?" Krista held out her hand and pulled Ada to her feet. "How are you feeling?"

"Kinda weak. I can walk if you stay with me, though."

"Of course I'll be with you. I've been by your side all this time, and I'll be at your side through this too."

"I don't like the sound of that," Ada said. "That's how you cheer up people when you know they're dying."

"Now don't go jumping to conclusions, sister." She took her arm and helped her into the kitchen. Mark and Micah bounded up the steps and to the island.

"Hey, Twink! Wanna take a little ride, see the countryside and all that?" Mark asked.

"Ooh, that sounds thrillin! Can we stop at the hospital first and treat my radiation poisoning?"

His face sagged. "Oh. I thought you didn't know. I didn't wanna get you worried." He grabbed his pistol and keys from the island. "So much for the cover story. If everybody's ready, let's roll."

Ada leaned on Krista's arm. They shuffled toward the front door, but Mark stopped them at the foyer. "Mikey, could you help Twink out to the car? I gotta talk to Krista for a minute."

"Sure." He held out his arm to Ada and helped her through the front door. When it closed, Mark pulled his keys from his pocket and unlocked a door in the foyer. He opened it and Krista staggered back – the closet was packed with guns of every type hanging from wire racks on three walls, and a shelf above held an armory of ammunition. He flicked a light switch and pulled a small silver revolver off the rack.

"This was one of Hunter's favorites. The forty-four Nighthawk snubnose, seven rounds of takedown power. Things are weird, and I don't know how safe you are right now. Everybody saw you on *Freedom's Bell*, and there's still a huge bounty on your head, and we're going to a public hospital where everybody can see you." He pressed the pistol into her hand. "Take this. I'll try to protect you, but in case I can't, you need to be able to protect yourself."

She handed it back. "I don't like guns. They give you a false sense of power and make you do strange things."

"It'd make me feel better knowing you've got firepower if you need it. Listen, there's a lot of scumbags in this world, so you gotta go out prepared. Please?"

She took the pistol, stuffed it into her waistband, and closed the hoodie around it. "Okay, but I won't use it."

"I hope not. C'mon, let's hit the road."

Mark weaved through the narrow streets until they drove off the island, and then he turned north toward San Rafael. Fifteen minutes later, he pulled into a parking lot at Marin Wellness Hospital.

The emergency room was crowded beyond capacity, and patients sat on walls outside the entrance and held yellow tickets. Krista and Ada walked inside and waited in a long line, reaching the reception desk twenty minutes later. The nurse asked for the patient's name, wrote it on a clipboard, and handed her a ticket.

"How long will it be?" Krista asked.

"We're treating number 422 now," the nurse said.

Krista looked at the ticket, which had '524' printed on it. "How long will it take to go through a hundred patients?"

The nurse shrugged. "It happens when it happens. You might want to get some lunch. You're in for a long wait."

"But she's sick," Krista protested.

"She's ambulatory, and that's better than most of the people ahead of her," the nurse said as she waved to the next person in line. "We're operating under Civil Emergency rules, and I can't move her up in line unless she presents a serious condition. Now move to the side."

"But..." Krista said.

"Or I'll call Security. Move to the side, ma'am."

Krista shuffled through the bodies jamming the counter and helped Ada through another crowd blocking the emergency room door. Outside, they found Mark and Micah sitting against the trunk of a palm tree.

"Is there anywhere else we can go?" Krista asked. "This place is mobbed. It'll take forever for them to see Ada."

"There's only one hospital in Marin," Mark said. "The next nearest hospital is in San Francisco. It's usually even busier than this."

Krista helped Ada sit in the grass and then sat beside her. "Well, this sucks."

"Yeah, that's for sure," Mark said. "The best thing to do is wait, though. They'll get to her soon."

Krista leaned back against the palm tree, and Ada rested her head on her shoulder. She was fast asleep within seconds. Right after that, Krista rested her head on Mark's shoulder and started snoring softly.

Micah sat cross-legged on the grass. "Well, we've got some time on our hands," he said. "So how'd you lose those windows in Wrestler's car?"

"Got blown out leaving Sacramento," Mark said with a yawn.

"Yeah? How'd they get blown out?"

"Scumbag tried to shoot me." He laid his head against Krista's and closed his eyes.

"So who tried to shoot you?" Micah asked, but Mark didn't answer.

THE LAWN SPRINKLERS SPURTED TO LIFE at four in the afternoon, and they awoke with a start and scrambled for dry ground.

"Jaysus," Krista said, dripping water on the pavement. "I think this place just wants to make things as inconvenient as possible. I was getting decent sleep."

Ada squeezed water from her hair. "Talk about a rude awakening."

"Sorry, I shoulda thought about that," Mark said. "Anything that's green here has a sprinkler near it. I guess I was too tired and wasn't thinking real straight."

"That's all right," Krista said. "At least I got some sleep." She pulled a sodden yellow ticket from a hoodie pocket. "Maybe they're ready for us now. Are you up for a walk?"

Ada took her arm. "Sure. It might do me some good."

Krista flashed a smile at Mark and Micah, and they walked back into the emergency room waiting area. It was even more crowded than before, and Krista swore when she saw the board displaying the patient numbers. "455? They're just up to 455? This'll take all night!"

"Krista, don't get worked up. I can wait."

"I detest red tape, and we're wrapped in it now. Well, I've had enough. It's cutting time." She slicked back her hair, patted the water from her hoodie, and took Ada's hand. "C'mon. I'll fix this."

She strode through a pair of doors into the emergency treatment room and found a chair for Ada. "You sit here. I'll be right back."

After looking around the busy room, she spotted the doctor's dictation area in a corner and sidled up to a man in a white lab coat.

"Can I help you?" he asked.

"I'm Krista Warner, editor of *The Rake*, and I'm here to interview the chief of this department. That would be you, am I correct?"

"No, I'm just a staff physician. Dr. Paton is the chief."

"Really? Well, you fooled me. I'm an expert at finding the man in charge, and you've got that aura of sober command I usually see in men who run the show."

He grinned and leaned back against the wall. "People tell me that sometimes. But no, I'm still low on the totem pole."

She leaned toward him. "Between me and you, it won't be long before you're at the top. I've seen this a thousand times – men like you rise to their level of competence. They always have."

"I'd like to think so."

"So where can I find Dr. Paton?" She glanced around the emergency room.

"You'll never find him in this madhouse. I'll take you to his office. I'm going over that way."

She followed the doctor through a maze of corridors, curtains, and beeping machinery, and stopped at a small, glassed-in office tucked in a corner. He opened the door and leaned in. "Someone to see you, Lou."

"Little busy here," a voice said from behind the door.

"She's a reporter. Says she wants to interview you."

"Oh, okay. Send her in."

The doctor opened the door for her, and Krista thanked him with a soft smile. Inside, she found a bald, chubby man sitting behind a desk mounded with folders. He wore a midlife-crisis tie with grinning blue dolphins cavorting across bright yellow silk. "Dr. Paton? My name is Krista Warner. I'm an MRC-licensed investigative journalist."

They shook hands. "How do you do?"

"I'm writing an article, and I need your help. California is facing unprecedented public health emergencies, and our emergency medical professionals have been thrust onto the front lines of a new and unexpected battle. The public should know about the work you're doing to save lives at this critical time."

"That's absolutely true," he said. "It's unfortunate that it takes a crisis of this magnitude to draw attention to what we do every day, though."

"Well said, Dr. Paton. May I quote you on that?"

"Yes, but first, may I see your identification? Wellness Corp rules say we can only give interviews to confirmed MRC-licensed reporters."

She leaned across the desk. "I was near Sacramento when the bomb went off, and I lost my purse there. You can check my credentials on the Internet, though." She recited her MRC identification number and prayed that the slow bureaucracy hadn't revoked her license yet.

While he tapped on his monitor, she scanned the office for information she could use. She saw a tan line on his finger where he'd recently worn a wedding ring; in the corner, a few boxes of books and clothes were stacked haphazardly with pairs of shoes jumbled beside them. A box for a new Advanced Heuristics tablet sat on a credenza, its phone number written on the side.

He scrutinized her face, and then he squinted at the monitor and frowned. Krista tried to maintain her composure, but she knew what that look meant: The MRC had already pulled her license, she was about to get tossed from Paton's office and turned over to the Federals, and Ada would die because of humanity's indifference. In the deepest reaches of her heart, she wished for the world to stop sucking so much.

Suddenly, she felt a jolt of chillybones like in Seven-Up. Paton shivered, and then he looked at the screen and smiled. "Ahh, there you are. Yes, your credentials are in order. The name and the face are familiar, though. Aren't you that –"

"Certainly not. Really, I get that all the time. I'm just plain ole me." She let out the breath she'd been holding and then noticed that yellow dolphins now swam across his bright blue tie. She rubbed her eyes and looked again.

"What's wrong?" he asked.

"My eyes are just tired. I haven't slept in days."

He sat back in his seat. "Nor have I. So what would you like to know? I only have a few minutes, and then I'm on floor duty."

"How has your department responded to the flood of victims coming from the Sacramento area with radiation poisoning?"

"That's not an emergent condition, and we don't treat that in the ER. Radiation illness is a blood disease. Those patients get referred to Hematology."

Krista tapped on her tablet. "And who would I speak to there?"

"The chief of that department is Dr. Sangha."

"May I have your permission to speak to him?"

"Oh, you don't need my permission. We have equal status."

"I don't want to rub anybody the wrong way, though. May I say that you sent me to him? That would make my job easier."

"Of course you may."

Although she had the information she wanted, she interviewed him for another five minutes to maintain her cover story, every now and then sneaking a glance at his tie. When she was done, she weaved back through the chaos to Ada, who was curled up in her seat and hugging herself. "I got a flash of chillybones a few minutes ago. Did you do your tumbleweirds thing again?"

"Dunno, but at least I sliced through a little red tape." She pulled Ada to her feet, and they walked through the emergency room and into the main hospital. After checking the lobby directory, she found the Hematology department and dragged Ada to the second floor. The waiting room was crowded, but Krista found an open seat for her and walked to the reception desk. "Krista Warner to see Dr. Sangha."

The nurse tapped on her monitor and frowned. "I don't have you on the schedule. Do you have an appointment?"

She shook her head. "I was referred by Dr. Paton, Chief of Emergency Medicine. Call his personal tablet number if you'd like to confirm it." She recited the number she'd seen on the side of the tablet box. "Lou's a really close friend. He won't mind."

"They hate when we do that. I'll have to call his office and confirm the referral, though. It's usually done through the system."

"He said we shouldn't wait for the paperwork, and we should see Dr. Sangha immediately. My friend has radiation illness, and that's a condition they don't treat down there."

The nurse dialed Dr. Paton's office phone. "He's not picking up."

"Well, the emergency room's a madhouse. Really, I'm sure Lou won't mind if you call his personal tablet. The number is –"

The nurse held up her hand. "I like being employed. I'll just ask Dr. Sangha if he wants to make an exception for a department chief referral." She dialed again, murmured into the phone for a few moments, and hung up. "Dr. Sangha will see you in Exam Room Six right now – that's the third door on the right, down the hall."

Krista collected Ada, and they shuffled down the corridor, looking at room numbers. "Will a doctor see me?" Ada asked.

"It looks like it," Krista said. "By the way, if you hear me say some strange things, don't correct me, okay? I'm lying my teeth off, and I'm on a roll right now."

"You lied your way in?"

"I lied my way across the country. Why stop now?" She opened the door to Room Six and they walked in. "Go with the flow, sister."

"All right." Ada trudged to the examination table and sagged onto it. "I'm so tired. I wouldn't have the energy to fight this if it wasn't for you. I love you so much."

"I know."

"I'd be dead without you." She laid back and closed her eyes. "But you shouldn't try so hard to save me."

"Keep talking that crap, and I'll paper your feckin forehead with zombie patches. No more suicide palaver. I had enough last night."

"I won't off myself, all right? Just don't tell me I should feel wonderful about being on this freakin planet, though. I don't."

"I don't, either. I wouldn't expect you to."

"Good," Ada said. "I need you to promise me something – if the news is bad, don't fight the inevitable. If this is my fate, I can't avoid it."

Krista pointed a finger in her face. "Don't you go hiding behind Fate."

"*You're* lecturing me about Fate? You? You're freakin kidding me!"

"I'm just saying you shouldn't use it as an excuse. If you don't like the fate you've got, go find yourself a new one. And you can stand up to Fate and win, sister. I did it, and I found out that it's just a bully. Don't whine about it. Don't let it control your life. End of inquiry."

"I don't think I can stand up to anything right now." She let go a long sigh and closed her eyes. "I'm done. I'm too exhausted to fight."

Krista plopped into a chair next to the exam table. "If you start singing *Swing Low, Sweet Chariot*, I'll pop you right on the nose."

"This is serious. I've made my peace with my end, okay? Don't make it harder, and don't get in the way. Promise me."

"I absolutely *will not* make it easy for you to die!" She jabbed a finger at her with each word. "Now shut yer feckin gob and get better. That's your mission, and you'll complete that mission if you love me! Got it?"

Ada smiled weakly. *"Jawohl, mein Führer."*

"There you go. Now stop talking nonsense." She sat back, crossed her arms, and glowered at a picture on the far wall.

"I like it when you get tough with me."

"Oh, shut it."

The door opened, and a short, dark-skinned man in a lab coat strode in. "I am Dr. Sangha," he said with a melodic Indian accent. "I understand you are here by Dr. Paton's referral, is that not true? That is an irregular procedure, you must know."

Krista smiled and made a mental note of his tie color: beige with brown chevrons. "Well, Lou and I are very close." Remembering the tan line on his finger, she added, "Especially in this delicate time of…his emotional transition."

"Ahh. I have heard the rumors." His gaze ran up and down Krista's body and lingered on her breasts for an awkwardly long moment. "I see his transition has resolved to his satisfaction."

"I hope so," Krista said, trying to recall Liza Wetmore's bimbo voice. "Women should just be proud – damn proud! – to comfort great men like you and Dr. Paton in times of crisis so you can do your –"

"Achh!" he cried. "You need not butter me. I will see the patient because of Dr. Paton's request."

"This is my daughter, and she needs –"

"*This* is your daughter? Please do not lie."

"She was in a –"

"I can see for myself." He ran a finger across the flashburns on Ada's face. "She has been exposed to intense radiation." He spotted the bacon roll in her nostril, reached into a drawer, and pulled out a pair of forceps. "Tales from old wives," he muttered. He yanked the roll out and threw it into the trash, and blood began to pour from Ada's nose. He inserted a pen-shaped instrument into her nostril and squinted into it, and then the pen flashed and the room filled with the smell of scorched bacon.

"There. The bleeding has ceased. Now follow me to the diagnostics room." He turned on his heel and left.

Ada sat up and rubbed her nose. "I just love that guy. Can I make him my honorary uncle? He's so warm and huggable."

She helped Ada stand and took her arm. "That's why I can't stand the sciency types. They don't have any hearts. Only good thing about that guy is that his tie didn't go all kaleidoscopey on me."

"Hunh?"

"I'll explain later." She took her hand, and they walked down the hall. Dr. Sangha stood by a machine, tapping his foot.

"I've had a terrible science day," Ada said. "I need a break."

"Just put up with it a little longer," Krista said.

Shiny steel machines lined one wall of the room and a row of chairs lined the other. An assortment of elderly patients watching wall-mounted televisions lounged in them.

A nurse helped Ada climb into the machine, and steel bands clamped around her arms after she sat. A monitor descended in front of her face, and the sound of children's cartoons started up. Ada groaned and asked someone to change the channel, but the nurse had walked to the other side of the room.

"It will be thirty-one minutes," Sangha said, and he disappeared through a nearby door.

Krista stood in front of the machine, unsure what to do, and then she ambled back to the waiting room. She dithered there until the patients began to stare at her, and then she walked downstairs to get Mark and Micah.

KRISTA LEANED AGAINST THE WAITING ROOM WALL and tried to be invisible. She pressed closer to Mark's side while watching the seconds tick by on the clock. "Are they still looking at me?"

"I think a few of them figured out who you are," Mark said. "I warned you about *Freedom's Bell*."

"You'd think the haircut would throw them off."

He leaned over and whispered in her ear. "Hey, it sure throws *me* off."

"Look, this is driving me nuts. Between the waiting and all these people…"

"Why don't you go back to Diagnostics a little early? Waiting here is killing you."

"You'll be okay?"

"I'll be fine," he said.

She kissed his cheek and started for the diagnostics room. Wanting to be with her best friend, but also not wanting grave news, she walked down the hall in a hesitant stutter step.

She found the machine still enveloping Ada, but it was clicking and emitting the smell of glue, so whatever it was doing was almost complete. The monitor arm rose with a hiss, and Ada lay back against the headrest and groaned.

"Are you all right?" Krista asked, kneeling next to her.

"Half an hour of singing cartoon pigs. It was torture."

"You seem okay. I was worried. I never trust these machines not to eat me by accident."

A door behind them clicked open and Dr. Sangha strode to Ada's machine. "I have the results."

"Can you open these clamps?" Ada asked.

"I will call a nurse when we are done." He slipped a tablet from his lab coat and scrolled down the screen. "Yes, here we are. The subject has acute radiation illness and concomitant aplastic anemia, and significant reductions in hemoglobin, thrombocytes, leukocytes, and lymphocytes. It would be difficult to keep the subject free of infection long enough for a recovery of blood components. I recommend pastoral care and terminal symptomatic treatment. If you give me the number of your pharmacy, I will send a prescription for an opioid to relieve her symptoms until expiration." He dropped the tablet into his pocket. "Is there anything else?"

"There sure is. I didn't understand one feckin word of that," Krista said.

"You should make final arrangements. She will die within a week." Ada gasped and started to cry, and he patted her hand. "We must all die, child. I am quite sad, of course, that you will die so young. Now I have many duties that require –"

"Whoa, you're not done here, pal," Krista said. "You're not dropping that bomb on me and sashaying off. What can you do to help her? This is supposed to be treatable."

"Indeed it is. However, she would need a platelet infusion and colony stimulating factors, which are quite impossible at this time."

"Let's talk about making it possible. What would it take?"

"I am very sorry, but the apheresis equipment is booked, and we have insufficient blood components. It is impossible." He moved to walk around her, but she placed a hand on his chest.

"What? You can cure her, but you won't because of a scheduling problem? A feckin scheduling problem? Are you shittin me? You'll let her die because of that?"

"You must understand. I cannot unbook –"

"I'll pay what it takes!" she yelled, her nose an inch away from his. "I'll give you whatever you want! How much easier do I need to make this?"

"I am sorry, but it is not possible! Now please lower your voice and let me go!"

She pulled out her pistol and pressed the barrel into his forehead. "Getting that healing feeling now?"

"What are you doing?" He raised his hands and stepped back toward the wall. "This is not sensible!"

"It's completely feckin nuts. But crazy or not, I'm still pointing a heater at your noggin, boyo. You'll be ending up a foot shorter if you piss me off." He tried to back away, but Krista pushed the barrel even harder into his skin. "We all must die, right? So pick your time – now or later? Whaddya say?"

"I cannot unbook the waiting patients! They have been scheduled for weeks! It is not –"

"Is it okay with you guys if I cut in line?" Krista yelled, and the waiting patients chorused a hearty 'YES!' and nodded enthusiastically. "There we go, problem solved. Ada's first on the list now. Save her life or I'll blow your feckin brains all over this pretty wall! Ya follow?"

"You would not shoot me."

"I sure would. I offed a hundred guys just the other day, and I wasn't nearly as pissed."

"But you need me to operate the equipment!"

"I'll have Ada figure it out," she said. "Hey, now *there's* a think! I don't need you at all. So just tell me where to send the flowers, and I'll take –"

"Hands in the air!" a man yelled from behind her. "I'm armed and authorized to use force!"

"Bullshit!" she called over her shoulder. "Shoot me and I'll pop this guy's head like a zit!"

"This is your last warning!" The voice was higher and shakier this time. "Put your hands in the –" The man emitted a strangled gurgle and then hit the wall behind the machine face first.

Mark knocked the taser out of his hand and lifted him by the collar, and then he flashed his gold Highway Patrol badge in his face. "This is official State business, and this is my jurisdiction."

"You can't –"

"Well, I just did, Sparky. Remember that when you wake up." He grabbed the guard's hair and bashed his head against the wall, and he crumpled to the floor.

"Officer, do something!" Sangha croaked, trying to see behind him. "This woman is mad!"

Mark looked at the pistol in Krista's hand and then at the quaking physician. "What's the problem here, ma'am?"

"The problem is that he can save Ada's life, but he won't," she said. "So I'm reminding him how fragile *his* life is."

Mark stroked his chin. "Nah, that won't work. These Punjabis are real stubborn. You'll have to shoot him." A strangled croak escaped Sangha's mouth. "But this is whatcha call a teachable moment. I'll show you how to do a proper headshot. First, never place the muzzle against the skull. Keep two inches clear at all times." He drew his pistol and aimed it at Sangha's temple. "Like this. If you don't keep your clearance, his brains might blow back into the barrel."

"It's messier that way?"

"Oh, yeah. Makes the skull pop like a shook-up coke. If his brain pulp gets inside the barrel, you could get a misfire the next time you shoot. You might even damage the weapon."

"Got it. I'll keep two inches clear, Officer."

"Good. Now, second," he said as he shoved Sangha to the wall, "there's a reason why you always cap a guy when he's standing against a wall. Watch." Sangha's eyes rolled up into his head, and he slid down the wall, collapsing into a heap beside the unconscious guard. "Great, I scared him to death. I was never good at menacing."

She knelt next to the doctor. "You were acting?"

"Sure, weren't you?"

"I wasn't." She pressed her fingers to Sangha's throat. "He still has a pulse. He just fainted."

"Good. I know how to wake him up." He ran to a medical supply closet and rummaged through the cabinets. Krista knelt by Ada's machine, while Micah held her hand.

"How are you doing?" Krista asked.

"I'm okay." Ada sniffed, and then she broke into tears. "I don't wanna die anymore, I was feeling sorry for myself, but I didn't make my peace with it and I don't wanna die, I can make up for all I did and I'm just sixteen and this isn't fair…" She tried to draw a breath through her tightened throat with a wheeze. "Oh, no, here it comes again…"

"Easy, easy." Krista pulled her to her chest and Micah took her hands in his.

She drew a few racking breaths, closed her eyes, and gripped Micah's hands, but her panic attack never materialized. After a few minutes, she could breathe freely again, and she opened her eyes and smiled shakily. "Thanks," she whispered.

"Now there you are," Krista said. "You're okay, and you're going to be okay, and you shouldn't worry. Mark and I, we've got this covered. Once we work around this little hitch, we'll take care of you."

Micah grabbed a tissue and wiped the tears from her cheeks, and she forced a brave smile on her face. "You can do it. I trust you with my life, Krista."

"Good. Just don't trust me with Dr. Punjabi's life. I might still pulp this douchebag's head."

"You should. He gives science a bad name," Ada said, and then she looked into her lap and spoke in a small voice. "Am I a cold-blooded ass like him?"

"Absolutely not! You're the wild, passionate, mad-scientist kind of ass!"

Ada sniffed, and a small, uncertain smile crept to her lips. "You mean that?"

Dr. Sangha gasped, and Krista turned to see Mark waving a glass ampoule under the doctor's nose and tapping on his cheeks. "I can't bring him around. Maybe we gave him a brain attack or something."

Krista spotted an automatic defibrillator on the wall above Sangha. She pulled the rubber paddles from their cradles and pressed a button, and the unit's capacitors whistled as they built a thousand-volt charge. "This'll wake him up," she said, kneeling next to Sangha and raising the paddles to his ears.

"Sure, but he'll wake up with his brains dripping out his ears."

She pressed the paddles to his temples and waited for the yellow blinking lights on the handles to turn green. "So he can join the bloody circus or something when we're through. I don't care." The light changed to steady green, and as the paddles began to hum and vibrate, he twitched and his eyelids flew open. With a strangled scream, he tried to wriggle away, but Mark pushed him against the wall and pinned him there.

"Stick around, pal," Krista said. "I want an answer to my question. Will you help Ada or not?"

Sangha glanced sideways at the paddles and tried to shrink down the wall. "As I have been trying to tell you, we do not have the blood components for a platelet infusion –"

"I'm not liking the sound of this. Get some and save her."

"I cannot. The hospital has only thirty liters of blood left, and none is B negative. The subject requires –"

Krista pressed the paddles even harder. "Her name is Ada."

"Yes, yes. Ada requires B negative components, which are very rare under normal conditions, but the Sacramento incident has depleted the blood supply statewide. There is no chance of finding four liters of whole blood of any type, much less B negative. I could transfuse platelets from a B negative or O negative donor, but since only two percent of people –"

"I'll do it," Micah said, standing up.

Krista looked over her shoulder at him. "You'll do what?"

"I'll give her my platelets," he said. "I'm B negative."

As DR. SANGHA SENT HER DAUGHTER into mortal fear fifty miles away, Victoria Lang was raising and lowering a plastic cup. "I didn't drop it this time. My strength's coming back."

"Good, good," the doctor said as she made a note on her tablet. "You shouldn't be here too much longer."

Victoria looked around the gymnasium at the rows of cots. "When will you tell me what happened?"

"I'll make you a deal," the doctor said. "If you can get up and walk to my office, I'll tell you all about the…event."

"Event?"

She unplugged the IV and held out her hand. "Walk first. You need to move, or else –"

"I'm a physician. You don't have to explain," Victoria said as she climbed to her feet. "And what I see here puzzles me. Some sort of public health emergency occurred, didn't it?"

"Yes, it did." The doctor smiled and took her arm. "Lean on me if you have to." They walked through the cots to a wall of bleachers and turned toward a pair of doors.

"Is this a quarantine?" Victoria asked. "It looks like an isolation hospital. Has the virus hit here?"

"No, not yet."

"I'm vaccinated anyway."

"Good, good," the doctor said as she opened a metal door. "We'll talk in here."

Victoria shuffled into a concrete-block room lined with racks of basketballs. The doctor sat at a desk and motioned to a chair. "My name's Connie," she said, extending her hand.

"Tori," she said. "So…?"

"Yes, yes, the event." She arranged a row of boxes on her desk, avoiding Victoria's eyes. "This is hard news, the hardest ever, and I'll give you a sedative if you need one."

"I can take hard news. Give it to me straight."

"All right," she said. "Tori, a nuclear bomb exploded in Sacramento last night. That's how you got here. Everybody's brakes failed, not just yours. There were countless collisions."

"A nuclear bomb? Are you serious?"

"Yes."

"Why on Earth would anybody…" Victoria bit her lip and leaned forward in her chair. "Forget that. What happened to Sacramento?"

"It's completely gone. I'm sorry."

Victoria slumped back in her seat. "My daughter…"

"I know how you must feel." Connie took her hand. "And I'm so sorry for your loss, and I wish to God you never had to go through this. I know how bad it feels. Would you like that sedative now?"

"No. My daughter…she might not have been in Sacramento," Victoria said. "I wasn't sure where she was."

"Well, I hope she wasn't within two miles of the fairgrounds. That area was wiped out."

"I don't know exactly where she was. She might not have been in the city itself."

"Good, good. There's reason to hope."

"Yes," Victoria said, standing to her full height. "And I'm going to look for her now."

"No, you aren't."

"Indeed I am, doctor, unless you tell me I'm a prisoner here." She flexed her fingers; Connie would be unconscious two seconds after her lips stopped moving, and then she'd put on her lab coat and walk through the front door as if she were staff.

"No, no, you're free to go whenever you want," Connie said. "But Victoria, there's nothing left of the city. If your daughter was anywhere near it, you should prepare for the worst. Please, don't hurt yourself by going on a futile search…what's wrong?"

Victoria had doubled over, and she staggered back to her chair holding her head in her hands. "Omigod, no!"

"What are you feeling? Do you have a headache?"

"My baby's dying," Victoria moaned.

"How do you know?"

"I feel it. I can't explain why." She took a deep breath and let it out shakily. "She's dying, but that also means she's still alive." She stood on quivering legs and reached out to the wall with one hand. "Somewhere, she's alive, and I *will* find her. Get my clothes."

"As your physician, I recommend –"

"Get out of my way, Connie. She might be lying in a cot, just like I was, and she could be around here. She needs me, and I'm going to find her." She walked to the door. "Where would the seriously injured be taken around here?"

"All right." Connie reached into a stack of plastic bags and pulled one out. "Your clothes. If she's in serious condition, she would've been taken to a regional trauma center. Probably Lodi, Fairfield, or Vacaville. They're the nearest ones that are still operating."

"Can you call them and find out if Ada Lang is there?"

Connie shook her head. "Everything electronic is shot. It's like the eighteenth century around here."

"Then I'll do it the old-fashioned way." Victoria pulled the IV out of her arm and threw it into the trash. "I'll walk to each one and find her myself."

A NURSE FIDDLED WITH THE CONTROLS on the blood-analysis machine and released the arm clamps. Ada climbed out and jumped onto the gurney an orderly had brought.

"I'll see you inside in ten minutes," Krista said. "Micah will stay with you, okay?"

Ada lay back on the gurney and sneaked a glance at him, and then she turned to her with an impish smile.

"That's the spirit." Krista smiled back and squeezed her hand.

"Hey, thanks for going all Jedi-knight on Dr. Sangha for me."

"My pleasure," Krista said. "Now Mark and I have got to keep an eye on Dr. Strangelove, okay?"

Mark and Dr. Sangha had already left the room, and Krista hurried to catch up. They rode the elevator to the top floor, walked down a narrow corridor, and opened a door into a small, darkened room with a large window. Krista glanced through the glass into a white-walled space housing a bulky stainless steel machine wrapped in hoses.

Sangha sat at a desk in front of the window and tapped on a monitor. "If you will excuse me, I must change the settings from infusion to transfusion."

"Fine," Mark said. "I guess we'll sit against the wall here. You're bogarting the only chair."

"You may sit in the waiting room," Sangha said.

"No way, doc," Mark said. "We're all staying here till the girl's turning cartwheels."

"There is no need to observe," Sangha said. "The equipment is controlled by a computer. Everything is automatic."

"We're staying. Make yourself comfy."

"This will take six hours!"

Mark raised the gun to his head. "We gonna have a transformative encounter, you and me?"

"I do not wish to be transformed into a man with no head. This I have already said."

"Then maybe you oughta shut the fuck up."

"How does one shut a fuck? Is this another American vulgarism for mouth – ?" Mark cut his question short by jamming his pistol into Sangha's tonsils. The doctor's eyes doubled in size and he raised his shaking hands.

"There you go, Doc. You're getting the hang of it." Mark pulled the gun from his mouth and wiped it on the doctor's lab coat. "See, even smart people can still learn."

A door at the end of the apheresis room opened, and Micah walked through wearing a blue paper gown and a cap. He peered at the machine and then reached to touch the hoses encircling it.

Sangha pulled a microphone to his lips. "Do not handle the equipment, young man. Please lay on the gurney. This is all you may touch."

Micah walked to the window and shaded his eyes, and Mark flipped him the finger.

"It is one-way glass," Sangha said. "That is a futile gesture."

Panic crossed Micah's face, and he stood back and patted the air in front of him, his fingers groping to find the edge of the invisible wall he'd encountered.

"He knows I'm here," Mark hissed.

Micah grew more frenetic as he tried to find the opening in the invisible box.

"I hate it when that sumbitch mimes me up." He rapped the glass with the butt of his pistol, and Micah fell back onto the gurney laughing and holding his sides.

"He's actually good at that," Krista said.

"He's just doing it to piss me off," Mark growled. "He knows I hate mimes, so he went and learned mimery, the bastard. I just put up with him in case I ever need a kidney."

"Is your blood type B negative?" Sangha asked.

"Naw, it's O positive."

"Then successful transplantation would be most unlikely."

Mark swore and grabbed the microphone. "Hey, Trial Size! Cut it out! I got no reason to keep you alive anymore, punk!"

The door opened and an orderly wheeled Ada's bed beside the machine. A nurse pulled a small cart between Ada's and Micah's beds and spoke to them for a few seconds, and then they rested their forearms on top of it. Large metal cuffs emerged from inside and engulfed their arms so only their hands showed.

The nurse fussed over a control panel and left the room, and then Dr. Sangha tapped a few times on the monitor and sat back in his chair. "The process has begun. There is nothing more to do for six hours."

ADA AND MICAH HAD BEEN LYING on the transfusion table for the better part of an hour. They'd run out of small talk, and the clicking of the apheresis machine was grating on their nerves.

"Thanks for saving my life, Micah," she said. "I know that sounds lame."

"What's wrong with lame? You should hear the things I say sometimes." He gritted his teeth as another thick needle pierced the skin of his arm. A tube connected to the machine filled with his blood.

"Lame's all I've got. I'm sorry."

"Wow, you're real depressed," he said. "You oughta cut that out."

"That's how it works with us freaks. We try to pretend we're normal, and then something happens reminding us we're not, and that's when it gets depressing."

"You think you're a freak? You seem normal to me."

"That's cuz you don't know me. Inside, I'm all freak, and everything about me is twisted and bad and broken. It's stupid to think I can ever have a normal life." She looked up at a picture of mountain meadows that was stapled to the ceiling. "At least I don't have to watch those freakin cartoons."

"If you think you're so weird, there's really no coming out of that."

"I know there isn't."

"But what if you're wrong? What if you're not weird?"

"Micah, other people dream of puppies and flowers. I dream of sub-nucleonic particles. My brain never turns off, and sometimes I wake up and have to spend an hour writing down what I was dreaming about. Tell me that's not freakish."

"It's not. In fact, I think that's real interesting."

"Yeah, it's real interesting how freaks think, isn't it? I should be in a sideshow." She turned her face away and barked a short laugh. "All the normal people can watch me and be grateful they're not as messed up."

Another needle jabbed into him and he hissed. "Do they sharpen these needles here? Okay, so if you're not normal, maybe you're trying too hard to be normal. Mark says you're brilliant, like some über-Einstein-grade genius, so you're unique and that's a good thing. Maybe you oughta stop fighting that."

"So I should go out and celebrate my freakitude? Yeah, thanks. Just let me slit my wrists right now."

The machine ticked and whirred, and then it rumbled so loudly that they couldn't hear each other. After a few minutes, it stopped and burbled happily.

"So why'd you wanna kill yourself?" he asked.

She turned her head to look at him. "Did Mark tell you that too?"

"No. You said you didn't wanna die anymore, so that means you did once, right?"

She studied the mountain meadows for so long that he thought she wouldn't reply, but after a few minutes, she drew a deep breath and looked in his eyes. "Did Mark tell you what I did? Did you talk about Sacramento?"

"He doesn't wanna talk about it yet."

She looked up at the meadows again. "I designed the bomb that destroyed Sacramento. I'm responsible for the deaths of a million people. I'm a monster that unleashed another monster. And not only that, I'm a coward and I tried to run away from what I did by killing myself." She let out a ragged sigh and settled onto her pillow. "And that didn't work, so now I'll have to wake up screaming every night for the rest of my freakin life. Now, aren't you glad you asked?"

KRISTA STOOD AT THE ONE-WAY GLASS and watched Ada and Micah. "She looks pissed," she said. "I wonder what they're talking about."

"Good thing she's in there with Mikey," Mark said. "That boy never gets worked up over anything."

She took his hand and leaned against his shoulder. "Maybe he can help. I'm not doing any good anymore. After that suicide attempt, I wonder if she needs somebody else to help her."

"Maybe Mikey can help. Maybe the little asshole has a reason to live after all."

"Okay, so that's a lot to unpack," Micah said.

"Go ahead and unpack away," Ada said. "When you're done, I'll understand if you wanna unhook from this thing and leave me here."

"I'm staying hooked. You didn't drop the bomb, you just designed it. And somebody else woulda designed it if you didn't, so stop thinking you're responsible."

She grimaced and let out a soft growl. "I wish everybody would stop saying that! The device worked cuz only I could make it work, Micah! I had to go to Los Alamos and show them how to do it, so no Ada, no bomb, all right? A million people would be alive right now if I'd just blown the particle accelerator engineering, but no, not Ada, she can't do anything wrong."

They lay side by side, and for a few moments, the room was quiet except for the bubbling of the machinery. "I'm real impressed you did that," he said. "I made a particle accelerator once."

"You've gone to the Dork Side too?"

"Actually, my class made it for a science fair in freshman year. But when we got to the fair, they told us we couldn't go in cuz they thought it was radioactive."

"Idiots. Accelerators are less radioactive than sunshine."

"Our science teacher told them that, but they didn't wanna listen," he said. "The thing did look kinda scary. It was this huge-big seven-foot-wide donut. Barely fit in a pickup truck. How big was yours?"

"About the size of a real donut."

"Wow. I bet you could do lotsa stuff with something that small. In my science class, my teacher was talking about how someday we'll be using particle accelerators all the time in medicine, but they're too big right now.

But someday, every doctor will have one, and they'll use them to fix all sortsa things."

"Theoretically, sure. You shoot cancerous cell DNA with a trillion fast mesons going at lightspeed, and it's gone, baby. Totally obliterated without affecting healthy cells. You'd just have to figure out how to focus the particles with an electromagnetic array and a medical imager."

"Isn't that like proton therapy? Everybody does that."

"Proton therapy? Gimme a break. That's like slicing cheese with a baseball bat. There's no comparing the magnitudes –"

"All right, all right," he said, holding up his one free hand. "Anyways, how many lives you think that would save if you made it? A million?"

She looked at him sharply.

"Helluva lot more than a million lives, I'd guess," he said.

"Huh." She pursed her lips for a few moments. "I wish I could, but my accelerator is a military secret. If I ever designed one for civilian use, they'd execute me."

"If you lived in the States, they would," he said. "But once we secede, you'll be in a foreign country!"

She grinned. "Yeah, I would, wouldn't I?"

ADA YAWNED AND STRETCHED as far as the arm restraint would allow. "So, what grade are you in?"

"Just started junior year, but I bet they cancel school now," Micah said. "How about you?"

"I'm a junior too, but I cut class most of the time. It's so boring."

"I guess being a genius and all, it's all low weight and high reps for you."

"I don't know if that's it," she said. "I have a problem with structured learning. I cut classes at Stanford too. I just log on when it's time to take a test, which pisses off my professors, especially when I get all A's."

"Stanford?"

"Yeah, I'm working on my second doctorate there."

He propped himself on an elbow and gawped at her. "You've got a Ph.D?"

"But just in quantum chromodynamics. QCD is the study of –"

"The electromagnetic charges of known quarks and theoretical sub-atomic particles."

"Sub-*nucleonic* particles," she said. "Protons and neutrons are sub-atomic nucleons, and they're composed of quarks –"

"Okay, so I said it wrong, but I know it's like the hardest science on the frickin planet." He lay back on the pillow and grinned. "And you're still going to high school. I thought *I* was fucked."

"The Commander still thinks my life can be normal, so she wants me to keep going. It's so freakin stupid. I mean, I've already written three dissertations, for chrissakes, and she *still* expects me to sit through Chemistry 101 and stay awake. That's the stultimate."

"Yeah, chemistry is total snoredom."

"It's a freakin crayon science." She looked up at the ceiling and laughed. "High school's screwed up, but whatever. I'm dropping out. So tell me, if you're Mark's brother, why do you look so different?"

"I'm his half-brother. His father was Wrestler and mine was Bigfoot, though it gets kinda weird when you try to explain it. Bigfoot raised Mark, and Hunter raised me."

"I'm lost. Something doesn't make sense here."

"Oh, that's for sure," he said. "It never did, and it's hard to explain."

She glanced at the wall clock. "I have five hours. Give it a shot."

"All right, I'll try to make it simple." He took a deep breath. "My mom's got bad luck with husbands. Her first husband, Lucky, shot himself two years after they were married. Mom met one of Lucky's friends at the funeral and they hit it off, and a year later, there was baby Mark. But the guy was a pro wrestler, and that's what killed him. One day, he choked to death in the ring."

"Somebody choked him to death at a wrestling match?"

"Naw. His sponsor was Laughing Pig Sausages, and his contract said he had to eat one of their hot dogs in the ring after every win, but that day somebody slapped him on the back while he was eating. He choked on it."

"Omigod! That's really tragic!"

He shook his head. "That's the genes Mark inherited. Wrestler wasn't real bright, and I think it spooks him that he might end up the same way. I give him credit for trying hard to get smarter, but really, it's kinda futile. He is what he is."

"Yeah. You know what my favorite Chinese proverb is? 'You may someday scoop butter from the desert sands, and you may someday drink from the mirage's waters, but you will never conquer stupidity.' I'm not saying he's stupid, but he's never gonna be Sir Isaac Newton no matter how many big words he uses."

"He's been doing the Word Builder thing with you, huh?"

She chuffed and laid back on the pillow. "Dear God, yes."

"Well, you better get used to it. So anyways, Mom was wrecked, so she ran off to the Yucatan with baby Mark. She was gonna make a new life, but she met an anthropologist from Berkeley there, and they got married and came back here. About ten years later, I showed up – she still calls me Baby Oopsie sometimes – and everything woulda been chill if my father didn't like playing pranks. One day he went up into the redwoods dressed up in a Bigfoot costume, fixing to play a prank on another professor, and…this is where it starts getting weird."

"*Getting* weird? This is way off-planet already."

"Oh, it gets worse. A lotta people up in the redwoods swear they've seen a Sasquatch. They've been trying to bag one to prove they're not crazy."

"Uh-oh. Did somebody shoot him?"

Micah nodded. "He was dead before he hit the dirt. So anyways, at the funeral, the guy that plugged him comes up to Mom and apologizes, on his knees and everything. Mom said it was like poetry, and she fell in love on the spot."

"She meets a lot of guys at funerals."

"Yeah, it's like hanging out in a bar to her."

"And she fell in love in a funeral home," she said. "With the guy who killed her husband. Next to his freakin coffin."

"Look, it wasn't Hunter's fault. He'd been looking for a 'squatch his whole life, and then one just walked right in front of him. And Bigfoot had on the best 'squatch costume ever. Anyways, Mom and Hunter hit it off, and she married him the next month."

"You're kidding!"

"And Hunter was a real great guy. He raised me from when I was only a year old, and I loved him. Mark couldn't stand him, though, I think cuz he shot Bigfoot."

"Well, duh!"

"He never gave him a chance. Hunter was a little unpolished sometimes, but he had a big, beautiful heart. No kid could ask for a better father."

"All right," she said. "I notice that Hunter's not around anymore."

"His gun blew up when I was twelve," he said. "Killed him on the spot. That was the worst day of my life."

She took his hand. "I'm sorry."

"That's okay. I'm over it now."

They lay on the gurneys and gazed at the ceiling, savoring the sensation of each other's hands. "Your mom's had four husbands?"

"Five. After Hunter, there was Freefall, but he didn't last long. After the wedding, he and Mom went skydiving to celebrate. She jumped outta the plane a bride and landed a widow."

She grimaced and covered her face. "Why does she marry these deathwish types?"

"I think she just likes the risk-taking types of guy, and sometimes the risks don't work out."

"I guess that's true," she said. "Sometimes the breaks don't go your way."

Downs was walking along El Camino Avenue in Sacramento when his tablet rang. He scanned his perimeter for threats and then picked up the call.

"Hey, Bob, I have intelligence for you. Can you take it now?"

"Hey, Raf. Yes, I can. What did you learn?"

"It was hard, but here's the address – 151 Golden Gate Avenue in Tiburon, the residence of Marissa Savu. We think that's Mason's mother, and that's the only known associate he has west of Sacramento."

"You *think* that's his mother? Raf, with our capabilities, we should know what she had for dinner on the night he was conceived."

"My friend, this is one convoluted family. That house is owned by some corporation that belonged to one of her many husbands, and she goes by five or six different names now. If that's not confusing enough, we can't find her birth records, so she's probably been in the country illegally for decades. And she's an odd one – she's president of her local quilting club *and* a seventh-dan *Hinoken* black belt."

"Caution is required, then."

"Yeah, those quilters can be real fanatics."

"I was referring to her martial arts skills, Raf. How could quilting –"

"It was a joke. Y'know, one of those things, makes people laugh and stuff?"

"Whatever." He tapped the address into the tablet and called up a map. "The first reaction to a traumatic experience is to return home, so that's where they must be. I'll be there tomorrow, and I'll extract information from this Savu woman if I don't find Warner."

"You brought your interrogation kit?"

"Of course I did. What Executive leaves without one?"

ADA CURLED A FINGER INTO MICAH'S PALM and stroked it, savoring the feeling of his warm hand. She risked a quick glance at him, a thought flicking into her mind: *I don't ever want to let go. I want to stay here forever.* She shook the thought away. "Micah's a nice name."

He laughed. "It's better than what Mom was planning to name me. She was going to give me a name that meant 'intellectual' in Samoan."

"Yeah? What's that?" she asked.

He looked over at her and grinned. "Hardon."

"Ouch! Holy shit, that woulda hurt!"

"I know! I woulda been totally demolished by the sixth grade," he said. "As it is, they eat me alive cuz I'm short."

"You're not short. You're like a giant to me."

"Wow, I've never heard anyone say *that* before. Hey, maybe you can come to my school and testify that I'm normal. Those dudes are merciless."

"It sounds like your school's a lot like Fort Washington High. Everybody's always trying to eat you alive. And even that got boring after a while."

"It's a huge waste of time, and I can't wait to get out and get on with my life, y'know?"

"Boy, do I ever know that."

"Yeah. It's just one big party there, anyways. All the juniors and seniors wanna do is screw their brains out and drink, and I'm not into that."

"I'm *really* into that," she said.

"You are?"

She blushed and looked away. "No, I mean, yes, I like to drink."

"And?"

"And I like to drink, okay?"

"And?"

"Drop it, chump."

"Okay," he said. "I don't like to drink. I tried it once and got wasted."

"You just did it wrong. There's a real art to getting a high buzz without going profundo blottissimo."

"Help me, Ada-wan. Show me the light."

"Oh, it's easy. You start with a full bottle of brandy…"

"Yeah?"

"…and you end with an empty one."

He snorted and looked up at the ceiling again. "*Ass*hole."

"But the magic comes inbetween. If you build up your blood alcohol slow, you get this feeling like you're some slayin hellah butterfly emerging from the cocoon into a world where everything's in tune. And the buzz lasts for hours if you do it right."

"Wow. Would you show me how? Whaddaya say?"

She smiled at him. "Sure. I'd like that."

"*They're falling in love,*" Krista sang.

"It looks like it, doesn't it?" Mark asked.

"Mmm. It's contagious, watching them." She gave his hand a small squeeze and then laid her head against his chest.

"You're right. It's real contagious. They're sending out major soft-porn vibes."

"You know what's happening? The Life Force is rushing back into her now, and it's flowing through us too."

"That's great. She came way too close to offing herself."

"Way too close. She saw her own death, Mark. I've been there myself, and if you survive that, you hunger for life." She wiped a tear from her cheek. "That's what's happening now. Micah's handing her a new life. I'm so happy for her, and I'm so sad for you."

"Me? Why?"

"Because you'll be seeing a lot more of her now."

He ran his fingers through her hair and chuckled. "That's okay. Don't tell her this, but I actually like the little snot."

"I knew you did." She kissed his cheek, rested her head against his chest again, and saw Ada and Micah looking into each other's eyes. "She won't be able to let go of him, y'know. Her life is becoming intertwined with his. Whenever she sees Micah from now on, she'll see a reason to live and to hang on. She won't be able to resist him." She squeezed him tight. "Like I wasn't able to resist you in McPhee."

"Actually, you jumped *me*, remember?"

She pressed her head closer to his chest, hoping he wouldn't see her blush. "I was feeling a little primal, okay? I've never done that before."

"You were just using me for sex?"

"It was complicated, and…aww, screw it. You were hot and I was horny, and I'm sorry if I –"

He kissed her on the top of the head and then bear-hugged her so hard that she couldn't breathe. "Best damn compliment I ever got. Thanks."

She blushed even more fiercely. "Sure, you earned it."

"You know, McPhee was fun, and I'll remember it forever. I love that place. The lodge, not the town, of course. When this is over, we oughta go back there and take a long vacation."

"Never. I'll never go back." She shuddered violently. He let go of her, and she stood back and wrapped her arms around her chest.

"What's wrong?"

"That's a nightmare place. I almost killed myself in that hellhole."

"You did?"

"I was only a few minutes away from doing myself in. If you hadn't come out when you did…" She shuddered again and bit her lip. "It was horrible. I felt the deadness climbing over my skin and crawling into my pores. With every breath, I was breathing out life and breathing in death, and all I had to tell me I was still alive was the pain. That's nothing to live for. Dying was better."

He pulled her into his arms and rubbed her back. "I didn't know."

"And you saved me. You were my living, breathing lifeline."

"I'm glad I came out when I did. It sounds like you were real desperate."

"More desperate than I've been in my entire life, Mark."

"And you desperately needed some guy to pull you back, and I was the nearest one."

"Not just *any* guy! That's not all that happened –"

"Hey, I'm not griping about it. I'm kinda generic. Happens to me all the time."

"That's not it!" She pulled away and looked into his eyes. "Do you really think it was just sex? After all we've been through, can't you see we were planting the seeds of something good?"

"I wish we were planting something good. I wish it wouldn't end. I wish for that a thousand times a day."

"Hunh? You're saying we don't have a future?"

He shook his head and puffed out his cheeks, looking at the floor. "I don't know what you see in me, and I start every day expecting to end it without you. And that's okay cuz every day's like a lifetime to me. But we're too different. What kinda future could we have?"

She leaned back against the glass and crossed her arms. "We could have a wonderful future if we wanted to."

"It's not that I don't want to. God, I'd do anything if we could, but…" He sat on the desk and studied the floor tiles again. "Okay, let's call it for what it is. I'm not in your league. I'm just a basic rank-and-file guy, and you're a rich and famous celebrity. I know what I see in you, but what can you see in me? We're like a different species."

"How can you say that?" she asked in a small, tight voice. "You won't give us a chance?"

"Chance? Chance doesn't have anything to do with this." He breathed out slowly and his shoulders slumped. "I wish it wasn't this way, but look, I know how this is gonna turn out. You're gonna be the Queen of Something someday. Your picture will be up on billboards, and you know where I'll be? I'll be at the bottom of that billboard citing some dude for a broken taillight."

She blinked back her tears and looked away with her lower lip trembling. "That's all you think of me as? This is all about status? You can't give me a chance and get past that?"

"Krista, please, don't cry…"

"Why shouldn't I cry? Why should I feel good about something so fucking stupid?"

"Don't get worked up. Nobody can fix this."

"Is that so? Well, just watch!" She yanked out her tablet and stabbed at the screen, swearing under her breath and sobbing. When she was done, she threw it on the desk and leaned against the glass. "There, all done."

"What's done?"

"I just gave you half my money. Now you're a millionaire too. We're equal."

He slid halfway off the desk. "Hunh?"

"I just transferred thirteen million bucks into your checking account. Problem solved."

"Hunh?"

"Done. Can you stop being so insecure and love me now?"

"I…uhh…well, take it back!"

She crossed her arms and shook her head.

Sangha slapped his palms on the table. "Enough! She is beautiful *and* she is giving you large sums of money! This is not the behavior of a rational…" Mark yanked the pistol from his waistband and pulled back the slide, and Sangha huddled over his monitor. "…and yes, before you ask, I am shutting my fuck now."

Mark jammed the pistol back into his pants and then rubbed the knots from his neck. "Krista, please, don't be angry and don't do anything foolish. It's not about money. Our lives are just too different. This is just a dream, a real wonderful dream, but it's not real."

"What's wrong with dreams?"

"Cuz one day you're gonna wake up and see me and realize you can do better, and that's gonna hurt like a sonofabitch. Hell, that's gonna be like having the heart ripped right outta my chest, and it'll just hurt worse the longer we pretend. But that's okay, cuz that other guy you find, he'll take you places I can't. He'll make you happy, and that's all I want." He shook his head slowly and looked through the glass. "It's okay. Good things don't just happen to folks like me. I don't expect them to. It's like Fate or something."

"Screw Fate." She swallowed and sniffed. "I love you."

"Hunh? You do?"

"I love you and nothing will change that, not ever." She sniffed again, tears welling in her eyes. "You're my guy. You're my other half. I don't want anybody else and I won't ever do better because you're The One and I don't care what's right or wrong and I don't want anything to get in the way."

"C'mon, don't cry," he said, taking her into his arms. "I don't want to hurt you. Please, don't be sad. I want you to be happy."

"Then stop all this stupid talk and love me, Mark." She looked into his eyes. "Do you love me?"

He kissed her and then rested his head on hers, playing with her hair. "If I say that, the clouds will open up and some huge cosmic foot will come down and squash me."

"Stop being so damn superstitious," she murmured.

"I'm not being superstitious. It's just that Fate and the unknown, they kinda scare me sometimes with what they can do. They can be vicious."

"And that's not superstition?"

"No," he said. "The world works like that. You're asking for trouble if you cross it."

"I know trouble. I can take it."

He ran his fingers along her shoulders and felt her warmth on his chest. "You really love me?"

"I really do," she said. "And I know you love me because you're not denying it."

He wound his fingers into her hair and looked through the glass. "I'm not denying it with all my heart."

"How's it feel to have me in you?"

Ada gasped. "Micah!"

"My platelets, I mean."

"That's not what you meant."

"Gosh, then what *did* I mean?" He batted his eyelashes. "Please tell me."

She pinned him with her most potent laser-intensity glare, even narrowing her eyes to amplify the effect, but he gave her an easy smile instead of looking away. "You've got the most gorgeous eyes," he said. "I could look at them all day long."

"Hunh?"

"They're so deep and dark, like a well that holds mystical secrets and wonderful treasures for the one brave enough to dive in."

Her color rose fast and she looked away. "Micah…"

"They're beautiful, but I'm sure everybody says that."

"Nobody's *ever* said that," she whispered.

"Well, they should. They're the most soulful eyes I've ever seen, and I wanna get lost in them."

She felt his pulse throbbing under her fingers. *I wonder if his lips are as soft as his hands. I'll bet they are.* She mused about kissing him, imagining her tongue exploring the texture of his mouth, and then a thought exploded in her mind: *I want him to make love to me.*

A horn squawked, lights flashed on the machine, and Dr. Sangha's irritated voice boomed from the speakers. "Your blood pressure is 150 over 100, young lady! Whatever you are doing, you must stop, or the procedure cannot continue. The machine is not magic! I do not wave my wand and, *poof,* you are healed!"

Ada lifted her head and smiled at the mirror, and then she lay back and glared at Micah. "Cut it out, chump."

"Didn't mean to get you in trouble. Sorry," he said. "I meant it, though. You do have beautiful eyes –"

The horn sounded again, and she shot him another dark look.

"All right, all right, I'll chill." He scowled at the ceiling as if he'd just bitten a pickle dipped in lemon juice. "This is so freakin gongshow."

"Let's talk about something else," she said. "What's your school like?"

"It's okay, I guess, but I don't really fit in. All everybody talks about is the college they're going to, and since I can't even afford to go to MMU…" He sucked his teeth for a second and shrugged. "Whatever. The worst part is that my best friend moved away this summer. School's pretty lonely right now."

"Why don't you give him a call and talk?"

"I did for a while, but I haven't been able to get through." He looked away quickly. "His family moved to Columbus, Ohio."

She squeezed his hand and bit her lip, unsure of what to say.

"He's probably dead," he said. "*Midnight Sun* says Columbus was wiped out by the virus."

"No way. I was there, Micah, and it wasn't that bad."

"He used to lie to make me feel better too."

"He's probably okay. The phones aren't working, that's all."

"Thanks, but I know what happened there." He stroked his finger along her palm. "I could use a new best friend. You know anybody who might fit the bill?"

She coughed into her hand. "I've got some ideas."

"Well, let me know. I could use a real friend."

"I could too. Krista's the first real friend I ever had. Once I got to know her, I realized how deluded I was about how real friends behaved. I actually thought friends betrayed and screwed each other. That's all I ever knew. After I met her, I realized that I'd never had a friend before."

"That musta hurt. Maybe you should make more friends," he said. "Like with someone your age."

She turned her head on the pillow, wearing a small smile. "Do you know anybody who might fit the bill?"

He smiled back. "Yeah, I've got some ideas."

VICTORIA LANG WALKED THROUGH THE MAIN DOOR of Lodi Hospital and sat on a bench outside. Although they hadn't admitted anyone matching Ada's description, she wasn't bothered. Perhaps it was the sunset bathing her in warm light, or the westerly breeze blowing the burning city's stink away, but she felt optimistic.

The mortal fear and dread that gripped her earlier felt comfortably distant. She'd walk to Fairfield Hospital, but if Ada wasn't there, she'd just keep trying until she found her. With the first smile her lips had seen in weeks, she began the thirty-mile walk to Fairfield.

"I like having you in me," Ada said. "Your platelets, I mean."

"I get that a lot," Micah said. "People stop me on the street and tell me I've got slayin platelets."

"Oh, I can see why. They're easy to get along with and they're funny."
She ran her finger up his palm, barely touching the skin. "And they're cute.
They're my kind of platelets."

He blushed and tried to will his heartbeat to slow down before the
horn blared again.

"They make me feel brand new." She sighed and looked up at the
ceiling. "I'd like you in me again sometime."

He gulped as his pulse raced to the warning line. "Umm, are we still
talking about my platelets?"

She smiled dreamily and settled into her pillow. "Platelets?" she asked,
and the horn squawked again.

"No, time travel is simple," Ada said. "Gravity, energy, and time fields
all function by the same laws but with different particle popula. Interstitial
space-time-energy perturbations are common as muck. And cuz toron
particles in dyadic opposition are syzygetically mated – they synchronize
across time as well as space – it'd be easy to induce local temporal
perturbations…" She looked at Micah, who was gazing at her with soft eyes
and a small smile. "You weren't even listening. Okay, it's all done by magic.
Electro-magic fields make time travel possible."

"Sorry. Whenever I see your face, it's all I know and my mind shuts
off. I really *was* listening, though. What you're saying sounds a lot like
Einstein's Spooky Action Hypothesis."

"You know about that?"

"Hey, science nerd here. Of course I do."

Her eyes glittered for an instant, and then she looked away and said,
"Well, for one thing, it's not a hypothesis anymore. I've seen it in action,
and I think I know how to work it. All I need to do now is modulate the
truon feed, and then I can produce a stable swarm of oppositioned torons –
which I call a toroid -- and move across time. Actually, you wouldn't move
in time, but the toroid would suspend the timeflow and open the
concurrence plane in the center, where everything happens at the same
time, kinda like some cosmic train station where all the tracks meet. You
find a track and go back as far as you want, then you disperse the toroid and
voila! it's like going back in time."

"Okay, yeah, I totally see that. So if you can do time travel, how come you haven't tried it?"

"There's a few small consequences I don't know how to control," she said. "I need to find a way to constrain the toron array so the toroid doesn't get too large, and I have to know that before I test my theory. If the toroid expands, you could get a bazillion-megaton explosion. If the toroid collapses, it could suck the solar system into a black hole."

"Shit," he said. "You shouldn't be fooling around with this stuff."

"Oh, don't worry. The chances of that happening are tiny. I'm just planning for the worst-case scenario, that's all."

"As worst-case scenarios go, that one's toppa the list. It's like a twelve on the Rectum Scale." She didn't answer, and he turned his head to see her glaring at him again with her lips pressed together. "What'd I say wrong?"

"I won't destroy the world, Micah. I might be undisciplined, but I'm not sloppy. Stop being a weenie."

"All right, I'll try to ignore that whole end-of-days gig just to make you happy."

"Don't get theatrical," she said. "It's totally safe if you do it right, and I just need to get the truon feed to work. I actually figured that out once, but Krista lost my math. But I'll figure it out again. Once I do, there'll be no limit to how many times you could move back and forth cuz one truon propagates two torons…"

She stopped suddenly, and Micah glanced at her – she was gaping at the ceiling as if it were the eighth wonder of the world. "Ada, what is it?"

"That's the answer. No matter which way you do it, it would work."

"What would work? What are you talking about?"

"Recombin destroys Neovirus by hijacking its shell proteins and making copies of itself with them," she said. "Each Neovirus gets cannibalized to make two more Recombin viruses. That's how you can make a lot of the vaccine – you feed Neovirus to Recombin, and it reproduces so fast that it almost gets out of control, like my toroid!" She smacked her forehead. "Why didn't I see it before? It was right there in my mom's papers the whole time. I could make so much Recombin that it'd be like opening a tap!"

MICAH OPENED THE DOOR and walked through with a weary Ada on his arm.

"How are you two feeling?" Krista asked.

"Tired and hungry," Micah said.

"I'm tired, but I feel a lot better than I did before," Ada said. "I have some slayin platelets now and lots of interesting ideas, so I'll be okay."

"You will recover fully in five days," said Dr. Sangha. "Now, may I go, please? There is nothing more I can do."

"Yeah, I guess you did your part, doc. Thanks." Mark opened the door for him, and outside, a hulking Highway Patrol sergeant in an immaculate gray uniform stood rigidly at parade rest. A muscle in his jaw twitched, and his dark, angry eyes locked on Mark.

Sangha ran to him and grabbed his sleeve. "I was held hostage for hours, Officer!" he said. "Arrest these two criminals! I will press charges! They held a gun to my head and forced me to perform –"

The officer laid a meaty hand on his shoulder. "I'll take care of this, sir. Please move on." He scurried around a corner, and when he was out of sight, the sergeant turned to Mark with his eyes narrowed.

"Don't gimme that face, Espinoza," Mark said. "You always look like you're squeezing out a hard dump. Just sayin, y'know?"

"I should cite you for going stupid in a smart zone, Mason. You made a real mess here. And speaking of messes, have you forgotten what the business end of a razor looks like?"

"Blow me. Go iron your underwear or something."

"I can't. I have to clean this up. You broke at least five ordinances and pissed off a hundred locals. Somebody's gotta talk them down."

"I'll clean it up myself," Mark said. "I'll square this with Captain McDougal when it's all over."

"You won't have time. DaCosta sent some National Guard troops to pick you up, and they'll be here in ten minutes. I'll have to do it."

Concern flashed across Mark's face, but he covered it quickly with a grin. "Hey, I'd love heavy security for a change, Spiz. We've been in there for hours, though, and the girls need a smoke."

Espinoza curled a lip. "A vile and unnecessary habit."

"Right, yeah, you don't wanna be around," Mark said. "That stink will never come outta your uniform. I'll take them down to the loading dock and meet you at the pick-up point after. Where are we meeting?"

"Outside the main entrance in the parking lot. Make sure you're there. I have orders from the lieutenant governor himself to get you all into their hands."

"Hey, dude, I wouldn't miss it for the world. I need some peace and quiet," Mark said. He was halfway down the corridor when he turned back. "Hey, Spiz! You got a smudge on your shoe!"

Espinoza looked at his feet with a scowl, and they hurried to the elevators. When the cab arrived, Mark pressed the button for the first floor.

"The loading dock is on the L Level," Ada said.

"We're not going there, Twink. No way we're gonna let this DaCosta clown get his hands on us. He doesn't understand the word 'no', and I barely talked him outta locking us up on a base and taking everything over. And now he's fixing to do it again."

"But this is our chance to make a deal," Krista said. "We give him the vaccine, he lets us go free, and we all drive to Mexico or something."

"Nuh-uh," Mark said. "It's not just the vaccine I'm worried about now. Twink has the Doomsday bomb in her head, and what if DaCosta knows that? He's a real prick, and I'm not sure he isn't a scumbag. We gotta keep Twink away till we know for sure nobody's gonna pry open her head."

"I was thinking of getting a hatch put in my skull just to make it easier on me," Ada said.

"Yeah. On top of that, I don't wanna spend the next few months in Fresno. Now we're gonna act real casual-like and mosey on out through the Emergency Room before the troops get here, okay?"

The elevator couldn't have moved slower if the shaft were full of jelly. Micah and Ada huddled at the back and watched the floor numbers tick by, whispering about Doomsday bombs. After an eternity, the elevator doors opened on the first floor, and they scurried to the Emergency Suite.

They edged through the crowds to the exit and ran to Mark's car. As it started, three Humvees drove into the parking lot.

"Okay, it's the perfect time to be somewhere else," Mark said. "Everybody hang on!"

DISPATCHES

Midnight Sun
News Post of October 10, 2043

Russia's Defense Minister, in an unprecedented step, has released the locations of its entire strategic submarine fleet as of 6:36 PM PDT Thursday. None were stationed within a thousand miles of Petropavlovsk, Russia, where the Russians believe the missile was launched.

In addition, a Soviet Bloc fisherman has published a video on the SatNet that shows the purported underwater launch of a cruise missile off the Russian coast Thursday afternoon.

Professor LaRonde of the University of the Upper Northwest has studied the Aleksei Kunitsin video: "This video undeniably shows the launch of an American Lancet missile. No other missile in service has this ram-air intake or can fly at such astonishing speeds. The Lancet missile carries the W104 warhead, which is as Warner describes: 950 kilotons yield and sea-launched.

"The only question about this video, in my mind, is whether it was taken on Thursday afternoon as the fisherman claims."

Canadian Defense Intelligence officers have reviewed the video, and they state privately that its geolocation and time tags place the fisherman eighty miles southeast of Petropavlovsk, Russia, on Thursday afternoon local time.

White House officials have yet to comment on these new developments, although a press availability is expected later today.

A PRIVATE MATTER

Day 53
Saturday morning, October 10, 2043
Pacific Ocean, 420 miles east of Petropavlovsk, Russia

Lieutenant Commander Tala Ripley stepped through the hatch into the Control Room and leaned against it, her face even paler than usual. She looked around for Commander Quinn.

Durgan saw her and pulled off his headset. "If you're looking for the Skipper, try the acoustics nest. They're tracking something in there."

"Thanks." She walked around the command podium to the rubber-lined acoustics room near the front, where Quinn stood with a headphone up to one ear and a finger in the other. She waved a hand in front of his face. "Skipper, may I have a few minutes of your time?"

He looped the headphone on a hook. "Sure. Fire away."

"It's a private matter. Can we discuss this in the forward conference room?"

He searched her face for clues but found none. "Yes, of course." He walked to the command podium and scanned the status monitors. Finding everything in order, he turned control over to the Tactical Warfare Officer and followed Ripley.

"What's up?" he asked, but instead of replying, she opened the conference room door and held it for him. Inside, two men sat at the table: Bailey, the chief missile technician, and Goldblum, the communications security officer. Both men wore the same pale, poker-faced expression as Ripley, and both clutched glasses of whiskey.

Quinn walked in and rested a hand on the back of a chair. "This looks bad."

"Please take a seat, Skipper," Ripley said. "We've cracked the launch controller and identified the target we struck on Thursday." She sat and tapped on a table monitor a few times, and a map appeared on the bulkhead screen. It showed a red line connecting Petropavlovsk to Sacramento.

He studied the map, showing no reaction; just his eyes moved, tracing the line back and forth. After a minute, he drew a deep breath and swiveled the chair to face Ripley. "Confidence?" he asked.

"One hundred percent. Goldblum, Bailey, and I verified the target coordinates independently."

He looked at Goldblum. "What are the chances of a decryption error?"

"Zero," he said. "Two other techs checked my decryption, and these are the coordinates we were ordered to strike."

"Bailey? Could this track be an echo from a previous exercise?"

"No. The controller we pulled isn't used for gaming or exercises. It's a mirror backup to the primary launch controller, used only during live releases. These are the only coordinates on it."

"I see." He looked at each one in turn, but their faces didn't reveal that this was an elaborate joke. As his mind accepted the truth, he squeezed his hands together until his knuckles turned white. "I admire your self-control at a time like this. I'm finding it difficult not to swear and punch a bulkhead."

Goldblum held up a bandaged hand. "We're all human, Skipper."

Quinn nodded and looked at the missile track again for a few long seconds, and then he turned back to the sailors. "So this happened. All right. Thank you all for your extraordinary efforts." He toggled the intercom. "Captain to the forward conference room."

BRICKER UPENDED HER GLASS and then looked again at the map. "Tala, disable that damned Missile Release Control System. We will *not* do this again under any circumstances."

"Julie, that's mutiny," Quinn said. "It was a valid release order, and under Article 94 –"

"It was a valid order from an insane president! That makes it wrong!"

"Would you argue that at your court martial?"

"Yes!"

The room fell quiet, and everybody avoided each other's eyes for a few moments. Then Quinn leaned back in his chair and said, "It's the only sensible argument. When they drag me before the mast, that'll be my defense too." Ripley, Bailey, and Goldblum nodded.

"This is my boat and my decision. I'll take the consequences," Bricker said. "The rest of you, clam up and play dumb."

"No way. I'll shout the truth to anybody with ears," Ripley said.

"Same here. I'm looking forward to that fight," Goldblum said. "I just hope my fist heals in time."

"Fuckin A," Bailey muttered. "We're the Blue Crew. We fight together. You don't take our heat."

"Looks like you're stuck with us, Julie," Quinn said.

Bricker swiveled her seat to study the map again, but in the light from the monitor, Quinn thought he saw her blinking back tears. Suddenly, she stood and leaned on the table with both fists. "We're getting ahead of ourselves. Our immediate priority is to disable the MRCS. Tala, exorcise it, bury it at sea, beam it to Mars, I don't care. Just get that damn thing off my boat."

"Aye, we'll look into it, but the fifth controller is located in the aft signaling pod. That's outside the pressure hull, and we can't send a diver out there to open it at this depth. It may not be possible."

"It just looks impossible. I'm confident you'll find a way. Now everybody get to work." Ripley and the chiefs left the conference room, and Bricker refilled her glass and sat beside Quinn. "Fuck, Ennis. What the hell's going on?"

"It explains why the *Rockefeller* is tracking us, doesn't it?"

"Are they still paralleling our course?" she asked.

"I was listening just before I came in here. There's no change."

She sat back in her chair and rubbed the twisted muscles in her neck. "They were there before the release, Ennis. Somebody knew this would happen and positioned them to destroy us."

"But why haven't they? If we're the sacrificial pawn, why are we still here?"

"I have no idea. I can't connect the dots on this." She picked up a pencil and twirled it in her fingers. "But the political machinations are immaterial. The *Rockefeller* is still out there, and it may be hunting us. What do you know about it?"

"Not much," he said. "I know what it sounds like, but I've never seen it. It's a littoral combat vessel launched last year from Pascagoula. It was built under high security, and the scuttlebutt says it incorporates some innovative technologies. Beyond that…" He shrugged.

"That's all I've heard too," she said. "I don't know what the ship is capable of. If it's stalking us, I need to know."

"Adam might know."

"He might, but with the *Rockefeller* out there, I don't even want to come to mast depth to contact him."

"If you're that concerned, why are we making ourselves an easy target?" he asked. "We should lose them and stay invisible till we know the situation on the surface."

"I agree." She called up a seafloor chart, tapped her lips for a few minutes, and then pointed to a spot near the end of the Aleutian Islands. "They won't expect us to sail right into American coastal waters. The shallows between Attu and Agattu Islands are bedded with magnetite deposits, and gray whales migrate through that passage this time of year. We'll be invisible in all that acoustic and electromagnetic noise. Once we're through, we'll head for Kiska Island and settle into a basin for a day or so, listen to the environment and see if we're clear. Then we'll try to get home." She stood and straightened her jumpsuit. "And remain calm, Ennis. Act like nothing unusual has happened."

DISPATCHES

Midnight Sun
News Post of October 10, 2043

CATACLYSM IN SACRAMENTO: DAY THREE

California Office of Emergency Services managers arrived on the scene early this morning. Our Witness in Auburn spoke to one and reports:

"The state didn't lose the whole government when The Bomb went off. The guy I talked with said the staff moved to somewhere in the Central Valley – he wouldn't say where – before the bombing. He said Lieutenant Governor DaCosta didn't trust President Cheyn to not do something stupid, so he moved the key departments out as a precaution. But I don't think he expected this.

"Governor DaCosta's running this emergency government, and at least they finally got their act together and showed up here. The Emergency Services managers are already working with the 184th Infantry to cut through the confusion, and now we're making headway on the rescue and relief operations."

Red Cross officials state that the crisis has exhausted California's reserve blood supply. Blood transfusions can make a life-or-death difference to someone suffering from radiation poisoning, and they urge all citizens west of the Health Cordon to donate blood as soon as possible. Our Witness in San Francisco reports that donation centers in San Francisco are already congested, and that the line at the Red Cross center in the Marina district extends for seven blocks.

FALLOUT FORECAST

Meteorologists forecast that the fallout plume will reach Mono Lake tomorrow, Las Vegas on Monday, and Flagstaff on Tuesday. After that, they fear that it might mix with Hurricane Andy Boy, which is predicted to make landfall on the Texas coast and then turn north into Missouri and Illinois, carrying the radioactive fallout to prime cropland. Winter crops may become tainted and inedible, as may meat production in Nebraska.

The governor of Nevada ordered the evacuation of Las Vegas this morning, but it will be managed by the California Office of Emergency Services. The California government appears to be directing Nevada's response to the viral and nuclear crises, and some speculate that western Nevada has been ceded to California. We are unable to confirm this assertion.

California officials advise Las Vegas residents to seek refuge near the California border due to the number of viral cases confirmed in eastern Nevada. Neovirus is now reported on the eastern edge of the Reno area, and residents of Southern Nevada are urged to avoid the north.

The State of California website is operating again, and it says that the health cordon will remain in place despite the fallout crisis. California border forces are rushing to construct a shelter at Barstow to handle the Las Vegas refugee influx.

WATER SUPPLY CRISIS IN THE OFFING?

Contaminated rain is falling in Yosemite State Park and the Hetch Hetchy reservoir, the primary water supply for San Francisco and the Bay Area. Experts say the water will soon become undrinkable unless it is filtered properly. Boiling the water will not remove the radioactive elements.

Midnight Sun is consulting water treatment experts, and we will update our readers in the afternoon edition.

VIRUS UPDATE

Reno's refugee shelter at the abandoned Hughes National Airport now holds about ten thousand displaced persons. Refugees escaping the Neovirus pandemic have been gathering there in the hope that California will distribute the vaccine that the Warner party brought into the state early Thursday. However, Warner has not mentioned the vaccine since the blast, stoking fears that it may have been destroyed.

Our Witness in Reno reports that residents there are anxious but optimistic:

"California is taking care of us now. We get daily shipments of food and water, and while you'll never get fat on almonds and avocados, you can live on it. Despite that, everybody here is having fun. It's great to see that. It's like spitting in the eye of Death.

"The city put together the new shelter just in time. I heard that a few refugees out at the old airport are infected, and the National Guard has designated a wing of the building to house the infected so it won't spread among the refugee population. They call it the Hot Wing. Great gallows humor, guys.

"California is supplying food and water to the refugees at the old airport as well as Reno, so conditions there are good.

"And we're all relieved that the fallout plume is headed somewhere else. A lot of people say it's because we're a lucky town, and everything goes our way. I hope that's true."

IT'S NOT ME, IT'S YOU

Day 53
Saturday afternoon, October 10, 2043
Site Q Leadership Continuity Shelter, Liberty, Pennsylvania

President Gabriel Cheyn fidgeted in his armchair. His morning meetings had exhausted him, and he'd been planning to relax in the small, dank presidential study with a newly published history of the Peloponnesian War. However, unwinding was proving impossible.

He sighed and looked around the room. Despite the plush carpeting and leather furniture, the study resembled a long-neglected prison cell: White dust streamed down the concrete walls from a recurring leak, and black and green mildew stains dotted the carpet. The mildew filled the air with the reek of sour rot, and his nose twitched as he suppressed a sneeze.

The study wasn't the only thing flattening his mood. He'd only been reading for fifteen minutes when a suffocating blanket of depression descended on his soul: The fragile Athenian democracy's destruction, and the ensuing civil unrest, were what America would suffer if he lost his war against Hayborn and the Archangelists.

Unlike the Athenians, who debated raising an army as Spartans marched over the horizon, Cheyn had sharpened his sword and limbered up when he learned about the Arkie's overthrow plan. The laws and the Constitution were useless defenses – both had been tossed overboard back in the Clune Administration, and he'd been the one heaving them into the sea. However noble it had been to silence the whining Democrats so Clune could transform the nation, the lawlessness of his White House had provided a roadmap for the Arkies to take power. Now only the feral rules of simple survival defined the coming war to preserve a semblance of the America that once was.

While his challenges were unprecedented, all wasn't lost. The rescue of democracy could still work if he pruned the Tree of Liberty, for so long over-nourished by the blood of patriots, and if he removed the ex-employed from the economy. Only then could American workers match the productivity that the corporations were exploiting offshore. Only then could he show the corporate oligarchs that democracy, not autocracy, was still the best political environment for capitalism. Only then could he show the Russian oligarchs that a strong and resilient democracy could survive even their machinations.

If his strategy worked, the prospect of paying penurious wages to sweatshop workers would attract Corporate America's wandering eye, and they'd bring their operations back home. American workers would have to endure this lesser democracy until the virus ravaged the Asian workforce, but after a few difficult decades, the resulting labor shortage would raise wages again.

However, that wasn't his immediate concern. All he wanted now was to avoid what a President Noah Hayborn would usher in: He'd immolate democracy and free the corporations of all regulation and responsibility for as long as they paid obeisance to Archangelism. This vile half-breed of theocracy and oligarchy would infect the planet and spawn centuries of war and strife. Billions would die, and even more would suffer. If he defeated Hayborn, though, the Russians and the Corporate-Americans would abandon them, and they'd return to being a bizarre and ridiculous sect.

He was devising new ways to amplify Corporate America's doubts about the Arkies and pinch off their money pipeline into Arkansas when someone rapped on the study's door. Sara Hogue opened it and peeked in.

"Sara! Come in, come in," he said, pointing to an armchair. "I could use some pleasant company for a change."

"Thanks." She settled into the chair and rubbed her eyes.

"You look exhausted."

"I haven't been able to sleep. There's been so much to think about. My bunk is hard as a rock too." She leaned forward in the chair and rested her elbows on her knees. "Listen, I've figured out that the Activists have a mole in the Navy. I talked to a few Navy guys in the dining room, and they said Warner's information on the W104 was exactly right, even down to the version of warhead we deployed. Only a handful of people in the military know that. But she also didn't know that the missile launch was accidental, which means her mole isn't on the operations side of the Navy but somewhere inside the supply chain. This narrows the search down."

"You should have come to me first. I know who her mole is."

"You do?"

"Of course. It's that pest Ada Lang. She headed the W104 trigger team, so she knows everything about it," he said. "She was the best asset Project Blue Ball ever snagged, but also the biggest troublemaker."

"Lang works at Los Alamos? Seriously? She's a National Security asset?"

"No, she's *the* National Security asset. Blue Ball blackwalls everything in her life so the Reds don't learn about her. If they get her, we'll be speaking Russian within a year."

"So just throw her kill switch. Isn't that what it's for?"

"I'm not ready to give up on her yet, and kill chips aren't a perfect solution anyway. Electromagnetic pulses screw them up, so if the Reds toss her in a full-body MRI and fry the gizmo before I trigger it, I've lost her. They'd know to act fast because they also chip their key scientists – and they know that the first thing we do is zap them when they defect." He pursed his lips and gazed into the corner of the room, and then he shrugged. "I can't protect her anymore. I just hope the Reds don't get her first. If I can bring her in, I'll lock her down in Level Nine this time – if I can keep the damned NSF from killing her first. Do you know how hard it's been throwing them off her track? They're a single-minded and bloodthirsty crew down there."

"It's not a job for the timid…wait, you've been interfering with their pursuit?"

"Of course. She's no good to me dead. I need her back in Los Alamos building nasty little bombs, and allowing the Reds to snatch her would be a strategic disaster. It was the only course that made sense."

"So *you've* been helping them make those miracle escapes!"

"Only for the past two weeks. After her tracking chip went silent and the FBI started poking at her cover identity, Blue Ball came running to me with their hair on fire and ready to go to Defcon Fifty. I assured them that their precious asset was probably still safe and sound."

"Why didn't you just joint-op the Watch Room and Blue Ball to find her? We're good at that."

"I couldn't trust the NSF. They would have told Hayborn, and the Reds have so thoroughly infiltrated the Arkie organization that it would be tantamount to handing her to the Russians. Nor could I tell them to let her go because that quisling Hayborn would have used it against me. So I told Blue Ball to throw the Watch Room off the trail with a few cyberbombs, knowing they'd believe it was another Activist ploy. I figured if those Blue Ball kids could crack the Nizhny Novgorod computers, the Watch Room should be a snap."

"I was wondering how Warner kept getting so lucky, but it turns out it was another Gabriel Cheyn nine-dimensional chess game. I wish you'd tell me about these gambits of yours."

"I have so many plates spinning, it would be impossible."

"Still." She rubbed her temples and then snapped her fingers. "*That's* how that mayberry found her! Some California cop came outta nowhere and saved Warner just as we were closing in. Was that you too?"

He smiled and shrugged. "I told Governor Rodriguez where Warner was crossing the Rockies and that they could keep the vaccine if they found her. In return, Rodriguez agreed to attach so much regulation to the tenpez recall bill that it would never work – *and* he'd return Lang to Los Alamos."

"You don't want Warner anymore?"

"No, she's nothing now. I called in some favors in Ottawa, and they'll ensure that the videos never get released. Not that anything would change if they *were* aired." He leaned back in his chair and laced his fingers behind his head, his eyes smiling. "American apathy. It's a force to behold, isn't it? As pervasive as gravity and as easy to neutralize, I dare say. Warner shouts all over the SatNet that the Ranks are being systematically excised from the body of humanity, and all they do is yawn and change the channel."

Hogue shook her head. "Dickhead Downs used to say that lower-class apathy worked so well, it had to be engineered."

"It actually was. Back in Clune's time, we needed a nationwide mechanism to dissolve the lower-class social cohesion that would eventually lead to all-out class war. The PASS Act wasn't effective – the chronically poor couldn't afford enough marijuana and alcohol to fragment their communities – so the MRC decided to give them a safe, synthetic class war instead. They called it Engineered Tribalism: broadcasting a fictional class conflict every evening paired with a wargaming app for an immersive, round-the-clock experience that even earns some pocket change. That's how *Fight for Your Life* was born. The MRC engineers predicted that the lower classes would become obsessed with battling fictional upper-class warriors instead of burning cities. And it worked, much to our surprise, even though no legion has ever brought the Tessera Orb home in eighteen seasons, and none ever will."

"I knew that. I mean, I didn't know that *Fight for Your Life* was a government initiative, but I always scheduled my inner-city redactions for eight PM when the show was on. My Executives usually had a clear operational perimeter then."

"Ah, apathy. How could we get anything done without it?"

"We couldn't. And speaking of alcohol…" She stood and stretched, and then she walked to the bar and poured a tumbler of bourbon.

"I wish you wouldn't do that," Cheyn said, curling a lip. "It's so bad for you."

"So's working for the Dickhead." She took a long sip and then sighed. "You and Rodriguez kissed and made up? I thought you'd given up on him."

"The political winds changed, and I changed my course correspondingly. I'll follow whatever course leads to a stronger and more secure American democracy," he said. "And this deal was so sweet. Recombin is damnedly difficult to make, and California would never be able to make enough before the virus jumped over their cordon, giving me nothing to lose. And I'd get that pest Lang back where she belongs, which is critical to founding a Great American Century."

She barked a short laugh. "C'mon, Gabriel, she's just a little girl. I was a teenager once, and my head was so far up my ass…" She saw Cheyn eyeing her over the top of his glasses. "You're serious?"

"Indeed I am. The Lang girl was born with a revolutionary knowledge of quantum physics already wired into her mind. She's so brilliant, the Stanford physicists still haven't deciphered her doctoral dissertation. And the fusty Los Alamos pipe-smokers would kill to get her back because she can lead them across the frontier into an entirely new science, and I'm sure they also want to rub her little belly and feel smarter. Incompetence is a substance lighter than air, Sara – it always rises, and the Los Alamos leadership is proof." He drew a long breath as if he was planning to continue, but then he pulled up his glasses and cleared his throat. "But I digress. That little girl can give us the proverbial Big Stick we need. She talks about a device called Big Sister in her sleep, and Los Alamos is convinced it's a thirty-megaton warhead a Joe Slick could deliver. And America *must* have it. A thirty-megaton groundburst can bust even a hardened silo, making every Russian land-based missile vulnerable to a stealthy first strike."

"What about your disarmament deal with Premier Rutskoy, though? Is this another course correction? To tell you the truth, nuclear disarmament appeals to me, especially now, and I think you're nuts if you're going back on that."

"Oh, no," he said. "I'll honor the disarmament agreement, of course. However, Rutskoy's regime won't last five years, and then another strongman will take over. Before that strongman can re-ignite the arms race, I'll inform him that I have four hundred stealth silobusters aimed at his country, and that he should dismantle his nuclear arsenal – and the Soviet Bloc as well. And he'll capitulate because he wouldn't stand a chance against our throw weight, stealth, and accuracy. Thus the Great American Century begins with us as the sole superpower. And the world will see that democracy is, and always has been, the strongest political system."

Hogue sat up and perched stiffly on the edge of her chair. "You're running a long con on Rutskoy. You just wanted to weaken them so you could gain a military advantage. You were never anti-nuke."

"I guided Rutskoy to where America needed him. That's my job." He sat back in his chair and laced his fingers, looking off into a corner of the room with an unfocused gaze. After a few moments, he picked up his tablet and began tapping the screen. "But it's time to accept that the odds of getting the Lang girl back are growing dangerously long. This being said, she now represents a risk to this nation by freely gallivanting about California, practically begging to be snatched by the Reds. But I'm confident that we can progress into the Great American Century without her, even though it will be more difficult and time consuming."

"Okay, then get rid of her. Trigger her kill chip and move on."

He tapped one last time and laid the tablet on the side table. "I just did."

∞∞∞∞∞

AN HOUR LATER, Cheyn had read no more than ten pages of his history book. As he closed his eyes for a short nap, a gunshot echoed through the hall outside. He toggled the intercom switch for the security office. "What's going on?"

"Someone discharged a firearm, sir."

"I know that, oaf. That's why I'm calling. Why did someone shoot a gun in here?"

"We're investigating, sir. A guard should be there soon. Please remain in your study for the duration."

He walked to the door and heard people running by outside. A few seconds later, a young Secret Service agent opened it. "Sir, please remain inside for the duration –"

"I've heard that already!" Cheyn snapped. "Why are people shooting down here?"

"We're investigating –"

"Oh, for God's sake!" He pushed the door closed, returned to his chair, and turned on the intercom. "Give me a straight answer right now! What's happening?"

"It appears there was an incident in the lounge, sir. We're containing the area now. I'll brief you when I know more."

Cheyn snorted and walked to the door again, where he heard people talking outside. The knob turned, and Hogue slipped into the room with two pistols in her waistband and an assault rifle in her hand. "Sara, thank God. Maybe you can tell me what's going on. I heard a gunshot."

Hogue looked up him briefly and then pulled the magazine out of the rifle. "I killed Admiral Cardozo," she said, tossing the empty rifle into the corner.

"You...you what? You shot...?"

"A Navy officer told me Cardozo instructed one of our subs to destroy Sacramento. I asked Cardozo, and he said he did, so I killed him." She pulled a black, long-barreled pistol with a silencer from her waistband and aimed it at his face. "But before he died, he said *you* ordered the attack."

"Sara, please..."

"Did you?"

"The political winds shifted, Sara. I was forced to change course."

"So you wiped out Sacramento before they could vote for secession. You lied to me."

"Sara, I know this is a shock, but please understand that I only did what was needed. I didn't make it necessary, and I'm as much a victim as anyone in Sacramento. We're all pawns in Hayborn's game."

"Game? You call this a fucking *game?*"

"Yes. It's a deadly game, one where the only rule is to win. Winston Churchill understood that. He willingly sacrificed the city of Coventry to protect his Enigma decoding device and win World War Two. Sacramento is no different."

"Churchill's enemy bombed Coventry. *You* bombed Sacramento. That's an enormous difference."

"But nobody will know that. The victors write history, and history will say a crazed Arkie submarine captain nuked Sacramento to punish California for its wasteful liberalism. My team's concocted a compelling backstory for Captain Bricker, and my surrogates have been sowing it in the media. By tomorrow, the court of public opinion will be ready to lynch her. And then I'll play the victim-in-chief, assuring that I'll win the election and receive a mandate to lead America into greatness again."

"Wrong, Gabriel. Historians aren't stupid. They'll say you slaughtered a million people for your own political gain."

"My gain? Mine? This was never about me. This is about preserving democracy and laying the cornerstone of the Great American Century. And don't pretend to be moral now. You knew about the RVE Initiative and Economic Selection. Don't weep over the loss of a million lives when you have the blood of ten times more on your hands."

"Hold on, pal. *I* didn't kill them."

"Oh, no, Mother Nature killed them off, right? And you can be pure and principled again just by denying you ever believed in Economic Selection."

"I loved you too much, and I forced myself to believe you. You were a master of mindfuck. Day after day, argument after argument, you injected your psychosis into me till I couldn't see the difference between a natural pandemic and a man-made one, till I believed that bad was good."

"You make it sound like I wanted to do this."

"Oh, for fuck's sake! It was the most fun you ever had! Be honest with yourself!"

"I relish the challenge, true, but I had no choice except to fight. The only way to save America is to pare it down and build a new economy." He reached to take her hands, but she shrank back. "Don't overreact. All births bring pain, but the birthing of a new and healthier democracy must be done regardless of the pain. The RVE Initiative merely induced this birth. If you think explaining that is mindfuck –"

"It *is* mindfuck!" She glared at him with bloodshot eyes. "All that comes from your fucked mind is nightmares that get worse and worse. I wanna be out of your life and away from this madness!"

"Don't get so damned emotional about it!"

"Am I supposed to be as inhuman as you?"

"I'm as human as anyone else, and it broke my heart to sacrifice Sacramento, but it didn't break my resolve. I reached beyond common sentimentality and found a greater order and purpose. Rise up and see that. Then you'll understand it's not as terrible as you think."

"I don't need to *think* about nuclear war! I saw the pictures! I saw the injured!"

"And I feel their pain." He thumped his chest. "I feel it all here, and I hold them in my thoughts and prayers. I'm not happy I had to do it, but I *had* to. California was ready to secede. I had to stop that." He sank into his chair and rubbed his eyes. "And if I were impeached and removed from office, it would be democracy's end, Sara. Hayborn and the Arkies intend to found a theocracy so total that it'll make the Persian caliph look reasonable. They'll wipe out any science or beliefs they don't like and throw this country back to the eighteenth century. Everybody will have to become an Arkie because they'll control the economy and dispense the jobs, which they're practically doing now. Religious and political freedom will be erased, and nobody will even remember what those phrases mean. America will become a land of holy kings and lowly serfs, and the only person standing between them and that future is me."

"Then nominate a vice president to carry on. Resign and hand all this over to him. You're not fit to lead."

"Don't talk like this, please, Sara. The Senate won't confirm my nominees. You know that."

"Okay, then do something else! I don't care what, but find another way to fight Hayborn instead of blowing up innocent cities cuz you're shit-scared of him!"

He drummed his fingers on the arms of the chair. "Don't push me…"

"Admit it!"

"I'm not afraid of *him*! I'm afraid of what he'll do! He'll crush this republic under his heel! It's my sworn duty to protect the country from zealots like him!"

"Even if you have to kill a million innocent Americans?"

"This is war, Sara! Anything goes! We're lucky we only lost a million!"

"What?"

"Sixty million died in World War Two, and they weren't fighting religious nutjobs and Russian provocateurs at the same time! Sacrificing *only* a million was a bargain!" He leaned forward and stabbed a finger at her. "And don't you dare cast me as some invertebrate dastard. I did what needed doing, and I was the only one with the balls to do it. The last six presidents just twiddled their thumbs as the economy became a welfare system for the wealthy. Economic Selection just cleans up their damn mess."

"Don't use history to rationalize your atrocity. Sacramento didn't need to be nuked. If you'd killed Hayborn years ago –"

He jumped up, and the chair crashed into the wall. "That's ridiculous! We talked about that, and it wasn't a viable option –"

"And nuking a million people was?"

"Yes!"

"You needed to grab Hayborn's throat and choke him till the life went out of his eyes, just to learn the basic rule of combat – every battle is man-to-man. When it comes down to the snuff, there's just you and the guy killing you. But you couldn't do that, and that's why you just sacrificed a million people." She leaned forward until their noses touched. "You're a fucking coward, and I despise cowards."

"Watch what you say…"

"You're a cowardly poof who doesn't have the balls to carry the fight through to the kill. We shoulda rubbed out Hayborn, and then the guy who replaced him, and then the next guy, till the goddamn Arkies got the message that we'd keep going till they were extinct. Even the damn Aluminati woulda backed off when they felt the hands around their throat cuz ideology disappears *real* fast when you can't breathe. But you don't have a taste for the kill. You're all brain and no balls, so you slaughtered a million people cuz it was easier than throttling one."

"Calm down —"

Someone knocked on the door, and she aimed the silenced pistol at it without taking her eyes from Cheyn. It coughed twice, blowing two neat holes in the center of the door. A woman screamed and footsteps scurried away. "You shoulda stayed in college. You're not built for a world of brutes and blood." She pulled a long plastic zip tie from a back pocket. "You're worse than Hitler. At least he wasn't afraid to get his hands dirty and get the job done."

"Hitler I am not, Sara. If I fail, future historians may compare me to him – if there are any non-Arkie historians – but I'm doing what needs to be done, even if it's difficult and troubling. And I'm doing it all alone. It's just me."

"Exactly, Gabriel. It's just you. Now cross your hands."

"What?"

"Cross your hands. People like you shouldn't be running my country, and I'm gonna do something about that. You'll help by being my human shield, or I'll shoot you right now."

"You wouldn't kill me."

She aimed the pistol at his forehead, keeping the barrel two inches away. "Your only tactical value is that you can stop a bullet meant for me. You'd be dead already if it wasn't for that."

Sighing, he crossed his hands, and she looped the tie around it. He winced as Hogue pulled it tight. "Jesus, Sara, all right already."

She turned him around, pulled out a silver pistol, and then wrapped an arm around his chest so it was aimed at the fleshy underside of his jaw. With the other hand, she jammed the silenced pistol under his armpit so only the tip showed. She dragged him to the door, pulled it open, and then kicked the legs of two unconscious agents away from the doorway. Her path clear, she grabbed Cheyn tight and pulled him into the hallway.

Two Secret Service men crouched at the far end of the hall with their pistols drawn. As one opened his mouth to call out, the silencer under Cheyn's arm spat twice. Both agents dropped their guns and fell to the floor holding their knees.

Keeping Cheyn in front, she edged along the wall until they reached a corner, and then she kicked their pistols far down the hall. "We good here,

Jeff?" she asked one man, who was rocking back and forth and grimacing. He nodded while mouthing misogynistic slurs. "Make sure they take you to University Hospital. That's where we go for gunshot trauma. They're the best." His mouth twisted into an anguished grin, and he nodded again.

She pulled Cheyn back to the wall and edged to a thick concrete column at the crossing of two corridors. Glancing in the dome mirror on the wall above, she saw that the corridor leading to the entrance was empty except for two agents with their pistols drawn, both hiding behind a desk by the massive blast door.

She fired again and blasted the mirror into a cloud of shiny plastic. Before the pieces hit the floor, she'd spun around the corner holding Cheyn in front of her. Both men crouched even more and leveled their guns.

Keeping pressed against the wall, she and Cheyn slid sideways toward the blast door. When they were only a few feet from the desk, though, a voice called out from by the column, "Release the hostage, ma'am! You have no way out!"

"You've got a magic bullet in that gun, pal? Something that can hit me in the head or the spine and guarantee I won't blow the president's head off? Something that won't hit Gabe by accident?"

A door across the corridor swung open, and a young woman jumped out and into a shooting crouch, aiming at Hogue. The gun under Cheyn's arm spat again. The woman's hand exploded, spraying her face with blood, and her pistol clattered to the floor. "A magic bullet like that? You've got one in the chamber?"

"I'm a marksman! I have a clear shot!"

"Then take it! Impress me!"

"EVERYBODY SHUT UP!" Cheyn shouted. "We've lost. Sara could slaughter us all with only a post-it note, and you may have noticed that she's brandishing two pistols. One of them is burning a hole in my damn armpit, so everybody STOP MAKING HER SHOOT! Just lower your weapons. She'll do me no harm."

"You too," Hogue called to the man hiding behind the column. "Place your weapon on the floor and kick it over here where I can see it. And that goes for the noob next to you with the nasal condition. Jesus, I can hear you breathing all the way over here, kid." The noob swore softly, and then two pistols skittered across the concrete and stopped near the injured woman curled up by the door, who was clutching her bloody hand and glaring at Hogue. "You two over by the desk. Open the blast door and collect all these weapons and drop them outside."

One agent glanced at Cheyn, who nodded. He entered a code into a wall monitor, and the massive steel door groaned open. Another man picked up the pistols and flung them through the opening.

They stood aside as Hogue and Cheyn backed through it. "Y'all need a few weeks on the hostage course down at Quantico," she said to one of the agents. "This was way too easy."

"You just had the element of surprise, that's all."

"It's called 'maintaining a superior tactical posture.' Look it up." She kicked the pistols further down the tunnel and said, "Close the door."

The massive door's motors whined, the hinges groaned again, and the door slowly swung shut. After the locking bars slammed home, she pulled the pistol from under his armpit and pushed him forward. "Put some lotion on that burn. It'll be fine in four days," Hogue said. "Now walk."

"Are you going to kill me?"

"No. I won't help that creep Hayborn become president, and that's the only reason why I'm letting you keep breathing. But I'll hurt you, Gabriel. Believe me on that."

They walked in silence down the long tunnel until it turned hard to the right. Soft green daylight streamed through a faraway entrance, where four Silverbacks were parked along the tunnel's wall.

They walked to the one closest to the entrance. She laid her thumb on its fingerprint reader, and the big engine rumbled to life.

She climbed in and then glanced outside at Cheyn, who looked confused and lost. "You still here? It's over. Get the fuck outta my sight."

"I'll happily vanish." He turned and took a step down the tunnel but then stopped. "Sara, keep some perspective. Don't do anything inadvisable, okay?"

She closed the door, rested her elbow on the windowsill, and looked back at him while wearing a half grin. "I'll be starting at inadvisable and working my way up. Watch the news, Gabriel."

OVERPRESSURE

Day 53
Sunday morning, October 11, 2043
Pacific Ocean, 110 miles south of Attu Island, Alaska

Captain Bricker handed a thumb drive to Durgan. "When we get to mast depth, bounce this off the satellite and straight to Admiral Harris' tablet. As narrow a signal as you can get."

"Nobody will pick it up, Captain," Durgan said.

"And download nothing except the news packet. Send that to my cabin, my eyes only." She called to Commander Quinn. "I'm going aft to check on Propulsor Two. Call me there if you have any problems. You have the conn."

"XO has the conn," Quinn said. He sat at the command station and reviewed the status monitors, and then he leaned to the side and called into the Acoustics nest. "Jackson, what do you hear out there?"

"A pod of blue whales swimming south, that's all. I haven't picked up a peep from the *Rockefeller* since yesterday."

"Maybe we lost them when we turned east." He rechecked their location; the boat was approaching the Aleutian Ridge, nearly four hundred miles from where they should be. "I think we're clear. Pilot, rise to mast depth."

Ten minutes later, Quinn raised the photonic mast and scanned the horizon. He saw no surface traffic, although thick fog obscured his vision to the south. Still, since Jackson heard nothing there, the fog bank was probably empty too. "Comm, raise the mast and send the captain's message."

He swiveled the mast camera around to the fog bank again, which was thick enough to hide an aircraft carrier. Suspicious of the cloud, he switched the camera to infrared and spotted a heat source inside it. When he zoomed in and changed back to visible light, a dark smudge appeared on the screen. The haze obscured any detail, though, so he captured the image and enhanced it.

The reconstructed picture materialized on the bulkhead monitor and displayed the outline of a large ship. He estimated its location with the laser rangefinder. "Jackson, I have a visual at 10,900 meters, bearing 170. You sure you don't hear anything there?"

He answered a few seconds later. "Nada. It's a surface vessel?"

Quinn pushed the magnification higher. "Yeah, maybe three, four thousand tons. You really don't hear anything?" He walked to the acoustics nest, picked up a pair of headphones, and pressed them to his ears.

As soon as he put them on, Durgan called, "Missile release order!"

Ripley checked her screen. "Aye, we have an MRO, Skipper! Twenty seconds to change lockout!" When Quinn didn't acknowledge her call, she looked over her shoulder and saw that he wasn't at the command station. She searched the Control Room and found him leaning against a bulkhead in Acoustics.

"Skipper!" she called, and when he didn't answer, she sprinted over.

He saw her coming and pulled off his headphones. "What's –"

"Missile release order!"

He glanced at the Strategic status monitor and saw the countdown. "Abort it!"

Ripley ran to her station and stabbed the Abort icons, but the launch screen appeared. "Changes locked out! Tubes One, Twelve, Two-Three and Three-Four selected!"

"Four of them?" he asked.

"Aye, four!"

Quinn glanced at the countdown for the first missile, which would launch from Tube Three-Four in less than three minutes, and then he whirled to the helm. "Pilot, emergency dive! Down bubble forty-five! All ahead flank! Rig for angles and dangles! Comm, sound general quarters!"

A klaxon blared, and a mechanical voice called out the alarm: "Dive! Dive!" The deck tilted as the boat began its descent.

"Missile Release Control System has accepted the task. Launch controllers engaged," Ripley called. "Self-arming enabled. Pre-release sequence initiated. Ejection booster vessels charging."

"Pilot, display time to 250 meters depth," Quinn said. "Strategic, display time to first release on the Command monitor."

"But the MRCS won't be able to launch below 250 meters…" Ripley began. "Oh, right, got it."

Quinn tapped the intercom button. "Captain to Control."

"Hatches opening in ten seconds," Ripley said. "All indicators nominal."

"Acknowledged," Quinn said, watching the countdown. The first missile, in Tube Three-Four, would launch fifty seconds before they reached 250 meters. At that depth, the MRCS would suspend the launches because the water pressure would be too high to eject the missile pods. For that strategy to work, though, they needed to get to 250 meters fifty seconds faster. "Ballast Control, emergency blow aft trim tanks, emergency flood forward trim tanks." The forward tanks rumbled as seawater flooded the chambers, and the deck tilted. He sat and buckled his seatbelt, watching the boat's trim diagram change. The hull trembled as four hatches opened.

Jackson called from the Acoustics room. "Skipper, the planes are cavitating! We're blowing more bubbles than a Mardi Gras float, and those hatches are like whistles!"

"Acknowledged." He turned to Communications. "Where's the Captain?"

"Here," Bricker said, sliding across the slanted deck to Command. She grabbed the edge of the charting table and looked at the launch screen over Ripley's station. "Holy shit!"

"Reactor at eighty-nine percent!" the Reactor Control Officer said. "Approaching the lockout at ninety percent!"

Quinn tapped numbers into his chair monitor. "Lockout released. Exceed the limits."

"Skipper, we have cold rods in Cell Two, and it could scram if –"

"Exceed the limits, sailor," Quinn said. He rechecked the countdown, and Tube Three-Four was now only forty seconds ahead. Bricker stumbled to the chair and gripped the back.

"Four release orders and I'm diving below –" Quinn started.

" – the launch floor. Got it," she said. "You should also flood the forward main ballast tanks."

Quinn issued the order, and the deck tilted even more. Pencils and coffee cups rolled across the deck, and the monitors shook as the hull slammed through cold-water layers.

"150 meters," the pilot called.

"Ejection booster vessels are pressurizing to compensate for depth," Ripley called. "I'm reading a fault on Three-Four's primary booster vent. Pressure is increasing beyond containment parameters."

"Will it prevent the release?" Quinn asked.

"No. MRCS isn't acknowledging the fault. It'll release the bird," Ripley said. "Targeting transferred and pre-launch sequence complete. Inertials spinning up. Tube Three-Four is thirty seconds from release, Two-Three is sixty seconds."

Quinn leaned toward Bricker. "I don't know what else to do," he said. "We'll get below the launch floor for the second release, but I don't know how to stop the first."

Bricker started to reply, but then the Reactor Control Officer called out. "Number Two cooling pump failure! Cell Two is scramming. Control rod insertion fifty percent, powerplant generation dropping to eighty-five percent."

"Rig for minimum power," Quinn ordered. The main lights switched off, and battery-powered lights bathed the Control Room in an orange glow. He rechecked the launch screen: Tube Three-Four was twenty seconds from launch, and the boat was forty seconds from the missile launch floor.

"We won't make it," Bricker said. She swiveled the chair monitor toward her, tapped a long string of numbers into it, and then reached to touch a flashing red icon. Before she could press it, though, the hull shook and threw her to the deck.

"What was that?" Quinn grasped the chair's armrests and scanned the overhead status monitors. "Was that an early release?"

"No, the bird's still in the tube," Ripley said. "But I'm reading zero pressure on Three-Four's launch booster vessel. Maybe the primary vent blew. MRCS still isn't reporting faults."

"If the booster vessel's damaged, the missile pod won't launch," Bricker said as she climbed to her feet. She watched as Three-Four's countdown reached ten seconds, and then five. She was holding her breath when it reached zero.

The boat was silent. The Control Room crew looked at each other, and at the monitors, but nothing indicated that the missile had launched.

"Three-Four must be damaged," Ripley said. "The launch controller doesn't know what happened to it either. MRCS is trying to release it, but it's still in the tube."

"Midships keel passing through 250 meters," the pilot called.

Ripley swiveled around in her chair. "The Missile Release Control System has suspended four missile releases and advises that we rise above the launch floor."

Quinn let his breath out and sagged in the chair. "Pilot, all ahead half, twenty degree down bubble, make your depth 275 meters. Ballast, blow forward tanks, come to zero bubble at depth."

He unbuckled his seatbelt and stood, and then he leaned against the charting table and rubbed the kinks out of his neck. Bricker took the seat and turned the monitor toward her, and then he saw what was on it: a diagram of the *Henry* he'd never seen, one with blinking red dots throughout the Mushroom Farm. Below the diagram, flashing red letters said IMMEDIATE SELF DESTRUCT Y/N. "I didn't know you could…" he started.

"Some things even an XO doesn't know," she said as she blanked the screen. "And some things an XO should forget."

EXCEPT FOR LOSING A REACTOR CELL, the emergency dive only caused minor damage.

Quinn oversaw the shutdown of reactor Cell Two while Ripley and Chief Bailey ran a simulation of the explosion in Tube Three-Four. She'd built a computer model of the tube and the missile, and they were simulating the effects of abnormal air pressure inside the ejection booster vessel, which was designed to propel the missile pod to the surface with a concentrated jet of air. While the booster's steel walls could withstand extreme pressures, the primary vent's rubber seals were notoriously fragile. Ripley was modeling a vent seal failure.

She squinted at the numbers on her screen and then leaned back to watch the simulation on her upper monitor. The image showed the tube colored placid blue, and then a wave of red suddenly flashed out of the ejection booster and engulfed the missile pod.

"That was it," Ripley said. "That had to be what happened." She stood and read the numbers in the model. "With pressures this high acting on the pod's aft end, it would've been severely damaged."

"Why didn't it eject?" Quinn asked.

"The positioning arms are still engaged. The bird can't move until they retract just before the release," Bailey said.

"Which made the damage worse," Ripley said. "The port winglet got hit hard. Also maybe the tail. They're folded against the fuselage right here." She ran her finger along the model of the missile pod. "The airspeed and angle of attack pitot tubes in front of the left wing probably got sheared clean off too. They burn off at scramjet speeds, but the flight controller needs them on ascent so it knows when to light the engine."

"And that's not all," Bailey said. "I'll bet the air pressure blew out the sea diaphragm. I measured the tube shell temps, and Three-Four is thirty-seven degrees cooler than the rest. It's probably flooded."

"Even better," Ripley said. "The solid rocket booster propellant doesn't take well to seawater immersion. It's probably as combustible as jello now."

Bailey tapped the screen. "This bird can't fly. I'm sure of it."

Bricker looked at Ripley. "I agree," Ripley said. "I can think of a dozen reasons why this bird can't achieve or sustain flight."

"That's the first good news I've had today," Bricker said.

"It's just a hypothesis, though," Ripley said. "I wouldn't rely on it. We have to stay below 250 meters anyway to keep the other missiles in their tubes, but later on..."

"Later on, we'll have major headaches," Bricker said. "Right now, we need to focus on other priorities." She called Quinn to the Command podium, and then she sat in her chair and eyed the two officers, tapping her fingers against the armrest. "Tell me how we ended up with this fine FUBAR."

"It was my fault. I left Command," Quinn said. "I didn't hear the missile release order come in, and I didn't have the time to abort it."

"I was also at fault," Ripley said. "I left my station too, so I wasn't able to get back in time."

"You're the finest officers that ever served under me," Bricker said. "And officers with your level of discipline don't leave their duty stations without a reason. Explain."

"I was scanning the horizon and found a contact, a large vessel to the south-southeast," Quinn said. "Acoustics hadn't picked it up, and I was curious why not. I made an error by going to Acoustics and listening for myself, and that prevented me from hearing the call."

"That was an amateur mistake, Commander. I expect better from you," Bricker said. "But despite that, you were right to be curious about it. Play back what you saw."

He tapped on a monitor and called up the playback from the mast cameras. The fog bank materialized on the screen, showing the dark smudge of the ship inside it. He displayed the enhanced image next to it.

Bricker called Jackson over and pointed at the picture. "You didn't hear this? It has to be four thousand tons if it's an ounce."

Jackson shook his head. "After the Skipper gave me its bearing, I focused on it, but I didn't hear any hull, wake, or propulsion sounds. It might be a stealth hull."

"Interpolate this image, Ennis," she said.

Quinn worked on it, and a few seconds later, a clearer picture flickered onto the screen. Bricker stood and pointed to a spot on the vessel's flank. "This is an antisubmarine warfare ship. See these rings on the hull? These are torpedo launchers." She crossed her arms and frowned. "Eight on this side alone."

"It doesn't look like any Soviet Bloc vessel I know of," Quinn said.

"Right. This isn't a Red ship design," Ripley said. "The bow is too swept, and the Reds like every ship to double as an ice-breaker. This was built for speed."

"I agree." Bricker pointed to the hull. "It's also a catamaran hull, and the Reds don't use those because they foul in the ice. Have you looked for a match?"

"I didn't have time," Quinn said. "We received the release orders a few seconds later, and I was scrambling to prevent that."

"Do it now," Bricker said.

Quinn set the ship recognition program to find a match. The program found it after a few minutes, and he grunted like he'd been punched in the chest. He sent the image to the forward status monitor, and Bricker drew a sharp breath – printed beneath the fuzzy picture of a twin-hulled ship was USS ROCKEFELLER LCS-93.

"We *are* being hunted." Bricker turned to the Engineering station. "Systems, enable quieting measures." She tapped on Jackson's shoulder. "You, go find me the thermocline."

"Under quieting measures, I can't use active instrumentation, so I can't confirm –"

"I want a thermocline, sailor, not excuses."

"Aye aye." He scurried to the Acoustics room and slipped on his headgear.

She leaned over the charting table and called up the seafloor hologram, which showed that the Aleutian Ridge was less than a hundred miles away. "We can lose them in the Ridge if we get under the thermocline. The cold water should scatter their sonar rays."

"They didn't use active ranging to find us, so there's another technology in play," Quinn said. "Until we know what that is, we don't know how to evade them."

"Right. Come up with some ideas, Ennis."

Jackson leaned back in his chair. "I think I hear dead water just below, and that could be denser, colder water. I'd say the thermocline starts around 300 meters."

"Good. Pilot, make our depth 350 meters, down bubble ten."

"Once we're in the shadow zone, we should change course," Quinn said. "If they're tracking us, they know we're going to Attu."

"We'll let them continue on to Attu. While they're chasing a ghost, we'll loop under the thermocline and head south for an hour." She pointed to an undersea canyon in the side of the Aleutian Ridge. "Then we'll turn east and head for Coulee Canyon. It's a notorious sound trap, and it'll provide acoustic camouflage. After that, we'll sail around Kiska Island and head home."

"Yes, but what if they drop sonobuoys through the thermocline? That's what I'd do. In fact, when I was skipper of the *Astor*, it was one of the first measures I took. We went through dozens on an average float."

"I expect that," she said. "But the *Astor* didn't have the advantage of stealth, and the *Rockefeller* does. I'm betting they won't give up that advantage just to pop off sonobuoys. That'll give us time to get away."

"I hope you're right."

"Just hope and pray, Ennis. It might make a difference."

BACK AT THE BASE, Admiral Harris strode down the catwalk at the Explosives Handling Wharf and ducked beneath the gantry beams. The *Ethan Allen*, tied to the wharf below, was having a Joe Slick replaced. A Missile Service Unit hovered over one of its tubes.

He checked the conference room windows until he found where Captain Caldwell was meeting. A dozen men sat around a plastic conference table, and the base's Chief Missile Technician was pounding on it. "It's a design flaw! The Missile Service Units always shoulda had cameras at the bottom! It's impossible to lower a five-ton missile ten meters down – blind – and nail Betty in the boop!"

A gray-haired man in a perfectly tailored suit leaned across the table. "Nobody expects you to hit it on the nose. We designed the MSU with a thirty millimeter radial tolerance."

"And at forty millimeters, you have the primary vent for the ejection booster vessel. If you even tap that thing, you could distort the seals and it could explode!"

The suit snorted and sat back in his seat. "That's never happened. It's a pure hypothetical."

"Hypotheticals happen all the time in this man's Navy," Caldwell said. Harris cleared his throat, and he stood and put on his cap. "Excuse me for a moment. Keep in mind that assigning blame is way above our paygrade. We're only preparing a Design Modification Request, and we need a clear description of the problem and workable solutions. Discuss that while I'm gone."

He met Harris out on the catwalk. "Sometimes I think we need a war so everybody can take their aggression out on an enemy." He glanced at Harris' clenched jaw and flushed face. "But something tells me we have bigger problems."

Harris pressed his tablet into Caldwell's hands. "I just got this."

2317Z 2043-10-09; ORIGIN: V; ENCRYPT: NAVMIL9C

RCV: HARRIS, ADAM, COMSUBPAC
SND: BRICKER, JULIETTE, COMSSN807
SUB: WHISKEY TANGO FOXTROT?

HENRY RELEASED ONE JS AT 0206Z YESTERDAY PER RELEASE ORDER
ISSUED BY WHITE HOUSE OFFICE OF NAVAL OPERATIONS. THE
ORDER WAS SIGNED BY ADMIRAL CARDOZO. WE CRACKED A LAUNCH
CONTROLLER, AND IT SAYS THE TARGET WAS SACRAMENTO. I HOPE
TO GOD IT'S WRONG. DID WE HIT IT?

THE ROCKEFELLER WAS SHADOWING US. IT WAS THERE BEFORE THE
RELEASE AND PARALLELED OUR COURSE AFTER. I SUSPECT THEY'RE
THE HANGMAN IN THIS GAME. WHAT PILE OF SHIT DID WE STEP IN?
DOES THE NAVY THINK WE'VE GONE ROGUE? HAVE WE BEEN SET UP
TO TAKE THE DROP? ADVISE ON OUR STATUS ASAP.

WE'VE SHAKEN THE ROCKEFELLER. WILL RUN THROUGH ATTU
SHALLOWS AND THEN LAY DARK AND DEEP OFF KISKA FOR A DAY.
AFTER THAT, WE'RE COMING HOME. WILL SURFACE EVERY SIX
HOURS FOR CONTACT.

JULIE

PS: FRIDAY HARBOR. HAVE YOUR LAUNCH READY WHEN I DOCK.

Caldwell reread the message and handed the tablet back. "This is hard to believe. Are you sure this isn't Red disinformation?"

"It's authentic," Harris said. "Only Julie knows what that postscript means. She probably put it in to validate the message."

"All right." Caldwell leaned against the railing and crossed his arms. "What the hell's going on?"

"That's your job to figure out, Captain. Analyze this for me."

"Well, the good news is that our Slick didn't hit Sacramento because of a machine intelligence flaw. Although, when one starts calling something like that 'good news', one is utterly fucked." Caldwell puckered his lips and looked across the water. "Let's see. First, there was that college camera footage of the flash, then that fisherman's video of the Joe Slick, and now

Julie just confirmed what Warner wrote word for word. And all four of those accounts are independent of each other. Thus, the shit has officially hit the fan. The *Henry* really did reposition and attack Sacramento at the direction of the White House." He looked down through the metal grating of the deck and watched sailors work on the wharf below. "But what the message implies is even more disturbing."

"That's what has my guts in a knot, Zack. Stitch it together."

"In other words, you want me to jump to unsupportable conclusions based on unverified information so I can confirm what you already think."

"Precisely."

He pulled off his cap and played with the gold braid on the bill. "If the *Rockefeller* is shadowing our boat, it means somebody in command knew that the Sacramento strike would occur and deployed it to monitor – but not prevent – a strike on American soil. That means there's a conspiracy between the Pacific Fleet and the White House. This wasn't the act of a lone lunatic."

"That's what I figured two rums back," Harris said. "All right, I'm done playing games. I'm flying down to Pearl to find these SOB's, and then I'm dragging them –"

"Whoa, Adam! Do that and you'll just make yourself a target!"

"I *want* to be a target! I want to meet the scumbag behind this so I can reach down his throat and pull up his asshole!" He slapped a roof beam, glared at it, and then balled his fist to punch it.

"Adam, calm down. You'll accomplish nothing by going down to Hawaii hot. Besides, you're making too many assumptions. This still could be a massive FUBAR."

"What are the chances of that? Really, Zack, can't you read the writing on the wall?"

"There's *no* writing on the wall. We know nothing, and we're guessing at everything. And maybe it was just an accident after all, and we're jumping to conclusions about a conspiracy. We don't have any hard evidence either way."

"Right," Harris said. "You're right. We need to know more before we start bending nooses. I'll make some discreet calls to Pearl and see if I can sniff something out. Wrap this meeting up and come to my office as soon as you can. We need to woodshed this problem fast, Zack. We're too damned far out of the loop already."

THE *PATRICK HENRY* HAD BEEN SAILING EAST under the thermocline for five hours with no sign of pursuit. Their speed was limited to twenty-one knots with only two cells of the reactor producing power, but they'd be enveloped in the acoustic camouflage of Coulee Canyon within a half hour and speed wouldn't matter then.

Bricker leaned back in her chair and studied the map on the conference room bulkhead – four red lines curved from the *Henry's* position to the west coast of the United States. "Two days ago, I would've thought something like this was only a Hollywood fantasy," she said. "Portland, Salem, Olympia, and Seattle. That's even too absurd for *Mushrooms over Moscow.*"

"This is really happening, Julie," Quinn said. Ripley and her two chiefs sat quietly and tried not to be noticed.

She swiveled to face the conference table. "All right, Mister Ripley, now that you've given me the bad news, hand me the good. Tell me you've discovered how to disable this accursed Missile Release Control System."

Ripley looked down at the table. "It's not possible, Captain."

Bailey spoke up before Bricker could reply. "We can't find a way to access the fifth launch controller. That's the key to disabling the launch system."

"If the fifth controller remains online, it'll release the remaining birds once we rise above the maximum launch depth," Ripley said. "But we've come up with an alternative that effectively neutralizes the launch controllers. We propose to keep the MRCS online and false its inputs so it believes we're at 300 meters no matter what our depth. That should keep the launches suspended."

"Every depth sensor on the boat needs to be rigged to false its depth reading," Bailey said.

"Why can't we just find the sensor it's using and rig that one?" Bricker asked.

"The MRCS uses quintuple redundancy," said Goldblum. "It draws its positioning information from five randomly-chosen sensors. If we just rig one sensor to show 300 meters, the MRCS will ignore it as being wrong. We need to rig all fourteen of them."

"We'd be without any depth sensors at all," Quinn said. "On the other hand, we have the pressure sensors, and we can pull gravimetry from the inertial navigators. Those can approximate our depth. We wouldn't be totally blind."

"Do it. We can't stay down here forever. If that's our only choice, we'll work with it." Bricker leaned back and clasped her hands behind her head. "Ennis, Tala – you need to break the Sacramento news to everyone in the Control Room and the Executive Department. Take Chief Izu with you and talk to them one at a time. If anybody makes trouble, confine them to quarters. All right, people, go get this done."

Bailey and Goldblum stood to leave, but then a soft, watery ping rang through the hull. Everyone in the room looked up.

"I'd bet that's the *Rockefeller*," Quinn said. "And she sounds close."

Bricker swore and stood. "How'd she find us again? All right, everyone back to your stations. We have work to do." She hustled them out of the room, and then she ran down the short passageway to Control and called Jackson. "Where are they?"

"10,400 meters, bearing 282, 24 knots."

"It's the *Rockefeller*?"

"Aye. I have screw sounds now. They've abandoned stealth."

"Comm, flash battle stations," Bricker said. "Sonar, was that ping enough to locate us?"

"No." Another ping resounded through the ship. "They know about where we are, though. They're coming our way."

"All right. Tactical, load a Mini-Me into Starboard Tube One and a Squid into Tube Two. Set them for heading 090, half thrust, 100-meter depth, rig for countermeasures at three thousand meters. Make ready to shoot on my order." She studied the hologram of the seafloor: Coulee Canyon wasn't far, but the bottom was still two thousand meters below. She spotted the Van Der Houck Rocks, a spur in the canyon's ridge that would cast a strong acoustic shadow they could hide in. It was still five thousand meters away, though. "Pilot, come to heading 020, all ahead full," Bricker said.

Jackson leaned out of Acoustics. "Sonobuoy in the water, bearing 280!"

"It'll ping below the thermocline, Captain," Quinn said.

"I know. Pilot, make your depth 290 meters, twenty degree up bubble." The deck tilted, and she watched the sea temperature rise as they climbed above the thermocline. As they leveled out, the sonobuoy pinged.

"It's gone active, and I think I hear remote listening vehicles out there too, bearing 210 and 140," the sonar operator called. "I think that's how they're tracking us. Those drones are listening to our hull scatter, but the thermocline is deflecting the sonar rays. They're not getting any joy. I doubt they can see us up here."

"What's the ping life on these sonobuoys?" Bricker asked.

"130 seconds," the sonar operator said. "They have 102 seconds left."

"Understood. Pilot, in 103 seconds we're diving below the thermocline again. Once the sonobuoy stops pinging, that ship will go back to active sonar, and I want to be invisible." Bricker checked the seafloor hologram again. "I hope this chart is accurate. We'll have to snuggle up to this spur."

"We'll rely on Jackson for the fine details. He can hear anything," Quinn said. "I'll assist him when the time comes."

"*If* the time comes," Bricker said. The sonobuoy stopped pinging, and she looked at the clock. "Pilot, thirty degree down bubble, make your depth 650 meters. Rig for angles and dangles."

The deck slanted down and Quinn gripped the charting table. "I don't have to tell you that's close to our crush depth."

"You don't," Bricker said. "But I know my boat, and I need to get behind this spur before they –"

A loud ping rang through the Control Room.

"Before they paint us good and square like that?" Quinn said.

She leaned into the Sonar Room. "That sounded like a solid hit."

The sonar operator nodded. "The sonobuoy was eighty meters to starboard. They could read the numbers on our sail with a ping that close, stealth hull or no. Now they're changing course directly toward us. Range 8,200 meters, bearing 272, speed 24 knots."

"Tactical, shoot the Mini-Me. Pilot, hard starboard, heading 092," Bricker said. The floor shook as the decoy torpedo jetted from its tube. Once it traveled three thousand meters, it would broadcast the sound profile of the *Henry* at flank speed and leave the same heat and chemical disturbances in its wake. "Tactical, shoot the Squid." The deck quivered again and the chaff torpedo followed the decoy, releasing sheets of sonar-absorptive nylon that mimicked the *Henry's* hull absorption.

The Control Room shook as the boat plunged through the cold-water layer. Shortly after, the *Rockefeller* dropped another sonobuoy behind them, which began pinging below the thermocline. "It might not pick us up," Bricker said to Quinn. "It's pinging off our stern, which doesn't present much cross-section to get a bounce off. Let hope this works." The sonobuoy kept pinging for a minute and then went silent.

Another sonobuoy started pinging, but the sound was weak and distorted. "Good, they're above the thermocline. Pilot, come to heading 350." She rechecked the hologram: The spur was only two thousand meters away, and they were paralleling it. In two minutes, she'd pull hard to port and slide behind the rocky outcropping.

The ship pinged again. It dropped a sonobuoy, but it was even further away.

"They've lost us. Pilot, hard port, heading 210," Bricker said.

Two minutes later, they passed behind the spur. She slowed the boat to a crawl and walked to the charting table, where Quinn was hunched over a hologram with headphones pressed to his ears. She tapped on his shoulder. "We're here. Is this chart accurate?"

"Mostly," he said. "The main wall seems to be where the chart says, about forty meters south and rising forty meters above our sail. Of course, you can't hear details, but the gravimetry matches what we're...wait, I hear something."

"Fish in the water!" Jackson called out. "Three torpedoes, Mark 54's!" A faint ping rang through the hull. "One's active sonar. I don't know what the other two are. They might have passive seeker heads."

"Pilot, all stop. Tactical, enable anti-torpedo batteries," Bricker said. "What's their bearing?"

Jackson closed his eyes and listened. "They're not coming at us. It sounds like they're searching for a contact. I don't think they're picking us up."

The pilot asked, "Captain? Why's our own ship shooting at us?"

Bricker leaned against the charting table and drew a long breath. "Back at Attu, I defied an order to attack four American cities. Instead of court-martialing me, the Fleet has apparently decided to sink this boat. Don't ask me why. I don't know."

Everybody in the Control Room turned in their seats, and Jackson leaned out of Acoustics. "Where did our Vilyuchinsk bird hit?" he asked.

Bricker pursed her lips for a moment, and then she said, "We can't confirm its target."

Around the room, sailors raised their eyebrows. Durgan mouthed a silent curse, and Jackson punched the rubber-coated bulkhead.

"But what I can confirm is that the *Rockefeller* has initiated hostilities against this boat. Now I need you to perform your duties better than ever. The enemy may fly an American flag, but it's still the enemy. Eyes front, sailors." She turned to the young woman at the Tactical Warfare console. "Prepare a Mark 58 for Starboard Tube One. Three kilotons, self-arming."

She nodded and tapped on her screen. "Aye, Captain. I need three Command authorizations to enable self-arming of a nuclear munition."

Bricker punched her authorization into her monitor and waited for Quinn and Ripley. "We'll only get one shot at this target. If we have to take it, it better count. I promise I won't shoot this fish if I don't have to."

Quinn and Ripley nodded and tapped codes into their monitors. "I hope it doesn't come to that," Quinn said.

"Nor do I," Bricker said. "If they withdraw after their fish are expended, we might get off easy. We'll know in a minute."

"The passive seekers turned east. I think they're tracking the Mini-Me," Jackson said. "No, they're circling around to us...no, the active one peeled off to the south, and the other ones...I can't tell what's going on. They're all in the same area, and it sounds like they're just circling. The active seeker is diving deep now, straight down –" A distant explosion rattled the Control Room monitors. "Yep, it was self-destructing. Another one is diving, and now the third one." Two more explosions rattled the hull. "Three up, three down. Captain, all three were armed with conventional warheads."

"They intended to destroy us," Bricker said. "That confirms the rules of this engagement. Where's the *Rockefeller* now?"

"7,100 meters, bearing 165, speed 24 knots," Jackson said. "It sounds like they're moving away."

Bricker smiled for the first time in hours. "Maybe those fish were their last crack at us."

Overpressure

"This feels wrong," Quinn said. "Why hunt us and then back off? Were they ordered to withdraw?"

"We'll know more soon," Bricker said. "We'll hold this position and listen for threats. I don't see any reason to move."

"*Rockefeller* is 8,100 meters at bearing 165, speed 24 knots," Jackson said. "I hear a splash…big-ass bubbly thing, sounds like a garbage can, and it's dropping through a hundred meters…bearing 170, range 3,200 meters. I've never heard anything like this. Skipper, can you figure this out?"

Quinn picked up his headphones. As he put them on, a thundering boom shook the hull and the boat rolled until the deck was nearly vertical. Officers who hadn't been strapped into their seats were flung across the room into the Engineering control stations. The boat rolled back, and Quinn, who had landed atop the Reactor Control console, slid off and fell to the deck. The orange emergency lights flickered on, and then a monitor from an overhead rack crashed next to him, peppering him with shards of sharp plastic.

After a minute, the rocking slowed and he tried to stand, but a bolt of pain shot up his leg when he put weight on his foot. As he rubbed the sore ankle, he looked around the Control Room – only the pilot and the Ballast Control officer were still strapped into their seats, but the ballast officer's head lolled at an unnatural angle.

A pile of sailors was jammed into corners behind Quinn. He hobbled over and helped the uninjured ones to their feet. Two officers lay under the reactor console, unconscious and bleeding, and he pulled them out onto the deck and checked their vital signs. He found the intercom switch on the reactor console and toggled it. "Corpsman to Control, medical emergency!"

Ripley was wedged between the seat and console of the Strategic station with her leg stuck in the arm of the chair, and he pulled her out and helped her into a seat. He spotted Bricker crumpled next to the charting table, her jumpsuit bloody around the neck and chest, and he ran to her side. As he was reaching to roll her on her back, a corpsman knelt beside him. "I got this, Skipper. You got other things to do right now."

"Okay, doc. Take good care of her." He rose to his feet shakily, leaned against the charting table, and looked over at Ripley. "You okay?"

"Think so." She blinked her eyes a few times. "Vision's a little blurry."

"What the hell happened?" he asked.

Ripley rubbed her head. "It felt like we got hit by an overpressure wave. I think it was a depth bomb, a B87 or a B91. Those are twelve kiloton nukes, but they haven't been deployed for –"

"They dumped a nuke on us?" Quinn asked.

Ripley nodded. "Think so. I'm a little pixelated right now. Don't rely on my judgment."

"Okay, sit there and take it easy." He stumbled to the Acoustics Room and found Jackson rubbing his neck and shoulder. "How are you doing?"

"Shook up a little."

"Get unshook fast. I need to know where the *Rockefeller* is."

"Yeah, soon as all these tweety birds flying around my head go away, I'll get right on it."

Quinn checked the Sonar Room, where the operator was leaning against the rubber-lined bulkhead, flexing his arm. "The hell was that, Skipper?"

"Ripley thinks it was a depth bomb. Listen, I need you to receive the damage control reports. I want a summary in two minutes."

He returned to the Control Room and counted heads, and the Reactor Control and Tactical Warfare officers were missing from their stations. "Mister Ripley, take Tactical," he said. "And get Corbin up here to take over the reactor. Pilot, can we maneuver?"

"We have planes and rudder, Skipper. What we don't have is propulsion power."

Quinn checked the reactor status monitor: The reactor control computer had automatically safed the nuclear pile, and power generation had dropped to three percent. The reserve power situation was even worse – only two of the ten battery banks were delivering power, and both were discharging fast. He tapped out a message to the battery room and then swiveled his chair to the helm. "We won't have propulsion for ten or fifteen minutes at least. Jackson, any idea on the whereabouts of the *Rockefeller?*"

"It's still out there, but it's hard to hear anything with all the echoes and the turbulence. Whatever exploded stirred up a lot of seafloor gunk. My best guess is that it's about where it was. I can't tell if it's moving." A soft ping rang through the Control Room. "Okay, they've gone active again. 9,800 meters at bearing 170. I hear screws now. It's moving."

"Toward us or away from us?"

"Toward us. If they ping again, I'll range it."

"So they're not giving up. They'll keep after us till we're sunk." Quinn hunched over the holographic chart and watched the dot representing the *Rockefeller* approach their hiding place; trying to evade a hunter this good would be futile, and he wouldn't risk the lives of his eighty-seven crewmembers on the slim chance they could slip away.

But while the *Henry* couldn't rely on stealthy evasion anymore, the *Rockefeller's* attack had given Quinn a critical tactical advantage. Their commander hadn't known his prey's location and figured blowing holes in the sea would compensate for the lack of intelligence. That tactic had failed, but it had succeeded in scrambling the undersea acoustics, giving its prey cover for a counterstrike – and that prey carried six nuclear-armed torpedoes.

However, he could only shoot one of them. Since it was his only shot, he needed to get that torpedo within range of the *Rockefeller* before being detected and swarmed with countermeasures. To pull that off, he needed to create a diversion.

He tapped his fingers against his lips, trying to think like the *Rockefeller's* commander: He'd dumped a nuke on them to either crush the *Henry* or force it to flee. If the *Rockefeller's* commander expected to catch the *Henry* on the run, the best diversion was to let him think that was happening. "Tactical, load a Mini-Me into Starboard Tube Two. Set it to heading 270, ascend to one hundred meters on one-quarter thrust. Run it quiet. At three thousand meters, start broadcasting our sound profile and increase to maximum thrust. I want it ready to shoot in two minutes. Jackson, what's our sound environment out there?"

"High and scattered, echoes everywhere. They musta heard that boom at McMurdo."

"Could you hear torpedo motors with all that noise?"

"Only if they were screaming at their max."

"Good. If you can't hear them, your counterpart on the *Rockefeller* won't either," Quinn said. "But spool out the sonodrone and try to get a better read on the environment. Maybe we'll get a better picture if we get it above these rocks." Jackson pressed an icon on his screen, and a small door opened on the sail. The tiny sonodrone whirred out and began rising above the boat, trailing a cable behind it and listening to the sea's sounds with its omnidirectional receivers.

Another ping sounded and Jackson called out, "Skipper, the *Rockefeller* is coming toward us at 16 knots. Range 8,800 meters."

"Acknowledged." Quinn turned to Ripley at the Tactical Warfare station. "Tactical, report the status of Fish One."

"Fish is sitting dry and awaiting targeting parameters," Ripley said.

"On my order, send it at one-quarter thrust, inertial guidance, at heading 090 for a thousand meters. Then turn to the *Rockefeller's* last confirmed position, maintaining inertial guidance. At five hundred meters from the target, engage active sonar ranging and go to maximum thrust. What's the yield on that warhead?"

"It's set for three kilotons."

He rubbed a sore spot on his shoulder and read the incoming damage reports – four sailors were dead and hundreds of small leaks had sprouted throughout the boat, but all essential systems were still functioning. Nevertheless, the hull couldn't take any more overpressure waves, not when they were so close to their crush depth. "Select a detonation depth of one hundred meters beneath the midships keel. Set the yield for ten kilotons."

A sailor ran in and sat at the reactor control station. After scanning the monitors for a few seconds, he tapped on his console. "Skipper, I can have half power in ten minutes."

"Understood. Make it faster if you can."

Ripley looked at her monitor. "Skipper, targeting complete on both Fish One and Fish Two."

"Acknowledged. Flood both tubes. I want a silent shoot."

After a minute, Ripley called out, "Skipper, both starboard tubes flooded and ready to shoot."

"Good. Tactical, shoot Fish Two."

Ripley double-tapped a small icon on her screen, and the Mini-Me motored quietly from the tube and turned west. "Fish Two away."

On the map over the Tactical console, he watched the blue dot of the decoy move slowly west. When it had traveled about a thousand meters, he sat and reviewed the status monitors a final time, tapping his fingers to his lips again. He drew a deep breath and let it out slowly. "Tactical, shoot Fish One."

She double-tapped again, and the nuclear-armed torpedo whirred from its tube and turned east. "Fish One away," she called, tightening her seatbelt. "Detonation in about four minutes."

Quinn buckled his seatbelt. "Pilot, extend the roll stabilizers. Acoustics, retract the sonodrone. Rig for angles and dangles. Comm, flash the collision alarm." Alarm lights blinked and seatbelts clicked throughout the Control Room.

"Three minutes to detonation," Ripley said.

Quinn leaned over to the Acoustics Room. "Jackson, any reaction from the *Rockefeller?*"

"None I can hear, Skipper. I can't hear our fish myself, and neither did the sonodrone. The water turbidity is obscuring it, I think."

"Pilot, prime the propulsors," Quinn said. "I want to move as soon as we have power." He rechecked the Tactical monitor: The Mini-Me would go live soon, and the Mark 58 had turned toward the estimated location of the *Rockefeller*.

"One minute," Ripley called.

"Fish in the water!" Jackson called. "A spread of six, no, eight, all active, heading 170. They heard the Mini-Me!"

"Acknowledged."

The pinging of the torpedoes echoed through the hull, and Quinn bit down on his knuckle, resisting the temptation to jam his fingers into his ears. "Ripley, did our fish get lost?"

"No –"

"Trash can!" Jackson called. "Bearing 170, range 3,000 meters! I think they popped another depth bomb on us! Shit, I hear another one! There's two!"

"Everybody hold on!" Quinn yelled. An overpressure wave slammed the hull and the deck tilted. It was leveling out when two more overpressure waves hit and turned the boat upside down – and then the spur they were hiding behind crumbled, and tons of rock fell toward them.

QUINN FELT LIKE HE WAS SLIDING SIDEWAYS while upside down and rolling at the same time. Before he could order the pilot to right the boat, though, it returned to level and trash fell back to the deck.

He unbuckled his belt and ran to Sonar. "I want a damage report..." he began, and then something thudded against the outer hull. The boat lurched sideways, and he bounced off the bulkhead and fell to the deck. "The hell was that?" he asked, rubbing his shoulder.

"Maybe they're throwing their damn trash at us too," the sonar man muttered. "Did we actually roll over?"

"Think so." Quinn stood slowly and looked around the room: Everybody seemed unharmed except for the Reactor Control Officer, who was lying back in his seat with his arms dangling. He ran over and felt for his pulse; the man was alive but unconscious, with a bloody gash on his temple. Above the station, the status monitor swung from side to side, tethered only by its wires. He jammed it back into its mount and flicked the intercom switch. "Corpsman to Control! Powerplant, get Donley up here to run this reactor! Sonar, damage report!"

"No fatalities, multiple injuries," Sonar said. "Hundreds of leaks, and we have a small pressure hull breach in the port torpedo room. The pumps are handling it, but the engineers say they'll burn out in maybe an hour at this depth. Power is out to both galleys."

Quinn glanced at the reactor control panel; the reactor had safed again, and the powerplant was generating at three percent of its capacity. "Nobody's getting any juice if Donley doesn't get up here and unsafe –"

"Right here, Skip," Donley said. He bent over the panel and tapped the monitor. "I got this."

"All right. Jackson, any sounds from the *Rockefeller*?"

"Nothing, but I don't trust the sound environment. I hear undersea landslides rumbling all along the Aleutian Ridge, and I'm having trouble discriminating with all the noise. Gimme a few minutes, okay?"

"Sure, sure." Quinn rubbed his sore shoulder and turned to the helm, where the status monitors blinked on and off. While they were on, though, the icons for Propulsors One and Two showed red. Two electronics mates ran into the room, cracked open the propulsion control panel, and began pulling on wires, muttering about rebooting the propulsion computer and switching out circuit boards.

He scanned the room, and everything that should be done was being done. The *Henry* was a tough boat, far tougher than he'd imagined; she'd taken the brunt of four shockwaves and survived despite being near their crush depth. Still, he didn't want to test her endurance any further.

"Skip," Jackson called. "I'm getting no machinery sounds from the *Rockefeller*, but I hear cavitation noise and debris hitting the bottom. I think we got it."

The boat suddenly jolted sideways. Quinn checked the status monitors for the cause, but the boat's condition hadn't changed. "What was that?"

"Displacement wave," Jackson said. "It's from the landslides. More coming. Somebody's gonna get a wicked tsunami."

Quinn nodded again and turned on the charting table as the boat rocked again, gentler this time. The seafloor hologram blinked into being above the table, and then a thin stream of hydraulic fluid trickled from an overhead pipe and the image disappeared. He dried the projector plate and turned it back on, and just as he was calculating the distance to Eareckson Naval Air Station on Shemya Island, the pipe wet the table again.

He opened a chart cabinet stuffed into a nook behind the helm and pulled out plasticized charts of the Northern Pacific. After finding one for the Western Aleutians, he returned to the charting table. He opened a seldom-used door in the side of the table that held plotting tools, and he began measuring the distance to Eareckson.

Shemya Island was only two hundred kilometers to the west-northwest, a distance an anti-submarine aircraft could cover in thirty minutes. He had to assume that Eareckson would hunt them like the *Rockefeller* and that they'd scrambled their planes after the first detonation fourteen minutes before.

The electronics mates cheered, and he looked up at the propulsion status monitor – all indicators showed green on both propulsors, but then the screen flickered and Propulsor Two's indicators turned red. "What's happening with Two?" he asked.

"We rebooted it, but we can't get any flow through it," the pilot said.

"I think I know what happened," Jackson called. "The acoustics outside are different now. I'm not picking up ambient reflection from the Van Der Houck Rocks anymore. I think the shockwaves turned them into the Van Der Houck Gravel. That's the thump we heard."

"That could be it," the pilot said. "Propulsor Two's intakes are on the port side, and that's where the thump came from. Two's intakes could be clogged with mud and gravel. The roll stabilizer was extended, and that coulda funneled it into the ports."

"Retract the stabilizers and see if that frees up the intakes."

The pilot pressed a button on his console, but then a red icon flashed. "Starboard stabilizer retracted, but we're getting a fault on the port stabilizer."

"All right, reverse thrust and try blowing the blockage out."

"We tried that, but there's no water flow in any direction. Both ports must be clogged, Skipper."

"Understood." He studied the numbers on the propulsion monitor and then checked his chair monitor; the battery room said they would need an hour or more to bring all the battery banks back online. The two functioning banks were down to fifteen percent, which could only power the propulsors for a few minutes.

The *Henry* needed to vanish before the anti-sub aircraft began searching the area. He guessed that they could move a few thousand meters on batteries before the powerplant began generating again. "Pilot, ahead flank on Propulsor One, come to heading 010, ten degree up bubble, make your depth three hundred meters. Donley, give me juice *now*. We have hostiles on the way."

"Skip, you don't wanna rush nuclear fission. Procedures are clear on rod withdrawal timing –"

"I hear a ping!" Jackson called. "Active ranging, bearing 310-ish, range over twenty thousand meters. Multiple sources. Sounds like sonobuoys."

"Company's coming, Donley, and we're the main course…"

"The pile startup procedures call for an eleven-minute rod withdrawal."

Quinn checked the battery levels and saw that they'd dropped to thirteen percent already. He guessed that they'd last another five minutes at the most. "I've done it in four minutes without affecting pile criticality. I don't care about the nucleation noise and turbine pressures. We'll be an oil slick on the waves if we don't have propulsion soon."

"I know you wanna get going, Skip, but I've got to follow –"

Quinn thumped his fist on the charting table. "Enough, Mister Donley! Make it happen or you'll be Fish Two!"

The crosstalk in the room stopped, and the Control Room crew pretended not to listen for the retort that would make Donley the world's first human torpedo. He just turned back to his monitor and tapped the screen, though. "Aye aye, Captain," he muttered.

Quinn looked at the monitor over the Tactical station and checked the boat's armaments inventory. "Tactical, load a Mini-Me and a Squid into Starboard Tubes One and Two, and a SLAM into Port Tubes One and Two. Set the SLAM's to engage any aircraft below 20,000 feet. Make ready to shoot on my order. I'm going hot before Eareckson does."

"Aye aye, Captain," Ripley said, and she turned back to her station wearing a half-smile.

He laid the chart on the table, picked up his grease pencil and divider, and started plotting their next course. After that, he watched the red bars on the battery monitor – they'd dropped to nine percent power and were discharging faster than he'd estimated. His eyes flicked between the battery monitor and Donley, who was working the control panel, and his gut tightened more with every point the battery percentages dropped.

When they reached five percent and began blinking, he decided to take over the reactor and withdraw the control rods himself, but then the battery charges began rising. "Skip, the powerplant is generating," he said. "At ten percent and climbing. We can reach maybe fifty percent in thirty minutes, eighty percent in another hour."

"Good. That's enough for one propulsor." He looked at the lines on the chart and nodded. "Pilot, come to heading 050. We'll go around Kiska Island to the north. If we're lucky, Eareckson won't look for us there."

GAMES OF CHANCE

Krista opened the door to the guest bedroom and found Ada sleeping so soundly that her pillow was soaked with saliva. She pulled the blanket over her shoulders, taking care not to wake her.

She tiptoed into the bright kitchen, followed her nose to the coffeemaker, and poured a mug. Sipping the drink, she looked through the windows and saw Marissa standing on the balcony. She topped off her cup and walked out to join her.

"Well, you're finally up," Marissa said. "I'm surprised you didn't sleep all day."

"Mark and Ada are still completely out," Krista said.

"Markie's a champion sleeper. He can sleep for twelve hours straight sometimes. As for me, I feel dopey if I have more than five hours sleep a night." Marissa smiled at her. "The sex probably wore him out."

Krista blushed and looked away. "Jaysus, just come out with it, wouldja?"

Marissa slurped her coffee. "It's nice having you here. You really liven things up. Last night was exciting, all of you stumbling in here after midnight, checking to see if the National Guard was chasing you."

"I'm surprised we got away with it. I don't even want to think of how many laws we broke at the hospital."

"But you have friends in high places," Marissa said. "Mark thinks the governor will clean things up in exchange for the vaccine."

"Or he'll take me into protective custody," Krista said. "That's almost like being in jail. I don't consider him much of a friend."

"So don't get caught, and everything will be peachy."

Krista watched the top of the Golden Gate Bridge float on a dense cloud of fog. The sight mesmerized her, and she had to pull her gaze away from it. "Right. So I thought the state government was wiped out."

Marissa shook her head. "The rumors on the SatNet are that DaCosta went to a National Guard base in Fresno with an auxiliary government the day before the Sacramento thing, and they're operating down there now. I hope Cheyn doesn't hear that. He might nuke it." She took a sip of her coffee and sighed. "Not that anyone would miss Fresno, but I'd like to have somebody running this place."

"Especially at a time like this."

"It's terrible," Marissa said. "I wonder how it'll all end. Did you know that even Washington and Oregon are talking about seceding now?"

"Are you kidding? I've got to read the news."

Marissa emptied her cup. "Why don't you make yourself comfortable and catch up? I have to get breakfast started. Those boys eat like spring bears when they wake up."

"The virus is right outside the border?" Marissa asked as she threw more bacon into a pan.

"That's what I read," Krista said. "It wasn't far behind us when we were out there."

"I had a BASE jump scheduled for New Year's Day at Royal Gorge," Marissa said. "I guess I can forget about that, what with Sacramento and that virus in the way."

Krista filled her mug again and sat at the island. "A BASE jump. You must love extreme sports."

"Oh, I do. It's like…well, I don't have to describe the incredible high I get from it. I'm sure you know."

"Actually, I don't."

"Really? You didn't get a tingle all those times you nearly died?"

"Not a single one," Krista said.

"Then why'd you do it?"

"Because I had to. And while it was happening, I kept wishing it was over. And once it was over, I wished it would never happen again."

"What a shame," Marissa said. "So many exciting opportunities wasted. Well, that's life – the people who want it don't get it, and the people who get it don't want it."

"I'm sorry to disappoint you."

"Not disappointed, just envious," Marissa said. She leaned over the island with her eyes glinting. "I'm bored. How about you and me take a ride and see if we can find some trouble?"

Krista snorted. "No need to waste gas. Trouble comes to me."

"Fantastic!" She cracked a dozen eggs and whisked them. "You're a danger magnet. If I'm lucky, you'll bring some here."

"Marissa, trust me, you'd hate the trouble I bring. It's no fun at all."

She smiled and reached into the refrigerator. "Orange juice?"

"Sure." Marissa poured her a tall glass, and Krista took a sip. "This is wonderful! Is there something special about it?"

"No, it came out of a carton, but it's fresh. I bought it yesterday."

Krista emptied her glass and set it on the counter. "It was divine. Maybe it's those California oranges."

Marissa refilled her glass. "Maybe that's it."

The bedroom door opened and Ada stumbled out. She staggered to the bathroom with her eyes closed, dragging one hand along the wall and scratching her right leg. A few minutes later, she shuffled into the kitchen, plopped on a stool next to the window, and sagged against Krista's shoulder.

"How are you feeling this morning?" Marissa asked.

"Bluh," Ada said. "Better than yesterday. I'll let you know when I wake up."

"You need coffee, sweetie." Marissa set a cup in front of her and reached for the carafe.

"I'd rather drink paint."

"What color, dear? We have red and yellow," Marissa said. "I think the red tastes yummy. Want some?"

"Hmm. Oil or latex?"

Krista noticed that they were dare-staring each other. "Try some juice," she said quickly before Marissa started filling cups with enamel. "It's made from California oranges!"

Ada nodded, and Marissa set a glass in front of her. She took a small sip and said, "What's the big deal? It just tastes like normal juice."

Krista held out her glass for more. "Well, *I* can't get enough."

Marissa turned on the stove and started whipping a bowl of pancake batter, and Ada leaned toward Krista. "I like her. She dishes it right back."

"I see how this'll go. You'll bond with her just like you bonded with Mark."

"Shut it!" Ada hissed. "I am *not* bonding with Skid. No way!" She scratched her right thigh again, this time digging her nails into the flesh. "This is driving me nuts. Ever get that feeling like you need to scratch your bones?"

"Never. Maybe it's a weird side effect of radiation exposure or the transfusion."

"I don't think so. It just started a few minutes ago, like somebody flipped the itch switch."

"I wouldn't be worrying about it. It'll go away on its own."

"Mmm. Hope so."

Footsteps thundered on the foyer steps, and then Micah bounded into the room. "Morning!" he called as he crossed to the kitchen, his eyes locked on the breakfast skillet. "I'm starving!" He reached into a cabinet and set a plate next to the stove, and Marissa hugged him.

"You're such a good boy," she said. "You saved Ada's life! You should be so proud of yourself! It must have been terrible being hooked up to a machine all night."

"Oh, no, I had a fantastic time, and I was real sorry when it was over. Ada's a lot of fun to hang with. She's totally different from any girl I've ever met and she's..." He lifted the lid from the frying pan, breathed the steam, and sighed. "She's got this huge-big ego, so don't tell her I said this, but I can't stop thinking about her."

"Sounds like you're getting a thing for her," Krista said, feeling the heat from Ada's blushing face.

"Hell, yeah. She's *the* ultimate scorching-hot NILF." He reached into a pan to scoop out some eggs and then froze when he saw Ada sitting beside Krista.

"Hey," she said in a tiny voice.

"Oh, hey," he croaked. He forced a shaky smile to his lips, and she smiled back and looked down at the countertop. "You guys are mean, setting me up like that," he said to the egg pan.

Marissa waved a hand in the air and coughed. "Wow, I can hardly breathe for all the hormones you two are pumping out. I bet I'll have to wash the windows now!"

"Ma…" Micah warned.

Marissa smiled and flipped a pancake. *"Hello, young lovers, wherever you are…"*

"Ma!"

"I just like that song, sweetie," Marissa said. "Now why don't you fill your plate before Markie gets up and eats all the food?"

MICAH WALKED ONTO THE BALCONY and handed a glass of juice to Ada.

"Thanks." She flashed him an extra-bright smile and turned back to Krista and Mark. "I was right. My mom tested Recombin on John Durant's blood, and the particle count exploded once it started feeding on Neovirus." Ada closed the packet. "If I had a bioreactor and some Neovirus, I could make the virophage at fourteen times the rate that Chalys was."

"Are bioreactors hard to find?" Krista asked.

"I know where we can find one, at least," she said. "When we crossed the border, they said we had to report to a lab in Davis, right?"

"Tanager Labs," Mark said. "We were supposed to be there yesterday."

"And why were we supposed to go there?" Ada asked. "Cuz they have bioreactors, natch. If I can find them and get a good supply of Neovirus to use for snacks, I could make lotsa this stuff."

"Davis looks like it's near the No-Go Zone, though," Micah said as he checked a map on his tablet. "The labs might not even be there anymore, or they might be damaged or radioactive."

"It's too dangerous to go back there anyway," Mark said.

"I don't want to go back," Krista said with a shudder. "I never want to see it again."

"I don't either. We oughta just get the vaccine into the governor's hands before he finds us and 'keeps us safe,'" Mark said, hooking quotation marks in the air. "That's the best way to go."

"It makes no sense to just hand the Recombin feedstock to him and hope they can make it. The place is a wreck right now," Ada said. "I can do it, and I can do it now."

"No," Mark said. "You're outvoted, Twink. Tomorrow, we'll contact DaCosta and set up a neutral place to hand over the vaccine. That's the only thing we can do. We gotta get rid of this stuff and lay low. Krista can put the plans for that bioreactor on *Midnight Sun,* and some other brainiac can figure it out. We've been rode a little too hard to go on another adventure."

"And I like the peace and quiet here," Krista said. "I agree with Mark. Our war is over, and we need to let this go."

"And you've got to take it easy for a while," Micah said. "After a nuclear bombing and a transfusion –"

She stood and threw the packet on the chair. "I feel fine. You guys are real weenies, you know that?" She stalked off the balcony and slammed the door behind her.

KRISTA SAT ALONE ON THE BALCONY and checked the news. After a few minutes of surfing, she decided that she didn't want to know what was happening. The stories from Sacramento brought back nightmarish memories in vivid detail, and the relentless spread of the virus was depressing.

Desperate for something different, she clicked on a video that a Russian fisherman had made of a sea fart. Instead of a diversion, she saw a Lancet missile erupt from the ocean and rocket toward Sacramento – and her – carrying its payload of death and destruction. It was a frightening apparition, with its hungry shark's-mouth intake and shark-gray color, and it looked too much like the fearsome, mindless predator it was.

She closed her eyes, and an image flitted into her mind of Gabriel Cheyn sitting in a submarine, holding the leash of his monster. He stroked its sharkskin head and told it how bad Sacramento had treated him, and how it deserved to die; at once, the shark leaped skyward, anxious to avenge its master, and Gabriel laughed in demented glee as it flew away.

After a few minutes of simmering in her anger, she started to write a post. When it was complete, she called Aaron Birnie of *Midnight Sun* and vowed to send him a box of bull testicles if he needed the balls to publish it.

The threat was unnecessary. The *Sun's* editorial staff had been stunned by Ottawa's spiking of the Cheyn videos and the pictures of the HHS list, and ministerial interference was worsening with every Warner post. When Aaron put the question of publishing the post to his staff, the vote was unanimous: They'd declare their independence by publishing Krista's act of sedition.

⌒━⌒━⌒

The Rake
News Post of October 10, 2043

ENOUGH
If we are to survive, this president must die

I will pay five million dollars for the head of President Gabriel Cheyn. The Destroyer of Sacramento must be destroyed.

In a land where guns outnumber people, there must be one man with hawk eyes and piano-wire nerves who will kill Cheyn and save America. There must be one man who knows that the tree of American liberty thirsts for the traitor Cheyn's blood. I will find this hero and make him wealthy.

Yet the work won't be complete with Cheyn's assassination. He isn't the only politician complicit in the Sacramento tragedy – the quislings in his foul golem of a government must also be turned out.

When injustice becomes law, revolution becomes duty. The Activists will fulfill that duty, and we've ordered our armies to rise and bring on this government's demise.

As the Founders did, we'll exile the weak-chinned, hemophiliac overlords of our political class. We'll bring down this president and overthrow this Congress. But if you want to get your freedom back – not the feeble 'freeishness' we've been spoon fed, but the real thing – we need your help.

History has called Americans to its stage, and Freedom's Bell can't be unrung. Join our patriots and chase the corrupt, cowardly curs of government into the sewers. Join our men on the march and trample that mindless golem into a dust that history's gales will forever disperse.

Stand and defend the democracy the Founders intended. Rise and strike wherever you can – a million small blows and modest victories will bring this giant crashing to the ground. Confront authority and smash it everywhere. Disobey orders, stay home from work, hack a computer, or build a roadblock.

Silence is no longer safe. It's your prison, and if you don't stand, it might be your coffin. Get loud while you still have a voice. Time's running out.

See that glow on the horizon? That's the fabled glimmer of hope and the rising sun of change. Our long night can be over if we act.

Rise with The Activity. Shoulder by shoulder, we'll march together into America's bright new day and change this miserable world.

-KLW

Outside on the street, Mark turned a screw on the 'Stang's carburetor and listened to the idle. He couldn't hear much over the Blac Sacrament music shaking Micah's bedroom windows, but he thought that the engine was stumbling. He was puzzling over what to do when he heard Winifred Williams' sugary voice behind him. "Hello, Mark. I heard you were back."

He reached into the car and killed the ignition. "Hey, Win."

"You're looking just great. You know, you haven't changed a bit in three years. Has it been three years?"

"You're looking great too," he said, although he didn't believe it. Win's face was so homely that no makeover expert could rescue it. Her watery blue eyes were so close-set that they'd touch if it wasn't for her nose – and that was so hooked that even her friends called her Wind Vane behind her back. The bags under her eyes were darker too. However, her lustrous auburn hair was still thick and shiny, just like Krista's. He suddenly realized why he'd dated her, and somewhere inside, he laughed until he cried. "Hey, so how's the writing going?"

"My last e-book sold three thousand copies. If I write one a month, I can afford to eat," she said.

"Was that *Hell's Cafeteria* or *I Left My Heart in Hell?*"

She unloosed a braying laugh and he cringed. "That was ten books ago. I wasn't proud of those. I was in a real dark space back then."

"That have something to do with Andramelech?" he asked, and she nodded and looked away. "Hey, you guys oughta talk more and work out your problems."

"Oh, we don't communicate verbally," she said. "Andy actualizes his Underworld channel tracings, and I follow them into his Hell-dominant state. Our communication is more like a symbiotic transference."

"Yeah, I figured that." He sat on the radiator grille and wiped the grease from his hands with a shop rag. "Anyway, Andy's always been important to you, and y'know, you gotta work at relationships."

"Oh, we are," she said, and her little eyes brightened. "We're getting couples counseling now, and I'm so happy. I'd go crazy if we had a non-positive relationship transition."

Mark drew a long breath and let it out in a silent whistle. "Okay, well, congratulations to you both. Say, where'd you find a counselor that works with arch-demons possessing your soul?" She glared at him, the skin around her eyes tight, and he raised his hands to ward off the coming salvo. "Yeah, right, this is Marin. I forgot, okay?"

"Turbulence is the antithesis of purpose, Mark, and you validate false paradigms by rejecting psycho-spiritual evolution. Enlightened professionals treat non-corporeal entities with dignity to disengage spiritual turbidity without judging, because where there's judgment, consciousness can't thrive. Your discontinuities are inhibiting our morphic resonances."

"Got it. I wasn't trying to knock Andy."

"Oh, he doesn't mind. For an arch-demon, he's real nice, even if he *is* a little sensitive. You know, he's collaborating on my latest book? He's giving me a first-person visioning of Hell's political dynamics. This book will be a bestseller." She sat on the grille beside him. "But enough of me and Andy. What brings you back?"

"The Sacramento thing."

"That was terrible. Were you there?"

"Don't wanna talk about that, Win. I'm in denial, y'know?"

She ran a hand down his thigh. "I'm glad you're back. I really am."

"Hey, Win?" He cleared his throat and looked down at the gravel. "Don't take this like you did last time, but I'm in a relationship now."

Her hand quivered, and she pulled it back into her lap. "Do I know her?"

"Probably. Everybody does now, I think," he said.

"Who is she?"

"Win, I can't say. Let's talk about something else."

"He can't tell me her name," she said to herself. "It's somebody well-known who wants to stay incognito –"

"Hey, so what's your new book about?" Mark asked.

She snapped her fingers. "It's that psycho from *Freedom's Bell!* What's her name – Crystal Wormer?"

"How'd you know I was with her?"

"I saw her in the car when you were driving up the hill yesterday. I just happened to glance out the window."

"Listen, Win, people move on and…"

"It's okay." She sniffed and wiped her nose. "She's a lot prettier than me. I can see why you'd go for her."

"I don't mean anything personal."

"I'm not taking anything personal." She wiped tears from her cheek and forced a brave smile to her lips. "I wish you both the best, and I won't get in your way."

"Hey, thanks. I appreciate that, Win."

She nodded and blinked away tears. "I'm getting used to being alone. It's not so bad, at least when Andy's around. But when he takes off for Hell, it gets a little hard."

He ran his hands through his hair. "I gotta go into town and get gas. If you wanna come along, we could get a soda or something."

"No, but thanks for thinking of me." She looked at her watch, strapped just above a row of scars running across her wrist. "Look at the time! The kitties get petulant if I don't feed them right at the stroke of four!" She stood and started walking down the road. "It was nice seeing you again!" she called over her shoulder. A minute later, she disappeared around a corner.

He looked down at the rag he'd twisted as thin as a shoelace. Swearing under his breath, he threw it to the ground and closed the car's hood. Micah and Ada walked out of the house as it latched.

"Whuzzup?" he asked.

"Hey, didja know that Krista is Blind Billy's kid?" Micah asked. "And he was just nearsighted, not blind. He only wore those black glasses on stage cuz seeing the crowd freaked him so much, he couldn't play. And she has all of Blac Sac's music on her tablet, even some stuff that never got released! But she never listens to it."

"She says it's too raunchy," Ada said.

"Heretic!" Micah hissed, making a cross of his fingers. "She has no taste!"

"Yeah," Ada said. "Did I tell you she has extended versions of *Sticky Stuff* too? And you should hear the drum solo they cut from *Escalator to Hell!*"

"I gotta hear those!" Micah said.

"And if you rub her head first, you pick up a Blind Billy vibe! It's like you're in the studio with them!"

"Aww, c'mon, guys, stop rubbing her head," Mark said. "It weirds her out."

"Hey, you don't have to worry about weirding *this* chick out." Micah thrust his tablet into Mark's hands. "You gotta read what she just posted."

Mark leaned against the car and read the *Midnight Sun* post. "Oh, jumpin Jesus, there she goes with the Full Metal Straitjacket stuff again." He read on further, his eyes growing wider with each passing sentence. "She puts out a contract on the president *and* calls for the violent overthrow of the government. Hey, what could go wrong with that?"

Ada laid her hand on his arm. "I told you – when Kick-Ass Krista goes all Hammer of Justice, the bad guys become a wet cleanup on Aisle Three. She's a lot of fun."

Mark shook his head. "Fun? I finally find the girl of my dreams, and all she wants is to get killed?" Mark handed the tablet back to Micah and lay back on the hood of his car. "All redheads are insane, bro."

"Blondes are a lot better, dude," Micah said. Ada slipped her hand into his, and they wrapped their fingers together.

"What kind of Kristan are you? Show a little more faith, Skid," she said. "She does a lot of things that sound crazy at the time but make sense later."

"She just committed sedition or something! That gets the death penalty, y'know!"

"How does she start a revolution without committing sedition? It's an occupational hazard for rebels, Skiddo. Just relax and stop worrying so much. Everything will turn out all right."

"No, it won't." He pressed the heel of his palms into his temples and groaned, still gazing up at the sky. "There's a god, I know it, and he's one cruel SOB. This is just sick, Mikey, sick."

"Yeah, but that's not the only sick thing about this," Micah said. "It's gonna get a lot worse. Wait till she starts getting all those heads in the mail."

BOB DOWNS PAID THE TAXI DRIVER and climbed Golden Gate Avenue toward the Savu residence. His tablet showed that he was only a quarter mile away, a distance he could cover in two minutes, but he wanted to identify insertion and recovery routes first. With almost three hours until dusk, he had ample time to gather intelligence.

Golden Gate was a one-lane road choked with rhododendrons and lined with small mansions of the near-elite. A perimeter intrusion system protected every home, which he was glad to see – the security would keep the residents inside as much as keep the intruders out. He concluded that this population fit the profile of the indifferent and paranoid wealthy who didn't know their neighbors and wouldn't interfere with his operation.

151 Golden Gate was a small, faded-glory mansion. When he was scouting escape routes on the road downhill from it, he'd clearly seen the home's western face, which was dominated by a long balcony and tall floor-to-ceiling windows. However, the railings were broken, the glass hadn't seen a cleaning in a decade, and unpruned rhododendrons in the yard below the balcony had grown into trees.

He passed a gate leading to another hidden mini-mansion and walked along a row of rhododendrons growing out of ivy beds. Footsteps clicked on the road ahead, and he hid behind a shrub and squinted down the road as a tall woman rounded the corner a hundred feet away. She walked through a beam of sunlight that set her auburn hair aglow.

He squinted and tried to make out her face, but his nearsighted eyes couldn't discern her features. Nevertheless, he was certain that an unsuspecting Warner was walking toward him from the target house. He lowered his rucksack into the ivy and loosened his muscles, listening as the tapping of leather-soled shoes grew louder.

The woman walked past, an auburn ponytail swaying across her back. He leaped from the cover of the shrubs and landed on one foot as he locked his arm around her head. Using the other foot as a fulcrum, he twisted her off her feet and flung her into the shrubs. She fell facedown into the ivy.

He slid out his assault knife, yanked her head up by the hair, and sliced the arteries in her neck. Dark blood sprayed across the green leaves, pulsing with each heartbeat and soaking the dirt.

Panting, he sat back and wiped his knife on her blouse. Warner would be conscious for at least a minute until she died, and he was tempted to turn her over to let her see that he'd won. However, that would be unprofessional. It also smacked of vengeance, which was reserved for missions of God.

Her purse lay a few feet away. He reached for it, hoping Warner had been carrying the vaccine and he'd completed the mission with one simple act. If so, he'd fly to Gitmo tonight and begin planning Cheyn's assassination, which would be far more engaging than hunting for a vaccine vial.

He loosened the clasp and pawed inside, but all he found was a large, worn wallet. Wondering how Warner managed to hold onto it after all she'd been through, he opened it and held it close to his eyes. It only held a small amount of cash – and a California driver's license in the name of Winifred Williams.

Dread clawing at his stomach, he turned the body over and saw a face that was nothing like Warner's: small eyes, a beaky nose, and thin, pale lips. He sat back and balled his hands into fists so tight that veins on his arms throbbed. A growl rose in his throat, and the tendons of his neck stood out like steel cables.

Everything about this mission felt wrong. Every time he thought he'd gotten Warner, every time he came close to success, the mission blew up in his face. He wondered if God had arranged this elaborate torture to drive him insane, or if Satan's hand was pulling him away from God's work – or if he was merely the shuttlecock in a game between the celestial beings.

Holding his breath to keep from bellowing, he pounded his fist into the ivy until it felt numb. After the worst of his frustration passed, he stood and assessed his situation: Since he hadn't killed Warner, his mission was still running, and he intended to complete it. He hadn't walked through the coals of Sacramento to abandon it now.

For the mission to succeed, he had to conceal the body. If it was discovered, police might swarm the area during his operation. However, hiding it would be easy because the woman was thin, and the undergrowth was thick.

As he was dragging her corpse behind the rhododendrons, though, the gate across the street opened, and a balding man walked through carrying a bulging trash bag. He froze and gawped at Downs and then at the limp body. A second later, he dropped the bag and ran back through the gate.

The plan had changed – police would respond within minutes, and the body would be found. He slashed her throat again to disguise the professionalism of his first cut and then sliced a pentagram into her abdomen. After wiping his blade clean, he slipped the wallet back into her purse to reinforce the perception of a ritual slaying, not a mugging. That would be enough to throw local cops off his track.

As he was sliding the knife back into its sheath, he heard distant sirens. He grabbed his pack and ran down the street.

MARK, KRISTA, ADA, AND MICAH had driven into town to fill Mark's tank and eat at an out-of-the-way Italian restaurant. They'd argued about Krista's post until their food arrived, but the boys dropped the subject when the girls crossed their arms and stared them down.

On the ride back, though, Mark brought up the possibility of getting lookalike Cheyn heads in the mail.

"It's a common idiom, for chrissakes," Krista said. "Nobody takes that kind of expression literally."

"Are you sure about that?" Mark shook his head. "I think every gomer with a gun and a cardboard box is gonna be sending you a head."

"You're right, you're right, I didn't think it through. I actually didn't think at all. When I get angry, the words sometimes just come out." Krista pressed her palms into her eyes and tried to push away a tension headache. "I'll have to write another post and clarify what I meant."

"Or you could collect the heads and open a museum over at Fisherman's Wharf," Micah offered.

"Hunh?"

"The tourists flock to *memento mori* museums. They've got a kinda Dahmer vibe that folks secretly like. There's three or four down there, and they make a ton of money," he said. "Anyways, I'm just throwing out options."

"I will *not* start a head collection, Micah!" She shuddered and looked through the window. "Jaysus, that's the stuff of nightmares."

Mark slowed when he saw police cruisers and an ambulance blocking Golden Gate. He stopped behind a patrol car, and an older officer with salt-and-pepper hair walked over. "You a local?" he asked.

"Yeah, I live up at 151 Golden Gate," Mark said. "What happened?"

"Homicide," the officer said. "We closed this area for the investigation. If you want to get home, you'll have to go 'round by way of Eucalyptus."

"Right," Mark said. "Can you tell me anything about it?" He flashed his Highway Patrol badge, and the officer leaned one elbow on the windowsill.

"Don't spread it around, okay? It looks like we have one of those nutjobs on the loose. The victim has ritual disfigurement. I hear we've got a witness, but the incident gave him the vapors or something, and he got a nervous breakdown. Had to take him to the rubber ramada."

"Who was the victim?"

"ID says it was Winifred Williams. She's that Satanist writer with all the cats, lives down the hill and keeps to herself." He noticed Mark's stunned expression. "You know her?"

"I talked to her this afternoon. Just before four o'clock."

"Where?"

"Up in front of my house," Mark said. "We chatted for a few minutes, and then she left. She went this way."

He looked closer at Mark's face. "Funny, she has a photo of someone who looks like you in her wallet. How well did you know her?"

"I saw her on the street now and then, that's all."

"And what did you say your name was?" the officer asked.

"Mark Mason."

"And you're going up to 151 Golden Gate now?"

"Yes, I am."

The officer stood and nodded. "All righty. You have to go 'round by way of Eucalyptus, then. You can turn in this driveway here."

Mark drove down the hill in silence and stopped at Eucalyptus. "Okay, we're screwed," he said. "First, I'm gonna have a squad of homicide detectives at my door in a few minutes. Win had a picture of me in her wallet, and I was the last one to see her alive."

"You knew her?" Krista asked.

"Yeah. I used to date her, and that makes me a person of interest. On top of that, I don't have an alibi for the time of death."

"Sure you do," Krista said. "You were with me right after four, and I can testify that you didn't have blood-soaked hands."

"Jumpin Jesus, the woman who just put out a hit on the president isn't a credible witness!"

"I've promised to kill the bastard a few times. I don't see why anybody should get all huffy about it now."

"Let's talk about that some other time. It's not our biggest problem, Krista. What's got me worried is that Win looked just like you from the back – same hair, same figure. I think somebody mighta mistaken her for you."

The car was silent for a minute, and then Ada spoke. "Here we go again."

THEY RAN INTO THE HOUSE and found Marissa standing at the cooking island. "Ma, we need to get going right now," Mark said as he walked over. "Go pack a bag. We don't have much time."

"What's going on?" she asked.

"Somebody's after Krista again. I don't know if it's a bounty hunter or an assassin, but I'm not sticking around to find out."

"An assassin?" Marissa asked.

"Yeah. You don't wanna run across one of those." He grabbed a plastic bag and stuffed cans of food inside. "I figure we can go up to Hunter's cabin. It'll be a tight fit, but it'll have to do."

"The cabin can't hold the five of us, and the power's been off for years," Micah said.

"Well, unless somebody comes up with a better idea, that's where we're going."

"I think we should go to Davis," Ada said.

"Back to Sacramento?" Mark asked. "That's even worse."

"No, it's the best security you can get," Ada said. "No sane person would look for us there. And if I can find the labs, I can see if they have bioreactors. It makes sense all around."

"Yeah, except the radioactivity part," Micah said.

"It's not radioactive that far from Ground Zero," Ada said. "Guys, please, I have to find out if I can do this. Let's just go and see, okay? If we can't find the labs, I'll shut up and go wherever you want."

"Okay," Micah said. "It's worth a shot."

Krista nodded. "She needs to do this."

"Whatever," Mark said. "As long as we're outta here. Everybody go pack and meet me by the door." He grabbed his mother's arm. "Ma, pack light, cuz –"

"I'm not going," she said.

"There could be killers on the way! You don't wanna mess with these guys!"

"I can handle them," she said, crossing her arms. "I won't scurry away from my own home like a frightened animal."

"Ma…"

"That's my decision, Mark Thomas Mason!" she snapped. "Now you go and get ready!"

He pursed his lips and let go of her arm. "All right. But I want you to keep a gun with you, okay? And call the police at the first sign of trouble."

"I can take care of myself. Now go."

They ran to their rooms and were soon standing in the foyer with an assortment of bags. Mark unlocked the gun closet and rustled around inside. "One last thing. We don't know what's happening, so everybody's gotta be armed." He pulled out two small pistols, which he handed to Micah and Ada, and then he stuffed a few boxes of spare ammunition into a bag. "I'll leave this unlocked for you, Ma."

She reached up and kissed him on the cheek. "Don't worry about me. Call and tell me where you are, all right?"

"I'll keep in touch," he said.

THE DETECTIVES LEFT MARISSA'S HOUSE after questioning her for almost an hour. She locked the door behind them and leaned against it, watching the sun set over the Coastal Range. Today, the clouds promised a technicolor sunset.

The golden light bathed her face for a few minutes and then faded to a dusky purple-gray. Sad that the moment was over, she sighed and gathered her thoughts – she needed to double-check that every window was locked downstairs and then set the alarm. Once the house was secure, she'd cook dinner.

The house was quiet with the children gone. The unwelcome silence chilled her so much that she felt a flash of fear about walking into the empty great room. She chided herself for being sentimental and superstitious, but then she heard a loose balcony railing creak.

She crept forward but didn't hear the sound again. When she reached the gun closet, she pulled the door open and lifted her favorite skeet shotgun off the rack. Walking back to the front door and the alarm panel, she broke open the weapon and confirmed it was loaded.

The darkening sky made the tall windows a mirror. In them, she spotted a figure against the wall near the kitchen. It was a man dressed in dark clothes, and he held out a pistol as he crept to the foyer.

She pressed the silent alarm and unlocked the front door. Inching back to the corner of the great room and looking into the window, she saw that the man was no more than ten feet away.

She raised the shotgun and aimed where his head would be when he turned the corner. Taking a slow breath, she pulled the trigger, but the gun didn't fire; it was equipped with a release trigger and would only discharge when she let go. Once she did, though, his head would be blown off his shoulders by an ounce of supersonic steel shot. The fun part would be over quick, and she hoped he'd take his time stalking her. She needed a break from the tedium.

He crept closer to the foyer, and then he whipped around the corner and dropped into a two-handed stance with his pistol drawn. He froze when he saw the big barrel leveled at his forehead. "Bad news, assassin," she said.

He looked at her, the shotgun, and the surroundings for ten long seconds. "I concur," he said. "You have me at a disadvantage, Miss Savu."

"I'm the one at a disadvantage. Didn't your mother teach you to introduce yourself to strangers?"

His lips quirked in a half smile. "Call me Bob."

"Well, Bob, do you realize what I have pointed at your face?"

He rose out of his crouch while keeping his pistol aimed at her head. "A Colchester twelve-gauge single-shot skeet gun with a release trigger."

"And I've pulled it. If you shoot me, I'll shoot you." An unexpected thought flitted through her mind – this assassin looked almost like her husband Hunter, even down to the hazel eyes, but Hunter hadn't been chiseled like a Greek god. Her heart stuttered for a few beats. "And yes, it *is* a Colchester."

"It's a fine weapon." A bead of sweat appeared at his hairline. "This is a delicate situation we have here, is it not?"

She watched his eyes for any warning of impending action, but he was a professional and wasn't giving much away. "You have the air of a dangerous man," she said.

"I'm the most dangerous man you've ever met."

"And how do you know that?" She stepped forward and he took a step back.

"If you'd ever met anybody more dangerous, you'd already be dead."

"If you're so badass, why don't you act? Don't you know a hundred ways to take this gun from me?"

"I apologize for being off my game. I can only think of four right now."

"That's three more ways than you need, so go on and take me out. Prove how dangerous you are."

He smiled again. "Not yet."

"I have a hot date tonight, and I don't want to be late. Let's get this over with."

"Why ruin this moment? Do you really want to hurry?"

Her heart thudded in her chest; she hadn't experienced an existential thrill of this caliber in years, perhaps even decades, and life felt as immediate and urgent as it had as a teenager. If it were her choice, it would only end when her heart gave out. "Yes, of course. I've made social commitments I intend to keep."

The bead of sweat rolled down his face. "You don't savor the exquisite feeling of being on the edge of death, all your life compressed into these precious seconds?" With a small smile, he raised the barrel of his pistol slightly as if he was taunting her to shoot him. "You do. Immensely. Your respiration rate is elevated, your pupils are dilated, and your flawless face is flushed."

He circled slowly to one side, but she refused to move out of his way and give up her position; she had walls to either side, and police would rush through the door behind her at any moment. She wanted him out in the open, with only one way to escape, no place to hide, and a maze of furniture to trip him.

When he came too close, she stepped forward and forced him back out of her reach. He stepped sideways and noticed the obstacle course of furniture behind him. "Since we have some time, may I be candid?" he asked. "Let me say that you're strikingly beautiful. Without exception, you're the most beautiful woman I've ever met."

"You cut a fine figure too. In fact, I'm thinking of shooting you in the heart so I can have one last look before the undertaker closes your coffin."

He barked a short laugh. "I appreciate that. Humor is hard to find in a state of high sexual arousal. However, I could be wrong – you could also be in a state of mortal fear. The symptoms are identical."

"Are they? Why is that, Bob?"

"I know why. So do you." Downs shifted his weight to his right foot while keeping the pistol aimed at her nose. "I can even smell the scent of your arousal. Come clean, Miss Savu: How alive do you feel right now?"

Her heart pounded even harder, so hard that she feared he'd hear it. Before her was the man she'd always sought, the man who lived for the thrill only near-certain death could deliver, as each of her husbands had in their separate ways. "More alive than you'll be if I lose my patience."

"It's me versus you, my skill and determination against yours, both our lives hanging on every breath, every move, every inflection. You're not living if life isn't this intense. Don't you agree?"

Lucky had said the same words the first night they'd played Russian roulette, and this man had to be the reincarnation of Lucky and Hunter rolled into one. She nodded slowly as a long-forgotten heat blossomed within. "You're a hypnotic talker. So hypnotic that I feel my trigger finger relaxing."

"That's just bravado, Miss Savu. You're enjoying the game, as am I. It's more of a high than five-chamber Russian roulette, isn't it?"

She hadn't expected to be read so easily and blinked a few times to conceal her astonishment. "One of us dies tonight. You call this a game?"

DOWNS WAS GETTING MORE AROUSED with each word that dropped from her delightful lips, but the time for words was ending – his hands and shoulder were throbbing, and he couldn't hold a shooting stance much longer. "A game of chance, yes, the highest-stake game we can play," he said. She could have acted at any time because her shot would reach him long before he could react, but she hadn't killed him for the same reason he hadn't killed her: The moment was too important to end.

The weight of the shotgun was making her shoulders sag, and he saw a gap between her arms and the gun. He'd duck and spin to her left because she was right-handed and couldn't swing the gun that way as easily; she'd react by jerking backward, and he'd thrust his arms between hers, turn her around, and pin her against the wall.

After that, he wasn't sure what he'd do. He knew he couldn't interrogate her anymore. That required rationality, and his rational mind had stopped working.

The totality of this deadly angel overwhelmed his senses. She seemed fantastical to him, nearly unreal: Her scent was pure adrenaline, her brown eyes glittered with a predator's intensity, and her skin seemed to glow. The effect might be a trick of the fading sunlight, his poor vision, or perhaps even the two Synthopias he took before climbing onto her balcony, but he didn't care. He'd have her long and hard, right here on the foyer floor, and then he'd explore every cell of her body to find out if she was real.

But she also was a black belt, and lean, tight, and fit. He realized that he might not survive a sexual encounter with her, and the thought sent an electric tingle dancing up his spine. What a glorious way to die. "We can be honest with each other in these last moments," he said. "I'll go first. After I disarm you, I won't kill you."

"Are you negotiating? You're that weak?"

"No, I'm telling you my plan," he said. "And once I've disarmed you, I'll have you till I'm satisfied. And when it comes to sex, I'm not easily sated."

"A man like you? Of course not."

"We'll climb peaks of ecstasy the steamiest romance writers can't even imagine. You'll fear it'll kill you, but you'll beg for more, incapable of caring whether you lived or died. And when we're done, you'll swear a vow of celibacy. There'll be no point in having sex again."

She laughed. "Your fantasies bore me."

"*Celibacy,*" he whispered, and her eyes widened. He sniffed the air; the perfume of her passion was strong, and he could take no more foreplay. And she was as ready for Nirvana as he was.

His muscles coiled for the strike, but then distant voices filtered through the front door. He felt a twinge of sadness as he realized that she'd been only stalling until the police arrived. Nevertheless, the sounds distracted her attention for a split second, which was enough time for him to drop to the floor and roll behind a couch.

Her shotgun boomed, the shot whistling over his head, but it only blew out a window. As the glass showered to the floor, he jumped up into a two-handed crouch with the pistol aimed at her chest.

She dropped the shotgun and raised her hands, taking a small step toward an open closet door at the same time. "So there it is. You win."

"Disappointed?"

"No. Everyone loses the game eventually."

He rose from his crouch. Slowly, he slipped his pistol into its holster, keeping his eyes on hers the entire time. A smile flitted across her lips and then across his. His fingers flipped the holster flap closed, and her eyes widened even more; when he snapped it shut, she flinched as if the sound were a gunshot. They stood rooted in place, each heartbeat seeming to last a lifetime, each waiting for the other to make the first move.

Someone knocked on the door, and she jumped toward the open closet. He started to run for the broken window but then turned when he heard a mechanical click behind him. Seeing her cocking a machine pistol, he sprinted for the balcony, yelping in joyous alarm. He leaped over the railing and fell into the trees just as bullets whizzed past him.

MARK TURNED ONTO THE ROUTE 80 RAMP after passing Vallejo and drove east. Ada and Micah sat in the back and talked.

"Do you think that post of yours will do something? You think somebody will go and assassinate Cheyn?" Mark asked Krista.

"I don't know. I hope so. I need somebody to shoot this bastard soon, or people will figure out there's no Activity. Propaganda has a short shelf life, Mark."

"I wouldn't get my hopes up," he said. "People are sheep. It's hard to open their eyes."

"Then they deserve to get screwed over by this douchebag." Her tablet buzzed and she looked at the screen. "I've got to take this. It's my attorney." She hunched over it and jammed a finger into her ear to hear over the noise from the open windows.

It was a long call, so he focused on the road ahead. The drive seemed like an everyday commute to the Valley; the traffic was light and the stores along the highway were brightly lit. Nothing indicated that a nuclear weapon had wiped out a city nearby.

After they passed through the hills, Krista folded her tablet, and then she lit a cigarette and stared through the windshield.

"Bad news?" he asked.

She nodded. "Cheyn just froze all my trust's assets. I'm poor again."

He took her hand. "Well, you coulda seen that coming, since that was where the five million was coming from. But hey, rich or poor, I still think you're wonderful."

"I don't," she said. "I'm not wonderful at all. I don't think things through. Sometimes it's like there's somebody else at the wheel."

"Guess it's good you gave me that money, then. You can have it back anytime."

"You hold onto it. If I touch it, somebody will take it away."

"All right. I'll be sure to save at least five million bucks. You'll have to pay the guy with the head."

"Oh, crap, I forgot to follow up on that post." She laid her head back and frowned at the ceiling. "Do you think they'll really send me heads?"

"Hey, don't worry. I'll open your mail for the next year. Dead guys don't bother me."

Her fingers trembled as she pulled the cigarette to her lips, and she took a long pull and watched the wind whip the smoke away. "There's more, though. He also raised the Snuff Order on me to five thousand tenpez, so he matched my five million dollars, that bastard. If I'd known how he was going to turn out, I would have strangled him back in grad school and saved us all this grief." She squeezed his hand and looked through the window. "The other news is really bad. I was just convicted of sedition too. Thirty counts."

"That was fast. That post is just a few hours old," he said. "By the way, that's a twenty-year sentence."

"The judge didn't bother with jail time. He sentenced me to the Foggy Bottom Ballet." She pulled up on an imaginary noose. "And I'm not the only one who got a death sentence, either." She nodded over her shoulder at Ada. "Six counts of murder. That's bullshit. When did she commit six murders?"

"They're making stuff up," Mark said quickly. "How'd they get to thirty counts? I can get up to only two."

"They're just piling on now because I'm not there to defend myself. My attorney wasn't even allowed to present a closing statement, and the jury only deliberated for five minutes. You're guilty till proven innocent these days."

"Look, they have a Snuff Order out on you. Why be bothered about the death sentence?"

She sighed and rubbed the bridge of her nose. "Maybe I still expect this country to be fair or something." She tossed her cigarette out and lit another. "I shouldn't have posted those bioreactor plans on *Midnight Sun* this afternoon. I just gave away a lot of leverage with the governor. Now I've got to find some way not to get extradited."

"You still have the vaccine, and that's the big red chip in your stack."

"Right. I'll have to use it now," she said. "I need to get in contact with him soon and cut a deal. If I can't, then I've got to get out of this feckin country."

"He's not the easiest guy to get ahold of." Mark stared through the windshield for a few minutes. "The National Guard knows him, so I should talk to one of their officers, be the intermediary. I'll negotiate the deal, and you can stay hidden till it's all worked out."

They passed through Vacaville, and Mark spotted a row of concrete barriers on the road ahead. He slowed and pulled up to a police cruiser blocking the opening. A young officer stood next to it, who walked over and leaned into the window. "You're at the Exclusion Zone, sir. Only authorized personnel are allowed past this point. Please turn around."

Mark flashed his badge. "Official business. I gotta report to Davis, but I don't know anything else. You know how it goes."

The officer nodded. "Well, there's an evacuation center at the university. I'll bet that's where you're supposed to report."

"What's it like up there?"

"Davis got hit hard, but the badlands start east of it. That side's hot, and you need radiation gear past Mace Boulevard. But stay near the university and you'll be okay."

"Thanks for the intel," Mark said. The officer rolled his cruiser out of the way and let him pass, and they continued toward Davis.

Micah leaned into the front seat. "Where's Sacramento?"

"About a mile over Yosemite, last I heard," Mark said.

"I mean, where was it?"

Mark pointed at the night sky to the east, which was dark now that the black cloud and the awful glow were gone. Sweet scents from nearby fruit farms floated on the air, almost masking the burnt plastic odor. "Don't go sightseeing, Mikey. You'd regret it."

"That's for sure," Krista said. "It's something you should hear about secondhand."

Five minutes later, they spotted an exit for the University of California, where another barrier blocked the highway. "I'll bet that's the No-Go Zone, so we'll see where this exit takes us," Mark said, turning onto the ramp. "It's the university you want, right, Twink?"

"Yeah, except I have no clue where these labs are. We'll need to find a map."

The ramp crossed over the highway, and they drove north on a wide boulevard until signs for UC Davis appeared. They took an exit for the college and merged onto a two-lane road. Bright lights glowed in a large meadow to one side, and as they passed a thicket of bare-branched trees, a compound of tan tents came into view that stretched for hundreds of yards.

Two helicopters sat in a grassy field beside the road, and people scurried to one of them. In the distance, the blinking lights of an approaching helicopter twinkled.

"I guess that's the evac center," Mark said.

"That's not where we're going, though," Ada said. "Look for a directory or something."

Mark peered into the darkness beyond his headlights. "I think there's an information center ahead. We'll try that." He pulled into a parking lot with a small stucco building at one end.

Its roof had been blown across the pavement, and the tires crunched over broken clay tiles as the car rolled up to it. He grabbed his flashlight and stumbled around the building until he spotted a campus map screwed to a wall.

It showed that the Science Complex was located a half-mile ahead beyond a four-story concrete parking deck. He peered that way and saw the darkened garage in the evacuation center's glow.

They crunched back out of the parking lot and passed the garage a few minutes later. He turned and then parked on a sidewalk. "That's the Life Sciences Building," he said, pointing to a pink stone building across a brown, littered lawn. "We'll start there."

They climbed out and stretched, looking at their surroundings – the trees were bare of leaves, cars were stalled on the road, and tan dust coated every surface, but the area appeared untouched by the blast except for that.

"We'll try the main entrance," Ada said. "Maybe they have a directory there." She took Mark's flashlight, walked across the leaves on the lawn, and ran around the building to the front entrance.

It had taken the brunt of the shockwave: The window glass was blown out of the frames and the front doors were twisted off their hinges. She stepped over the glass into a two-story lobby.

"I don't see anything called Tanager Labs," she said, running her finger down a directory board. "In fact, there's only a few labs in the basement, and the rest of this place is classrooms."

"So let's check out the basement," Mark said.

They found a staircase and checked every room on the lower levels, but the laboratories were only equipped for basic biology. They searched the next building down the street, and another after that, but they found no virology labs. As they left the last building, Ada spotted a few benches in a courtyard behind it.

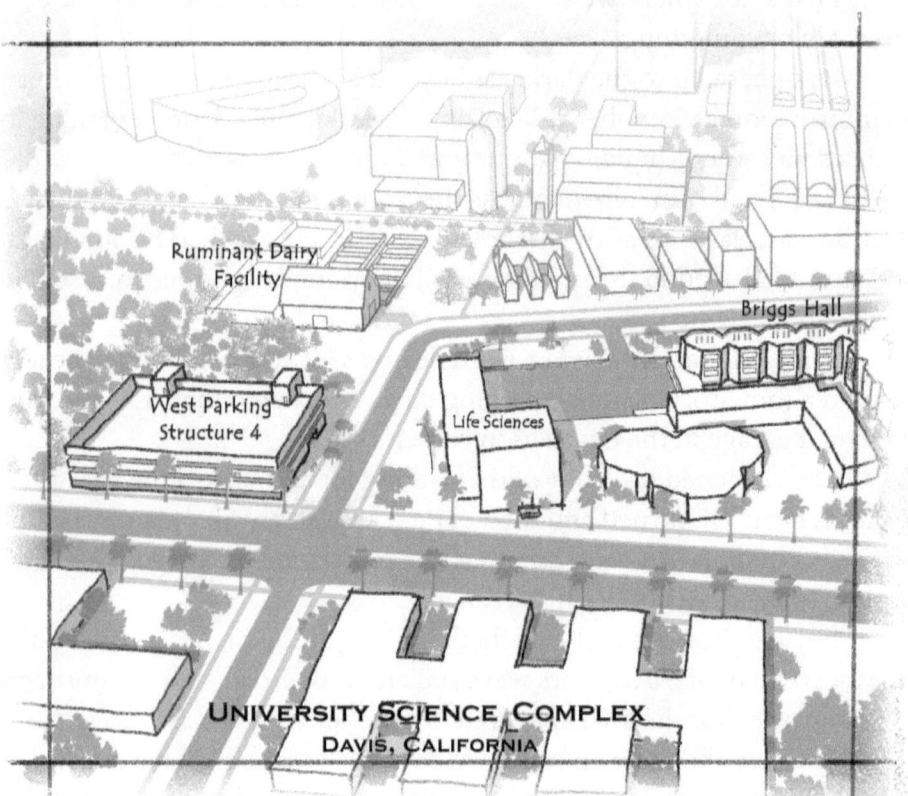

"I need a break. My legs are sore from all these stairs," she said. "Let's chill for a few minutes and figure out what to do next. We're running out of places to check."

Krista stood beside her and massaged her knees. "If I do any more stairs, these things are going to swell to the size of melons."

The courtyard was a grassy square dotted with trees and benches, lit softly by the skyglow from the evacuation center. They sat on a bench, and Mark pulled his shoes off and rubbed his feet. "Musta been a mile of stairs in those places. These people really love their science."

"We're running out of hard science buildings," Ada said. "After this, we start hitting veterinary labs and stuff like that."

     Games of Chance

Krista lit a cigarette and handed the pack to Ada. "Are you sure the lab was at the university? Maybe it was a private lab of some kind."

"UC Davis is what they told me at the border," Mark said.

"We'll just keep looking till we find it." As Ada blew a long plume into the air, she noticed something shiny above and behind the trees. She stood on the bench and squinted – a forest of metal stacks glinted in the light from the evacuation center.

"Whatcha see?" Krista asked.

"There's a row of lab vents up there," she said. "There must be a heavy-duty lab building on the other side of this square."

"Well, let's go over and check it out, "Micah said.

Ada hopped down from the bench, and they trudged across the square. When they reached the other side, they saw the outline of a dark, hulking building.

"I never woulda figured this was here," Mark said.

Micah looked at the dark gray concrete façade and black recessed windows. "It was made to get lost in the dark."

Ada pointed to a flight of low concrete stairs beside a sign that said BRIGGS HALL. "There. Let's see what's inside. It must have a lot of labs from the looks of those vents. This might be the place." She bounded up the stairs and through another pair of glassless doors. The others followed and found her inside the lobby shining the flashlight on a building directory. "None of them say they're the Tanager Labs, but this place has a ton of lab spaces, and it also has a microbiology lecture hall. Virology is a specialty in microbiology."

Micah listened to the empty building. "It has power. I hear a hum."

"The floor is vibrating." Mark knelt and pressed his palm to the marble. "It's coming from downstairs somewhere. The place must have emergency generators or something. I wonder why they're still working."

"Cuz this building is ancient and so are the generators, so they weren't fried by the electromagnetic pulse," Ada said. "Virology labs can't lose power. They need to stay pressurized all the time to keep the l'il buggies inside. I'll bet we have some hardcore labs down there." She turned in a circle and pointed to a door. "There's a stairwell."

"No more stairs," Krista whined.

"This might be the last ones." Ada held the door open.

They walked down a flight to the basement and continued to a sub-basement. At the bottom, they opened the door and walked into a dark room. Ada flipped a switch and ceiling lights flickered on, revealing a short corridor.

Doors set in gray block walls stretched to the right, but to the left, a metal desk sat in front of a concrete wall blocking the corridor. A shining steel vault door with an orange biohazard symbol was centered on it.

BIOSAFETY LEVEL 4 was printed in bright red letters above the symbol. TANAGER PERSONNEL ONLY was printed below it.

DISPATCHES

Midnight Sun
News Post of October 11, 2043

CATACLYSM IN SACRAMENTO: DAY FOUR

Relief and rescue efforts in the stricken area are gathering momentum. Emergency equipment from Canada has arrived on the scene, and the number of field hospitals has doubled overnight thanks to the donation of tents by Mexico and medical equipment by Japan. No Federal assistance has arrived yet, and Washington has yet to indicate if or when it will.

National Guard forces are preparing to enter the No-Go Zone later today and search for survivors. Members of Alpha Company of the 184th Infantry, who are equipped to work in radioactive environments, have arrived in Roseville and plan to undertake a two-hour excursion to the North Highlands area.

Survivors still stream from the No-Go Zone almost three full days after the blast. Many are seriously ill and not expected to survive.

Rescue workers are asking each survivor their location as of 6:36 PM. Most come from the ring four to eight miles from Ground Zero, which is where the National Guard will concentrate its rescue efforts.

FALLOUT FORECAST

Observation cameras in the evacuated village of Lee Vining, near Mono Lake, show no sign of ash or black rain, but radiation monitors have recorded significant levels of strontium-90, with dose rates peaking at three rads per hour. Emergency Services officials say the area will be uninhabitable for several months, although they may grant residents excursions of less than four hours next week to retrieve personal effects.

The fallout plume is forecast to reach the northwest Las Vegas suburbs by midday tomorrow, with dose rates approaching five rads per hour by early evening. The center of the plume should pass over North Las Vegas, but fallout is a certainty within the city itself because the plume front will exceed thirty miles wide.

Scientists consulting with California's Office of Emergency Services note that the aggregate fallout since detonation is far lower than expected. They express concern that radionuclides may be trapped in the plume by rising hot desert air, as the Southwest desert regions have experienced 110-degree-plus days continuously since mid-June. This raises the danger of heavy fallout once the plume encounters cooler air.

TSUNAMI STRIKES US WEST COAST AND ASIA

A tsunami struck the US West Coast in the early morning hours. Isolated reports from the affected areas say coastal cities from Newport, Oregon to Eureka, California experienced considerable damage to their harbors. No loss of life has been reported, although two people are missing in Port Orford, Oregon. Coastal cities in Japan and Taiwan also reported tsunami impacts, although property damage is minimal. Canadian cities have reported no damage from the event.

The Pacific Tsunami Warning Center (PTWC) in Hawaii issued its initial alert at 11:54 PM Pacific Time yesterday. Sources in Eureka, California, say that tsunami sirens sounded only a few minutes before the 12:22 AM arrival of the seven-foot wave. Fortunately, many residents were asleep at that time and the beaches were closed, so the region suffered no known fatalities.

Sources at the PTWC say that the tsunami was triggered by an earthquake along the western Aleutian Ridge that caused widespread underwater landslides. However, none of the tsunami detection buoys in the Northern Pacific reported the wave. The PTWC only identified the tsunami when it was reported by the US coastal detector array approximately two hundred miles off the US mainland. The tsunami was only thirty minutes from land at that point.

Japanese oceanographers detected the tsunami hours earlier than the PTWC and immediately reported the event to their US counterparts in Washington, DC. However, those officials did not pass on the warning to California or Oregon authorities.

VIRUS UPDATE

Along with her post yesterday, *Midnight Sun* correspondent Krista Warner also attached plans for the bioreactor Chalys Pharmaceuticals used to produce Recombin.

We have attempted to contact Chalys, which is in Maryland, but phone lines in the area are not functioning. Ham radio reports that the communications and power grids between Philadelphia and Baltimore have been experiencing rolling blackouts.

Communication is sporadic in Central California due to ongoing problems with the SatStream satellite. Despite this, we have talked to Krista Warner and can confirm that the vaccine survived the destruction of Sacramento.

HAVE THE ACTIVISTS BEGUN THEIR EASTERN CAMPAIGN?

Ham radio reports widespread work stoppages from Baltimore to Richmond. Public transit and sanitation services have been disrupted as operators and engineers refuse to work.

Power and communication outages are widespread throughout Washington and Northern Virginia today. No official explanation has been offered by the power companies or public authorities, although they admit privately that their computer systems were struck by a multi-pronged Internet attack.

Boris Campbell, Professor of Computing Systems Security at Vancouver University, believes that The Activity is responsible. "I've intercepted the malware used in the cyberattack on the power and communications grid, and I've seen this kind of deep-magic code before from the hacker group Warcode, whom I believe are network engineers for the anti-malware firm Cybernext in San Jose. It makes sense – who else could write the best malware than the people who fight it every day? Who can crack a government computer better than the folks who wrote their security software? If I ran an American government computer network, I'd be nervous."

The Activist cyberattack hasn't been limited to public utility systems. The websites of every major bank in Washington are 'offline for maintenance.' The White House website, which has repeatedly been hacked in the past week, just shows a video clip of two rabbits in the act of coitus.

Midnight Sun received three thousand emails yesterday asking what Warner's plans are, and how one might join The Activity. We repeat that she is merely a correspondent for this publication, and we have no knowledge of Activist operations and organization.

RUMORS OF NORTHWEST SECESSION

Our Witness in Olympia reports that the government staff appears to have departed the city. He believes that Washington State is protecting critical departments in the event of an attack on the state capital:

"The Capital Building is empty now. Nobody knows where they went or when.

"Families of government workers I know are out of town too, so I musta missed the memo. I heard Washington and Oregon were talking up secession, but I didn't think they were serious.

"I'm taking off for anywhere else, because if Cheyn's gonna nuke Olympia too, I wanna be far away. I'd rather see that on the news."

Midnight Sun has attempted to contact numerous officials in the Washington and Oregon governments for comment, but calls to their offices remain unanswered.

MIDNIGHT SUN OPERATING FROM UNDISCLOSED LOCATION

A power outage struck the block where our offices are located yesterday, which is an area of the city where blackouts are virtually unknown. Vancouver Public Utilities informed us that all three of our block's transformers failed simultaneously, and they are an unusual model only made in Ohio, USA. As that state was devastated by the virus, they say, it is unknown when power will be restored.

Together with the Revenue Ministry audit of our tax status, as well as two of our editors being recalled to active military duty to patrol the Arctic Circle, the message is clear: Canada wants us offline. Thus, we have moved our operations to an undisclosed location for the duration of this crisis and have activated a secondary uplink site.

THE TANAGER LAB

Day 54
Sunday morning, October 11, 2043
Briggs Hall, University of California at Davis

Ada sat up in bed and rubbed her eyes. She dressed and stumbled out to the small lounge, where Krista was hunched over a coffeemaker and threatening it with grievous harm.

"Good morning," Ada said as she poured a glass of water.

Krista punched buttons on the machine, which responded with a chirp. "Aha! I knew I could do it! Good morning." She reached into a cabinet for a clean mug. "How'd you sleep?"

"Like a baby."

"I did too. They treat their doctors well here."

"All the decent labs have day lounges," Ada said. "At Los Alamos, our lab days were thirteen hours long. After six hours of lab work, though, you're dead on your feet and you start making mistakes, so you have to nap. But their mattresses were hard as granite. I don't think they wanted us to get too comfy."

Krista held up her mug. "Coffee?"

Ada scowled. "I don't know how you can drink that stuff."

"It's what the gods drink to cheer up, sister," she said. "It turns ordinary people into geniuses and lazy people into workhorses. I couldn't have gotten through college without it." She took a sip and smacked her lips. "It's the ideal drink for when you need to learn."

"No, thanks." They leaned against the counter and sipped their drinks.

They'd spent an hour the previous night trying to open the steel door but couldn't bypass its biometric palmpad. Mark had thrown all his weight at the door, but he bounced off the immovable slab of steel and onto the hard concrete floor, cracking his head. After he came to, Ada said they needed to rest, and that she'd solve the puzzle of the door after sleeping on the problem. They explored the rest of the floor, found the Fellows Lounge at the end of the corridor with its two bedrooms, and turned in for the night.

Krista emptied her mug and pointed to Room B, where the men were sleeping. "They must be zonked."

"It was a long day," Ada said. "At least we found the labs. Now all we have to do is get in."

"I hope we can. That door looks pretty solid, and the wall it's in is solid cement. I mean, concrete."

"Yeah, that door's totally undefeatable, but the answer came to me last night. Don't worry."

ADA STOOD ON A DESK in an office and handed a ceiling tile down to Mark. "The floor above is supported by steel beams. That's our way in."

"How's that?" he asked.

"This wall is concrete, but they never pour it all the way up to the floor above. There'll be a gap at the top." She pulled him close to the desk, climbed onto his shoulders, and poked her head above the ceiling. "See? You *are* useful for something. You're a natural human ladder."

Micah snickered, and Mark shot him a dark look. "Stuff it, Short Stack, or I'll pound you down another inch." Ada shifted her weight, and her boot heel cut into his shoulder. "Oww! Watch it, Twink!"

"Almost there," she said.

"This is never gonna work," Mark said.

"You wanna do your hulksmash thing again and try to run through a solid steel door?"

"Did I really do that?" Mark whispered to Krista. She nodded and looked up through the ceiling.

The space between the floor beams was filled with flimsy wallboard that rattled when Ada thumped it. "Get me something sharp!" she yelled. Krista handed up a letter opener, and she stabbed holes in the board, making a large circle, and thumped it hard again. The circle fell out, and she tore the remaining pieces off and repeated the process on the other side of the wall. When the gap was clear, she peered through the opening.

"There's a ceiling just like this one on the other side!" she yelled. "Lift me up!" Mark grabbed her ankles and pushed her up so fast that she banged her head on the floor above. "Asshole!" she yelled. "Watch it!"

"What? I'm Mr. Useful, Twink!"

Air whistled through the hole and ruffled her hair. She grabbed a pipe on the other side of the wall and pulled herself through the foot-high opening, but then she lost her grip on the slick metal and fell. Squealing, she pinballed off a metal duct into a light fixture, became tangled briefly in some wires, and then she crashed through the flimsy ceiling. After bouncing off a lab table and crushing a rack of glass tubes, she tumbled to the floor.

She blew ceiling tile dust out of her mouth and plucked bent pieces of the metal grid from her legs. Looking around the darkened lab, she saw instruments sitting on tables that lined the walls, with a large table occupying the center. Broken test tubes were scattered across the floor, coating the vinyl with a glistening, polychromatic sheen.

The fall had pulled on her wounds, and her leg ached when she put weight on it. Leaning against the table, she limped toward a glass-walled airlock in the center of the room.

As she passed a freezer, she noticed racks of red metal tubes just inside the glass door. Curious about the unusual color, she pulled one out and read the label, which said 'RVE ENTIVIRUS ELLESMERE 2036'. She shrugged and slipped it back into the rack.

She pulled another tube from a rack beside it and rubbed the frost off with her thumb – and the label said 'FV EBOLAVIRUS SUDAN 2031'. With shaking fingers, she returned it to the rack and then glanced at the shattered test tubes littering the floor.

She hobbled to the airlock as fast as her injured leg would allow. Through the glass, she saw rubber biocontainment suits with plastic air hoses hanging from wall hooks. A showerhead in the center of the room dripped iridescent green fluid like antifreeze into a floor drain. On the door opening into the lab, a fluorescent yellow sign warned:

DANGER!
LETHAL AIRBORNE PATHOGENS
PRESENT BEYOND THIS POINT
BSL-4 PROTECTION <u>MANDATORY</u>

She banged her head against the glass wall and looked around the lab, pinching her nose with her fingers.

A HALF HOUR LATER, she opened the vault door from the inside. "Welcome to my lair!" she said.

"You left us standing out here while you took a shower?" Mark asked, looking at her dripping hair.

"In your clothes?" Krista asked.

"Why do you smell like floor cleaner?" Micah asked.

"I was in the mood for a full Silkwood, okay? Drop it."

"God, you're weird," Mark said, walking through the doorway. "This is the place?"

"Yep. There's a big lab on the left that has the bioreactors," she said. "Don't go into the lab on the right. It umm…doesn't have the equipment we need."

Krista noticed her reddened face and arms. "I'm guessing you felt dirty. It's like you scrubbed yourself with a stiff brush or something."

Ada mumbled a reply as she walked down the hall to a glass door. "Here we are! They have five countertop bioreactors and everything we need."

On the back wall, five large metal cylinders sat on a stainless steel counter. Mark walked to them and ran his hand along one. "It's like a combination pressure cooker and moonshine still. You sure it all works after the electromagnetic pulse and everything?"

"I checked them, and everything's fine. The steel frame of this building grounded the electromagnetic field."

"You really know how to use one of these things?" Micah asked as he squinted at a monitor attached to the cylinder. "This looks pretty advanced."

"Actually, I don't," Ada said. "I don't know all that much about virology. That's what The Commander does, so it was the last thing I wanted to learn." She frowned at the bioreactor monitor. "Now I wish I'd paid more attention."

"So we came all this way for nothing?" Mark asked.

"No, dummy," Ada said, spinning on her foot and striding to the door. "There's a library across from the day lounge with all the books I need. I'll just learn virology."

Krista caught up with her as she opened the library door. "Are you sure you can do this? It's okay if you can't. We could talk to the governor and see if he has experts."

Ada opened a book and pursed her lips, scanning the words and diagrams. "Science is my bitch. Gimme some Blac Sac and some time, and I'll totally spock this. In fact, I think I was meant to. My mind, the vaccine, the books, this lab – we were all meant to come together here and do something good. This is why I survived Sacramento when I shouldn't have, Krista. I know this'll work."

"If anybody can do it, you can." Krista laid a hand on her shoulder as she read and massaged the knots from her muscles. "Sure sounds like you're talking about the Life Force, sister. I never thought I'd hear that from you."

"Something bigger than me is at work. I better be nice till I see more evidence telling me what that is. I hope it's the Life Force, I really do. If it's the Archangel Michael, I'm gonna get chopped to bits cuz I've been a naughty girl." She pulled down another book and leafed through the pages. "But I'll worry about that later. Right now, I know what to do. This is that edge of chaos I was telling you about, where you bust out or break apart, and I do my best on the edge. Now lemme borrow your tablet." She snapped the book shut and threw it on the table, where it landed with a thud and raised a cloud of dust. "If I'm gonna rock, I need loud music."

TWENTY-FIVE MILES TO THE SOUTH, Victoria rubbed her eyes and yawned. Looking through the fire truck's windshield, she saw that the sun had risen high over the mountains. She'd slept for a solid twelve hours.

That wasn't surprising. She'd been exhausted when she'd climbed into the old fire engine the previous night, and the backseat had been more comfortable than she'd expected. Rising slowly, she peeked over the windowsill, but the gang of vigilantes that had driven her to take refuge in the firehouse had vanished with the dawn.

After leaving Lodi Memorial Hospital, overflowing with optimism and anticipation, she'd started walking west through the bayous to Fairfield. However, as the setting sun's light dimmed, so had her energy. Worse than that, dusk brought swarms of mosquitoes from the brackish waters beside the road, and she couldn't keep from getting bitten no matter how many she swatted.

As she walked further, she realized the terrible silence of her world: No planes roared across the sky, no trucks thundered down distant highways, no sirens wailed, and no children laughed. All that pierced the silence was the lonely whistle of the hot, dusty wind, which brought with it a thick, waxy stink of melted plastic that made her throat tighten and her sinuses ache. A poisonous thought crept into her mind: Humanity had perished once she'd left Lodi, and she was all that remained of the once-proud species.

That drained the last of her energy. She sat on the roadside, oblivious to the mosquitoes and wanting to wail her anguish into the night. However, after being bitten a dozen more times, she commanded her feet to walk, if only to escape the bugs.

As the moon rose four hours later, trees appeared in the distance, backlit by the light of a distant city. Feeling a fresh hope, she stepped up her pace and soon found a stand of oaks stripped of their leaves. Beyond them, the road rose to a river levee and crossed a low steel bridge to a small town.

When she was halfway across, she heard the lapping of water and looked down into the Sacramento River. A cloud dimmed the moonlight to a soft lambency, and she leaned over the rail and peered into the water. The river appeared to be a dull and lumpy stew instead of a living stream, and worse, it stank of week-old meat.

Then the cloud dimming the moonlight passed by, revealing an ashy, steaming river choked with dozens of bodies.

Her pulse started to race, and she pressed her fingernails into the gash from St. Elizabeth's to stave off the impending panic attack. A flash of white caught her eye, and she looked into the water again: The bloated, boiled body of a blonde girl wearing knee-high boots floated facedown, her wavy hair splayed around her head. She jammed her fist into her mouth to stop the rising wail, but it was too late and she shrieked. Panting, she staggered back to the roadway, knowing in her heart that the body wasn't Ada's but still jolted by the image of her child in death.

She'd just started walking off the bridge when she heard voices coming from the town ahead. Unsure what awaited her, she ran off the bridge and vaulted a guardrail into dry shrubs just as a pickup truck roared around a corner. She spotted men with guns squatting in the truck bed.

She slid down a weedy slope to a riverfront road. As soon as she thought she'd eluded them, though, a man leaned over the railing and shouted.

The pickup squealed around on the bridge as she dashed into the town seeking refuge. She found the firehouse soon after and hid in the fire engine's cab until the truck sounds faded. As soon as they had, she fell asleep.

She yawned again and peeked through the glass firehouse doors – no armed men walked the streets of the deserted town, and no truck engines revved. In fact, the place sounded as lively as a graveyard, which it might very well be.

After listening a little longer, she opened the door quietly and slid to the floor. She climbed the stairs to the kitchen and rooted in the cabinets, where she gleaned enough food to last her a day. She stuffed it into a shoulder bag that she'd found in the cab and then walked back downstairs.

Outside, the town was still quiet, and she decided it was safe to leave. After running through her mental checklist and confirming that she was prepared, she walked to the highway and turned west for Fairfield again.

KRISTA TAPPED ON THE LIBRARY DOOR and walked in. Ada sat at a desk with a stack of old paper textbooks at one elbow and an overflowing ashtray at the other, and Blac Sacrament's *Young, Wet, and Stupid* blared from her earbuds. The packet of Chalys bioreactor designs lay on the desk in front of her.

She pulled her earbuds out when she saw Krista, and Blac Sac thundered even louder. "I'm rockin the Budokan here. Stop pulling my plug."

"I found more sandwiches in the lounge refrigerator. They've got orange juice in there too, which is heavenly. Do you want me to put a lunch together?"

"You don't have to serve me, Krista."

"That I do. You're the star of the show, and my job is hero support. Besides, I've got nothing to do. We sterilized the bioreactors and laid out all the supplies you asked for." She sat across from her and looked at her face. "You've been at this for hours. Your eyes are bloodshot, and your face is flushed like you've got a fever."

"It's just a spock-sweat."

Krista laid her hand on Ada's forehead. "Jaysus! I could grill cheese on this!"

"The brain is a muscle, and I'm pumping iron. It oughta be hot."

"So warm down and take a break already, wouldja?"

"I can handle it." She looked down at the page and started reading again. "Food would be nice, though."

Krista returned a few minutes later with a plate of sandwiches and two mugs of coffee. She set one mug in front of her and sat.

"I don't drink ass water," Ada said, pushing the steaming cup away with one finger.

"You're starting right now," Krista said. "Drink up."

"The Commander drinks the stuff by the gallon. It just turns her into a bitch and gives her the worst breath cancer. On top of that, it tastes like diarrhea. Can you get me something that tastes better, like a nice, hot cup of diesel?"

"Here it is. Diesel for the brain." She leaned over the table. "It lights up your mind and makes the world go slow-mo. You need this more than ever, sister."

Ada wrapped her fingers around the mug and squinted at the black liquid. "Did you make this right? There's globs of greasy stuff floating on it."

"That's the liquid power. It floats to the top." Krista drummed her fingers on the table.

"All right. I'm doing this for you, though." She pinched her nose with one hand, lifted the cup with the other, and guzzled it down.

Too late, Krista jumped up and snatched the empty mug away. "You'll kill yourself like that! You're supposed to sip it, not speedball it!"

"It's medicine, right? So I took it like medicine," Ada said. "Now lemme –" She clutched her stomach, belched, and moaned.

"See? Don't knock back hot coffee. You'll get cramps."

Ada belched again and pushed the mug away. "Look, I did what you asked. Can I concentrate on my studying now?"

"Are you going to be okay?"

"I'll be fine," Ada said, rubbing her belly. "Close the door on your way out."

Krista returned to the lab, where Mark and Micah were sitting on a lab table looking bored. "What's up?" Mark asked.

"She's still studying." She jumped up on a table and swung her legs back and forth. "I can't think of anything left to do."

"We've done everything," Mark said. He checked Ada's list and confirmed that they'd completed all the tasks and collected all the supplies. The lab grew quiet, and after a while, Micah started to whistle tunelessly. Mark examined his nails, and Krista picked fuzz from her hoodie.

"Okay, this is going to drive me crazy," she said. "We should go explore this place in daylight, see if we can find food, see what's around, whatever. It's better than sitting here."

"I'm all for that." Mark jumped off the table and held out his hand to her. "You coming along, squirt?"

Micah shook his head. "I'll stay here in case Ada needs something. I wouldn't wanna leave her alone. I have my pistol if something bad goes down."

Mark grinned. "Yeah, that's the responsible thing. Tell you what – I'll stay here, and you can go exploring with Krista. I'm better with a gun."

Micah's eyes grew wide and he shook his head. "No, no, I have to…umm, autoclave these things again. You go on."

"You sure?"

"Yeah. I'll stay here." Micah picked up an instrument tray, and Mark and Krista left the lab.

"Why do you bust his chops like that?" Krista asked as they walked to the stairs. "You know he's got a crush on her."

"See, that's why I'm busting his chops. You really don't understand how guys work, do you? If you see a weakness, take 'em down!" He slugged an imaginary opponent with a sizzling haymaker. "That's how you toughen guys up. I'm doing him a favor."

"You're right. I don't understand that at all." She stopped at the library door and peeked in, and Ada hadn't moved an inch. "We're going exploring. Do you need anything before we go?"

Ada nodded and wiggled the empty mug in the air. "Get me more diesel, and put more liquid power in it this time. It helps me concentrate."

"One extra buzz coming up. I'll be back in a minute." Krista took the mug and closed the door behind her, and then she leaned against the corridor wall and grinned.

"You're pleased with yourself," Mark said.

"The world has a brand-new caffeine addict, and I'll never drink coffee alone again. Why shouldn't I be pleased?" She sighed and walked next door to the Fellows Lounge, and she returned a few minutes later with a steaming mug in one hand and a bottle of orange juice in the other. After delivering the coffee, she peeled the lid off the orange juice. "Okay, I'm ready to go 'splorin.'"

"You really like that stuff," Mark said, opening the door to the stairwell.

"I love it. It's the New Coffee." She took a gulp of juice and licked her lips. "I can't get enough. It's heaven in a bottle." She drained the container and threw it into a trash can. "I was thinking we oughta check the basement. We passed right by it last night."

"Makes sense." He pulled his pistol from his waistband as they climbed the stairs, and when he came to the door, he opened it slowly with the pistol aimed into the gap. "It looks clear," he said. "I see daylight down that way. Let's check it out."

They entered a long corridor lined with glass-fronted laboratories. Halfway down it, they spotted an alcove with darkened vending machines. One was packed with lunch sandwiches.

"Food. We need to get in there," she said. "Ada can pick these locks."

"Nah, there's an easier way in. Stand back." Mark plucked a fire extinguisher from the wall, pointed the nozzle at the lock, and sprayed it until it was rimed with white ice. He lifted the heavy cylinder above his head and slammed it onto the lock. It snapped off, and the automat's door swung open.

"That's a neat trick." She reached in and grabbed a grilled cheese sandwich.

"You can learn a lot from scumbags. Are you sure this food's good? The power's been off for days."

She sniffed the sandwich and then took a small bite. "It's fine. Maybe all this stuff was so irradiated that it won't go bad now."

He pulled out a roast beef sandwich and examined it. "Well, it's not furry, so it's eatable. Okay, we gotta empty this out on the way back and take it downstairs. Right now, let's go see what's outside."

They continued down the corridor and found a glass door that opened onto a loading dock. The first floor overhung the entire dock, cloaking it in soft, hazy shadow, and the parking lot beyond it was surrounded by high berms of brown grass.

"I should bring my car around here. This is the perfect place to hide it," he said.

"Do you remember where you parked last night?" she asked. "We wandered all over the place."

He pointed to a gray concrete parking garage a hundred yards away. "I parked next to that, I think."

They jumped off the dock, crossed the lot, and found the road to the garage. Small buildings lined one side, and the glass was blown out of every one; they checked a few, but they were empty of people or supplies.

As they approached a barn, they heard bleating behind it. They crept to the back and found a fenced yard with a dozen goats milling around. When they saw Krista, they trotted to the fence, and one pushed its muzzle through and nuzzled her.

"Hey, there, little guy," she said. "You're a friendly one, aren't you?" The goat stretched through the fence and sniffed a pocket of her hoodie. She pulled out the half-eaten sandwich. "Are you hungry? Can you eat grilled cheese?"

"They're goats," he said. "They're the Animal Kingdom's garbage disposal."

She ripped the sandwich into small pieces, and other goats crowded the fence. When her sandwich was gone, she asked Mark for his and tore it into small chunks. He watched her feed them, utterly content in the moment. "You love this, don't you? You look happy as a kid with an ice cream cone."

"I love feeding animals. I could do it all day and never get bored. I know it sounds corny, but it recharges me somehow."

"I can see that," he said. "Y'know, you look just like Keira right now."

"I *am* Keira."

"It's an amazing change. It's like ten years just came off your face."

She looked up sharply. "Do you think I look old?"

"No, it's just a saying. Relax."

"Sometimes I think I'm going all haggy," she said.

He kissed the back of her neck. "You're perfect and wonderful and you don't look old. I'll never see you as a hag. I'll always see you as a kid no matter how old you are."

"That's another reason I'm so hooked on you." She threw the last pieces into the corral and leaned her elbows on the wood rail. "We're the only ones who remember Keira, and I think that's why I feel like a kid around you. Before we met, I felt old and jaded and tired, and the world felt the same, but now...I've seen war and death, and I can see the good more than I did when we were at peace."

"Maybe it's cuz you're popping those painkillers like breath mints. They make a lotta problems go away, Krista. You know those things are addictive?"

"Definitely! They're the best!"

"No, you're gonna get a habit you won't be able to kick. You oughta slow down before it gets too bad."

"Nuh-uh. The pills end when the pain ends, and not one second before." She slipped her hand into her hoodie and clutched her pills. "But maybe they *are* affecting me. I've been having trouble articulating my thoughts lately."

"Articulating. What's that mean?"

"It means to express a complex thought coherently."

"Articulate. Ar-TIC-ulate. That's a word that rolls right off the tongue. I like it."

"You know what word I really like?" she asked. "Ganache."

"Ganache! That sounds great! What's it mean?"

"It's the chocolate cream filling they put in pastries."

"Even better! Ga-nosh..." He pursed his lips. "Now *that* feels nice on the tongue."

"You know what else does?" She reached up and kissed him. "How's that?"

He licked his lips. "Good, but it could use a little ganache."

She smacked his arm and then rested her head on his shoulder with a sigh. He laid his head against hers, and they watched the goats amble around the yard, indifferent to war or politics, their life struggle limited to finding their next meal. "I could stay here forever, just you and me," he said.

"Mmm. Me and you forever. I'd like that."

THEY RETURNED TO THE ROAD and found Mark's car. "I was afraid somebody mighta stolen it since it's got no windows or anything. I wanna get it under the overhang before it rains."

He started across the street and then heard helicopter blades beating the air beyond the parking garage. They ran into it and hid behind a column.

"What is it? Are they Popo?" she asked.

"Dunno. I don't think so, not here." The helicopter chuttered overhead, continued to the west, and landed in the evacuation camp. "It's best that nobody knows we're here, even the locals. Things are dangerous enough for you."

She snorted. "Don't worry about me. I've been in danger every second for the last month. I can handle it."

"That was last month, but lately you've been getting cocky, and that could kill you. You gotta be more careful, all right?"

"I'm not getting cocky, Mark. I'm just not cowering anymore."

"Fine, be brave, but don't be stupid," he said. "Walking around in the open and letting everybody know where you are is stupid. Walking into gunfire is stupid. Threatening to kill the president is stupid."

"Oh, so you think I'm stupid?" she asked.

"No, I think the risks you're taking are stupid."

"I'm taking the risks I've got to, Mark. You can't live without taking risks."

"But you gotta try to stay alive too. There's nobody except me on this damn planet that doesn't want you dead, and I won't lose you."

"You won't lose me. Stop being such a weenie."

He grabbed her shoulders. "Listen for once! You could get killed if you're careless! I've seen your dead face before, and I never wanna see it again –"

She kissed him hard, and then she rested her forehead against his and looked into his eyes. "You love me. You don't have to say it," she said.

"Look, I –"

"I love you."

He blinked his eyes a few times. "You're really throwing me off. Why are we talking about this?"

"I love you, and I don't care if Fate tries to smack me down. I've been dead before, and I'm not scared of it. Let's take chances, Mark, you and me. Let's find those stupid risks and take them together and to hell with everything else. Just don't be scared of who I am and what I do and it'll all work out. You can wake up to Keira every morning and put her to bed every night as long as you're not afraid of me."

He ran his fingers through his hair. "I feel a little dizzy." Yips, barks, and howls came from a field down the road. "Wow, even the dogs felt that. It was like an earthquake."

She ran her hands across his chest, but the barking grew louder. Biting his lower lip, he looked outside. "Something's wrong," he said, and he pulled her across the garage to a concrete stair tower.

"What is it?" she asked.

"Dogs. Too many of them." He pulled her into the stair, closed the door, and peeked through the small window.

A German shepherd trotted past on the road, followed by dozens of smaller dogs. Their fur was matted and filthy, and most wore collars around their necks. A black Rottweiler broke away from the pack and padded into the garage; the fur on its muzzle was caked with dried blood, and its flanks were scratched and bloody. It turned its head from side to side, sniffing for them, but it lost their scent and ran to rejoin the pack.

"A black dog. Splendid," she said. "This is like McPhee. They were running in packs there too."

"They're dangerous when they form packs," he said. "I've seen it happen before, but that was usually only three or four dogs. This has to be fifty or sixty."

The dogs passed by, and they crept to the end of the garage. Just as they reached it, the dogs started barking and sprinted for the barn, and then they heard panicked bleating from the goat pen. Krista pulled out her pistol and started toward it, but Mark grabbed her arm and yanked her back.

"What?" she asked. "I'm supposed to let them slaughter the goats?"

"Stop and think! This is one of those stupid risks I was telling you about!"

"But I've got a gun!"

"There's too many of them! You can't stop this and you have to let it go! Do it for me, okay? Please?" The goats squealed one last time, and then the barn was silent except for the wet sound of tearing flesh. "It's too late anyway."

"Crap. I hate dogs," she muttered. "Man's best friend, my ass. They're not pets. They're savage animals."

"They're pets that got abandoned," he said. "They got hungry, and they gotta eat too. You can't blame them for reverting to their nature."

She leaned against a column and crossed her arms, glaring down the road at the barn. A few dogs had already eaten their fill and waddled away up the sidewalk, their muzzles covered with blood. "That's the way everything is anymore – kill the weak so you can live," she said. "I hate this new world."

"I don't like it, either," he said. "That's why you need to be careful and not become somebody's meal. There's always a predator out there that wants to snack on you."

BOB DOWNS POPPED ANOTHER SYNTHOPIA and limped along a road paralleling Highway 101 in San Rafael. He was pleased with his endurance: His instructors in the Applied Political Science program had said he showed promise as an Executive, but that he lacked the stamina the art demanded. They'd change their minds if they could see him now.

A bomb had exploded only feet away from him, yet he'd still infiltrated California in search of his target. He'd been blown through the air by a nuclear blast, but he got onto his feet soon after and walked halfway across the state in pursuit of his quarry. He'd survived the sensuously homicidal Miss Savu and the fall through her rhododendron trees. He was scratched, slashed, broken, and bent, but he was still on his feet and mission-capable. No other Executive could tolerate that much abuse.

Rolling his shoulders, he realized that he didn't feel the ever-present knot of tension in his back. He wondered if that was because he wasn't standing still for twelve hours a day and watching the awful world flick by on the Wall.

He looked up at an eagle flying high above. Nature was bold and abundant here – puffy white clouds skidded across the deep blue sky instead of swirling yellow fug, and sweet scents of eucalyptus floated on the wind instead of the rotten egg bouquet of Washington. He drew a full breath of fresh air and exhaled his worries.

However delightful Nature was, though, it was also trying to kill him. He examined the blisters on his hands, which were now seeping foul-smelling white pus. When Warner had laid the vial on the floor and set off in a stumbling run, he'd thought that she was just intimidated – but then he discovered she was playing him again when he picked up the silver vial of supposed vaccine.

It was so hot that it melted into the skin of his right hand. He realized instantly that it was a bomb and pried it off with his left hand, and then he sprinted for the office. The device detonated when he was almost there, though, and the pressure blew him off his feet and sent him cartwheeling through the blastproof door. He huddled behind it for an hour until the explosions stopped.

When he opened the door, every building on the base was flattened, replaced with twisted piles of scorched steel and charred wood. He picked a path through the rubble to the gate access road and called out for survivors, but nobody answered. After listening for the sound of rescue equipment and hearing nothing but the whistling wind, he shrugged his rucksack over his shoulder and walked to the airstrip.

An NSF cargo aircraft buzzed the field a few hours later but was blown apart by a SAROC from somewhere out in the desert. He was too numb to react – it had been that kind of day – and he just watched it auger into the ground a mile away. After that, he walked to the midfield maintenance shed and waited for the Pocatello stealth helicopter.

He bit the inside of his cheek and returned his attention to current time. Walking around a curve in the road, he spotted a sign ahead for the

Vacancy Motel, which didn't look as crowded as the other lodgings he'd passed. Taking a few deep breaths and summoning his last energy reserves, he doubled his pace.

After a moment of surveillance, he found a tiny lobby tucked in a corner and walked to the bulletproof glass at the reception desk. The clerk, a young woman wizened by Base-M, gazed at him foggily; she was so Rocked that she'd never remember his face. He'd be safe and anonymous here.

With his key in hand, he stumbled to his room, which smelled like a forensic investigator's wonderland. The bathtub was an ancient metal thing as wide as a pond, and as it filled, he leaned against the wall and checked the political news.

Warner had raised the ante yet again by ordering Cheyn's assassination. That the Activists also wanted him dead pleased him – the more laser dots dancing on the man's forehead, the more likely one would be the kill shot – but he hoped her operatives stayed out of his way. After all he'd been through, he deserved the honor of snuffing the monster.

The other news on *Midnight Sun* was astonishing: The Activists had unveiled their Eastern Campaign and had thrown the East into chaos. He imagined how busy the Watch Room must be right now. The Watch was always electric when events were fast-moving and unexpected, and more was unfolding in the country now than had been for decades.

After all the years of boredom, the Watch had finally become exciting, and he was missing it. He frowned, but then his face brightened as he imagined laid-back Raphael trying to fend off a full-scale cyberwar.

With a chuckle, he climbed into the tub and replayed his extraordinary encounter with the deadly Miss Savu. The more he thought about it, the more certain he was that she'd been attracted to him and hadn't been stalling until the police arrived. And she hadn't killed him, although she easily could have. That had to be love.

Love. So this is what it feels like. He closed his eyes, saw every detail of her face again, and smiled.

KRISTA, MARK, AND MICAH SAT CROSS-LEGGED on the lab floor in a circle, playing cards and drinking coffee as they had all afternoon. They were planning another excursion aboveground to break the tedium when the corridor door slammed open, and Ada strode through holding her Cryogenie. "Wake up, sleepyheads!" she called. "We have work to do!"

Mark helped Krista to her feet. "So does this mean you're a virologist now?" she asked.

Ada turned on a bioreactor and read the numbers on its monitor. "Piece of cake, despite the crappy textbooks."

"Garbage in, genius out, is that it?" Krista asked.

"Story of my life." Ada scowled at the numbers on the screen and tapped on it, calling up a menu. "I can think of lotsa ways to improve these bioreactors, though. God, it's like they were designed by cavemen." She pushed a few buttons on the side and poured a bottle of blue liquid into a hole in the top.

"You think you can pull this off?" Krista asked.

She squinted at a glass tube, frowned, and flicked it with her fingernail. Happy with the results, she tapped on the monitor again. "Virology, another crayon science. You just tell Nature what to do, and it does it. Try moderating nanoplasma chaos in a white matter p-vortex. Now *that's* hard."

"Right. It always gives me conniptions."

Ada nodded and wound a piece of hair around her finger, watching numbers scroll down the screen. "Mmm, yeah, the Matsuri Paradox makes the math messy," she mumbled. Suddenly, she opened her Cryogenie, stabbed a large syringe into a vial and withdrew most of the clear fluid, and then injected it through a rubber seal into the machine.

She pulled up a stool and cracked her knuckles. Her fingers flew across the screen, multicolored shapes and rows of numbers flickering across it almost too fast to see. Soon, she and the machine were two halves of a whole.

Krista snapped her fingers next to Ada's ear, but she didn't flinch. "She's gone down the rabbit hole."

"Yeah, she's off in her own world now," Mark said. "I guess we're gonna stay here, then. We can forget about Hunter's cabin."

"I'm okay with that," Krista said. "We're safe here. We've just got to avoid that dog pack."

Ada worked the bioreactor screen for two hours. Krista took a coffee break after an hour and brought Ada a cup, and she sucked it dry without acknowledging her. The trio sat on the floor and played cards again.

Finally, Ada stood back from the machine and leaned against the table. They rose and looked at the screen, where a twisted, spiky helix was displayed next to a column of letters and numbers. Ada stroked an imaginary beard. "There it is. This is Recombin. It's a work of art, isn't it? If there's beauty in science, this baby is it. It had to be nano-built, protein by protein, from the ground up." She looked up, but every face wore an expression of utter befuddlement. "Okay, never mind. What matters is what comes outta the business end of the bioreactor. If it looks like this, we're good to go."

"Okay." Mark rubbed his hands together. "Let's give it the old college try. When do we start this up?"

Ada leaned back against the counter and grinned. "I just did."

KRISTA SQUINTED INTO THE GLASS-COVERED CHAMBER on the front of the machine and waited for the first drop of Recombin. "How much can you make?"

"I'm just replicating the feedstock in this bioreactor right now. That's a slow process," Ada said. "In one day, I can make about three liters of pure Recombin. About a thousand doses."

"That's a good start," Micah said.

"I think I can make a lot more – as much as 108,000 doses a day. In ten days, I can make over a million doses." She leaned back against a lab table. "All I have to do is breed Recombin in Unit One, Neovirus in Unit Five, and mix it all together in the other three units. A little reconfiguration here, a little reprogramming there, and the virophage will pour out of the machines. 240 liters a day if I'm right, and I'm right."

"Wow," Mark said. "You could vaccinate all the first responders with that and still have some lots over."

"Sure." She sipped her coffee and eyed Krista over the rim. "I just need some Neovirus and I'm ready to go."

Krista stiffened. "Why are you looking at me?"

"Cuz you and Mark have to get it," she said. "Micah and I need to reconfigure the reactors and keep making Recombin feedstock. Besides, we're both still convalescing."

Krista rubbed the bridge of her nose and groaned. "I'll have to do something ghoulish, right? Dig up gross dead guys and drain their blood?"

"Oh, no, the donors have to be alive." Ada shrugged. "Hey, at least you won't have to kill time playing cards."

"Splendid, just splendid."

"I just need twenty pints, though."

"Why didn't you say so? Why am I worrying?" She puffed out her cheeks, slumped against the table, and looked at Mark. "The nearest place to find live virus victims is in Nevada. We've got to return to the States."

They listened to the humming of the bioreactor while they mulled over their options. After a minute, Mark slapped his hand on the lab table. "It has to be done, so let's figure out how to do it."

"Right. I can't think of any way around it," Krista said, crossing arms. "Well, crap."

"We don't have to take any stupid chances, though," he said. "We gotta cross the border, so we're gonna meet the National Guard again, and this is the perfect time to negotiate a deal with the governor." He ticked off the points on his fingers. "One – no extradition to the States. Two – total amnesty. Three – protection from the Federals."

"For all of us, including you," Krista said. "All I ask is that we stay far away from Sacramento on the way."

While they were planning their trip, Ada reached into the bioreactor with a pipette and drew off a drop of liquid beading on the output nozzle. She inserted it into the protein modeler and pushed a few buttons. A few minutes later, an image began to take shape on the screen. "C'mon baby, be my Frankenstein," she mumbled as the details sharpened, and then she jumped up and pumped her fist in the air. "Yes! I am totally freakin awesome! I oughta patent myself! I love being me!"

Krista leaned over her shoulder and looked at the screen. "It's good to see your self-esteem problem is back. So did it work?"

"Did it work? It's a perfect match!"

"You rock, Twink," Mark said, bumping her fist.

"Congratulations," Micah said. He leaned forward and pecked her cheek, and she wrapped her arms around his neck and kissed him long and hard.

Mark lifted his pack and heaved it over his shoulder. "Hey, Mikey! Wanna help us take the gear out to the car?" he asked.

Micah waved a hand behind Ada's back, shooing him away.

"Or should I go pound sand up my ass?" he asked. Micah's hand flipped into a thumbs-up sign.

STONEWALL

Adam Harris strode onto Delta Pier through a swirling, foggy drizzle and found Captain Caldwell standing near the drydock. They walked to the *Nathan Hale's* berth, pulled aside the camouflage netting, and watched workers lower crates of canned food into the boat.

"Did Julie respond yet?" Caldwell asked.

"No," Harris said. "And I don't want to speculate about why not."

"All right. I heard that you called your boys down at the Pacific Fleet. So what's the story?"

"Story?" Harris snorted. "I got more stories and sunshine from the brass than a fairy-tale book."

"The shinier the brass, the shinier the lies."

Harris nodded. "They told me nothing about the *Rockefeller's* mission. Suddenly, I don't need to know. They were trying to stonewall me, but I found a way around it."

"How?"

"You remember that little lieutenant who was eyeballing you at the Christmas party? She was good for some scuttlebutt. By the way, you're having dinner with her the next time you go to Pearl." Caldwell turned his face up into the drizzle and mouthed silent curses. "Stop whining, Zack. I'm paying, so you can go to the Pearl Club."

"Thank you *so* much, Adam. I've been missing that one hairy eyebrow and those lips like two slabs of pork bellies." He wiped his face dry and sighed. "All right. Since I'm already consigned to a night of hell, what did she say?"

"She's sure the *Rockefeller* wasn't on a routine patrol but a mission. Authority unknown." Harris pulled up the collar of his coat and leaned toward him. "And guess what? They lost contact with her near Kiska Island."

Caldwell looked at him quickly. "Oh, fuck. The earthquake that caused that tsunami originated around Kiska…"

"…where the *Henry* was laying low. That so-called earthquake was probably Julie going nuclear and blowing the living shit outta the *Rockefeller*."

"Did Lieutenant Pork Belly know what happened to the *Henry?*"

"No, but I'm sure they came out of the engagement okay. Eareckson has anti-sub planes looking for them all across the Pacific, but two haven't returned from a patrol northwest of Kiska. They were lost well after the quake, so the *Henry* must have taken them out."

"Thank God." Caldwell let out a long breath. "Y'know, one small piece of verified data would be nice. The merest mote of information, the feeblest fact, would be better than all this crystal-ball gazing. Here we are, at maybe the most consequential time of our lives, and we have nothing but supposition and rumors to base critical decisions on."

"These are the times when you gotta go by your gut, bud."

"I don't digest thoughts with my gut, just like I don't digest sushi with my brain."

"Stop whining and evolve. You wanna hear the rest? I need some brainwork from you on this."

Caldwell nodded, and Harris leaned against a piling. "She said COMPAC diverted four littoral combat ships up to the Aleutians, and two fast frigates to the Strait of Juan de Fuca. No salvage vessels – just combat ships. I think Pacific Fleet Command knows exactly what the *Rockefeller* was doing and what happened to it, and they won't stop hunting the *Henry* till she's on the bottom. And they're laying a trap for Julie in case she tries to come home." Harris looked into the fog over the Hood Canal. "Fill in the colors for me, Zack, before I start believing crazy conspiracy theories."

Caldwell made a show of drying off his cap. After a minute, he sighed and jammed it on his head. "All I have are crazy conspiracy theories. One, the Pacific Fleet really did conspire with a batshit-nuts president to attack Sacramento, now they're trying to bury the evidence at sea, and they're stonewalling us because we'd call bullshit if we knew. Two, the Pacific

Fleet wasn't involved in any conspiracy and they believe the *Henry* went rogue, they're trying to blow her out of the water before she does it again, and they're keeping us in the dark because they think we're in on it too."

"That's absurd. It's impossible for our boats to release missiles whenever they want. They'd have to override the Missile Release Control System, which can only be done dockside with special equipment – and only with my authorization."

"Exactly. In Crazy Theory Two, they'd have to assume this base went rogue along with the *Henry*," Caldwell said.

They walked to the *Nathan Hale's* bow and stood at the end of the pier. A tugboat chugged toward the Explosives Handling Wharf, and they watched it cross behind the *Hale* and stop beside the *Allen*. "So if they think we modified the *Henry* to attack American targets, why are we still breathing?" Harris asked.

"Because they know we didn't modify it." Caldwell crossed his arms and glared out at the Hood Canal. "Only Crazy Theory One makes sense: COMPAC knew about the attack, they supported it, and now they're trying to cover their ass. This is pretty much a fact. And because you tipped your hand sniffing around Pearl, now they know that we know. We might not be breathing all that much longer." He filled his lungs and savored the scents of seawater and submarine. "I've grown rather fond of respiration, Adam."

Harris turned and walked back down the pier. "So this is it. All right. The chain of command can't be trusted right now, Zack, certainly not with nuclear weapons." He looked at the dark bulk of the *Nathan Hale*, which was already loaded with Joe Slicks. "Remove the MRCS on the *Hale* and the *Allen*. I'll call Jimmy Three-Balls on the *Revere* and tell him to abort any missile release orders he gets. The *Revere's* the only boat in range of the Continental U.S., right?"

"Right, but that's a tough sell. Jimmy Columbo might be a swinging dick, but he's a loyal commander who's been trained to follow orders. And if you convince him to defy those orders, you're weakening our Pacific nuclear deterrent –"

"So I won't copy the goddamned Reds on the memo! As long as they don't know, we still have a deterrent in place!"

"Relax, Adam –"

"This is the wrong time to overthink the problem!" He took off his cap and shook off the raindrops. "Stop worrying so much. I'll figure it out as I go along."

BLACK SWAN

Day 54
Sunday evening, October 11, 2043
National Tranquility Center, Fort Belvoir, Virginia

It was time for the evening Watch change, and both crews had gathered in the Watch Room to brief each other. Cochon stepped onto the podium. "How's it going, Raf?"

"Hey, Phil. We've accomplished almost nothing today, as I'm sure you've guessed. The CIA computers were hit by a Warcode service attack this morning, and it didn't just shut their site down but breached their firewalls. They found at least one logic bomb inside, so we cut our link. The NSA and FBI computers are still up and running, but they're extremely slow. Mochyn thinks they were both hit with a distributed denial-of-service worm that's consuming computing capacity, so we cut those links too. Oh, and the cafeteria's closed. The civilian staff didn't show up for work today."

"The commercial websites are down too. I went online to pay my student loan this afternoon, and all the site showed was a video of a defecating elephant."

Raphael chuckled. "At least The Activity is being entertaining while they wreck the country. They're a formidable enemy, with both Warcode and Blue Ball on their side. I tell you, Phil, we're entering really interesting times."

"Have our computers been attacked directly?"

"Blue Ball's been annoying us with puny attacks all day long, but Mochyn killed each one in seconds. Our biggest problem is that we're starved of input because we cut our links to the external systems. We're blind except for our own visual data sources. Fortunately, though, the Sacramento bombing stunned the country, and nobody seems to be acting up, so our suppression activity –" A picture flashed onto the Wall of a preteen Ada Lang in a lab coat displaying her middle finger, and Blac Sacrament's *Messin with Mister Law* throbbed in the background. "And here we go again. Mochyn, take care of this."

The image disappeared from the screen. "Got it," he said. "It's that Blue Ball crowd again. I backtracked their last attack and found out it originated from a burger joint in Santa Fe, so I'm about to worm every damn computer in town. Maybe that'll shut them down and keep them down."

The lights flicked off, throwing the Watch Room into darkness except for the glow from the Wall. A few seconds later, the emergency generators triggered and the lights turned back on.

"Wonderful. The power goes out just when my shift ends. Now my air conditioning won't work. I'll roast all night long." Raphael glanced at the wall clock. "I'll also miss the presidential speech. Cheyn's supposed to be making some earth-shaking announcement at 2100 hours. Do you mind if we play it on the Wall?"

"No," Cochon said. "I'm curious too. The pundits say the White House figured out who bombed Sacramento."

"I'd like to know how they found out when we couldn't. Whoever did it left no fingerprints."

"I still think it was Cheyn, but I think they'll blame another government," Cochon said. "The distraction of an external enemy is too great to pass up. That means there's a high probability we'll be going to war."

"Good. More war protesters means more work." Raphael yawned and stretched. "Keep a close eye on his background. I'd like to know where the guy's been hiding for the past week. He hasn't been spotted at the White House or Camp David."

Buta picked up the NewsHub political feed and displayed it on the Wall. The presidential seal appeared a few seconds later followed by the grave face of Gabriel Cheyn. "My fellow Americans," he intoned, but then he wandered into the historical precedent for his remarks. When he began lecturing about the Teapot Dome scandal of 1921, most of the Watch Room staff found other things to do.

"Love those eyebrows," Raphael said. "You know that you can get implants just like them?"

"Why would anybody want to?" Cochon asked.

"Power, baby, power," Raphael said. "Chicks love it. See, this guy is one of the five most boring men on the planet, but I guarantee that most women in the audience wanna blow him right now. It's the eyebrows."

Ryan Beckmann walked up beside them. "Mind if I watch?"

"Did you bring the popcorn?" Raphael asked. "Looks like Gabe's gonna be spewing ozone all night. I could use a snack."

Beckmann opened his lunch bag and pulled out a foil package of popcorn.

"Man, I was just joking." Raphael tore open the bag and smiled. "Now this is the life, big-screen TV and popcorn…wait, I think he's already getting to the big reveal."

Wearing a grim expression, Cheyn leaned forward and gazed into the camera. "Our investigations leave no doubt – the city of Sacramento was destroyed by an American weapon launched by the USS *Patrick Henry*, a Navy submarine. The crew was not authorized to launch this missile, and we believe it was a unilateral action taken by the commanders of the submarine. The captain of the vessel, Captain Juliette Bricker, has longstanding emotional and psychological issues resulting from her rigid Archangelist upbringing, and we believe she launched this devastating attack to punish California for being what Archangelist cultists call a 'tainted, mongrel liberality decaying from sheer lack of moral fiber.' The executive officer, Commander Ennis Quinn, is a veteran of the Persian Regional Conflict and suffers from post-traumatic stress disorder and hallucinations, and he may have conspired with her to launch this weapon. Every asset of the Pacific and Arctic Fleets has been deployed to find the *Patrick Henry* and destroy it before it can do more harm…"

"Oh, bullshit," Beckmann said. "Submarine crews go through ridiculous psychological screening before they're even allowed to set foot on the base. If Bricker had any issues at all, they wouldn't have let her on a sub. And I know Quinn personally. He doesn't have PTSD."

"You're saying the president's lying?" Raphael asked.

"Definitely," Beckmann said. "I know that Quinn would never crack. Him, Adam Harris, and I were tortured for eighty days straight at the Hotel Hamadan. I finally gave in, but Quinn and Harris never did no matter what the rug jockeys tried. If Persian pros can't break a man, nothing will."

"What do you know about Harris?" Cochon asked.

"He's a good man, abrasive and impetuous but loyal to a fault. Why?"

"Because too many Activist threads lead back to him. He's the commander of the *Patrick Henry*'s home base, which just launched a nuke at California. Tala Ripley serves on the *Henry,* and she's connected to Warner and the Maryville bomber. And what about Lang? No, his base is an Activist stronghold, if not its headquarters."

"C'mon, Harris is no rebel," Beckmann said. "Arrows want to be as straight as Adam. Really, you're barking up the wrong tree with this guy, Phil."

"I agree," Raphael said. "It's all coincidence in this case."

"There are too many coincidences centering on this man," Cochon said. "I know your gut tells you otherwise, but for him to not be involved is improbable, Raf."

"But not impossible. It's what we call a black swan event, where everything comes together like there was some over-arching design at work, but it all turns out to be coincidence," Raphael said. "They happen from time to time. Trust me, nothing ominous is going on at that base."

Cochon stepped back looking as if he'd been slapped in the face.

"Take my advice, Phil," Raphael said. "Let this go."

BITTER'S END

Day 54
Sunday night, October 11, 2043
Bangor Naval Submarine Base, Kitsap, Washington

Zachary Caldwell stood on the south docks and watched the governor's yacht idle into the berth. A deckhand tossed him a rope, and he wrapped it around the dock cleat and pulled the boat in.

Harris stood on the aft deck deep in conversation with a slender, middle-aged Asian woman. A powerfully built, dark-skinned man stood beside them listening intently. As the boat turned, Caldwell saw that he was Bryan Pettit, commander of the *Ethan Allen's* Gold Crew. When the yacht hit the bumpers, Harris shook her hand, and then he and Pettit jumped up onto the dock.

"What are you doing skimming the surface, Bry?" Caldwell asked.

Pettit forced a smile to his face. "I've got things to do, so I'll just let y'all talk." He turned and walked down the dock toward the road.

Caldwell looked at Harris. "Talk about what?"

Harris unwound the rope and threw it onto the boat. "Let's take a walk, bud."

They strolled to the end of the long dock, which overlooked the Hood Canal. The view from there was spectacular on clear days, but all they saw tonight were the twinkling lights of houses on the opposite shore. A fog bank lurked thirty feet above the water and glowed in the light from the houses.

"I guess you heard Cheyn's speech," Caldwell said. "I tried to get back, but you were gone by the time I got here."

Harris grunted. "I watched it in the Officer's Club with Bryan and Paige. It got a little intense. When Cheyn unloaded that BS about Julie, Paige actually swore. I've never heard her curse."

"If anybody knew Cheyn was lying, it's Paige Pangelis. She was Julie's XO on the *Louisiana* for years."

"And Bryan was Julie's XO before Paige." Harris' tablet buzzed, and he pulled it from inside his windbreaker and hissed. "Not *her* again."

"Wang's already stalking you?"

"No, it's Elise Ripley."

"Who?"

"Tala Ripley's mom. Cheyn wasn't even done saying 'Patrick Henry' before she called to find out if Tala was safe." The tablet vibrated again.

"Wow, that's one persistent mama," Caldwell said.

"No, this time it's Wang." Harris looked from the tablet to the lights across the canal. "Yeah, I bet I could skip this sucker all the way across and break a window on the other side. Whaddaya think?"

"I think you need to stop giving out your personal number." They walked along the dock listening to submarine hulls creaking against the bumpers and smelling the sharp cedar scent on the breeze. "When you're this quiet, it usually means you're pissed beyond words. And after Cheyn's speech, you should be," Caldwell said.

"Damn straight I'm pissed," Harris said. "The president lied, and the Pacific Fleet backed him up. The Fleet damn well knows that the *Henry* didn't go rogue and Julie's not nuts, and saying the opposite is proof they're covering up a conspiracy with that bastard Cheyn. That was it for me, so I figured it was time to have a chat with Governor Stalker."

They walked to a concrete bench by the canal, and Caldwell sat and pulled up his coat collar. "You're right, of course. There's nobody else to turn to now."

Harris nodded and sniffed the air coming off the water. "This is why I went into the Navy. It was this simple – I loved the smell of salt water and the sting of the spray in my face. I never wanted anything more, but I never got it. And you know why, Zack? Because I went wherever the tide took me. Now here I am with two stars on my collar." He breathed in the salt air and held it for a few moments, and then he shook his head. "After the Persians released us, the Navy wanted a hero. They picked me, and I did everything they asked. I signed every autograph book, shook every hand, ate every hot dog at every damn county fair. Sure, I didn't have time to save my marriage, but I had to be a good sailor and go with the tide."

"Everybody has regrets when they get to middle age, Adam. The life you could have led is always better than the life you did. You can't be bitter about that. It'll corrode you."

"I'm at bitter's end, Zack. I'm at the end of my rope, and below me is an abyss." A gust of wind blew sea spray on them, and Harris smiled. "But that's good. That's good."

"I can't understand how."

"It's good because my delusions are gone, and my course is clear. I know what'll happen now, Zack. Cheyn will come for me and pop a bullet in my head. He'll come for you too."

"Because we know the truth," Caldwell said. "He couldn't trust us to remain quiet or support his lies."

"And he'd be right. It's also clear Cheyn won't stop with Sacramento. He'll destroy more cities, because once you've delivered nuclear Armageddon, there's no reason to stop. What's the difference between destroying one city or ten?"

"None," Caldwell said. "The horror of the act is absolute, and you can't multiply an absolute."

"Precisely."

They watched the lights of the governor's yacht glide toward the Hood Canal Bridge. When they were swallowed by the fog, Caldwell stood and walked to the dock's edge. "I can't see any good course out of this."

"There are no good courses," Harris said. "But there are right ones."

"If you know how to get out of this trap, let me know."

"Would you let go of the rope and fall into the abyss, not knowing where you'll land? You have to be sure that holding on is worse than letting go."

"Don't get lost in your metaphors, Adam. Getting a bullet in my skull is an undesirable personal outcome. I'm open to better ideas. Tell me what you have in mind."

Harris crossed his arms and gazed across the canal. "Somebody needs to force Cheyn back into his box. I can do that. I have control of a nuclear arsenal and the means to deliver the warheads. I have the power to balance this confrontation and prevent the death of more innocents, and I have the moral obligation to use that power. I'd be as much a monster as Cheyn if I didn't. I want you to help me, and I need you to. Pick a side, Zack. You can walk if you want, but I really need you with me on this, bud. Are you?"

"You're allying with Wang?"

Harris nodded. "They're almost ready to break away, maybe in a week or two. And they're working less on the secession politics than the consequences that'll follow. They figure that war with the States is inevitable. They have the National Guard and the 81st Armored at Fort Lewis to handle a ground attack, but they don't have a nuclear deterrent. And like you said way back when, they need one – Cheyn nuked Sacramento, so he'd nuke Seattle. Governor Wang needs us to give her that deterrent."

"You'd give her the keys to the Strategic Weapons Facility?"

"No, the SWF is off the table. I'll lock it down and figure out what to do with the warheads later. I'd retain full control over the nuclear weapons deployed at sea, though, and I'd never use them offensively. They're just a deterrent. With two hundred megatons afloat, I can stop Cheyn from throwing around nukes like firecrackers."

"Zero megatons of which you can actually launch."

"Sixty-eight, at least. Bryan and the *Allen* are in if you are, and so are Paige and the *Hale*."

"Why me?"

"Because you can't help making shit work. You make Bangor tick like a Swiss watch, and it's not even your job. You're my adjutant, but everybody thinks you're the base commander. Hell, *I* don't even know who's supposed to be running this place."

"Captain Johnny Whitland."

"Never heard of the guy."

"He's out on the links a lot."

"Because he has nothing to do. *You* make Bangor work. And Bryan and Paige trust you to make this work too. That's a compliment."

"Yeah, what an honor." He examined the fog bank above, puffing out his cheeks. "You never go halfway, Adam."

"There's no halfway on this, and there's no going with the tide," he said. "We're the only ones who can stop Cheyn. The reactor of this country has gone supercritical, and we're the control rods. We have to scram this reactor now before things get worse."

"You've got to stop with these metaphors. You're making me dizzy. Or maybe what's making me dizzy is that I'm beginning to understand what you're proposing. Rebelling is irrevocable. It's mutiny if we lose, and that's a mandatory death penalty."

"You're just as dead if you don't do something. Look, your own president would execute you for no greater crime than knowing the truth. Your own president would kill eighty-seven loyal sailors on the *Henry* just for doing their duty. Tell me who's the real traitor in this picture and who's the real patriot."

"This is where I get dizzy. I'm an American, Adam, not a rebel."

"Well, those days are over. The old America is gone, and it's time to accept it. This is the new normal, and we've got to adapt or die." Harris looked at the twinkling lights on the far shore. "And that's tough to do, bud, I'll admit that. We were boring naval officers only last week, and now we're rebels fighting tyrants. Yeah, it's not easy wrapping your head around *that* concept, but it's true. Face it: We're all that's left of the America that was. Now it's *our* duty to protect it from Gabriel Cheyn."

"Now you're making stuff up. Our duty is to defend the Constitution, not interpret it the way we want."

"I'm not freestyling here. Our oath says we'll defend the Constitution against all enemies foreign *and* domestic – and if there was ever a domestic enemy, Cheyn's the guy. He's pissing all over the Constitution and doing whatever he wants. That leaves *us* with the duty to defend what's left of that democracy from the enemy inside our walls."

"I don't see it that way. I took my oath expecting to obey the orders of properly constituted civilian authority, not parsing the Constitution's wording."

"I'm not parsing anything! Nothing in our oath or the Code of Military Justice says we have to do *anything* an unhinged president says!" He strode across the dock, running his fingers through his hair, and then he whirled around. "Screw this legalistic bullshit. I'll never get to say that at my court martial anyway. This is all the trial I'll get." He made a gun of his fingers, aimed at his temple, and pulled the trigger. "Bam! Case closed! That's the America we're sailing for, Zack, an America where anybody can get the axe but nobody gets a trial – not me, not you, not a single virus victim, not a soul in Sacramento!"

Caldwell leaned against a piling and crossed his arms, his lips pursed as he looked across the canal. "Somewhere in the middle of that impassioned rant, you stumbled across an important truth that says why we have this Cheyn shitshow – he's at war with something. He's behaving like a battlefield commander who can decide who lives and dies to achieve his objective. Nobody gets a trial on the field of battle, either."

"Precisely! This is definitely a war, but it's not between nations. It's between Cheyn and whoever crosses him. And that's not my America, and that's not the country my buddies on the *Vanderbilt* died to defend, and I WILL BE DAMNED if I let them be proven wrong!" A seagull alighted on a nearby piling, and Harris kicked the wood post hard. The bird squawked and flew into the fog over the canal, leaving a puddle of wet guano on the dock.

"You're getting a little hot," Caldwell said. "Cool down. If you keep this up, the seagulls will start dive-bombing us."

"Look at it the other way. Maybe *you* need to heat up."

"I don't do hot. You know that."

Harris turned away with a snort and watched the twinkling of the house lights, rolling his shoulders and taking deep breaths. After a few moments of silence, he spoke softly. "Anger is therapeutic, Zack. It simplifies your thinking. Being cool-headed only lets you delude yourself into believing that this shitshow isn't important enough to react to. But you have to react. You have an obligation to everybody who wore that uniform and died defending America, and Cheyn is pissing all over their devotion, and that should make you mad."

"It does. It enrages me."

Harris turned quickly and peered at him.

"Well, what should I do, scream and yell and wave my arms like a gorilla in gastric distress?"

"Oh, no, not you. You might wrinkle that compulsively neat uniform."

Caldwell smiled, and then he brushed some dust off the bench and sat. "A man without standards is merely *homo erectus*."

"All right, listen, we signed on to fight this fight no matter how hard it gets. And if we don't, the America we knew just becomes a footnote in some history book. This is bigger than you and me, bud, and I don't think you see that."

"You're jumping to conclusions again." Caldwell straightened the wrinkles in his pants carefully, and then he looked up. "Adam, you're giving a stirring eulogy for America and democracy, but they aren't dead yet. We have an insane president, and yes, he's a dirtbag and a traitor. But we'll get past what he's done. We'll move on and recover."

"Okay, you're a circumspect guy. I respect that. Your cautiousness saved my ass more times than I can count. But follow your gut and not your head, Zack. Tell me if you see the band getting back together after Cheyn cratered a major city and uncorked this virus. Tell me if anybody will ever trust Washington to run things again."

Caldwell leaned forward, his elbows on his knees, and stared at his hands with a faraway gaze. After a few moments, he sat back and sighed. "You really think there'll be a shooting war?"

"Absolutely. General Pendleton was on Wang's boat. He's the Force Mobility commander at Fort Lewis in Olympia. Before he left for the meeting, he received mobilization orders for the 81st Armored and all his Stryker units, which means ground action is imminent. But his airlift wing didn't get mobilized. And the 11th Armored at Fort Irwin, down in Southern California, they got the same orders."

"So whatever they're preparing to attack, they're driving to get there. Tehran's a long commute from Olympia, Adam."

"Exactly. Cheyn's preparing to occupy Western cities. Armored columns won't be rolling into Seattle because Pendleton's on our side, but what happens if tanks roll into San Diego or LA?"

Caldwell leaned forward again and looked at the dock planks. "That would be the point of no return. Such an act would inflame their secession movement and push it into violent resistance. That unrest would spread to other states, and Cheyn couldn't suppress widespread rebellion. He'd become desperate to win and would employ destructive measures that damage the country even more. Finally, everybody will say 'Fuck it' and start blowing each other away, and we end up in total war by Halloween." Caldwell pulled a flask from his pants pocket and took a big sip. "Yep, the America we knew is toast."

"It sure is. So you're in?"

"Not so fast, Adam. If everything's swirling down the shitter, why should I fight to rescue what's left? If I'm not defending mom and baseball and apple pie, why paint a bullseye on my ass? If I'm a man without a country, why shouldn't I just go to Mexico where Cheyn can't blow my brains out?"

"Weren't you listening? We're at the business end of history, Zack, and we've been called, and we've *got* to answer that call."

"All right already! I get it! You want me to throw my body over the barbed wire of history because everybody else did! But what if the freedom they were fighting for is gone? Why throw myself over the wire for a lost cause?"

"It's not lost!"

"How can you be sure?"

"Cuz I'm still breathing! And the enemy won't win while I am!"

"Oh, the hero speaks! He can save the world all by himself!"

"No, I'm not saying that! I can't do it myself!" Harris sat beside him on the bench. "This doesn't sound like you, bud. We're always on the same frequency. It's like you're right inside my head half the time. What's going on?"

"I'm just evaluating my alternatives. Normal people consider the pros and cons. Only the heroes rush in irrespective of consequence, and I'm no hero." He leaned forward on his knees again and screwed the cap on his flask. "For years, I've been trying to explain this to you. For years, I've been trying to make you a better leader, and you still don't get it. For the rest of us, your brand of fearlessness isn't a natural skill – it's something we train ourselves to learn and discipline ourselves to do. We consciously commit to it."

Harris scowled. "The more you think, the more you'll come up with excuses to be afraid."

"Reason isn't cowardice!" Caldwell jumped to his feet and strode to a nearby piling. "Can you even try to make that distinction?"

"I get it. But when the shit hits the fan, reason is the road to inaction. And it's time to act." Harris walked to the edge of the dock and stood beside him, and he rested his hand gently on his shoulder. "How can you walk away? How can you *not* fight back? This is one of those moments that prove what you are and what you're made of. And you'll remember how you faced this challenge all your life, trust me. This is the time to fight your war, bud. This is the time to find your balls."

"Balls?" Caldwell whirled around, knocking Harris' hand from his shoulder, and he jabbed a finger in his chest. "Watch it, Harris. While you were playing hero in Bushehr Bay for all of ten minutes, I was at the tactical warfare station on the *Tulsa* keeping my fish hot because two *Qalif*-class frigates were stalking us. For three of the longest hours of my life, I sat there and didn't make a sound. Every muscle in my body wanted me to climb out a hatch and swim for safety, but I stayed. That's real bravery, pal, when you keep doing your job even when you want to run. And not just for ten goddamn minutes, either!"

"You're outta line, Caldwell! Try getting punched in the face every morning for three months! Then you can lecture me about commitment!"

"Try putting up with your shit every morning for ten years! I should be sainted for that!"

Harris' lips moved, forming a reply, but then he turned and walked back to the bench. He sat slowly, pulled off his cap, and fingered the brim. "We've been friends too long to be talking like this."

"Maybe we *have* been friends too long."

"You know me, Zack. You know I'm an ass, and that's why you stick around. I'm the ass you can't ever be."

Caldwell leaned back against the piling and crossed his arms. After a minute of glaring at the dock planks, he said softly, "Well, all the great leaders throughout history have been flaming assholes. That's why they got to be leaders." Harris looked up quickly. "Hey, I'm not saying you're right, Adam. I'm just agreeing that you're an aggravating ass. That's a compliment considering my emotional state right now."

"All right, all right," Harris said. "Listen, we've got to get past this. Events are moving too fast for this kind of pissing match, so here's the bottom line: Rebellion is the only option I can live with. I've got that Bushehr Bay feeling right now, that the course is clear and right and urgent, and I've got to do this. I want you by my side, Zack. I know I'm walking into a minefield, and I don't want to feel the trap's jaws clamp around my ankles. I need your scheming mind to find all the traps for me."

Caldwell pushed his thumbs into his temples and sighed. "You would step on a *mine* in a *mine*field, for the love of God."

Harris watched the waters flow by for a moment, and then he spoke softly. "But I won't browbeat you into getting on board. Truth is, there's no way I can talk you into war. Nobody takes up the sword because it makes sense. They do it because it's better than not fighting." He rubbed his bent nose. "You know why I never got this fixed? Because I like it this way. I didn't have to take the abuse I did, y'know. I could've given Flea Fucker what he wanted. I was just a junior nuclear engineer, so what military secrets could I divulge? That radiation is dangerous? Yeah, I could've taken the easy route, but I would've come home with a straight nose but a crooked soul. There's no surgery to fix that." He rubbed his nose again and looked across the water. "I prefer this. I can shave this face in the morning and not wonder about the man behind it. But maybe doing what's right doesn't matter as much to you."

Caldwell snorted and looked away.

"And that's okay, Zack. Unexpected and unwelcome, but okay. I'll just have to fight Cheyn without your help, I guess. Now I said you could walk and I meant it, so go. Send me a damn sombrero or something when you get to Mexico."

"There you go, jumping to conclusions again," Caldwell said, stepping away from the piling and straightening his shirt. "I'll walk up to the bluff and try to clear my head of all your bullshit. Maybe I'll come back. Or maybe you'll get a sombrero in the mail."

CALDWELL PLOPPED ONTO THE BENCH AND SIGHED. "I get the trots whenever I go to Mexico. Besides, life would be boring without all your drama."

"Good! Excellent!" Harris slapped his back so hard that Caldwell's cap flew off.

"And rebelling cancels my dinner date with Lieutenant Pork Belly too," Caldwell said as he picked up his cap from the dock. "Trust me, that was no small consideration. So what do you need me to do?"

"First, figure out how we can take over this base and command it under a new flag. If we can, then you and I need to meet with Wang and General Pendleton. He's in charge of tactical defense."

Caldwell stood and paced along the dock's edge. "We'll need to talk to Major Shelby first. We need his Security Battalion to take physical control of the base."

"His brother lives near Sacramento," Harris said. "It won't be hard to convince him. Just show him Julie's message."

"If we get the Marines, then we can find out who'll come over to our side. Those who won't have to be confined until we have complete control of base operations."

"We'll use the convention center as a brig if we have to. Let's put first things first, though."

HARRIS STRODE UP THE OFFICE STEPS nine hours later thinking about his testimony before the joint legislatures of Washington and Oregon at Fort Worden. He'd told them he was ready, willing, and able to seize Bangor and provide the new nation a nuclear deterrent. He *was* ready and willing, but his ability to do it was still in question.

He opened the door and found Caldwell sitting on the edge of his desk. "Give me good news, Zack. I could use it right now," he said.

Caldwell poured rum into his glass and swirled it around. "Shelby and his staff are in."

Harris whistled. "You're kidding."

"I'm not. I wasn't sure at first. I presented my case, and Shelby's staff just glared at me the whole time. I didn't know if they were angry at me or Cheyn. I wish you'd been there."

"Because the senior officer usually gets shot first?"

"Exactly. I would've been out of the building by the time you hit the floor."

"Ahh, the ties that bind." Harris poured a drink and collapsed into his chair. "I would have preferred a firefight to sitting in a room with six hundred politicians. By the way, it's official – the vote was 556 to 8 in favor of secession at 4:30 this morning." He leaned back and gazed at the ceiling. "And Wang took those eight dissenters into custody. What's this world coming to?"

"Nobody needs sand in their lube. We'll have to do the same."

"I know, I know." He sat up, sipped from his glass, and then set it down on the desk with a thunk. "Now tell me all about the Shelby meeting."

"Those were some pissed-off gyrenes, Adam. As soon as I was done, Shelby said he was in, and the rest followed. The vote was unanimous, and they're hot to fight back at something now."

"Marines always feel better when they have a target. I do too. So what firepower can Shelby give us? Will that be enough force to take the base with a minimum of casualties?"

"He thinks he can persuade more than half his rifle company to go along. That's a hundred and twenty Marines, which he says is enough to sack Seattle, never mind some 'li'l ole fishin hole like Bangah,' as Shelby put it."

"Arrogant jarhead." Harris rubbed his face and groaned. "Forget I said that. I meant to say he should be commended for having so much confidence in his troops."

"R-r-right. Anyway, I was surprised at how restive the Security Battalion was. If there's that much ill will toward Cheyn among the administrative and command staffs, this'll be a piece of cake."

"Let's not get too brash," Harris said. "We have to make a list of the personnel we'll need first. We should talk to the commands of the *Jones* and the *Adams* too, even though they won't be ready to sail for a month."

"When we tell them what the *Henry* is going through, they'll come right to our side. I don't doubt that."

Harris sipped his drink and sat back in his seat. "Once we get the key staff on board, we can start turning the wheels. I want to keep knowledge of the takeover confined to senior staff, except for Shelby's Marines. At Zero Hour, we'll declare a Hotbox alert and take the base, and we'll throw anybody who gets out of line in the brig then."

"Some won't go along. I can give you names now."

"Get them off-base beforehand, but we won't know about the fence-straddlers till it's go time. Right now, we have to lock in our loyal core. When the time comes, we'll seize this base with just them."

ADAGIO IN A

Day 54
Sunday evening, October11, 2043
Near Auburn, California

The drive around the north side of Sacramento took longer than Mark expected. Only the local roads were open, making a one-hour trip nearly three hours long, but he turned back onto Interstate 80 outside Auburn at last. "Thank the Lord! A highway! Open road!"

"How long till we reach the border?" Krista asked.

"About half an hour," he said. "Now, when we get there, I'm gonna stop a little short and walk up to the National Guard guys and get in touch with the governor. I'll work out a deal, but you gotta stay outta sight. You're my ace in the hole, okay?"

"Got it."

Five minutes after they passed Auburn, a pair of headlights appeared in the rearview mirror. "First car I've seen for miles," he said. "I've never seen the road this empty."

"That's because it ends in disaster whichever way you go. There's a post-nuclear wasteland on one side and a virulent pox on the other."

"True." He squinted in the mirror. "Tailgating's a six-point offense, buddy! Get offa my ass!" The car pulled out to pass, and then he saw a green Humvee in the next lane. A soldier in the front seat waved for him to pull over. "Well, there goes my bitchin plan," he said.

"It didn't last long."

He pulled onto the gravel shoulder, and the Humvee stopped behind them and beamed a spotlight through the rear window. "Assholes. I'll handle them. I'll act innocent and say we're not us."

"They know who we are. That's why they pulled us over."

"Okay, okay. How about this – as soon they get outta that truck, I'll peel out."

She opened the door and climbed out. "Let's do something unexpected. Nobody expects that." She stalked back to the Humvee and thumped on the hood. "C'mon, let's see a little action out here, boys!"

A soldier climbed from the driver's seat. "Please don't strike the vehicle, ma'am."

"I'm Krista Warner, and I've got things to do! Hop to it!" She snapped her fingers. "C'mon, chop-chop!"

"Back away from the vehicle and stand by the side of the road, ma'am," the soldier said. "We have orders to take you into protective custody. Please don't make a fuss again."

"The hell you will! Get your boss-man on the blower right now!" She crossed her arms and tapped her foot. "We're gonna chew the fat, him and me, ya follow?"

He removed his helmet and scratched his head. "Not really."

"Call Governor DaCosta, dummy! I've got important intelligence to pass on! Get the lead out of your ass, or I'll put it in a sling!" The soldier blinked a few times but didn't move. "I said MOVE IT, soldier!" she roared.

He ducked into the truck and spoke to someone inside, and he returned a moment later with a field radio. He stood by the roadside, talked into it for a minute, and then handed it to her. "This is Krista Warner," she said.

"Warner?" a brusque voice asked. "Ric DaCosta. How are ya? Hang on...*if they got tents, get 'em up there, and get me some buttermilk now!* ...Okay, I'm back. This place is a madhouse. We got tsunamis all over the coast, zombies stumbling across the mountains, and a friggin glowing crater inbetween. What a country I gotta run, huh? Who do they think I am, William-friggin-Churchill?"

"What country?"

The other end of the line was silent for a moment. "Forget you heard that."

"Wait, has California already seceded?"

"Keep this under your wig for the next three days, okay? Look, that party at the Fairgrounds was a show. The Legislature and Governor Rodriguez actually signed the Articles of Secession on October 1 in a secret session...*Hey, I'm tawkin here! Keep it down!*...so it's all legal, and now I'm the

Grand Poobah of the California Republic. You oughta see the big hat they gave me, the feathers are huge. Woo-hoo. You know I only took this job cuz Rodriguez needed the SoCal vote? Tawk about a raw deal, but hey – he was a world-class ass-kisser, bless his heart. But how's that important to you? It's not, so let's move on. Now, you made it outta Sacramento, but you got some allergy to going someplace safe, right?"

"I'm not a drug mule, Governor. I didn't bring the Recombin across the country just to get thrown in jail."

"Hey, I had orders to grab you and that Lang kid back then. Rodriguez had some sorta weird deal with Cheyn. But whatever that was, it's in the fossil farm now. Toes up, ticket punched, checked into the wooden Waldorf. Deal lasted as long as a hard-on in a nursing home. Things are different now, so let's tawk. Find some common ground, forge a connection, hammer out a deal. First, how about the vaccine?"

"I've got it. Not with me, of course."

"No, you got your head screwed on. Didn't expect you'd carry it around. By the way, we got your plans, and we're making some big whatchamacallits down in Torrey Pines, so two weeks max we can make this stuff. All we need is the vaccine now, so whaddaya want for it?"

"First, I want immunity from prosecution for any crimes committed by me, Ada Lang, and Mark Mason."

"Like the hospital antics? Hey, that's all clean, don't do it again, hang on…*No, I'm not giving any interviews! Tell them to come back after I have my psychotic break and I think tawkin to reporters is a good thing…yeah, that should be tomorrow at this rate. And where the hell's my buttermilk? …*Okay, I'm back, sorry, the place is berserk. And my ulcer – don't bring it up, you don't wanna know, but it's gonna pop any minute. So yeah, don't screw anything else up, and I'll wipe the slate clean."

"Second –"

"Blanket immunity's not enough?"

"I've got the vaccine. You don't. You're in no position to negotiate."

"Wow, that's direct. I mean, I'm a movie producer, and I can tell you about direct, but you – right for the jugular. Ouch. But you got that Midtown accent, so you're from New York, so I forgive you. You grew up in that shithole and survived, God knows you earned it. And hey, if you're gonna screw me over, call me Ric. Screw jobs feel better if you pretend you're friends. Okay, what's your number two?"

"I want protection from Federal agents."

"I'll give you a lotta beef to escort you this time. How's that work for ya? Hey, what happened to the guys I sent with you last time?"

"I don't think they made it, Ric. We couldn't find them after the place blew up, and things were crazy…"

The phone went silent for a few seconds, and then DaCosta cleared his throat. "Okay, we tawk about that, I'm gonna open a vein. Jesus, the thing burns a hole through my heart. When this is over, I'm going out to Seal Rock, gonna bawl my eyes out."

"Can I come along?" Krista asked.

"Sure. You, me, a million others. But right now, I've got the living to take care of, thank god or I'd go nuts, so let's move on. Hang on a sec…*Buttermilk, people?…Oh, yeah, thanks.*" He glugged down the milk and slammed the glass on an unseen table. "Ahh, buttermilk, the Mucus of the Gods. Where were we? I forget. I haven't slept in two weeks, and the stress is killing me. Be lucky to make it to November. When I kick the fuckin bucket…pardon my Brooklynese…when I kick the *friggin* bucket, you'll have to read my eulogy. You're the only person in the state that doesn't hate me. Everybody says I'm too tense. These people, I love 'em, but this friggin sun gives them mellow-noma. So where were we?"

"You said you were giving me an escort."

"Right. I'll give you a whole fuckin…a whole friggin platoon. We got a deal?"

"Not yet. Now, third –"

"Holy God, you're killing me!"

"Third, I want a guarantee that you won't extradite me, Ada Lang, or Mark Mason to the States."

"The hell? Why would I send you back there? After *Freedom's Bell*, the voters would string me up if I did – torches, pitchforks, the whole ball of wax. You're a PR gold nugget, baby! By the way, they sentenced you to death, you know that? 'Course you do, it's the kinda thing a person knows. You've got my promise. No way we'll ever send you back. Now when do I get my vaccine?"

"You say the bioreactors will be ready in two weeks, so you'll get it in two weeks."

"What *is* this? Stop stalling and deliver the goods, babe. That's how deals work. Quid pro quo, right? What good's the vaccine gonna do you?"

"Well, Ric, while we're waiting for your equipment to get built, we can start making more vaccine. My friend Ada is a genius, and she thinks we can cook it."

"Huh. I wondered why Cheyn had such a hard-on for the kid, if he can get his piss-pump to stand up and salute at his age, which I doubt, which explains lotsa things. I'm older than him, and I can still get a boner – only every other Tuesday, but hey, small favors, amirite? But why are we tawkin about dicks? Listen, what can one little kid do?"

"Ada's like a Vulcan with round ears. She can do anything. Except build bombs. She, umm…she can't build nukes or stuff like that."

"Good for her. Okay, we need to vaccinate, hang on…*Lenny, how many doses for the first responders?*…So yeah, could you kick out five, maybe ten thousand doses?"

"We can make more than a hundred thousand doses a day."

"A hundred thousand? *A day?* Seriously? You do that and I'll marry you. I'll put a statue of you in every town square and give you the Medal of Honor, if we have town squares, which we don't, so I'll build one and plunk the statue in the middle, hang on…*Lenny, we need a town square! Somewhere in San Francisco! Hook up with your architect friend and have him design a Medal of Honor too!* …I'm back. Hey, you can do that, do that. Get the vaccine to Reno. The cordon won't hold, and we need to draw the infected away from the border. Hang on…*Lenny, how many doses we need in Reno? We might be able to make a firebreak out there, yeah, Warner's got some dream team that can cook it*…okay, I'm back. You get a quarter million doses out to Reno, you're my hero. You're in my personal friggin pantheon. You could save the whole state or whatever we are now. Whatever you need is yours, so do it. I'll give you my personal tablet number, anything you need, you call me and it's done."

"What I need tonight is to get into Reno. Infected blood is critical to the process. I'll really need your soldiers if I'm going back into the States –"

"You won't be. We annexed Reno and Vegas. They're part of the California Republic now."

"Really?"

"Yes, really. Forget you heard that, okay? It's hush-hush, sub rosa, on the QT. I wasn't supposed to tell you, but sometimes my mouth just keeps running, hang on…*more buttermilk, please?*…I'm back. Only part of me that works anymore, so I won't complain about it. What were we tawkin about?"

"Can you hold on for a second, Ric?" She tried to recall New Detroit's location, but her memories were jumbled.

"You there?" he asked. "Tawk to me, babe. I hate dead air."

"All right. Fourth, I want you to annex Tonopah, Nevada, and everything, umm…everything a hundred miles around it."

"What?"

"That's my final demand."

"That's a helluva demand. Hey, Blue Eyes, I'm not the King of the friggin West here. I can't go grab whatever I want. Besides, the deal with Nevada was that we'd only cover Reno and Vegas, not the desert. I dunno if they'd go for it."

"There's something there I need to protect, Ric. It can't be in the States anymore, and this is important to me."

"You're a pushy one, I'll tell you that. But I like you. You got moxie. Hang on…*Lenny, where the hell's Tonopah? Holy God, she wants that flyspeck? Really, we'd get Area 51 with the deal?* …Okay, who can say no to little green men? I'll have Lenny Darwin tawk to Carson City. He's smart, he can work out anything workable, best rainmaker there is. Now we have a deal. I can't give you any more."

"All right. Deal."

"I love deals," he said. "Now, I've got an offer for you…"

Mark leaned against the car and watched Krista talk to DaCosta. Everything seemed to have gone her way, and now they were having a good laugh.

"You can't be serious," she said. "All right, you've got the right of first refusal…are you sure you want it? Hell, what would I do with it? Okay, I think I understand…right, here he is." She handed the radio to the soldier and walked back to the car.

"It went well?" Mark asked.

"He gave me everything I asked for and more. Ric's a real nice guy." She sat on the trunk. "It's exhausting talking to him, though."

"Ric? You two are buddies now?" he asked. "He seemed like a hardass when I talked to him."

"Ric's from the East Coast, and everybody's a little abrupt there. Inside, he's just a fuzzy little teddy bear, though."

"Okay, I guess I didn't see that side of him. So what did he want there at the end?" he asked.

She shook her head and laughed. "Get this – if I actually get Cheyn's head, he wants to make an offer on it before anybody else does. He plans to make it the centerpiece of a Ground Zero memorial."

A COOL BREEZE BLEW from the eastern mountain passes, and Boreal Ridge Camp was cold. Krista stood in the lee of a Humvee and shivered.

A corporal tapped her shoulder and held out a paper cup of coffee. "Thanks, I can use this right now." She took a sip. "Not too bad."

"No, they feed us well up here. If you want a hot meal…?"

Krista waved him off. "I don't want a full stomach, not with what I'm about to do. Really, I'd just like to get going."

"Your escort should be here in a few minutes," he said. "Last I heard, they were leaving the Donner Pass checkpoint. That's only ten minutes away."

Krista nodded and leaned against the jeep. The camp at Boreal Ridge was immense: The soldiers had taken over an old ski area, using the lodge for a combination command post and mess hall, while a few hundred tents were sprinkled among the trees. Campfires roared in front of them to chase away the high-country chill. Another breeze blew down the highway, and she pulled her sweater tighter.

Green trucks of every size and shape lined Route 80, leaving just one lane open for traffic driving to the border. The checkpoint there was so brightly lit that she could read the writing on her coffee cup in its glow even though the cordon was a half mile away.

Dozens of soldiers walked around the camp, but despite that, the place was quiet. When soldiers met and talked, they did so softly, and not one laughed or raised his voice. "It's spooky quiet here," she said.

"Yeah. It's depressing duty. It gets everybody down." The crack of a gunshot echoed from the pass and he twitched. "Shit. It always gets worse after midnight. The DeePees think that night makes them invisible or something." The gun cracked again. "Sounds like a bad night up there. I'd rather throw on a rad suit and go into Sacramento than do that shit."

Krista shook her head. "Trust me, you wouldn't."

"You were there, weren't you?"

"And I don't want to talk about it, okay?"

Engines rumbled up the hill, and headlights appeared on the road a minute later. A Humvee rolled into the rest area and stopped, followed by another, and then another. "There's your platoon," he said.

She glanced at the mob of soldiers climbing out of seven Humvees. "There must be a hundred of them."

"Twenty-six." He waved to one of the soldiers, who waved back and walked over. She took in his black hair, piercing blue eyes, and strong jaw, and tried to remember where she'd seen his face. "Lieutenant, this is your guest," the corporal said. "Krista Warner. Mark Mason's in the chow line."

He held out his hand to Krista. "Jon Gilsig, Lieutenant, First Platoon. Good to meet you."

"Krista Warner, Commander, Activity." Now she remembered where she'd seen the face – in a comic book, over a flowing red robe and a pair of tights. "You didn't grow up in Smallville by any chance?"

"No, Modesto. Why?" She shook her head, and he shrugged. "Whatever. I have orders to go where you go. I'm told you have an operation over the border tonight."

"I do. I've got to collect twenty pints of infected blood so we can start reproducing the vaccine. Do you know where I can find it?"

"Sure, out at the airport," he said. "I talked to the governor, and he says you can make enough in a few days to vaccinate Reno. Can you really do that?"

"I can."

"We need to do it fast," he said. "Half my men won't shoot the DeePees anymore, and the other half won't last long. And with Able and Charlie Companies being sent down to Sacramento, we've only got one man to cover every three miles of border. Some infected DeePee is gonna walk right through this cordon soon, and we won't be able to stop him. I suggest we get moving, ma'am."

MICAH SET ANOTHER ARMFUL OF BOTTLES on the lab table beside the hundred others he'd already found. The bioreactor chimed, and he snapped on gloves and reached into the sterile chamber on the front, where another bottle had already filled with Recombin. He screwed a lid on, slid it into a refrigerator in the corner, and then sat on the table and rubbed the spot where Ada had injected him with the new batch of Recombin earlier.

Ada was leaning off a ladder attempting to connect two glass tubes. After a few tries, she sealed them together, and then she climbed down and examined the tangle of silver-wrapped tubes and wires crisscrossing over the machinery. "There we go! What do you think of my work of art?"

"It's wicked steampunk," Micah said. "But I don't get it. What's it do?"

"It crossfeeds Neovirus and Recombin and optimizes serum temperatures to accelerate replication in the three breeding bioreactors, essentially functioning as a continuous-tube apparatus without the need for periodic growth media replenishment."

He gave her a blank look.

"It speeds everything up." She raised a coffee mug to her lips, and it shook in her trembling hand.

"You gotta cut down on that stuff," Micah said.

"Not till I reprogram the controls. I need to be sharp for that." She started to take a sip but yawned instead. "Wow, where'd that come from? I better make more coffee."

He looked up at the lab clock. "Not now. It's one in the morning already."

"No, I'll stay up till it's done." She gulped her coffee and shivered. "This'll keep me going."

"You gotta sleep," he said.

She shook her head. "I can sleep when I'm dead, or I make a million doses, whichever comes first."

"That sounds like a death wish. Are you sure you're over that?"

"I'm not trying to kill myself, Micah. If I want death so bad, it's not hard to find." She turned to the lab table, started arranging the bottles into neat rows, and then said softly without looking up, "I overheard Krista saying that the States sentenced me to death last week."

"What? What for?"

She slid another bottle across the table and aligned it with the others.

"It's okay if you don't wanna talk about that," he said. "I'd be a little rattled too."

"It's not just the death sentence, Micah. It's the doom game I was playing that bothers me too. It never did when it was all abstract, when death and destruction were just the game pieces." She drew a deep breath and looked into his eyes. "And I loved that game, Micah, so much that I couldn't stop playing even after I started making real weapons. I was addicted to living on the edge of chaos like you wouldn't believe. But Sacramento…" She looked into the distance for a moment and began lining up the bottles again. "Sacramento showed how much the dark has poisoned me. I only saw that after killing a million people, but at least –"

"You didn't kill anybody."

"Yeah, I did." She pushed the bottles away. "I've gotta freakin own that."

"I think you actually wanna own it."

"No, I'm not a freakin masochist. I don't –" She leaned back against the table and crossed her arms. "Whatever. What I want is irrelevant. A fact is a fact, and I need to accept Sacramento before I can start making up for it. And I need to make up for it fast. Death's coming for me, Micah, and it's coming from lotsa different directions. I can feel it snapping at my ass like a hellbeast, and it's getting closer and closer, and it'll suck me back under if I don't immunize myself against it. I've got to serve Life for once, not Death. That's the only way to fight the hellbeast off. If I don't…if I don't, it's like committing suicide."

He walked to her side and leaned against the table. "I've been to a lot of funerals and I think I know. After the organ music stops and I go home, I just wanna live hard. Real hard, desperate hard, like I'm trying to prove something to The Reaper himself. It's not a good feeling, and if you've got the same thing, I can see why you're beating yourself up like this."

She wrapped her fingers into his and gave him a quick peck on the cheek. "It helps to be with somebody who understands."

"Yeah, believe me, I get it. And if you gotta get to a million doses, I'll do anything I can to help."

She kissed his cheek again, this time letting her lips linger for an exquisite second, and then she turned to walk to the bioreactors. Before she could move a foot, though, he grabbed her arm with both hands. "Now, the best way to get to a million doses is to get some sleep!" She tried to wriggle out of his grasp, but he pulled her back and hoisted her into his arms. "Don't mess with me, woman! I'm taking you to bed and that's it!"

She stopped struggling and quirked an eyebrow. "You are?"

"Umm, I'm taking you to *your* bed, not *my* bed. I wouldn't even think of doing that…I mean, I would, cuz you're sizzlin hot, but I wouldn't…aww, forget it." He carried her through the lab door and staggered down the corridor. "Women are so difficult sometimes."

"Do you like this, getting all Neanderthal and stuff with me?"

"No!"

She rested her head against his arm. "I like it."

He pulled the lab vault door open with a foot, made sure he bumped her head on the jamb, and then stumbled toward the lounge.

"You're blushing," she said.

"You're heavy," he wheezed. "Heavier than…I thought."

"You're stronger than I thought." She rubbed his bicep. "You're a big boy."

He kicked open the door to the Fellows Lounge and dropped her in front of Room A. "Now be a good girl and go to sleep. Please. You need it."

She batted her eyelashes. "Are you ordering me, sir?"

He growled under his breath and stalked to the other bedroom. "You're infuriating! Just go to sleep!" He waved at her door. "Go! Give it a try at least!"

She smiled at him and opened the door. When she heard his door click shut, she tiptoed out and knocked on it. "I left my room! I need to be disciplined!"

"Go to sleep!" he roared.

She grinned and walked back to Room A, stripped off her clothes, and slid under the covers.

KRISTA SHIMMIED INTO THE RUBBER BIOCHEM SUIT. "Why have I got to wear this? I'm vaccinated."

"Your clothes aren't," Sergeant Swensen said. "We'd have to burn them when we got back if you weren't wearing a gumby suit."

"It's so uncomfortable."

"Sure is." He grinned. "Just don't fart in them. It never comes out."

"Now you tell me," Mark said.

They drove to the Boreal Ridge checkpoint, where a soldier pulled a truck out of their way. Seven jeeps roared through the opening and into the bright lights, the broken road of the no-man's-land rumbling under their wheels, and then they passed through the barrier on the other side. The darkness was almost absolute away from the lights, but Krista spotted a few people hiding behind trees.

Lieutenant Gilsig did as well. "These folks here, they'll probably be dead tonight. This is where the DeePees hang out and build up the courage to jump the barrier, maybe try to con themselves into thinking it'll be different for them." He looked through the window. "But it won't be. They'll get shot and dumped into a trench like all the others, and they'll be ashes after we do the morning burn. I sure hope you can get your vaccine out there, ma'am. I'd love to stop shooting these folks."

"I'll do my best," she said. "How long till we're there?"

"Thirty-five, maybe forty minutes."

Interstate 80 was empty all the way to Reno. The lights of the casinos flickered and flashed, but few cars traveled the highway even in the city. Soon after passing Reno, they arrived at the old Hughes National Airport terminal, a crumbling but still impressive Art Deco masterpiece festooned with more chrome and fins than a '58 Eldorado.

The convoy stopped in the pickup area, where the soldiers climbed out and donned their gumby helmets. After a few tries, Krista sealed hers to the suit, and Swensen nodded in approval. "Your headset is on all the time. We can hear you, but if you want to talk to someone outside, you have to touch the button on your helmet, okay?"

Mark and the soldiers pulled coolers with blood-drawing supplies from the back of the jeeps, and they walked into the terminal. The airport had been abandoned for years, and a thick layer of dust coated the luggage carousels; small tumbleweeds drifted to the side as they rolled the coolers toward a bank of escalators in the Center Terminal, where the only operating lights in the building shone. Refugees sat on blankets in the shadows and watched the group warily.

They climbed the long-unused escalator to the second floor and walked past a restaurant. Its golden arches still glowed, casting yellow light across the dining area, and people sitting at the tables watched the procession pass. Swensen continued to a cluster of soldiers in gumby suits at the Concourse B security checkpoint and pulled one aside.

"This is the Hot Wing," Gilsig said to Krista. "There are about a thousand people here with the bug. Be careful because a lot of these folks are unstable, and they can get ugly sometimes. Stay between two of my men at all times."

Swensen returned with the soldier he'd been speaking with. "This is Lieutenant Kidd of the 92nd. They specialize in chemical and biological threats, and he has rules for us to follow."

"Okay. These people are in distress, and you can't upset them," Kidd said. "Nobody in this wing will survive another two days, but you won't say that. If they ask if you're a doctor, you are. If they ask if they'll get better, they will. If they reach for you, back off and my men will handle it."

He looked at Krista. "Pick your blood donors, and we'll restrain the subjects first. Got it?"

Krista nodded and followed him into the concourse. Mattresses filled with moaning men and women lined a floor-to-ceiling glass wall overlooking a weedy aircraft apron. Kidd led them to a gate at the far end, where fifty to sixty people lay on bloodstained mattresses.

"These are the pre-terminals," he said. "They'll start bleeding out in a few hours. We'll move them down the jetway then. It's easier to hose that area down, and nobody sees us load the bodies on the truck too. So who do you want?"

Krista tapped the transmit button and pointed to a stringy, middle-aged woman on a mattress near her feet. "Let's talk to her first."

Kidd motioned to his men, and three of them pinned her to the mattress. She struggled weakly and moaned.

"What are you doing?" Krista asked.

"You have to restrain them, or they can hurt you. You can draw your blood now," Kidd said. "Don't worry. This is how we administer sedatives. They're used to it."

"This is inhuman!" She pushed the soldiers away, knelt next to the woman, and tapped on her microphone. "Hey there. I look and sound scary, but I'm really not," she said. "My name's Krista. What's yours?"

The woman blinked a few times and tried to peer into Krista's mask. "Doreen. You a doctor?"

"I am. I'm here to ask a favor."

"I don't do favors no more," Doreen said. "And I don't want no more lies."

Krista studied her seamed face, one that had endured countless crises and tough seasons. "I won't bullshit you, Doreen. I know you like to hear it straight."

"Don't have no time left for bullshit. Tell me, am I gonna die?"

Krista wrapped her gloved hand around hers. "I'm so sorry, Doreen."

She looked away. "You're the first one that tole me the truth since I been here. Ever'body's a liar here, and I don't truck with no liars." She raised her head and looked into Krista's eyes. "It gonna hurt? When the end comes?"

"It won't," Krista said. "You won't feel a thing, I promise."

"Least I got that." She rested her head on the pillow and sighed. "Awright, whatcha want?"

Krista leaned forward so Doreen could see her eyes. "If I can draw some of your blood, I can make a vaccine that'll save the lives of others. You can save thousands of people, Doreen."

"Thousands, huh? More good than I ever done livin." Her lips rose almost imperceptibly. "Be nice to go out on a high note and all."

Krista smiled, although the mask hid it. "I did that once."

"Now how you done that and still be here?"

"I drowned. I died, but somebody brought me back. I saved forty thousand lives that day."

"Wow. Now there's a high note for ya. Bet that felt good."

"It didn't feel good. It felt right, like I finally did something worthwhile." Krista held up a cannula, and Doreen nodded. She handed it to a corpsman kneeling beside her, who swabbed the crook of her arm. "It felt like I completed something I had to."

"What's it like?"

"What's what like?" Krista asked.

"What's the other side like? What's there?"

"Oh, there's nothing there." Krista winced as sadness flickered in Doreen's eyes. She yanked off her helmet and leaned forward so the woman could hear. "Sorry, my microphone crapped out. There's nothing there but joy, Doreen, unimaginable joy – it's magical and glorious and wonderful. And you know what the best part is? Everybody you've ever loved and lost is there. I saw my mom and dad on one of the clouds, but I got yanked back to this world before I could get over there. I was actually kinda sad to come back."

"Yeah?" Doreen's head sank into the pillow again, and she gazed at the ceiling with a faint smile. "Bobby, Jenny, Ricky...been real hard these last few weeks. Be good gettin back together agin."

"You'll see them all," Krista said. "They're waiting for you. You'll be so happy on the other side."

"You ain't makin this up, right? This all true?"

"It's all true, Doreen. I swear to God."

Doreen closed her eyes and winced as yet another pain shot through her weakened body. She smiled and opened her eyes, and pink tears welled in them. Krista slipped off her biochem glove and took her cold hand, and they sat like that until Doreen left to rejoin her family.

AS KRISTA COLLECTED BLOOD IN RENO, Ada fidgeted under the sheets in Room A. She hadn't slept alone for weeks, and the bed felt empty and cold without Krista in it. She willed her body to relax and slipped into fitful sleep soon after.

Dream Ada floated through the infinite blackness of sub-nucleonic space and orbited the knobby orange nucleus of a plutonium atom. A swarm of neutrinos flowed above, a glowing silver river coursing into far infinity. As she watched the eddies swirl, one of the plutonium's electrons pierced the river and dragged a silvery comet's-tail of neutrinos behind it. Beyond the river, a canvas of brassy blue and coppery green and vivid gray quarks stretched in every dimension.

She turned her head, and the sound was there again – the tinkle of a thousand wind chimes swaying in the faintest of breezes. Sub-nucleonic space was a vacuum, though, and she was always puzzled about why she could hear sounds, or why she could breathe when an oxygen atom was the size of Jupiter to her.

Because you're dreaming, idiot, she thought. *Don't try to make sense of the night magic.* Shaking her head, she noticed a wave of energy rippling across the Universal Canvas. When the ripples neared a silvery time well, most parted like the well was a rock in a stream. This golden stream was pure energy – or at least she believed so. While the flow appeared syrupy and slow, she knew that it was formed from tiny particles traveling at lightspeed, and someday she'd understand why they flowed that way. It was near the top of her list of things to do.

An energy tendril trickled into the time well, and the shining truon cluster floating over the well released a stream of glistening silver truons that dripped into the opening like gelatin on a string. The truons would fuse with the energy inside the well, casting off a swarm of oppositioned torons and generating a temporomagnetic field – and anything inside that field would be freed from the constraints of time. If she could build a device generating those fields, time travel would be as simple as pushing a button. And that was at the top of her list.

Quintillions of multicolored particles filled her world, a vast Pointillist painting where each spinning, twinkling dot had its place and served the whole. As she drifted further away, the dots coalesced and shimmered into a vivid picture. A bubble of contentment burst within her: Of all the humans who had ever lived, only she'd been allowed to witness the breathtaking splendor of the Universal Canvas. She'd never told anyone except Victoria that she had, either. This was her world, and hers alone.

A fat purple plasmon zoomed beneath her, and she jumped onto it and grabbed its corona. In the distance, a huge Cooper Pair of yellow electrons danced around each other, red energy crackling between them like soft, tame lightning bolts.

The plasmon turned toward the electrons. They grew to the size of planets, and a black, unmoving dot on their surface grew just as fast. As she drew closer, she saw that the black dot was two linked octagons. She closed her eyes and braced for impact.

She struck something hard and opened her eyes to see a dirty plaster ceiling lit by a flickering greenish fluorescent tube, like the rest stop in Ohio. Grimy red tiles covered the floor.

Sitting up, she looked through the windows at an alien land with burning, cindery soil. Waves of heat rippled into the air and rose to an infinite black sky. The heat seared her face, and fearing she'd burst into flame, she crawled away until her back bumped into a wall of plutonium atoms. The cinders were terrifying but also hypnotic; every time she tried to turn away, they beckoned her to look at them once more.

She squinted through the funhouse-mirror air and spotted something moving on the horizon, something huge, something coming her way. The thing had eight legs beneath a thick black body, legs that strolled through the million-degree coals as if they were meadow grass.

It stepped through the heat ripples and into the cooler air surrounding the rest stop. She saw it clearly but then wished she hadn't – it was a spider the size of a house, with a gray, hairy trunk swaying from side to side, its nostrils sniffing the air.

Its eight glowing red eyes scanned the rest stop, and then one spotted her. The spider slowly crouched lower. One by one, the other eyes turned to see, and their heat singed her arm hair. She tried to draw a breath, but the oxygen had been baked from the atmosphere, and her lungs crackled from the scorching dry air.

The trunk tapped the glass door, which vanished into a cloud of sparkling motes, and then it insinuated through the opening. She pressed against the wall of plutonium atoms, but they pushed her toward the spider. The trunk reached her boots, and then its nostrils opened wide and wrapped around her feet. They sucked her boots off and drew her legs in even more until they reached her knees.

Then the slimy maw bit off her feet. A thousand tiny teeth chewed away her ankles and started on her shins, and she clawed at the tiles and tried to pull away with what little strength she had, but it did no good and all she could do was close her eyes and be eaten alive, and then an earthquake shook her and she shrieked for all her life –

"Ada!"

She opened her eyes – the spider was gone, and so was the rest area. Micah sat beside her and gripped her shoulders. "What's wrong?" he asked. "You okay?"

She threw herself into his arms and sobbed. "It was horrible! There was a Base-M spider and the whole world was burning!"

"It sounds like you just had a nightmare."

"I never have nightmares!" She squeezed him so tight that he grunted. "I *never* do. It was so scary! Like it was real!"

"That's how nightmares roll," he said. He ran his hand up her back and into her hair. "It musta been real bad. You're totally soaked."

"It was terrifying," she mumbled into his shoulder. She pulled up the bedsheet with one hand, glanced at her feet, and let out a shaky breath.

"You're okay now," he said in a soothing voice. "Nightmares don't come back in the same night." He pulled away, but she just squeezed him harder. "Okay, okay, I'll stick around."

"Don't go."

"I won't." He weaved his fingers into her hair and then slid them down the nape of her neck and over her naked shoulders. "I'll stay here as long as you want. I don't mind."

"Thanks." She sat up to wipe her nose, and he saw her breasts. With a squeal, she jumped a foot away and covered her chest with a pillow. "You didn't look, did you?" A wide, happy grin spread across his face, and she blushed like a spring rose. "Oh, hell," she mumbled, pulling a sheet over her shoulders.

"It's okay," he said. "I know you didn't mean to flash me or anything."

"I didn't," she said.

"Do you want me to leave now?"

"No." She looked down at her lap. "I'm still a little freaked."

He slid across the bed until their thighs touched and held out his hand. After a moment's hesitation, she took it and leaned her head on his shoulder.

MICAH SAT ON THE BED and handed her the mug. "I don't know if I did it right. This coffeemaker doesn't work like my mom's, so I put in extra coffee just to be safe."

She took it and watched oil droplets dance across the steaming surface. "Lotsa liquid power. Good."

"Maybe this is why you're getting nightmares, drinking all this coffee," he said. "It can't be good for you."

"Well, those spiders are worse for me, bub." She slurped the top layer of coffee and shivered. "Oh, yeah. That'll keep me awake. If I drink enough, I won't sleep, and if I don't sleep, I won't see those freakin spiders. From now on, it's a million doses or bust."

"You said they were Base-M spiders. Did you ever take —"

"This coffee is just what I needed! Thanks!"

"I've heard lotsa stories about those Base-M hallucinations and they sound —"

"This is one slayin cuppa joe! You oughta be a barista!"

"All right," he said. "You don't wanna talk about it, we won't."

"If I'm lucky, I can forget all this crap someday. Maybe I can go to a shrink and have the memories repressed or something."

"You've suffered a lot. You oughta treat yourself better, not abuse yourself." He took her mug and set it on the desk. "Give yourself a break and take time to heal. I hate seeing you beat yourself up, Ada. You're not a bad person. In fact, you're one of the nicest people I've ever met. You should treat yourself like you're special."

"I know I'm special," she grumbled. "All freaks are special."

"Wow, you must really hate yourself."

"No, I just hate being a freak." She pulled down a lock of hair and chewed on it. "I'll always be a freak. Being kind to freaks is just pity, so spare me that, okay?"

"Are you sure you're a genius?"

She answered with a vexed look.

"You sure don't sound like one now. In fact, you sound a lot like a clueless idiot. You really can't see what you are?"

"I know what I am."

"Sure you do, except you're wrong." He took her hand and held it with both of his. "You're a gem. You're a rare gem, like one of those diamonds there's only one of in the entire world, and yeah, there's no other diamond like that, but that doesn't make it a freak. It's still a diamond, Ada, and cuz it's unique, it's even more precious. Listen – you're the smartest *and* most beautiful girl I've ever met, and you never find both at the same time. *Never.* Trust me, all the beautiful girls are stupider than a box of hair, and all the smart girls are uglier than a hatful of assholes. You oughta treat yourself like you're something exceptional, cuz you are, and that's just a plain fact."

She risked a quick glance at his face and then picked up her mug. "Really?"

"Yeah, really."

"I'm not good with emotions, Micah. Please, if you're playing a game with me –"

"I'm not playing a game. I'm saying what I feel."

She emptied her mug and studied the grounds coating the bottom. "Don't I scare you?"

"Why should I be scared of you?"

"I scare everybody else." The sheet fell from one shoulder and she pulled it back up. "That's why I've never been on a date or been to a prom. That's why I'm always alone. You might like me now, but I'm unpredictable and I do weird things and I'll scare you like I've scared everybody else and I'll end up all alone again."

"You don't scare me at all." He leaned toward her and whispered in her ear. "I'll tell you a secret – the part you think is scary, it turns me on."

"It does?"

"Really, it does. You invent things and take risks and live on the edge and never hold back. I don't have a clue what you're gonna do next, and that turns my crank. Nothing will ever be boring or predictable with you around." He brushed a lock of hair behind her ear and whispered into it. "In fact, that's one of the things I love most about you."

She gasped and looked at him, her eyes brimming with tears. "You...umm..."

"Yeah, I said it. And I'll say it again."

"But you don't even know me."

"Sure I do. We've spent every second together over the last three days. I know your baddest bads and your darkest darks, so I'll never learn anything worse." He squeezed her hand. "Everything I learn about you from now on has got to be good. Everything's just gonna get better and better with you. I know it."

"I wish this could all be true, but it can't. I'm not the lovable type, Micah."

"You're wrong." He kissed her cheek and whispered, "*I* love you. All I can think about is you. When you're not around, it's like somebody shut the lights off in my life. You come back, it's like sunrise. I love you so much that I'm totally lost in you, and you know what? I don't ever want to be found. I want to stay lost in you forever."

She searched his eyes for any glimmer of insincerity but saw nothing but earnestness. Her mouth worked to form an answer, but then her lower lip began to tremble. With an incoherent blubber, she curled into a ball and wailed.

"What's wrong?" he asked, wrapping his arms around her shaking shoulders.

"I don't know what to do!" she said between sobs.

"I'm sorry," he said. "I thought this was a good thing."

She nodded and wailed even louder.

He hugged her for a few minutes until her sobs calmed into snuffles. She sat up and leaned back against the wall, pulling the bedsheet around her. "I wish there was a manual for this."

"Umm...there isn't. You go with the flow, I guess. You say what you feel, and if you feel the same way, you say that back." He examined his hands for a moment and then looked up. "I thought you did, I mean, it was going so great, but it's okay if you don't. Well, no, it really isn't, but…" He ran his hands through his hair. "Do you?"

She blew her nose into a corner of the bedsheet and nodded once.

"Wow," he said. "Everything's awesome."

"No, it's not. I'll get so screwed. I'll get hurt and then dumped and then everything's going to shit and I can't do a thing to stop that cuz I have no freakin clue what to do."

"You think I'm gonna hurt you? Well, you're wrong again. I'm not."

"Love always ends in death or despair, Micah."

"No, you're wrong, it doesn't always –" He stopped and then leaned against the wall. "Yeah, you're right. It's pretty depressing when you look at it that way."

"The more you love somebody, the more you hate them when it's over." She sniffled and tears welled in her eyes, and then she laid her head on his chest and sobbed. "I don't want to hate you! I don't want it to end! I want it to be forever!"

"I do too." He stroked her hair until she stopped sobbing, and then he turned her face to his. "You know what it is? I think you've never seen what real love is like, and you're scared. Don't be. I'm the last person who'd hurt you, I promise."

"You promise?"

"Yeah, I do." He held out his pinky and tapped it against her hand. "I pinky-swear promise, even. I'll never, ever hurt you in any way, Ada."

She looked up at his eyes and down at his finger, and then she wrapped her pinky around his. "I'll hold you to this, pal, and I'm not somebody to mess with."

He laughed and kissed her cheek. "I screw up, they'll never find my body. I know that. I just won't screw up." He kissed her cheek and then her ear. "And you know why I won't screw up?" he whispered. "Cuz I love you too much to hurt you."

She nodded and ran her finger along the smooth, tan skin of his cheek and over his lips. "Say it again," she whispered.

"I love you."

"I love you too." The sheet fell from her shoulders when she turned to kiss him, but this time she didn't care.

DISPATCHES

Midnight Sun
News Post of October 12, 2043

CATACLYSM IN SACRAMENTO: DAY FIVE

National Guard units entered the No-Go Zone yesterday and returned with several hundred survivors from the North Highlands area. Guard forces will attempt to reach the former McClellan Air Force Base today, four miles from Ground Zero, to determine if it is safe for use by aircraft and unprotected personnel. If so, this would speed the evacuation and treatment of the stricken.

There is still no word from the White House regarding emergency assistance, and no Federal forces are present in the disaster area. However, Federal Emergency Management Administration aircraft have been spotted sampling the fallout plume approaching Las Vegas, presumably to gauge its impact on East Coast cities.

FALLOUT FORECAST

The fallout plume is approaching the town of North Las Vegas. Radiation monitoring stations there are reporting steady but light deposition of radioactive isotopes.

Meteorologists predict that the plume will pass over North Las Vegas by midnight and continue southeast until morning. At that time, the plume will mix with warm, dry onshore winds from Southern California and move due east.

EASTERN FOOD SUPPLY THREATENED BY FALLOUT

Hurricane Andy Boy, currently a Category 3 storm off Mexico's Gulf Coast, will make landfall in Galveston on Wednesday, and the fallout plume is likely to be drawn into its circulation when the two collide over northern Oklahoma early next week. If this happens, radioactive isotopes may fall on the prime croplands of Missouri, Illinois, and Indiana. While these farming areas are mostly depopulated due to agricultural automation, the food supply may be tainted.

Experts predict that these croplands could be unusable for as long as two years depending on the half-life of the isotopes that fall. Despite the high toll Neovirus has taken across the United States, this would leave inadequate food supplies even for the reduced population.

CHAOS ON EAST COAST INTENSIFIES

Due to the Media Regulatory Corporation's control of the newsfeeds, we have received no news reports of rebellion on the East Coast. However, the *Midnight Sun* staff has been using alternate sources to determine the state of events there, as Internet connectivity in the area has been decimated by the Activist cyberattacks. Ham radio operators have become our primary source for on-the-ground news, and many of them believe that The Activity has amplified its Eastern Campaign.

A radio operator in Baltimore says more than twenty car bombings occurred in the city early this morning. In addition, he notes that blockades have been built under the Jones Falls Expressway, isolating the east side from the city proper. He also reports that many people gathered at the Pagoda in Patterson Park this morning, in the center of the east side, and it is rumored that The Activity held a rally there.

An eyewitness reports that workers at the Point Breeze meat-processing plant in south Baltimore arrived for work at mid-day but blocked the entrances instead, shutting down operations. The mayor of Baltimore arrived at the plant and demanded that the workers report to the butchering floor. When they refused, he yelled, 'If you Ranks won't work, then why did we save your lives?' Police then attempted to disperse the workers, but as they did, a large crowd of armed young men overpowered them. The mayor and his staff were captured by this group, which vanished as quickly as it appeared. There has been no official word on the status of the mayor and the police officers.

However, another radio operator in East Baltimore says the operation was executed by the Activists, and that they're holding the mayor outside the city. He notes that resistance on the east side has become more organized with the arrival of an Activist leader called Commander Sara, and he confirms that she held a rally this morning attended by thousands of residents.

The communications and power grids are still experiencing blackouts due to Activist attacks, with thirty percent of the urban area between Baltimore and Richmond without power.

The *Midnight Sun* staff has tried to access government, financial, and commercial websites throughout the day, and fifty percent are offline, up from forty percent yesterday.

Midnight Sun is still receiving thousands of requests for information on how to join The Activity. We reiterate that Warner is only a correspondent, and *Midnight Sun* has no knowledge of Activist operations and organization. Please stop asking us. We don't know.

GROWTH SPURTS

Day 55
Monday morning, October 12, 2043
Briggs Hall, University of California at Davis

The convoy rolled into Davis just after sunrise and parked at the Briggs Hall loading dock. The soldiers climbed out, and Sergeant Swensen ordered two fireteams to search the area and secure the building.

Lieutenant Gilsig stretched the long ride out of his muscles and then ambled to the Humvee where Krista and Mark were unloading coolers. He kicked the shattered glass covering the parking lot with the toe of his boot. "Place got hit harder than I thought."

"This isn't so bad," Mark said. "It gets a lot worse closer to the city."

"Helluva place for a mission of mercy, I gotta say."

"The equipment we need is here," Krista said. "Trust me, I wouldn't have come back if I didn't have to. I'd like to be as far away from Sacramento as I can."

Gunfire cracked from the front of the building, followed by the yipping of dogs. Gilsig pulled up his headset and talked into it. "No problem. Just some mutts."

"Yeah, I forgot to tell you about the dog pack." Mark slid a cooler onto the dock and wiped the dust from his hands. "It's a big one, and they're vicious. Don't take any chances with them."

"No problem. I'd rather shoot dogs than DeePees anyway," Gilsig said. He hopped up onto the dock and lifted the cooler. "Show me where the lab is. Let's get on with the real work."

"Where do we go?" Gilsig asked, looking each way down the concrete-block corridor.

"The lab's through this big-ass door," Mark said. "I'll take you there."

"I'll make coffee," Krista said, heading in the other direction for the lounge. "I'll join you in a minute."

She opened the door to the Fellows Lounge and sniffed the biting stink of old, over-warmed coffee. Muttering, she turned off the coffeemaker and began cleaning it. When she tried to scrub the crust of baked coffee off the carafe, though, grounds sprayed out and coated the green T-shirt the soldiers had given her after the decontamination shower. She finished cleaning up and set the machine to brew a fresh pot, and then she walked to Room A to change into a clean hoodie.

She opened the door to the darkened room, turned on the desk light, and began to remove her shirt – and then saw Ada sprawled naked across Micah. "Oh, hell," she groaned. "What –"

Ada opened an eye and shrieked. She pulled the sheet from Micah and covered herself, exposing his naked body. His eyes fluttered open, and he grabbed the sheet with one hand and covered his groin with the other.

"I'm sorry!" Krista said, backing out of the room. "I didn't see anything!" She scurried back into the lounge and slammed the door behind her, leaned against the wall, and banged her head against it. "Strike me blind again, sweet Jaysus. I've seen too much," she mumbled with her eyes squeezed shut. "Can it get any more screwed up?"

The door creaked open. "Krista!" Ada hissed. "This isn't what you think!"

"It's exactly what I think! And you call *me* a slut! I leave you alone for one night with a boy…"

"Let me explain!"

"I know how it works, for chrissakes! I don't need an explanation!"

"Could you calm down?" Ada asked. "Stop acting like I did something ugly. It was beautiful and wonderful."

"So it's holy feckin communion when you do it? It's screwing when I do it? Is that the deal?" She waited for a reply, but Ada just snorted and closed the door. However, something clinked in front of her, and she opened her eyes to see two soldiers watching her intently. "Oh, hi. Been there long?"

One soldier inclined his head toward the closed door and raised his rifle.

"Really, everything's okay," she said.

"Heard screaming in here," the soldier said.

Ada opened the door and peeked out. "Is that Mark?" She looked down the barrels of two rifles, shrieked again, and slammed the door.

"That's what you heard?" Krista asked, and the soldiers nodded. She shooed them away, and they slung their rifles over their shoulders and tromped back to the lab.

When they were gone, Ada opened the door a crack. "Who was that?"

"I brought the Army with me. The governor wants us to have protection. There's like a hundred of them stomping around."

"Well, you coulda told me they were here."

"When? While you two were all twisted together like red and white on a candy cane?"

"Let it go, Krista. You're getting as stuffy as The Commander, for chrissakes." She poked her head out and glanced both ways. "Relax already. Try to find your mellow."

Krista breathed deep until the tension left her shoulders. "All right, I'll try. Holy crap, that was a hell of a shock, and I didn't need that, not today. Getting that blood was one feckin miserable job."

"You got it?"

"I did." She rubbed her temples. "That was brutal. I was like a feckin Halloween ghoul, complete with the scary mask, and on top of that, I didn't need to walk in on you two –"

"You got twenty pints?"

"Twenty-four pints. And it's got to be absolutely boiling with virus."

Ada whispered to Micah and then pulled her jeans on. "I'll come down to the lab right now. It's showtime."

A STEADY TRICKLE OF CLEAR FLUID DRIPPED from the spout of the bioreactor. Ada drew off a sample, inserted the pipette into the protein modeler, and set it to analyze the liquid.

She wiped her forehead with a towel and reached for a water bottle. Neovirus had contaminated the lab minutes after she'd centrifuged the blood and she was sweltering, but the soldiers were suffering more because they had to endure the virus sweats and wear heavy battle fatigues too.

Most were now working bare-chested, and Krista and Ada were pretending they hadn't noticed.

Only half the soldiers were assigned to the lab. Lieutenant Gilsig had split his platoon into two teams: The Security Team would stay upstairs, keep the complex safe, and procure supplies, and the vaccinated Bug Team soldiers would work in the lab, keeping a ten-foot distance from the others when they returned to the surface. This was to avoid exposing them to virus particles that might be clinging to the Bug Team's clothes.

The modeler chimed, and Ada squinted at the screen. After a few minutes of searching at the highest magnification, she found a colorful, twisted object that looked like a child's toy spring.

"Here it is," she said, and the people in the room crowded around her. She glared at them, and they stepped back a few feet. "This is Recombin-B. It's a nearly exact match to Recombin-A, except for some minor mutations."

The spout on the first bioreactor spurted and spat, and then the vaccine poured from it. A few seconds later, the second and third bioreactors started flowing, and Recombin-B dripped down the face of the cabinet and on the floor. "Get bottles under those spouts!" Ada yelled. "You're in the vaccine business now, folks!"

Once the bottles were filling, Gilsig leaned in toward the screen. "What's that?"

"That's our baby," Ada said.

"That's the vaccine? That spiky-corkscrewy thing?"

"It's not a vaccine. Recombin is a virus that attacks Neovirus, and it doesn't stimulate an immune response. I just call it a vaccine cuz everybody gives me a dumb look when I call it a virophage. It's more effective than some pansy-ass vaccine, though." She panned across the image and found a shape resembling a deflated beachball with suction cups sprinkled over it. "This is the Neovirus virion. A virion is the form a virus takes when it's hunting for a cell to infect." She panned across the screen more. "And this is what it looks like after it meets Recombin in a dark, dead-end blood vessel."

A gasp rose from the small crowd – the virus was rent into frayed chunks, and small stringy pieces floated beside it. Ada pointed to a few strands dangling off the shredded microbe. "Recombin tunnels into Neovirus and sucks out its RNA strands and reverse transcriptase enzymes.

Then it pillages its shell proteins and somehow rearranges all that stuff into two new Recombin virions. It doesn't attack body cells, though. I think Chalys engineered it to be vegan." She zoomed in on the mutilated virus and spun the image. "Kinda like some microscopic zombie movie. I'd love to see that in action."

"I would too," Micah said. "I love zombie movies." She gave him an admiring look.

Gilsig pointed to the Neovirus particle. "Will this hurt anybody?"

She shook her head. "It's totally inactivated. The Recombin ripped the brain out of it, so it can't do anything. It might prompt an immune response, though, and that's good. After all, it would be handy if the body had its own defenses against the virus instead of relying on Recombin to do all the work." She tapped her fingers against her lips. "I'll bet we could drop the dose from three cc's to two. That would stretch out the supply even more."

"I think we should test this Recombin-B on some of my men just to be sure." He called four soldiers from the Security Team and volunteered them to be test subjects. "Go upstairs and give it to those guys. If they don't seize up, we're good to go."

THE SOLDIERS HAD THE VIRUS SWEATS four hours later but showed no ill effects from Recombin-B. In the blood sample of one soldier, though, Ada found something unexpected: mutilated HIV viruses surrounded by mutated fat-and-happy Recombin particles.

She grabbed a new notebook, scrawled 'Recombin-C' on the cover, and then scanned through the rest of the sample for hours. However, she hadn't needed to take notes on the new mutation's effectiveness – every HIV particle she found was mauled.

She then announced to the lab that she'd discovered the cure for AIDS, and the news spread through the troops fast. The victory party that followed was raucous, especially after the formerly HIV-positive soldier, who hadn't known he was infected, found a keg of warm beer in the Student Center. After it wound down, Krista, Mark, and Micah returned to the lab to plan how they'd break the historic news to the world. They found Ada gazing at the modeler's screen, resting her chin in her hand and turning over possibilities in her mind. Gilsig leaned against her lab table and rubbed his temples. "Unbelievable. This is really a cure for AIDS?"

"Cure? This bad boy will make human immunodeficiency viruses extinct," she murmured, scrutinizing the colorful proteins on the Recombin-C shell. "I think it couldn't find any Neovirus, so it mutated to snack on HIV. That makes sense since they're both retroviruses, and that's Recombin's only food group."

"Congrats, Twink," Mark said.

"Thanks, but Recombin did all the work. I totally love this bug. It's the bad-assiest apex predator in the virus world. I can't wait to see what else it can do. I'll grab some Ebola from across the hall later and see what it does to *that*."

"There's Ebola across the hall?" Krista asked, glancing nervously through the glass at the darkened Level 4 lab.

"Oh, sure, there's tons of it in a freezer over there. I'll get a vial and see if we get another virus-on-virus smackdown. But Ebola isn't a retrovirus, so I'd guess nothing will happen."

"You won't do that on my time," Gilsig said. "This is great news, but it's somebody else's mission. Right now, we need to start planning how we'll get a quarter million doses to Reno."

"No can do, Lou," she said without taking her eyes from the screen. "We'll need a thousand bottles for that, and we only have three hundred and forty. And we'll need about two hundred liters of sterile water too. Maybe you oughta do something about that."

"Maybe you oughta help us find this stuff."

"Not me." She spun the image of Recombin-C and said to herself, "I am become Life, the creator of worlds, which is a fuckload better than hellbeasts snacking on my ass."

"What'd you say?"

"I said I don't have time to paw through busted glass. I've got tons of good stuff to do. Besides, I'm not in your freakin army. You can't order me around." Letters appeared on the monitor, and she wrote them in her notebook. "Be gone, soldier boy. Vanish."

"Actually, I *can* tell you what to do. This area's under martial law, and I'm the military authority here. I'm your judge and jury, young lady."

Ada yawned and twirled her finger in the air. Gilsig opened his mouth to push back, but then he pulled his radio from his pocket. He called Swensen and told him to search the entire campus for sterile bottles, making sure to bring a fireteam along in case the dog pack showed up again. "All right, there's my Plan A. Assuming that doesn't get us enough, where can we get more bottles?"

"We could ask Ric to send us some. He said he'd help," Krista said.

"The governor's too busy," Gilsig said. "He's barely holding it together. This is *our* problem." He picked up an empty 500-milliliter bottle. "I'm sure we can round up a thousand of these around here. We can go to local hospitals and offer them a bottle of Recombin in exchange for all the empties they have. I'd bet we find a lot that way."

"Marin Wellness Hospital was huge. I'm sure they have lots of bottles," Krista said.

"Vaca Valley is closer," Mark said. "Why don't we try that first?"

Ada looked into the glass front of the bioreactor, and the bottle was almost full. "Whatever you do, make it fast. I'll fill these bottles in nine hours and fourteen minutes, give or take, and I can't stop the flow now."

He unsnapped his walkie-talkie from his belt. "I'll have Swensen put teams together to go to Marin *and* Vaca Valley."

VICTORIA LANG TRUDGED ALONG THE SHOULDER of Route 80. Her destination was the new hospital in Vacaville; Vaca Valley Medical Center was supposed to have thousands of beds and the best trauma care in the area.

That was what the nurses at Fairfield Hospital had told her, and she had no reason to believe they were lying, although she wondered if they'd pointed her in this direction just to get rid of her. She'd made a commotion in the lobby and then had insisted on walking into each patient room to be sure an unconscious Ada hadn't been misidentified. The nurses were relieved when she left, and Victoria wouldn't be surprised if they'd given her directions to Hell General Hospital.

Another Humvee zoomed by and ruffled her clothes, but as with every other emergency vehicle that passed, it didn't stop to offer her a ride. The walk wasn't bothersome, though, because her strength was returning and she didn't feel as tired as yesterday. Also, Vaca Valley beckoned her; she didn't understand why, but she felt that it would be the end of her exodus.

IN THE VACANCY MOTEL, Bob Downs rolled over on the sweaty sheets and groaned. Every position was uncomfortable and sleep was impossible, but standing and walking was torture – his hands throbbed, and his heart pounded so hard that he became dizzy and disoriented. He'd almost fallen when he'd stumbled to the bathroom.

He examined his hands, which were more swollen than they'd been an hour ago. The pus had dried to a crust that cracked when he flexed his fingers, and worse than that, the veins from his hands to his elbow were inflamed and red. All the antibiotics he'd taken had failed to stop the infection, and it was now spreading throughout his body.

He'd asked Raphael to find a discreet NSF doctor in Marin County, but it was already four in the afternoon and he hadn't replied yet. He was becoming panicky lying on the bed and waiting for the tablet to ring. In a part of his mind, he wondered if Raphael would ever call back, or if he'd let him die in this squalid, no-name motel.

Looking at his swollen veins, he knew he couldn't wait any longer. He picked up his tablet and searched for the nearest public hospital. He found one only a mile away – Marin Wellness Hospital.

VICTORIA WAS SHOCKED when she spotted the exit sign for Vacaville because she'd only been walking for two hours. She hurried her pace, expecting to arrive at her destination within minutes, but the medical center was located on the far side of town. She had to walk another hour to get there.

She trudged to the main entrance of the hospital and into the lobby. The receptionist had no record of an Ada Lang being admitted, but he said they'd received many unidentified patients from Sacramento and suggested that she ask around the trauma unit.

Trauma was frenetic. She couldn't find a single staff member that wasn't responding to an emergency, so she decided to check every patient room herself. As she turned a corner and started walking to the patient wing, an orderly passed her pushing a cart piled with boxes of large bottles. He smiled and excused himself, and then he rolled the cart to a supply room halfway down the corridor. He leaned against the doorframe. "I found a few boxes of 400-milliliter steriles. That big enough?"

A woman's voice came from inside the room. "Prob'ly. They tole me they just want big bottles. I don't think they care lots 'bout the volume."

"Hey, you think I'll get the shot too?"

"Dunno," she said. "If there's enough, I s'pose you will."

He looked at the boxes. "They gotta be making a ton of the stuff if they want so many bottles."

"Yeah, the soldiers said they had some huge operation running up at Cal-Davis. They're making twelve liters of Recombin an hour."

Victoria stifled a gasp and stepped back into an alcove. She tried to control her breathing and strained to hear over her thudding heart.

"That's great news. I thought the vaccine got lost in Sacramento along with everything else."

"No, they said Warner kept it safe," she said. "And once the governor found out she had it, he gave her a battalion of troops and tole her to make it fast as she can."

"She knows how to make the stuff?"

The woman took a box from him. "Naw, she's got some whiz kid runnin the operation. She's some kinda Einstein or sumthin."

KRISTA AND ADA SAT at the end of the loading dock and watched the evening sky turn deep purple. Four soldiers stood nearby and kept watch on a few dogs lurking beyond the grass berm.

Ada laid her head on Krista's lap and lit a cigarette. "I'm whipped. It's been a hell of a day."

"At least you slept last night." She covered her mouth and yawned. "I begged dying people for their blood."

"That sounds awful."

"It was, it really was." She yawned again. "I don't want to talk about it. It's just another awful tragedy in a world of tragedies. All I want to know is when we can make that end."

"Well, we're making amazing progress with the Recombin-B," Ada said. "We filled thirty-one bottles in the last hour!"

"Gilsig's counting every one too. He's keeping an eye on where the Recombin is, and he's writing down how much is in every batch. I'll bet DaCosta gave him orders he hasn't told us."

"Of course he did. The vaccine's important, and he wants to make sure we don't run off with it," Ada said. "He can watch as much as he wants cuz we're beating even my expectations. We should be ready to take the stuff to Reno the day after tomorrow."

"I'm so proud of you." Krista rubbed her head. "You're a great person, you know that? Now I understand why you love yourself so much."

"There's just so much to love." She smiled and stretched her arms slowly. "Mmm, I'm more relaxed than I've been for years."

"I know what you mean. I always feel boneless for hours after, like I just had the world's best massage. Good sex makes all the little gripes vanish. Poof!"

"Mmm. I have a lot of gripes. I hope Micah's up to it. I wonder if he likes oysters."

"No need. Teenage boys are horny around the clock."

"Around the clock, hmmm…"

"Take it easy. If you cripple him, you won't get any."

"I'll be a good girl. Three, four times a day oughta be enough."

"You certainly love that Vitamin O, don't you?"

"It was like a pleasure bomb exploded in my tummy. I stopped counting my climaxes when I got to fourteen, and I came so hard on the last one that my calves cramped up. Is that normal?"

Krista looked up at the ceiling and scowled. "Sure, sure. Everybody feels that."

"Wicked pissin," Ada whispered.

"Well, Vitamin O is powerful medicine, kiddo." She took a long drink of orange juice and swirled it around her mouth. "There's a minimum daily requirement for that, I'm sure of it."

"There sure is." She took a long puff, watched it drift away, and then stretched languidly and sighed. "I think he just loves me for my body, not my mind. You don't know how that feels."

Krista rubbed Ada's head again and took another long pull from the orange juice bottle.

"I'm getting a tattoo when we get to San Francisco," Ada said. Krista coughed, squirting juice out of her nose and down her hoodie. "I want 'You're Not Done Till I Say So' tattooed right above my crack. In Chinese, of course. I don't want to be trashy."

"Oh, crap. Don't get carried away and do something stupid."

"You know, you're starting to sound like The Commander."

"Right, like you'd have this kind of conversation with her." She wiped her nose with her sleeve. "Gimme a break, sister."

"You're right." Ada held up her pinky. "By the way –"

"Hell, I won't tell her anything about this." She hooked her finger around Ada's. "I know nothing."

Ada nodded and watched the stars for a while. "I miss her more than I ever thought I would. There were times when I couldn't stand to be in the same town as her. Now, I can't even imagine that."

"When things settle down, we'll hire a detective and find her. I made you that promise, and I intend to keep it."

"I know, but I don't think we'll find her. I don't think I'll ever know what happened to her. What's scary is that I'm getting used to feeling that hole in my heart."

"It never goes away. Sometimes you can forget the hole's there, and that's the best you can hope for," Krista said.

"It sounds like you think she's gone too."

Krista swore to herself and wound a lock of Ada's hair around her finger. "I wouldn't say that."

"No, you wouldn't, cuz you're too nice to hurt me. And that's why I trust you with this stuff. Last night it hit me, though, lying in Micah's arms – my mom's the past and he's my future and nothing will ever be the way it was. It was a scary, cold feeling." She studied the ember of her cigarette for a few moments and sighed. "I know what it means now, taking the good with the bad."

"You have to," Krista said. "Nothing in the world of grown-ups is pure. There's always something screwy, even about the wonderful stuff."

"I wish it wasn't that way."

"But it is. Ignore the screwy stuff and focus on the good. That's what I do, and it usually works," Krista said. "Do you love him?"

She nodded. "He's my Nigel Goodbrass. When he's around, I feel like I'm not a freak, like everything about me is right and natural." She sighed

Growth Spurts

and smiled at the stars. "Nobody's ever made me feel that way, Krista. He has some sort of magic, I just know it."

"Not sub-atomic Love Particles?"

"Nope. Just magic, sister, pure freakin magic."

Krista smiled and then kissed her forehead. "I've been waiting so long to hear you say that. Now do yourself a favor and never try to analyze his magic. Just let it be and go with the flow."

"I get this feeling that if I tried to understand it, it would vanish."

"It would," Krista said. "If you don't respect magic, it walks right out on you and never comes back."

"Yeah." She took a puff and sent a few smoke rings into the air, where they wobbled and then shattered in a breeze. "I think I understand you a little more now. You're not so nuts. You just make sense in an unusual way."

"I guess that's a compliment?"

"It is."

"Thanks. Well, all I can say is that it works for me, and I think it can work for you," Krista said. "And here's another piece of advice I wish you'd follow – you deserve your happiness, and now that you've found it, grab it and never let it go."

Ada stabbed her cigarette out and ran her fingers through her hair. "But what if I screw this up? I wonder if I'm ready for this, or if I'm just a kid playing grown-up."

"Don't try so hard, and it'll all work out. Don't be scared if you make mistakes."

"Like driving a car – don't be afraid to let it wander and correct it. If you hold the wheel too hard, you'll crash. It's exciting but shit-scary at the same time." Ada reached up and took her hand. "You promised that you'd stick with me. I don't want to go through this alone, okay? You're my only famo now, Krista."

"I keep my promises, sister. You can count on me."

Ada held Krista's hand over her heart and gazed into the darkening sky. She watched a dot of light soar across it, and she told Krista it was the old International Space Station. They searched together and found a few more satellites, and Ada named each one. Eventually, the sky darkened to near black, and all that remained were the stars.

"Krista, can you do me a favor?"

"Sure. Whatcha want?"

"I don't believe I'm asking for this," she said. "Would you sleep with Mark tonight?"

"I'll bet *that* made your skin crawl."

"Nah. It's Opposites Month. Inverted realities don't freak me anymore."

"It's okay with me, but you've got to talk to Micah about it. If he hasn't told Mark, I'm not breaking the news," Krista said. "He might not have. Not everybody's comfortable talking about sex."

"I'll talk to him," she said. "I'm sorry, and it's not that I'm pushing you out of the way or anything. I'd never do that, not ever. It's just that, well…"

"It's just that you want to get laid again."

"Well, if you want to be crude about it, yeah, I do."

"*I'm* crude? What about the Cucumba Rumba? Docking the Boat in Tuna Town?"

"I'm sorry I said that," Ada said. "I didn't know it would be so personal, and like an ass, I made fun of something I didn't know. I won't talk like that anymore. I've learned my lesson."

"Ahh, my baby's growing up so fast," Krista said. "By the way, if you're going to be shaking the sheets this much, you need to think about birth control. Are you using any?"

"Sure." She held up her crossed fingers. "The same kind you're using."

"Ouch." Krista took a deep swig of orange juice and licked her lips. "All right, I guess I deserved that."

PULLING THE STRINGS OF THE SNARE

Day 56
Tuesday morning, October 13, 2043
Pacific Ocean, 715 miles WNW of Cape Flattery, Washington

Commander Ennis Quinn dipped his spoon into a cereal bowl and shivered. He pulled his sweater zipper up to his chin, but it did no good; the cold milk was chilling him from the inside out.

When the Eareckson anti-submarine aircraft cornered the *Henry* off Kiska Island, they dropped a spread of torpedoes. The anti-torpedo batteries intercepted them, but one detonated only thirty meters away, and the shockwave damaged the high-voltage transformers to the heaters and the galley cooking equipment. The boat didn't carry spare transformers, so the temperature had plummeted to forty-five degrees fast. Quinn had climbed into his topside gear, but the near-freezing water outside the hull sucked away his body heat no matter how much he wore.

He turned on the tabletop monitor and called up a replay of *Mushrooms over Moscow*, but his breath fogged the screen within seconds. After wiping the screen a few times, he switched it off. The movie wasn't funny anymore.

Ripley danced into the wardroom and over to the ice cream machine. She grabbed a waffle cone, filled it with a mound of chocolate-vanilla swirl, and then plopped into the seat across from him.

"It's moments like this when I hate you," he said. "Stop being so damn perky."

"Now, are we a grumpy-puss captain today?"

"Commander."

"Well, the crew voted you to be the Old Man. It was like somebody threw a switch at Coulee Canyon, and you knew exactly how to pull us out of that death trap. And even Jimmy Columbo couldn't have escaped all those anti-sub aircraft off Kiska Island."

"We didn't escape them. We blew them out of the sky." He shivered and reached for his cereal spoon with a shaking hand. "If I'd shot those SLAM's thirty seconds earlier, we'd still have heat. Did you know that I transferred to the submarine service so I didn't have to freeze my ass off anymore? Now here I am, shaking like a schoolgirl on recital night. I love the irony, I really do."

"Stop whining. You've earned the honor, Ennis."

"I don't want it, Tala. I'm done. As soon as I step off this boat, I'm walking to the nearest grocery store and getting a job in the produce section. Those are the only mushrooms I want to know about anymore."

"C'mon, you're the badass, swashbuckling Captain Quinn now! Why would you back out?"

"Why? I launched two nukes. I mutinied. I attacked my country and fellow servicemen. I even rolled over in a goddamn submarine, Mister Ripley, and submarines never roll over. That's enough trauma for one career. I've done it all, and I'm done with it all."

"That just makes you an experienced captain." She checked to see if any junior officers were listening and then leaned forward. "The scuttlebutt is that somebody overheard Bricker talking to the chaplain. She said that when we dock, she's retiring. The boat is yours."

He examined her eyes for a few seconds, and then he looked into his bowl and spooned some cereal. "That Vittler's Green down in Silverdale was hiring last time I was there."

"God, you're hopeless," she said. "Oh, hey, I have some news that'll brighten your cloudy day."

"Gah. If it doesn't have to do with warmth, I don't want to hear it. How can you eat ice cream when it's freezing in here?"

"It's never too cold for soft serve." She licked the drips off her cone. "Besides, it's neater this way. Doesn't melt as fast. So anyway, if you love irony, you'll love this: Acoustics has all its ears dialed up to eleven – the towed receivers, the sonodrone, the bow acoustic array, everything – and they think they just heard the *Astor* shredding water eighty thousand meters or so ahead, pinging away like a video game."

"They're in on it too? Figures." He dropped the spoon into his bowl and crossed his arms. "Well, they won't find us, either. Its sonar is like my grandma's hearing. I'm not impressed."

She leaned over the table. "And guess what? We finished falsing the depth sensor inputs, and we might be able to climb into warmer water. Impressed now?"

"*That's* the news I wanted to hear!" he said. "It's been tested at least three times?"

She nodded.

"When I get up to Control, I want to see those test results. I won't recommend breaking the 250-meter floor until I do." He leaned back in his chair. "How many seconds did we have to the next missile release before we dropped below the launch floor?"

"Twenty, thirty seconds. I can check."

"If I know Julie, she'll want to edge above 250 meters and see what the infernal Missile Release Control System does," he said. "Of course, we won't know exactly where 250 meters is."

"If the countdown resumes, we'll dive," she said. "We'll have thirty seconds or so to get below the launch floor. Totally doable."

"Right." He crossed his arms again and shivered. "And then what do we do?"

"Repeat every step of the process, Mister Ripley," Captain Bricker said. "That's the only way we'll know that the falsing was done right. Then, and only then, will we attempt to rise above the launch floor. Start your team on that now. And you have the conn for the next hour."

"Aye aye, Captain." Ripley sat in the Command chair and motioned to a cluster of instrumentation technicians, while Bricker hopped through the hatch and walked to the forward conference room. She studied a map on the widescreen bulkhead monitor while waiting for Quinn.

He opened the door a few minutes later and sat across from her. "You're late," she said.

"I was briefing the officers and the chiefs. Not much has happened since yesterday, but I want to keep them updated."

"That's always good. So how's everybody handling this?"

"The chiefs say the crew's beginning to accept that we nuked an American city on presidential orders, and that the Navy wants to sink us. What's bothering them now is that they don't know what's coming next. Chief Izu says he can't walk through the Mushroom Farm without getting asked about it a dozen times."

"Well, that's what we're going to decide right now." She adjusted her sling and wiped a thin film of condensation from the monitor with a towel. It showed five surface ships heading toward the same point they were, and three had been identified as old Arctic Fleet destroyers coming from the north – the *Astor,* the *Duke,* and the *Gould.* Two newer Pacific Fleet frigates were also approaching from the south, and Acoustics had tentatively identified them as the *Morgan* and the *Mellon.* All were headed for the waters off northwest Washington and the Strait of Juan de Fuca. "They've guessed we're going back to Bangor, and they intend to block us. If we continue at this speed, we'll only have to contend with the *Astor,* who'll get there two hours before we do. What do you know about her?"

"She's an interceptor equipped for speed, maneuverability, and surface interdiction, but not undersea warfare. And unless they fixed it, her sonar's deaf to port. The receivers on that side were damaged by submerged ice the year before I took command, and they never repaired them to my knowledge. The *Astor's* over seventy years old, and replacement electronics are hard to find, so I'd bet they still don't work. The *Duke* and the *Gould* haven't been in the Arctic Fleet as long, so they're probably in better shape."

"That's good intel." She scrutinized the monitor and the projected heading of the ships. "We need to decide now. We can proceed and try to outsmart or outgun the *Astor,* but if we fail, we'll only have an hour to disappear before the other four ships spring the trap. Have you developed alternatives?"

"Yes, but each has consequences."

"Not having an option carries even greater consequences, Ennis. The crew might mutiny if we don't have a plan."

"Well, the ice cream machines still work, so there's no chance of mutiny…" He looked up and saw Bricker glaring at him, and he studied his desk monitor intently.

"Answer me this, Commander: Why do submariners stay at their duty stations? Is it the low pay or the long hours? Or does the all-you-can-eat ice cream make up for all that?"

"No, of course not. Sailors will tell you a thousand reasons why they serve, but underneath it all, they do it out of loyalty to the country and with the belief that their Navy service secures our nation and protects our way of life. We all do."

"But how long will they feel loyalty to a country that slaughtered its own people? How long will they serve a navy that did its best to sink them at Coulee Canyon and Kiska Island? Not long, Ennis, not in a boat filled with the most rational minds you can find. So far, they're absorbing the events of the past few days, but once the shock wears off, they'll realize that patriotism is an obsolete motive. And when that happens, mutiny becomes a real possibility. In fact, it's already happened – both you and I have already disobeyed orders. I'll admit that I'm also thinking hard about alternatives to serving my country."

"So am I. And from what Chief Izu says, the rest of the crew will be asking that same question soon. So you're right to think that our clock is ticking."

"And we have to get this boat somewhere safe before our clock runs out. We're carrying enough throw weight to vaporize Europe, and this crew *must* remain disciplined and stable while we're at sea. We only have eleven officers and twelve chiefs on board, and we can't physically control sixty-four enlisted submariners."

"Fifty-eight now."

"Right." Bricker nodded slowly. "May God keep them and care for them."

"God has a special place for heroes, Julie. They'll be okay now."

"I hope so." She bit her lip and looked into a corner of the room. "What do I tell their next of kin, Ennis? How do I explain losing a loved one to friendly fire? How do I tell a mother that her child was sacrificed for no reason? How do I lie?"

Quinn looked down at the table while Bricker continued to glare at the wall for a few minutes, and then she swiveled her chair to see the monitor. "That's a problem for later. Let's focus on getting out of this trap."

Eighteen Hells | Alanson Rand · 271

"Okay. Our first option, assuming the falsing works, is to go home," Quinn said, displaying a series of maps on the bulkhead monitor. "We've discussed the challenges of that, so we'll move on to the second option, which also assumes the falsing works: sail through the Bering Strait, across the Arctic Circle, and down to Royal Navy Base Clyde in Scotland." He stood and ran his finger along a red line on the map. "But the Bering Strait passage will be treacherous with both the Reds and the Arctic Fleet looking for us."

Bricker opened a new window showing a map of the Bering seafloor. "Precisely. I had the same idea, and I located the confirmed hydroacoustic arrays in the Strait – both ours and the Reds – and I can't find a way to get through without being heard. If we didn't have four hatches open, *maybe* we could do it, but they're making a lot of noise."

"Jackson spooled out the sonodrone this morning so we could listen to our sound profile. Those hatches are generating noisy turbulence, and sometimes they even whistle. But we might be able to minimize that if we creep through at ten knots or less."

"Which is a workable plan until some Arctic Fleet swinging dick pops off a sonobuoy. Then we'll be stuck in fifty-meter-deep water with nowhere to maneuver, and we won't escape that trap. At first, I thought this was our best choice, but I now I think it's the worst."

"All right, then onto the third option, which we can do even if Tala's falsing doesn't work." He spun the map to display the Indian Ocean. "We can sail below the Equator, out of missile range, and dock at the old Air Force base on Diego Garcia. The problem is that pirates raid the nearby container shipping lanes, and reports say they use the lagoon to hide from the radars. We'd have to anticipate a confrontation."

Bricker shrugged. "If they become a problem, we'll send them our love in a torpedo-gram."

"Sealed with a kiloton?"

She granted him the most fleeting of smiles and then turned back to the screen. "Continue. I like this idea so far."

"The lagoon has a deep-water pier behind a breakwater where we can crack open the MRCS and toss it overboard. The missiles won't launch if they're out of range, so it won't matter if we make any mistakes. And it's always summer there, so we could take a break and enjoy a little sunbathing on a tropical island. We could even haul out the grills and cook our Halfway Night steaks. That might give the crew something to look forward to."

"I'd sure look forward to that." Bricker zoomed in on the island, and then she stepped back and tapped a finger to her lips for a few moments. "Maybe even for a week or so. We could exchange the boat's atmosphere and charge the batteries we're draining because of Cell Two's failure. And we can close those damned hatches. Or maybe we'll even stay there till Adam tells us it's safe to come home." She gazed at the island's image, her expression growing soft, and then she stood straight. "I'm deluding myself. We'd have a day at the most before the recon satellites pick us up, and then we'd have to go dark again. And where do we go after that? Around the Horn to Scotland? I'd only entrust this boat to the Brits, Ennis."

"We won't have to sail that far." He pulled the map over to the South Atlantic and zoomed in on a pair of large islands. "We can go to the Falkland Islands. Mare Harbour has a new deep-water jetty, it's out of missile range, and the Falklanders haven't had an extradition treaty with the United States since the Brit Split. However, the Royal Navy still operates Mare Harbour. We can just toss the keys to the Brits and hop a cab to Stanley City and request asylum. They'll probably grant it, but we won't be able to leave the islands without getting arrested."

"That's irrelevant right now. We'll handle the legal problems later," Bricker said. "It's also possible that we'll be arrested as soon as we step on the dock in Bangor. But I like my odds in a court martial with Adam and Zack as two of the three presiding officers. Even if we negotiated our return from the Falklands through some amnesty organization, I doubt we'd get a tribunal *that* friendly."

"That's a big selling point for returning home. And to be honest, I can't sell the idea of living in Stanley. I spent three days there once, and that was three days longer than I needed to see the whole place. It has one bar, one hotel, and a bazillion seagulls waiting to crap all over you." Quinn closed the picture of the Falkland Islands. "Given a choice, I'd rather sail down the *Astor's* throat."

Bricker dropped into her chair and pulled her sweater over shoulders, looking at the bulkhead monitor and the tracks of the approaching ships. "We should assume we'd end up engaging the *Astor*. However, we can handle that. They'll either make a hole for us, or we'll make a hole of them."

"These are the enemy, Julie. If they want a fight, let's give them one. But my gut says we can give them the slip."

"And if we don't?" She swiveled back to face him. "If we don't, it'll be Kiska all over again, but this time right off American shores."

"Right, but we won at Kiska. And we'll win this time." He reached into a wall cabinet, poured two glasses of whiskey and handed one to her, and then leaned against the wall. "Of course, we can avoid a confrontation by sailing for Diego Garcia and leaving all this behind."

Bricker looked at the monitor and tapped her fingers to her lips. "That's problematic. It'd take weeks to get there, and I'm not sure I can hold the crew together that long. And if we let them off on a lush tropical island, how many will get back on board so they can be exiled on some frozen, seagull-shit-crusted rock in the middle of nowhere? I might think twice about climbing through the hatch too. No, Diego Garcia is an option only if the falsing effort fails." She took a gulp of whiskey and let out a long breath, and then she tapped the monitor and zoomed in on the Strait of Juan de Fuca. "All right. Our first and safest option is to go home, even if we have to blow away five surface vessels to get there. If you can't come up with some clever evasion strategy, we'll draw these ships away from shore and go nuclear first. How many Mark 58's do we have left?"

"Only five. We'll have no room for error."

"Then we'll make no errors." She drained her glass and set it on the table with a thunk. "Prepare four Mark 58's and set them to a five-kiloton yield."

TERMS COMMONLY USED IN 2043

Aluminati: Pejorative slang for members of the Second Creation movement, an extremist group within the Archangelists. The term implies that they wore tin-foil hats, although there is no evidence this actually occurred.

Archangelist: a member of the Archangelic Church of the Son of Christ.

Arkie: Popular term for an Archangelist.

Base-M: A hallucinogenic street drug that was growing in popularity in the early 2040's. Due to eradication efforts, the drug disappeared by mid-century and is unknown today.

BoHo: Bohemian Homeless, itinerant urban artists of the working class.

Collateral Tactics Unit: The military arm of the National Security Forces, known popularly as the Ironshirts.

Corporate-Americans: Corporations. The 31st Amendment provided them all the rights and protections of human citizens, as well as exemption from taxation.

DeePees: A term for refugees, used by the California National Guard. Short for Displaced Persons.

Elders: Leaders of the Second Creation movement. See *Aluminati*.

Ellesmere A4: An enteric retrovirus weaponized by the US Army to incapacitate enemy forces. It readily mutated into the deadly Ellesmere A7 variant and was deemed too unstable for combat use. See *Neovirus*.

Executives: Elite operatives of the National Security Forces, often used for assassinations and surveillance.

Federals: Popular term for the National Security Forces.

Fug: A mixture of acidic coal smoke and ground fog, primarily affecting the eastern two-thirds of the country. The word is believed to be a contraction of the F-word and Fog.

Great Correction, The: A prolonged recession that eliminated the American middle class and placed all economic power in the hands of corporations.

Joe Slick: Navy term for the Lancet Missile.

Lancet Missile: A hypersonic stealth missile. See *Joe Slick*.

MRC: The Media Regulatory Corporation, a public monopoly formed to control the dissemination of news and information on the Internet and other electronic media.

MRCS: Missile Release Control System, an automated targeting and launch system installed on Patriot-class submarines. It was intended to reduce human error and the amount of manpower required to operate a missile boat.

Neovirus: Civilian term for the RVE viruses Ellesmere A4 and A7.

NSF: National Security Forces, whose primary mission is to uncover and suppress domestic dissent. See *Federals*.

Patriot Class Boat: A guided-missile submarine originally designed to carry Warhammer cruise missiles. The submarines were retrofitted in 2041 to carry the Lancet missile with the new W104 nuclear warhead. The Pacific Fleet boats in 2043 were:

SSGN 807 – USS *Patrick Henry*   SSGN 814 – USS *Ethan Allen*

SSGN 808 – USS *Paul Revere*   SSGN 815 – USS *Nathaniel Greene*

SSGN 809 – USS *Thomas Paine*   SSGN 816 – USS *John Paul Jones*

SSGN 811 – USS *Nathan Hale*   SSGN 817 – USS *Seth Warner*

SSGN 812 – USS *John Adams*   SSGN 818 – USS *James Otis*

SSGN 813 – USS *John Hancock*

Popobawa: Pejorative street slang for the National Security Forces, and particularly the Collateral Tactics Unit. It is believed that it was borrowed from the name of a mythical East African demon.

PRC: The Persian Regional Conflict, a naval and aerial war in which the United States sought to prevent the unification of Persian and Arab populations into one nation. It ended in a stalemate and an embargo on the shipment of Persian Gulf oil to the United States.

Ranks: The rank and file, or the lower class. This group once comprised skilled laborers but after the Great Correction came to include most of the surviving middle class as well. Also known as Breeders, Naggers, Mullets or Working Class.

Recombin: A virophage engineered to attack Neovirus.

SAG (Special Activity Group): Action squads of the National Security Forces, often used for pursuit, capture, and localized suppression efforts.

SLAM: Sea Launched Anti-aircraft Missile.

Soviet Bloc: Also known as the Group of Sixteen, those nations allied with Russia to achieve nuclear parity with the United States.

Stiffer: A person who has died on the street from an untreated illness.

Tenpez: A coin containing ten grams of gold issued by the State of California in the 2020's. In 2043, its value was approximately one thousand dollars. The name is believed to be inspired by a candy popular in the mid-20's.

Transition, The: Archangelist euphemism for a hostile takeover of the United States government.

Transportation, The: The forced resettlement of the urban poor from Detroit and Cleveland after a period of rioting and urban warfare in those cities. See *The Troubles*.

Troubles, The: A period marked by the broad repeal of civil liberties and repression of public dissent, spanning from early 2024 to late 2027. See *The Transportation*.

W104: A strong-fission/fusion weapon, which pound-for-pound delivered 21.2 times the destructive force of its predecessor, the fusion-fission W102 weapon.

www.ingramcontent.com/pod-product-compliance
Lightning Source LLC
Chambersburg PA
CBHW050014180626
46810CB00002B/417